CAPTURED BY LOVE

Lisa looked up at Nakon, her green eyes aflame with anger. "What do you know about fear? You have no idea of the torment I have been through since I met your people—nothing but hatred and fear and abuse. Do you know what it's like to be taken against your will, not by one man but four; and when you try to fight them, to be beaten for your efforts? Do you know what it's like to be made a prisoner when all your life you have been free to do as you please?"

Lisa began crying now, more out of frustration than grief. "Yes, Nakon, I am afraid of Kowano. I don't like to be beaten. I shiver at the thought of him touching me again. If you think me a coward, then that's what I am."

Nakon sat silently through Lisa's long speech and stared at her. He looked at the brilliant green eyes sparkling with anger, the color in her cheeks, her long, shiny hair streaming around her shoulders. In spite of the bruises on her face, he realized she was the most beautiful and alive woman he had ever known.

"I was afraid Kowano had broken your spirit which I so admire. If I judge anyone, it is myself, but never you. I promise you, he will pay for this, and until he does, he will not touch you again." He reached over as if to touch her, but pulled back and got up and left.

Lisa went to bed immediately after that, feeling much better. He did care, after all. Nakon blamed himself, not her. She lay back to sleep, secure with the feeling that this strange Comanche warrior was beginning to love her as much as she loved him . . .

SWEET MEDICINE'S PROPHECY
by Karen A. Bale

THE FOREVER PASSION

BY KAREN A. BALE

ZEBRA BOOKS

KENSINGTON PUBLISHING CORP.

ZEBRA BOOKS

are published by

KENSINGTON PUBLISHING CORP.
475 Park Avenue South
New York, N.Y. 10016

THIRD PRINTING JANUARY 1984

Printed in the United States of America

CHAPTER I

Lisa Jordan squinted and pulled the trigger of the rifle, hitting the Indian square in the face and knocking him from his horse. His body fell near the spot where she knelt behind the wagon wheel. She nearly retched at the sight of his face blown apart by her bullet, but there wasn't time to think of anything but making every shot count. She aimed again, waited until the next Indian was close enough, and fired. She was reloading when she saw the Indians retreat as they had been doing off and on for the last three hours.

She leaned back against the wheel and closed her eyes during the brief respite. Most of the women helped out with the wounded or with the reloading of rifles, but because she was an excellent shot with a pistol and rifle, she was on the firing line. She had never killed a man before and it was an awesome sight to see. She opened her eyes suddenly, aware that there was little time to rest. She checked to see if she had enough ammunition and reloaded all of her rifles and her pistols. She heard the sentry's shrill warning and the cries of the Indians as they charged again. The charge didn't last long this time and she was hopeful that they had retreated for the last time.

"Lisa." She turned to see Josh Wade, the train scout,

coming toward her. She got up and ran to him.

"Is it all over now?" she asked, leaning against him. She pressed her face against his chest. She felt his strong arms around her and she suddenly wished that she had let Josh make love to her that night not long ago. Now she might never know what it was like to be loved by a man. She pulled away, not wanting Josh to see her break down.

"Wish I could say it was all over, Lisa, but it's a long way from bein' over. They'll keep comin' till they wear us down, and then it will be one final, long assault. The Comanche are fierce and tough as hell and they're not afraid to fight at night. They won't give up." Josh looked at the look of fear on Lisa's face. She had a lovely face, small and oval shaped, framed by long chestnut hair, and enhanced by sparkling green eyes. More than anything, he wanted to take her away from here. He pressed his mouth against hers, drinking in its softness, feeling her willingness, and he groaned. He held her for a short time then pushed her away. She wasn't the only person on this train.

"Promise me something," he said seriously.

"Anything."

"Promise me you'll ride out of here if the situation looks hopeless. If I come back here and tell you we don't have a chance, you go. You're a helluva rider and you'll have a better chance out there than you will here."

"But how? How can I leave?"

"I'll have a horse tied on the back of the Brennans' wagon. Right out straight from there and you'll be headin' due east. You should reach the fort within two days."

"But can't you come with me?"

"You know I can't do that, Lisa, I gotta take care of

6

these people on the train. They're depending on me, even if there ain't much I can do to help them now."

"Then I'll stay, too."

"No," Josh said loudly, grabbing Lisa by the shoulders. "No, I want you to get the hell outta here if I say to. I'd rather kill you myself than let those Comanche bastards get their hands on you." He held her again. "Do it for me."

Lisa reached up and touched the shaggy blond beard and looked into Josh's gentle eyes. She kissed him tenderly.

"I'll do as you say, Josh, but only because you ask me to. I don't feel right leaving the other people here while I ride off. I'll never forget you. I just wish things could have been different between us that night." She watched him walk away, his thick build accentuated by the tight-fitting buckskins, his light hair contrasting with his brown skin. She had to clench her teeth to keep from calling out his name. She wiped the tears from her cheeks and walked back to her place by the wagon. She looked over at Mr. Bromfield, the elderly man who fought next to her. He was haggard and worn and tired. She walked to him and took his thin, wrinkled hand in hers.

"Can I get you some coffee, Mr. Bromfield?"

He looked up, his tired pale eyes brightening for a fleeting second.

"No thank you, my dear, coffee's not what I need right now. You're a fine shot, you know. If we had more marksmen like you, we'd have a better chance."

"Thank you, but I'm not doing any more than anybody else. Why don't you sit down for a while. The lookout will let us know in plenty of time."

Mr. Bromfield nodded absently and sat down in his

place by the overturned wagon, and Lisa went back to hers. She leaned back against the wheel and buried her face in her hands. Was this the excitement she had been looking for when she left Boston? Life in her stepfather's mansion, the frilly pastel dresses her mother made her wear, the young, proper lawyers, bankers, and stock-brokers her mother chose for her to be escorted by; suddenly life in Boston didn't seem quite so boring. She would have gone back in a second if it hadn't been for Josh. It was almost worth dying just to have known a man like Josh Wade.

Lisa had left Boston by stagecoach almost two months earlier. She had contacted a family out of St. Louis who were going to Oregon and she paid them to ride along. Once she got to Oregon, Josh Wade was to take her to Monterey, California, where her brother, Tom, lived.

She had been so excited when the letter from Tom finally came, stating that he was majordomo on a large rancho in Monterey and he wanted her to come live with him. She was thrilled because now that she was eighteen years old, her mother was trying much too hard to push her into marriage. She had decided to go west by wagon train rather than by ship around the Horn; a trip west seemed so much more exciting that way. That had proved to be the understatement of her life.

Lisa and Josh had taken to each other immediately. It had been barely two months since they had left St. Louis, but Lisa felt she had known Josh all her life, and she certainly felt more comfortable with him than she had with any man she had ever known, with the exception of Tom.

She thought of that night a couple of weeks ago when Josh had tried to make love to her, the way he had kissed

8

her breasts and ran his hands up under her skirt to rub her thighs. She had been frightened and curious at the same time, but fear won out in the end. Why in God's name had she been so stubborn? If only . . . The lookout's voice rang loud and clear and Lisa was up on her knees immediately.

She was astonished to see that the Comanche looked not the least diminished in number; indeed, they seemed to be everywhere at once. She knew without having to be told that this was it—they were all going to die. She heard screams and gunshots all around her and her head ached from her intense concentration. She felt a hand on her shoulder and gasped. It was Josh.

"Time to go. They've regrouped and they're stronger than ever. Ride like hell. Good luck, darlin'. God willin', I'll see you again." He kissed her deeply and then pushed her toward the opposite part of the train. She looked around her. She felt like a coward leaving everyone, but she had to admit, if she were going to die, she'd rather die free than as a tormented captive.

Lisa swung herself up on the mount Josh had left for her and headed eastward, away from the train. The smell of burning canvas and wood filled her nostrils and she turned to see almost all of the wagons burning. The screams of the women and children filled the air, and the fiery orange sunset created an eerie background for the gruesome scene. It was then that she saw the Comanche horseman, and she could see that he had spotted her. She turned and rode hard, urging her mount faster and faster. She didn't turn around to look at the Comanche, hoping beyond hope that he was not gaining on her. The sound of the Indian's thundering hoofbeats pounded in her ears but she refused to give up. It was not in her to give up.

9

Her horse tensed suddenly, crying out, and Lisa saw the lance that had landed in his flank. She and the horse went down quickly and when Lisa hit the ground, she came up running. She knew she didn't have a chance in hell on foot, but she hoped that the Comanche would tire of the chase and simply kill her. She was not so lucky.

She felt the weight of the warrior as he jumped from his horse onto her. She hit the ground with a thump but she fought with all her strength. She bit, clawed, screamed, and hit, but nothing was effective against the strong and determined man. He hit her against the side of the head until she was dizzy and then he yanked her to her feet by her hair and over to his horse. There, he tied her hands behind her and placed her across his horse, then he swung up behind her.

The constant pounding of the horse's backbone against her stomach and chest repeatedly knocked Lisa breathless and her head threatened to explode from the blood pounding in her ears. She smelled the smoke of the burning wagons and heard the guttural sounds of the Comanche as they yelled to each other. It wasn't long before the Comanche and their captives rode off, leaving what was once a wagon train with over one hundred people on it.

They rode for what seemed like hours to Lisa before they finally stopped and she was unceremoniously dumped on the ground. Her shoulders and arms were sore from being tied behind her for so long and she wished desperately that she could rub them. She watched as other prisoners were brought in, all of them women and children. Lisa counted fifteen in all: ten children and five adult women, including herself. All of the captives were placed next to each other on the ground with their

10

hands tied behind them, and a long rope was pulled behind them so that none of them could escape. They were all tied to each other. A large fire was built and the men sat down and began to eat and drink what looked like whiskey, which Lisa presumed they had gotten from the train. She hoped that what Josh had told her was true about children captives. Evidently, the children were the only ones the Comanche didn't mistreat. They were usually given to families without children and if they proved loyal, they were adopted into the tribe. But what of the women? Her eyes were drawn to a sudden commotion in the camp and the blood drained from her face as she remembered Josh's words.

"The Comanche seldom ever take male prisoners. Usually they torture and kill them so they don't have to take them back to their camps." Three white men were being drawn into the camp, and there was no doubt in her mind that these men would be tortured. Wooden frames were hastily erected and the men stripped naked. Their hands were tied to the frames above them and their feet to the ones below so that they were tied spread-eagled. Piles of leaves and twigs were placed between their legs and then the Comanche went back to their circle. It was obvious that these men were going to be burned to death and that the Comanche were going to take their time doing it.

Lisa closed her eyes again trying to blot out this reality, trying to think of happier times, but it was impossible. She could be thankful for one thing, at least; Josh had not been taken captive. That meant he was dead, but at least he didn't have to endure the torture these men would have to endure.

She must have dozed off for a while because she

11

jumped up when she heard the shouts of the Comanche as they began lighting the fires in front of the men. Lisa looked at them and each had look of pure terror on his face. As the fires grew in intensity the men tried to be as brave as was humanly possible, but as the Comanche kept adding more wood to the fires and the flames grew even higher, the men began to scream. Lisa watched as the fire crept up their legs causing large bubbles of skin to form, and then as the flames reached their genitals, they swelled and blistered from the intense heat. The bile began to rise in her throat as the skin of their legs peeled away and their bones were exposed, and she vomited on herself, unable to control the convulsive contractions of her stomach. She began to cry hysterically and prayed that they would die quickly, that God would have some mercy on them. She now wished with all her heart that Josh had shot her; death would be so welcome now.

The men's screams went on for a long time, until the Comanche grew tired of their game and let the fires die out. Then the camp was quiet, eerily so, but Lisa refused to open her eyes. She couldn't bear to look at the men. She lay down on her side, seeking as much warmth from the woman next to her as she could.

The Comanche roused the prisoners early the next morning and they were lined up single file on horses, with the same rope connecting them all. As they rode out of camp Lisa turned to have one last look at the tortured men, and it was a sight she would never forget. They looked half human, half skeleton with their bones exposed in various parts, the skin was charred and their scalps had been taken. The most horrifying thing was that they all died with their eyes open—they were large and bulging out of their sockets, showing the terrible

12

agony they had endured.

They rode all of that day and far into the night before they stopped to make camp. The Comanche seemed to regard their captives as little more than animals because they were all forced to perform their bodily functions in public and they were unable to clean themselves. They were given no food and only small sips of water, and forced to sleep out in the open with no cover at night. Lisa felt sorry for the children because they were unable to find comfort in anyone's arms.

The band continued on at dawn the next day and arrived at the Comanche camp before sunset. They were greeted by an odd assortment of old men, women, children, and half-starved dogs. The captives were brought forward and the women and children poked at them, tore at their clothes and hair and pinched them. The children were quickly divided up and taken away, but the women were left standing. They were forced to watch as the Comanche women fed their men and then fed themselves. Lisa's mouth watered as she saw scraps of food thrown to the dogs, but none was given to them. Shortly after that, she saw a group of warriors come toward them and she knew it was their turn to endure whatever the Comanche had in store for them. One of them walked over to her, a leering grin on his face, but the warrior who had taken her quickly pulled the man away. He untied Lisa and then ripped her blouse and chemise open and began to fondle and pinch her breasts until they were bruised. He pushed her to the ground and pushed her skirt and slip up above her waist and straddled her. She fought him, but again she was no match for him, and this time he beat her until she stopped. Then without further preamble, he entered her. The shock to her body

13

was enormous, the pain like nothing she had ever before experienced. The pain never diminished, but only seemed to increase with each grunting thrust of his body. When he finished with her, he motioned to another man and he took the first warrior's place. Lisa was raped by four of the warriors and by the time it was over, she swore to herself that she would either escape or find a way to kill herself. She would not endure this kind of pain and humiliation for long. She was sore and bruised and bleeding and she felt disgustingly filthy. She kept telling herself she was fortunate that she hadn't been tortured, but she felt that, in reality, being raped by four savage Comanche had been enough torture for her.

After that first night in the Comanche camp, time seemed to pass quickly. Lisa seldom saw any of the other captives but she imagined that they were faring no better than she. She had almost resigned herself to the nightly visits paid her by her captor, who she found out was named Kowano, and some of the other men. She never fought them anymore—she quickly learned that struggling only brought her more beatings. She feigned submissiveness and before she knew it, the ordeal was over. They never lingered long afterward, only long enough to sate their lustful cravings. She was quickly learning how to adapt.

The days were really harder on Lisa than were the nights. She was literally a slave to the wives of the men who used her; they treated her much worse than the men did. She was usually awakened at dawn and worked hard the entire day on minimal food and water. If she did not do as she was told or hesitated because she didn't understand, she was beaten on her back and legs with a thick stick. She wasn't even allowed to bathe or wash her face in the river.

The strain of being a slave to the Comanche women and a whore to the Comanche men was beginning to get to Lisa. She had been in the camp she supposed for five or six weeks, but instead of becoming more submissive to the women, she was becoming more rebellious toward them. One particular day, one of the women who was particularly fond of finding fault with her, Lakuna, sent her to gather wood at the edge of camp. When Lisa came back loaded down with the armload of wood, Lakuna stuck out her foot and Lisa fell face forward into the dirt, the wood going everywhere. She got up and saw all of the women laughing at her—it was too much. She was angrier than she had ever been in her life and with no thought to her safety, she walked to Lakuna, speaking in Spanish.

"Cabrona desgraciada," she spat. "Cowardly bitch."

Lisa heard the sighs of the other women and saw the surprised, then angry, look on Lakuna's face. She went up to Lakuna and before the other woman had a chance to react, slapped her hard across the face, knocking her backward. Lakuna screamed something in Comanche and lunged at Lisa. Lisa lost her balance and fell to the ground, Lakuna on top of her. The rolled around on the ground each trying to gain the advantage over the other; Lisa finally gained the advantage. She struck Lakuna with all the pent-up fury and hatred that had been locked inside of her for so many long weeks.

The women quickly formed a circle around her and Lakuna, and out of the corner of her eye Lisa saw some of the men come to the circle. She noticed one in particular, a tall young warrior she had never before seen, but she quickly looked back at Lakuna. She just hoped that

15

before they stopped the fight and punished her, she would at least get the satisfaction of beating the hell out of the woman. For the few seconds that Lisa had taken her eyes from Lakuna, Lakuna had gained the advantage and thrown her off, quickly scrambling to her feet. Lisa saw Lakuna draw her knife and she bent down and picked up a piece of the wood to defend herself. Although she was weak from little food, she was healthy and strong and she was driven by intense hatred, and she was able to out-maneuver Lakuna. They moved around the circle slowly, facing each other like two caged animals. Lakuna lunged at Lisa and managed to strike her shoulder with her knife. Lisa reached up to grab her shoulder, wincing at the pain shooting through it, but she kept alert, not willing to be taken off guard again. She decided she had better take the offensive or she wouldn't have a chance. She waited for the right moment, then feigned a quick move to the right and, catching Lakuna off guard, she brought the wood down on Lakuna's knife arm and then kicked her hard in the stomach. Lakuna fell on her back and Lisa jumped on her, beating her with her fists until all she could hear was the woman's screams. She stopped suddenly and looked up at the amused faces of the spectators, then down at Lakuna covered with blood and dirt. She stared at the faces of the people in the circle; everyone was watching her, but no one attempted to stop her. What she couldn't know was that the Comanche greatly admired courage, even in women, and this was seldom punishable.

Lisa was perplexed. Lakuna was one of their people yet no one tried to help her. She stood up and ran from the circle, not knowing what to expect and not really caring. She ran to the river-bank and stood perfectly still, watching the clear water as it flowed slowly. Her body

16

quivered uncontrollably and suddenly she fell to her knees and began to sob. It was at that moment that she sensed another presence. She knew she was going to be punished for her insolence but she felt no fear. She looked up and saw the brave she had seen for a fleeting moment in the circle.

"I have come to see for myself this wild, white woman," he said in Spanish.

Lisa sat down and looked up at him, her face dirty and tear streaked.

"There is nothing to see," she said coldly. She lowered her head onto her knees, absently rubbing her injured shoulder. She barely heard his footsteps as he walked over and squatted in front of her.

"Are you hurt?"

"Does it matter?" she said without looking up at him.

"It matters," he said firmly and took her arm, ripping the bloodied blouse away from it. She looked at him then, seeing how truly handsome he was. She watched as he deftly cleaned the wound and wrapped it with a piece of her skirt. "It is not too deep; it will heal in a few days."

She pulled her arm away from him and got up, staring down at the water.

"Why don't you punish me and get it over with," she said absently.

"There will be no punishment," he said, walking to her. "What is your name?"

"Lisa," she said without emotion and again she stared back down at the water. The name almost sounded unfamiliar to her.

"I am Nakon," he said, and reaching out he lifted her chin up. "You have green eyes. I have never seen a woman with green eyes." He stared at her for a moment

17

longer and then left without another word.

Lisa's eyes followed him as he left. None of the Comanche she had seen were so tall or well built. She wondered if he were full-blooded Comanche.

No braves bothered Lisa that night and she was even given a blanket to wrap herself in. She went to her usual place in the camp. It was located under a tree and provided some shelter for her. She lay down and rolled herself up in the blanket and she actually felt warm for the first time in weeks. She laid her head on her arm and thought of that afternoon. What had possessed her to act so foolishly? She had acted very much like a Comanche in her fierceness. She probably would have killed Lakuna if something inside her had not snapped and made her stop. Then there was the warrior, Nakon. He was unlike any of the Comanche men she had come into contact with. He had been gentle and caring but . . . No, he was still the enemy, no matter what he had done to help her. She mustn't let herself feel anything but hatred toward these people; hatred is what would give her a reason to keep going and find a way to escape.

The next morning when she rose to start her chores, the women ignored her and motioned her to go back to her sleeping place. She stayed there until a young girl came and took her by the hand and led her to the river. She was told to bathe and wash her hair and Lisa complied without protest. She quickly stripped off her old clothes and stepped into the cool water; she was sure she had never felt anything quite so wonderful. She spent a long time in the water and washed her hair with some of the soap the young girl gave her. She scrubbed her skin and scalp until they tingled. When she came out of the water she felt revitalized.

18

The young girl stared at Lisa with large brown eyes and smiled.

"You are very beautiful. I can see why you have been chosen."

"Chosen for what?" Lisa asked curiously.

"Chosen to become a wife to Nakon. You are very lucky." She helped Lisa to dry off and then helped her comb out her long hair.

"What is your name?" Lisa asked the girl. "My name is Lisa."

"I am called Raytahnee. This dress is for you."

Raytahnee helped Lisa slip into the deerskin dress. It fell almost to her knees and tied up the front with beaded leather straps, and it had long fringes that hung from the arms and hem. She was also given a pair of moccasins which laced up to her knees. She felt wonderfully clean and refreshed. When Raytahnee tried to braid her hair, however, Lisa adamantly refused. She let it dry loose around her shoulders.

"They will never make a Comanche out of me," she said stubbornly.

Raytahnee simply shrugged her shoulders and led Lisa back to camp, to a large tipi. The sun and a large, black eagle were painted on it.

"This is where you will live now," Raytahnee said.

The full impact of what Raytahnee was saying finally hit Lisa—she had been chosen by Nakon as one of his wives. What would his other wives think of her? Would they accept her?

"Will Nakon's other wives accept me, Raytahnee?" she asked apprehensively.

"Nakon does not have any other wives."

"But you said I had been chosen as a wife to Nakon."

"Nakon may decide to take other wives later, but you are the first."

Raytahnee led Lisa inside the large tipi. It was warm and roomy and there was a fire with a cooking pot in the center. Over on one side were robes laid out for sleeping. Lisa walked over to them and felt the soft fur. This was Nakon's bed. She turned to Raytahnee.

"I can't be Nakon's wife, I don't know anything about being a Comanche wife. I can't cook your kind of meals or make your clothes. . . ."

"Do not worry, I will help you. I will teach you all that I know. You will not be alone," Raytahnee said with a big smile.

"Thank you, Raytahnee," Lisa said, genuinely touched by the girl's warmth. Raytahnee was not her enemy.

Lisa and Raytahnee spent the rest of the day walking around the camp, while Raytahnee showed Lisa where to pick wild vegetables and how to catch fish with spears or her hands. They walked into the woods and Raytahnee killed a rabbit with her bow and arrow and showed Lisa how to skin it and cut it up for stew. They took it back to the tipi with some of the vegetables they had collected, and before long, they had a savory stew cooking on the fire.

Raytahnee left Lisa to go to her family's tipi, and Lisa nervously walked around the large tipi. The tipi frame consisted of several large poles which were bound together near their tops and then slanted outward from the center tie. Other poles were leaned against this frame work to strengthen it and a buffalo-hide covering was joined near the top with wooden lodge pins. An opening was left at the top as a smoke hole, and the entrance, which was at the lower part of the seam, had closable flaps. The flaps were left open in the warmer months to allow air to circulate freely. There were buffalo skins and robes used for sleeping which were rolled up against one side, and backrests made out of willow rod. Heated stones were in the center of the tipi and a copper pot hung over them, although most of the women still used buffalo-paunch pots, Raytahnee had told her. There was also firewood stacked next to the coals. Parfleches containing food, medicine, and other essentials hung from the sides of the tipi, as well as a bow, a quiver with arrows, and a brightly colored shield. There was also a hide pouch which contained awls, sinew thread, beads, quills, small bones, and paints, obviously things which the women used for making clothes. The tipi was a self-contained home, and much more comfortable than the bare one Lisa had been made to sleep in for so long.

She went back to the fire and again stirred the stew, the delicious odor making her stomach growl. It was the first real meal she didn't have to fight for in a long time. She heard a movement at the flap of the tipi and she knew Nakon had entered, but she was too embarrassed to turn around. She continued to stare into the fire.

"What do the green eyes hope to see in the fire?" She jumped at the sound of Nakon's deep voice. She turned around to look at him and couldn't restrain a smile when she saw him.

"Ah, you look pleased to see me," he said, sitting down by the fire. "I wondered how you would take the news that I had chosen you for my wife. You weren't very pleased to see me yesterday."

Lisa said nothing as she served him his meal. She waited, as was the custom, to feed herself when he was

21

through. During his meal, Nakon said nothing, but continued to stare at Lisa. She shifted nervously under his constant scrutiny.

"Must you stare all the time?" she asked finally.

"You look different with your face and hair clean," he said with an amused smile. "You look better." Lisa stared at him and she felt herself blush at his words. He fascinated her and she couldn't take her eyes away from him. He was tall and well built while other Comanche men were short and squat. His hair was dark and shiny while theirs was black and coarse. He wore leggings and knee-length moccasins, and the only thing which adorned his chest was a silver necklace. And his eyes— they were the bluest eyes she had ever seen—seemed to mesmerize. Never in her young life had she seen a man to compare with Nakon.

"You stare at me now, green eyes, but it does not bother me as it does you," he said suddenly. "Do I please you?"

"I'm sorry, I didn't mean to stare, it's only . . ."

"It's only what?"

"You don't look like the others. You have blue eyes and you speak so well. I thought maybe . . ."

"I am Comanche and that is all you ever need to know," he said coldly. Lisa looked up at the blue eyes that had suddenly grown cold, and nodded her head slightly. She hoped to get through to him somehow, to make him see her need to be set free, but she had made a mistake. Nakon was as savage as the others and she would never be able to get through to him. She cleaned up the bowls and quickly excused herself and ran to the river. She bathed and was sitting on the bank when Raytahnee came up. She brushed Lisa's wet hair. Lisa didn't mind the attention Raytahnee paid her hair because Raytahnee, like all of the other women, had hair cropped short. She learned the Comanche men were much more vain about their hair and many spent hours combing and decorating it.

When Lisa returned to the tipi Nakon was gone. She tried to busy herself with some handiwork that Raytahnee had given her, but she soon tossed it aside in boredom. When, hours later, Nakon still had not returned, she refused to go over to the robes that were spread out in the corner. She was afraid that Nakon would use her as the others had and she didn't think she could bear any such humiliation from him. So she cuddled up under her single blanket and tried to sleep as comfortably as possible. She awoke in the same position the next morning, her bones stiff and sore. Nakon was already awake and lighting the fire. He looked up when he saw her move.

"You won't last very long if you continue to sleep like that every night." He pointed to the lush robes. "They're more comfortable, and much, much warmer."

Lisa didn't miss the mocking tone in his voice.

"No, thank you," she said haughtily. "I prefer to sleep here."

"As you wish," he said.

After breakfast Nakon got up to leave.

"Nakon," Lisa said timidly. "What am I to do? I mean, what do I do with my day?"

He looked at her for a moment then said, "Do what all the other women do." Then he walked out.

"Oh, wonderful," she said to herself.

Not long after that, Raytahnee came to the tipi and explained that she would spend all her days with Lisa

23

until Lisa knew what to do. Lisa always laughed at the way Raytahnee pronounced her name. It sounded more like "Leet-sa" than Lisa.

That day they went into the woods by the river so Lisa could become familiar with the area. Raytahnee brought her bow and arrows to teach Lisa how to use them. They felt awkward to her at first, and she wasn't able to hit anything; but Raytahnee told her that she would learn to handle them in time.

Raytahnee also showed Lisa how to sneak up on a wild animal so her scent wouldn't be detected by the quarry, and Raytahnee killed two rabbits for their dinners. Raytahnee pointed out various wild foods—the prickly-pear cactus or las tunas, wild plums, grapes, and berries. If not eaten fresh, Raytahnee told her, they were beaten to a pulp, dried in the sun, and the sun-dried cakes were boiled and used in a variety of ways.

Although the tribe had enough pemmican, dried buffalo meat, to last them until winter, they still hunted fresh meat when it was available. The hunters and even some of the women would hunt for deer, elk, beef, or antelope. They would hunt bear if necessary, but usually as a last resort. The bear was usually used just for its sinew for sewing, for to hunt it constantly was too dangerous. That was why, explained Raytahnee, the women would help when they could by hunting for the smaller game.

By the end of the day Lisa felt tired but somehow better than she had in quite a while. It had been the first time in weeks she hadn't felt like a prisoner and everything Raytahnee taught her, she would remember and use when she escaped. The more she knew about survival in the wild, the better her chances for escape later on.

When it came time for the evening meal, Lisa roasted the rabbit on a spit over the fire. It smelled utterly delicious and she couldn't wait for Nakon to come back. She also put out some of the fresh fruit she had gathered that afternoon. It was the first meal she had prepared by herself and she was rather proud. She was learning to adapt to Comanche ways quickly, and she knew it was this adaptive quality which would help her to survive. When Nakon came into the tipi she looked up and smiled, and he smiled back.

"It is good to see you smile, green eyes, it brightens up your face."

She lowered her eyes and looked at the fire.

"Thank you," she said softly and gave him his meal.

After dinner Nakon complimented Lisa on the meal and she was delighted. It was curious to her that she wanted his approval. She supposed it was because he had taken her away from the others and she was grateful. When she started to leave for her evening bath, Nakon's voice stopped her.

"Why must you bathe so much? Our women seldom bathe. They think you very strange."

"I don't care what they think," she said bitterly. "I'm a white woman and I'm used to bathing often. I don't like feeling filthy. Bathing here twice a day helps me feel a little cleaner after what happened to me, although it will never wash away what I feel inside." She ran from the tipi, brushing tears from her eyes.

Lisa swam and floated in the water, luxuriating in its coolness. For the short time that she came here to the river each day, she was able to forget where she was and what really had happened to her. She floated on her back, opening her eyes to look up at the sky which was aflame

25

with the setting sun. They never had sunsets like this in the East, she thought. When she stood up to walk to the bank, she froze—Nakon was standing on the bank holding her clothes. He stared at her intensely, his eyes slowly going over every inch of her body.

"What do you want?" she asked tremulously, the fear evident in her voice.

"I wanted to see how clean you make yourself on the outside. Does it really make you feel any different?"

"Not on the inside, nothing can ever change that. I doubt I'll ever feel clean on the inside again." She walked forward and reached for her clothes but he held them back.

"Please, don't do this."

"Do what, green eyes?"

"Tease me."

"Is that what I am doing?"

"Oh, damn you. Do you enjoy humiliating people? Does it make you feel like more of a man to wield your power over defenseless people?" She lowered her head and spoke very softly this time. "Just do what you are planning to do and get it over with. Don't make me stand here like this." She tried to cover herself up with her hands but he pulled them away. She looked up.

"I am not trying to humiliate you, green eyes, and I will not force myself on you. Why are you so ashamed of your body? It is beautiful and there is no shame in beauty."

She stared into his light eyes and realized that he was sincere. He then slipped her dress over her head and tied it up for her.

"Pick up your moccasins and let's get back to camp. The sun is low. It's not good for you to be alone when the

26

sun is down. It's too dangerous."

They walked back to the tipi in silence. Lisa was even more curious about this man. He was big and powerful; yet he was gentle with her. He hadn't even laid a hand on her.

When they reached the tipi, he remained standing as if to go out again.

"Are you going out again tonight?"

"Why, green eyes, are you jealous? Do you miss me when I am gone?" he said, a smile playing around his mouth.

"What do you do when you are gone? I never see you during the day or evening. Where do you go? Do you have other wives?"

Nakon laughed, walking over to her.

"Well, I think you are jealous. You ask many questions. By our law I may have as many wives as I want, as many as I can support. I can support many." He saw her blush slightly and he stooped down next to her. "But do not worry, my wild, green-eyed beauty, you are the only one I have chosen so far. If you are very good and obedient, I may keep you as my only wife." She saw the huge grin spread out over his face and she ached to slap it off.

"You're a rotten son of a bitch and your mother sleeps with pigs!" she yelled at him in English.

Nakon stopped at the flap of the tipi, the grin still on his face.

"You'd better be careful, green eyes: your sharp tongue may get you into trouble someday." He walked out, his laughter ringing in the air.

She wondered if he had been able to understand her, but then decided that he had only guessed that she had

27

used some foul words. It was a habit she had picked up from her brother and his friends when she was a little girl, and now in moments of anger, dirty words were usually what came out of her mouth first. It was a habit that her mother had tried desperately to break, but to no avail.

When Nakon came back that night, Lisa was sitting up waiting for him.

"Why don't you let me go? Please, send me back to my own people. I'm worth nothing to you. Any woman in this camp could do the work I do and probably twice as well as I do it. What purpose do I serve?"

He looked at her silently.

"You do not serve any purpose, yet. But you will." She shivered slightly as she looked up and met his clear, blue eyes. She knew what he meant. He walked to his robes and sat down. Well, Lisa thought, she would show him that she wasn't worth anything as a woman. No matter what he did she would never respond to him. Never. And then he would grow tired of her and let her go.

"I'm tired," he said and opened his robes. "Are you sure you do not want to share my robes with me? They are warm and soft." She watched with envy as he stretched out on the soft bed.

"No, no, thank you."

"In that case, sleep well." She averted her eyes as he took off his leggings and moccasins. She rolled up in her thin blanket and lay down on the cold, hard ground. She cursed herself for her pride because every morning she woke up stiff and sore.

Lisa slept very badly that night, constantly tossing and turning. When she finally drifted off, her head was filled with thoughts of her capture and subsequent rape. Only

28

this time it was different. It was not Kowano but Nakon who was her captor. His blue eyes drilled into hers and then he knelt between her legs. He removed his breech cloth and she began to scream.

"You are serving my purpose now, green eyes," he said fiercely as he drove into her with incredible force. Then she saw the wooden frame and they were tying her hands and feet and building the fires. She began to scream and she couldn't stop until she felt herself being shaken. She opened her eyes and saw Nakon and she tried to pull away.

"It's all right now; you are safe. You were having a bad dream."

She looked up at his face and laid her head against his chest. Funny, he didn't seem like the enemy. Tears rolled down her cheeks.

"It was you, you were . . ."

"I was what?" he asked gently.

"Never mind, it doesn't matter now," she said sadly.

"But it does matter, green eyes, if it makes you fear me."

Lisa looked at him and seeing his sincerity, she told him of her capture, the torture of the men, and her rape by Kowano and the braves. She cried uncontrollably and he held her close. She felt oddly comforted by him. She was tired and emotionally exhausted by her capture. Nakon lifted her up and took her to the robes. She looked at him.

"Where were you when they brought me in? Why weren't you here?"

"I was on a raid and didn't return until the day I saw you fighting with Lakuna. I regret not having come back sooner." He saw the look of fear in her eyes as he

29

removed her dress.

"You will lie with me tonight, but don't be afraid. I find no need to rape my women."

Lisa turned onto her side shivering, unable to get warm. She felt the heat from Nakon's naked body as he moved closer to her. He pulled her to him, putting his arms around her, giving her the warmth from his body. She silently thanked him for his kindness and understanding. She was surprised she could feel this relaxed in his arms but she reveled in the warmth and security he gave her. She fell asleep not long after that, her head in the crook of his arm, her hand holding tightly onto his.

CHAPTER II

When Lisa woke up the next morning she stretched leisurely on the warm softness of the furs. She had slept well for the first time since her captivity, and she dreaded getting up from her cozy bed.

"Sleep well?" She heard Nakon's deep voice from across the tipi. She quickly covered her naked breasts and sat up.

"Very well, thank you."

"Good. You will sleep there from now on when we get back."

"Get back?"

"Yes, we're going on a visit to another band. After you have finished your bath, I want you to be ready to leave. I'll be back within the hour." He finished rolling up some things and left.

Lisa quickly dressed and went to Raytahnee's tipi so they could walk to the river together. She was very apprehensive about the journey.

"Why is he taking me on a trip with him? I don't understand. Do you think he's tired of me and wishes to trade me?" She bit her lip nervously.

Raytahnee smiled knowingly.

"Your thoughts are very clear. You tell me every day that Nakon means nothing to you, yet when you think that he might trade you, you become very worried. No, I don't think he'll trade you. War chiefs often visit other bands to find out news of the tejanos or the rangers, and to trade for supplies the others have that we may need. It is an honor when a man takes his wife along with him; it means that he does not wish to be without her." Raytahnee reached over and put her arms around her friend. "Don't worry, Nakon won't trade you. A warrior doesn't trade a woman he has paid four hundred horses for."

As they walked back to camp, Lisa's doubts were fewer. Secretly, she was very happy. She knew that a price of four hundred horses was very high, even for a full-blooded Comanche woman. She felt quite honored and resolved to be more friendly to Nakon.

They were a small group which left the Comanche camp that day, heading south, to a brother band. The group consisted of fifteen men and four women, the wives of four of the men, along with the pack mules and horses they took for trading. While they were riding, Lisa couldn't keep her thoughts away from escape. As she was out in the open for the first time, her eyes constantly roamed the countryside. As if reading her mind, Nakon spoke.

"I didn't bind your hands or feet because I didn't think you'd be so foolish as to try to outrun a Comanche on horseback."

Lisa didn't miss the veiled threat in his words. He was right, of course. One thing she had learned at the camp was that the Comanche were superlative horsemen. She wouldn't have a chance of outriding Nakon or any of his warriors. While she was grateful to him for all he had done, she still wanted to be back with her own people. But for the rest of the day, she concentrated on keeping her mind on the small group, temporarily pushing aside all thoughts of escape.

They camped the first night near a stream in a small wooded area. The four women cooked for all of the men and afterward they all spread out their robes and slept in the open. While the men sat around the fire and talked and drank whiskey and mescal, the women retired to their robes. Lisa put the robes she shared with Nakon toward the edge of camp so they would have some privacy.

Lying in her robe, listening to the laughter of the men, she was unable to sleep. She turned on her back and stared up at the stars. It was clear, so beautifully clear that the stars seemed to be bunched in large, white clusters. Tears were close to the surface as she thought of the times she had camped with her brother and he had tried to point out the various constellations to her. She wondered if she would ever see Tom again. She was so involved in her thoughts that she didn't hear Nakon as he came to lie next to her. He propped himself on his side and stared at her.

"What are you thinking?" he asked softly, almost caressingly.

Lisa answered without looking at him, her eyes still on the stars.

"I was thinking of the days when I was a little girl and my big brother would take me camping and point out the different stars to me."

"Were you very close to this brother?"

"Very. After my father died, he was not only a brother to me, but a father and friend, as well. It was he I was going to see when I was . . ." Her voice caught and she couldn't continue. She refused to cry in front of him again.

"Sleep now. We start early in the morning and we have a long day ahead of us."

Lisa stared at him, angry at the abrupt way he had dismissed her, as if he didn't want her to talk about her past. She thought perhaps he was cold-blooded after all, that he really didn't have any feeling for her. She turned on her side away from him, tormented by wondering what Nakon really wanted with her. She dwelt on this question long into the night before finally falling asleep.

The next day, setting off at dawn, they rode over some mountains and across numerous valleys and streams. In the afternoon they struck a wide, rolling prairie. Dividing it nearly in the center was a high, smooth ridge, its summit reached from both sides by a gradual ascent. As they crossed the prairie and approached the ridge, the small band was in a long, strung-out line. As the foremost horsemen reached the summit, they halted suddenly, making hurried signs, while two of them galloped to the others shouting frantically, "Apache, Apache!"

Nakon drew up suddenly and signaled for Lisa to stop. He told her to ride to some nearby rocks and seek cover. Before she left, he handed her his large knife and rode off up the ridge.

Lisa quickly rode to the rocks and dismounted, finding a hiding place among the small boulders. She huddled low among them, clenching the heavy knife in her hand. She watched as the Comanche formed a line at the top of the summit. Almost as quickly as they formed their line, she saw Apache, almost twice as many as the Comanche, come riding through. They fought hand to hand, some with lances, some with knives and hand axes. Silently, she hoped that the Apache would win, that they would then take her and trade her back to the white people. She had heard that many of the Apache spoke English and Spanish, and she felt that she could reason with them. What she didn't know was the immense hatred that existed between the two fierce tribes and that she would probably be better off dead than as a Comanche captive in the hands of the Apache.

She watched the top of the summit, her eyes seeking out Nakon's large paint. In spite of herself, she was afraid for him, for she knew he might be killed up on the summit. A shrill scream caused her to turn right in time to see an Apache tomahawk embedded in the head of one of the Comanche women. Unintentionally, she screamed at the brutal sight. She realized her mistake immediately. The brave heard her and turned his horse toward her, seeing another woman that he could brutalize. She looked for a place to hide, but she was trapped against the rocks. When he came riding toward her, she held the big knife in front, determined to fight to the end for her life.

The Apache rode quickly toward her, his tomahawk poised to throw, but after a second glance at the chestnut-haired beauty, her long hair streaming wildly around her shoulders, her green eyes flashing defiance, he lowered his tomahawk and picked up a rope. He rode closer to her, forcing her back against the rocks until she couldn't move. He bent down as if to grab her and Lisa swung at his arm with the knife, missing him, and the rope came down hard on her arm, causing her to drop the knife.

Seeing there was no way out, and not wanting a tomahawk in her head, Lisa did the only thing possible, she ran. She ducked out a small opening between the Apache and the rocks and ran as fast as she could toward

35

the summit, hoping that one of the Comanche would see her. She was frantic and she knew by the look on the brave's face, that she had been wrong in pinning her hopes on the Apache for escape.

As she ran up the ridge she heard the Apache behind her but she kept running. He caught up with her shortly, and swung her up in front of him. She struggled vainly. The Apache had a viselike grip on her, his arm painfully crushing her breasts. He screamed something up to some of the other Apache and then turned to ride down the ridge. It was then Lisa saw Nakon, on his paint, at the top of the summit. When she saw him something snapped inside—she was afraid she would never see him again.

"Nakon!" she screamed as loudly as she could, and before they rode off, she saw him turn and ride her way. She prayed he would save her, but she knew that her chances were slim. The Apache who captured her and about five of his other braves were riding down the ridge she and the Comanche had ridden up less than an hour before. She tried to turn to see if Nakon was following, but the Apache held her so tightly she was not able to budge.

As she looked up at the man who held her she was struck by the thought that the Apache were a handsome people. They were not much taller than the Comanche people, but unlike the Comanche, they were very handsome with husky bodies. But one thing Lisa was sure of, they were very definitely as fierce as the Comanche.

Her hope of rescue began to fade with every passing mile. She knew Nakon would not risk his life to save hers, and there was really no reason that he should. She was wrong. Slowed by the two people on his horse, the Apache began to lag farther and farther behind. When he turned to see if any of the Comanche had followed, he was shocked to see the big Comanche on the paint not far behind. He knew he stood no chance of outrunning him with the girl on his horse, so he decided to pull up and face the Comanche. He took out his knife and placed it at Lisa's throat, waiting.

Nakon stopped a few feet away from the Apache and Lisa—he knew that any movement on his part could cause her death. He also knew that the Apache would rather kill Lisa than give her up. The Apache smiled fiercely at Nakon while pressing the knife still closer to Lisa's neck, and he took the opportunity to fondle her breasts to torment the Comanche as much as possible. Lisa tried to remain calm, and she watched Nakon, a muscle twitching violently in his cheek as he spoke to the Apache in Spanish.

"Drop her and let us fight here. The winner will take her. If you don't fight me here, I will follow you until I get her back."

The Apache eyed Nakon warily and then a slow smile spread over his brown face.

"Why don't I just kill her now and save us the trouble?" Lisa made a choking sound as the sharp knife bit into her neck.

"Why waste such a beautiful piece?" Nakon asked calmly. "If you kill me, she is yours. Can it be that the brave Apache is afraid to fight me?" Nakon watched as the Apache's expression changed to one of anger.

"I am afraid of no one. But I wonder why you risk your life for a mere woman? You must care very deeply for her?"

Nakon's eyes caught Lisa's for a moment and then returned to the Apache.

"I paid a great deal for her and I don't wish to see my property stolen from me. Now, either we fight and the winner takes her, or I will follow you and hound you until you kill her or give her back. Believe me, she is worth keeping alive."

Nakon watched as the Apache pondered his last statement. He knew well the Apaches' desire for white women, especially beautiful ones. Nakon was sure he had gotten to the man—the Apache was probably thinking ahead to the times when Lisa would warm his robes.

Suddenly, without warning, the Apache dropped Lisa to the ground, where she fell on her hands and knees in the dirt. As the two Indians squared off to face each other, she quickly crawled out of the way. She felt weak from the loss of blood and reached up to her neck, which was bleeding profusely. He hadn't cut deep enough to sever anything vital, but he made sure that she was hurt and in pain.

She watched in terror as the Apache took out his tomahawk. All she could see was Nakon's head with that tomahawk in it, just as she had seen the woman. The Apache made the first move, screaming something, then riding at full speed toward Nakon, tomahawk raised. Nakon deftly swerved his horse to the side and leaned out of the way. The Apache missed him by inches. Then it was Nakon's turn. He watched as the Apache turned his horse, readying himself for another attack. Slowly, calculatingly, Nakon raised his lance and hit his target. The Apache was struck below the heart, and with a great gasping sound, he fell from his horse.

Quickly, Nakon turned his horse toward Lisa, who was still in the dirt, blood dripping down the front of her dress. When she saw him coming, she stood up and raised her arms. He reached down and easily swung her up in front of him. They looked at each other for a short moment and then Lisa pressed her face close to his chest, her arms wrapped tightly around his back. She felt him as he put one muscular arm around her and pulled her close.

They rode back to the others, quickly formed a tight group, and rode off again. In spite of the odds against them, the Comanche had sustained only a slight loss, four men and two women, unlike the Apache, who lost almost two-thirds of their men. It again served to prove that the Comanche were the best horse soldiers on the plains.

They made their way over the summit and within an hour had found a place to camp. Camp was hastily set up and the wounded attended to. Lisa had fainted from loss of blood and Nakon carried her to his robes, tending to her wound. One of the women came to help, but Nakon waved her away. He cleaned the wound, dressed it with some grass and ground-up herbs, and bound it in a thick leather strap. He covered her up and let her sleep. He was surprised by the deepness of the cut—proud that she had not uttered a sound. Hours later, Nakon woke Lisa and coaxed her to sip some broth, but she instantly coughed it up, her throat too sore to swallow. She turned her head away from him. He brushed the stray wisps of hair from her face and rubbed his hand on her cheek.

"You were very brave, green eyes. As brave as any warrior."

She turned her head back and looked into his eyes. She always got the strangest feeling in the pit of her stomach whenever she met those light-blue depths.

"I wasn't brave; I was just too scared to move." She lowered her eyes, afraid to meet his. "Thank you for saving my life. I was afraid you wouldn't come." She choked on the last sentence, extremely aware of this man, this man who twice now had saved her life.

Again Nakon reached out and gently touched her cheek.

"I need no thanks, you are my wife," he said simply. He got up to leave, but spoke again. "Rest now. Tomorrow the pain will be less."

Lisa's eyes followed Nakon's large form as he crossed the camp area. She lay back down in the robes and wrapped them tightly for warmth. His attitude toward her was puzzling. He had risked his life to save her because she was his wife. She remembered what he had told the Apache—she was his property for which he had paid highly. Yet she felt that it was something more, another reason, perhaps, that made him come after her. He treated her so kindly, and he, himself, tended her wound. He treated her with great respect and still, he demanded nothing in return.

She fell into a trancelike sleep, her head filled with thoughts of Nakon and her rescue. She saw again the way he came after her and lifted her up in front of him after his battle with the Apache. She remembered the way he held her close to him on the ride back.

"Nakon," she muttered his name softly, not seeing the smile that touched his lips as he sat watching her sleep.

They arrived at the Comanche camp the following night. Small tipis were hastily erected for the visitors. Lisa lost no time in settling into bed. The day had been long and tiresome, and her throat ached terribly. Nakon had been right; it did hurt less, but she continued to find it difficult to swallow.

40

Before Nakon went to join his friends, he came in to change the dressing on Lisa's neck. She sat very still, trying not to stare at him as he changed the dressing. Her heart beat wildly at his nearness. When he was finally finished, he laid her back down, covered her up, and to her surprise, kissed her lightly on the lips. He left without saying anything, but Lisa didn't mind. She reached up and touched her lips, as if she could still feel the touch of his lips. It was the first time he had kissed her; and she realized that it was not just gratitude she felt toward Nakon, but a deeply growing affection.

They spent another week at the camp. It went slowly for Lisa as she had nothing to occupy her time. She missed Raytahnee and she wasn't able to talk to any of the women here, since she found no one who spoke Spanish. She wandered about on her own during the daytime, taking little walks and looking at the different horses. She seldom saw Nakon during the day, but he did spend some part of the evenings with her. They would sit and talk outside the tipi. He told her that they came to this particular band because it was so far south, and because of its location they were able to obtain the latest information on the Texans and their new governor, who were waging all-out war on the Comanche.

On their first night in the camp, Nakon had pulled Lisa to him, and from then on, they shared the same robe. She loved lying next to him with the security of his arms around her. She felt no threat from him—he had not tried to force himself on her. She never thought of what the future might bring. She wouldn't let herself think about it. She concentrated only on the present.

They left the southern group after ten days and arrived at their own camp three days later. They encountered no

41

trouble from any hostile enemies on the return and the short trip was uneventful.

Lisa hugged Raytahnee fiercely when they returned to camp, so happy was she to see her friend. Raytahnee returned the gesture, and holding hands like small girls, they walked to the river to talk. Lisa told her of the trip and of the fight with the Apache. Raytahnee pointed to the mark on Lisa's neck and Lisa told her about the Apache and the way Nakon had rescued her. Raytahnee noticed the pride in Lisa's voice as she talked about Nakon, and she asked Lisa bluntly if she were in love with Nakon. Astounded, Lisa vehemently denied that she was, but Raytahnee knew better.

The next day, part of Lisa's daily lesson consisted of learning sign language. Lisa absolutely refused to learn Comanche, although she had already picked up a few words, so Raytahnee talked her into learning sign. This way, Raytahnee explained, she would be able to communicate with other tribes if none of them spoke Spanish or English.

As they sat on the bank of the river, the two girls heard a stirring behind them and turned. Lisa stared at the sight before her: it was a huge dog, almost wolflike in appearance, and he was completely silver-gray in color. Unlike the other dogs in camp, he was stocky and muscular and he had devilishly colored yellow eyes. They reminded Lisa of a lion's eyes she had once seen at a circus in Boston. She arose and started toward him but Raytahnee pulled her back.

"Don't go near him, Lisa; he's very dangerous. We of the camp stay away from him. He's very fierce; he allows no one near him. We call him Osolo, 'The Big Wolf.'"

"But, Raytahnee, he followed us. Maybe he wants to

42

make friends."

"No, he is not to be trusted. He is known to have killed two men who approached him. He's part wolf, you know."

"Why do you keep him around then, if he's so dangerous?"

"Because he's the best guard dog we have. He hears things the others don't. No sound escapes his sharp ears. Unlike the others, he hunts for his own food, so it costs us nothing to keep him here. He came to us a few seasons ago as a pup and has not left. We believe he was sent by the Wolf Spirit to protect us."

Lisa attempted to approach the wolf dog again but Raytahnee pulled her alongside as they walked back to camp. The next few days, no matter where the two girls went, Osolo followed. He always watched but never came too near. Once, when Raytahnee went into the woods to hunt for rabbit, Lisa walked over to Osolo. She was certain it was she that he was following, and therefore, she had no fear of him. She didn't hesitate when she saw him, but walked right up to him and placed her hand on his head. Osolo moved closer and moved his head under Lisa's hand, prompting her to pet him again. She laughed and began to pet him vigorously. When she sat down on the ground, he sat down next to her with his head in her lap. For some reason, Osolo had chosen Lisa as his human friend; she was greatly pleased.

Lisa walked back into the woods with Osolo looking for Raytahnee. When Raytahnee saw them both together, she immediately raised her bow and arrow, but saw that Lisa was next to the animal, her hand resting on his head. After that, Raytahnee had no doubts in her mind that Lisa was a witch. Only a witch could tame a wild dog like

Osolo. From then on, Osolo followed Lisa everywhere; further, he slept outside Nakon's tipi at night.

"I see you have found another friend," Nakon said to Lisa one evening while they were eating.

"Osolo?" Lisa asked with a smile.

"Yes. He's never before taken to humans. He is a smart dog." Lisa was not sure what Nakon meant by the remark, but she remained silent.

"Do you mind that he sleeps outside the tipi at night?"

"No. I'm glad to know you will be protected when I'm gone."

Not more than two weeks after they had returned from their trip to the other Comanche camp, Nakon informed Lisa that he would be leaving on a raid.

"We'll probably be gone at least two weeks. Maybe more. Don't worry. You'll be safe here. Be sure to keep Osolo with you when you go for walks."

"But what will I do when you are gone?" She couldn't hide the note of childish fear in her voice.

Nakon smiled at her, pulling her into his arms.

"The same things you do while I am here, green eyes. Except for this." He kissed her gently on the lips, lingering to taste their sweetness. Then he released her and left.

Lisa stood rooted to the ground for a few minutes and ran to find Raytahnee. She told her what Nakon had said.

"Our braves very often go out on raids, Lisa. There's no reason to worry."

"I am not worried!" Lisa said adamantly.

"Well, in any case, that's how they acquire the things we need. They scout to see if there are any rangers within the area of our camp but mainly they steal supplies and horses.

44

"But why must they steal, Raytahnee?"

"They like the excitement of stealing, but also to cause problems for the tejanos and the rangers."

Lisa was interested in the rangers.

"Do the rangers come around here very often? I didn't think many white men ventured into Comanche territory."

"They don't usually, but the Texas Rangers are different. They are tough and brutal and they seem to have no fear of the Comanche or of anyone else. They make it difficult for our braves to fight them because of a new pistol they use. It fires and fires and they do not have to reload it. They work for the government of Texas. They are trying to exterminate us."

Lisa looked thoughtfully at her friend and was amazed at her intelligence and insight.

"Why must the braves steal horses, Raytahnee? Surely, there are more than enough in this camp."

Raytahnee smiled.

"Yes, but the more horses a warrior has, the more powerful and rich he is. Besides, the Comanche is a great one for stealing. He finds it a challenge to sneak into an enemy camp, Indian or tejano, and steal horses beneath their noses."

"Do the men kill on these raids?"

"Yes, many of them do. Many of our warriors are very blood thirsty and kill just for the sport. But some, like Nakon, kill only when necessary. The men usually kill babies but will take children and women for slaves or to adopt into the tribe later on. Occasionally, they will bring a white man back for the women to torture, but usually they kill and scalp the white men on the spot. The women in camp make great sport of torturing the captives. I have

45

seen men with their eyelids sliced off so they had to stare into the sun; the heels ripped off their feet and forced to run over hot coals; and many men with their genitals cut off. Always, the torture is slow and the captives suffer greatly. It is a terrible sight."

"I know, I have seen such torture," Lisa said bitterly. "You don't agree with it, do you, Raytahnee?"

"It is the Comanche way and not for me to argue. There is nothing I can do to change it."

"But I sense that you don't agree with it, Raytahnee; that it is as ugly to you as it is to me."

Raytahnee was silent, nervously clenching and un-clenching her hands in her lap. Finally she spoke.

"I do not agree with their ways. I am Spanish. As you, I was captured and brought here when I was a child of ten. I was adopted into a family which had no children. They take it for granted that I am Comanche and have accepted their ways. But I do not. I will never forget what they did to my parents and brothers and sisters."

"Were they all killed?" Lisa asked gently.

"My parents and brothers were killed at our home in Mexico, but two of my sisters and I were brought here. One of my sisters died from their brutal treatment; the other was traded and I have not seen her again."

Lisa reached out and touched Raytahnee's shoulder.

"I'm sorry, I didn't mean to remind you of these things. It was thoughtless of me."

"It's all right. I think about these things all the time. It keeps my hatred strong. It's the first time I have been able to talk about it to anyone since my capture six years ago. It's good to talk about it."

"Do you ever think of escape?"

"I did at first, but now I wouldn't know where to go.

46

Most of my family were killed on the raid to our home, and I wouldn't know my other relatives if I saw them. Until I am old enough, I must remain here. Before long I will be taken to wife by a warrior and have a child. Then I will never be able to leave."

Lisa couldn't bear the sadness in her friend's voice.

"Don't give up hope; I never do. I think of escape all the time and wait only for the chance."

Raytahnee looked at Lisa in surprise.

"But why would you want to leave? I don't understand. I'd never leave here if I had a man to love me as Nakon loves you."

"Loves me?" Lisa stared at Raytahnee incredulously.

"Of course he loves you. Why else would he give up four hundred of his best horses, or risk his life to save you from an Apache?"

"Nonsense. He only considers me a piece of his property. He told the Apache so."

"Believe what you wish, but it won't be long until you realize the truth."

"I know the truth," Lisa said bitterly. "Raytahnee, was Nakon born in this camp? He's never talked about his parents or any family, and he doesn't look like the other men in the camp. He's so different from the other men. Have you ever seen a Comanche with blue eyes? Is Nakon part white?"

"I don't know and I've never asked. You don't ask about a man who is as important as Nakon. All I know is that he was here when I was brought in, and he was kind to me. He was one of the few."

Raytahnee then told Lisa that the members of the raiding party would paint their faces black and leave that night. Unlike other Indian tribes, they had no fear of the

47

night, and sought its cover when they left on raids. There would be a war dance that night to honor them; and later they would leave and ride for most of the night before they camped. There they would rest for awhile before continuing on their way.

After dinner that evening, Nakon packed some things in a roll and went out to tie them to his horse. Then he reentered the tipi and walked over to Lisa, pulling her up to him.

"I am going now, green eyes. Do not worry. Raytahnee will be with you during the days and will keep you from being lonely. Keep Osolo with you wherever you go. And don't stay down by the river after dark, ever."

He brushed her cheek lightly and leaned down to kiss her softly on the mouth, and before she knew it, he was gone. She had longed for more, but he had pulled away. She ran to the flap of the tipi and watched as he mounted his horse and rode through camp. He looked magnificent, his bronze skin reflecting the golden glow of the campfires. She let the flap down and walked over to the robes. She undressed and snuggled in the warm softness. Her hand reached out to the place where Nakon slept and she suddenly felt very lonely. It would be much too long a time until he returned.

CHAPTER III

Lisa was a good student. She worked with Raytahnee daily learning the use of the bow and arrow and how to use a knife. She wasn't allowed to have a knife of her own yet, but she used Raytahnee's whenever they went out. Lisa learned how to skin an animal quickly, in the most efficient way, without wasting any part of the animal. She also learned sign quickly and delighted Raytahnee by using it often. Lisa relished the time she spent with Raytahnee and the two were becoming like sisters. Osolo followed the two of them wherever they went and the three of them became a familiar sight around the camp.

Raytahnee took Lisa around to the different families and tipis, and showed her the different duties that were performed by the women. One woman was making deerskin dolls for her children. The hair of the dolls was made out of human hair and they were dressed in outfits similar to their human counterparts. One woman was making a cradle board, which was elaborately beaded and, Raytahnee told her, made in the traditional design of the tribe. Other women worked on shirts, moccasins, and skirts, which were all resplendent with multicolored quillwork and beads. The dyed quills were sewn or woven into the clothing along with the beads. Lisa was particularly taken with a buffalo skin, on which a woman

49

was painting horses, figures of men in combat, and buffalo. Raytahnee told her that this was their way of recording important events in a warrior's life.

When they left the women, Lisa persisted in knowing what the men did during the day, especially since she never saw Nakon during the day. Raytahnee told her that when the men weren't out on raids, they normally relaxed and indulged themselves in leisurely activities. Some of the men went to the sweat lodge, which was a rounded, hide-covered frame in which heated stones were arranged, and water was thrown on them to create steam. The steam was a way of purifying the men.

Raytahnee said, and Lisa noted that it was with a tone of disdain, that most of the men spent their time sitting around preening themselves—combing, oiling, braiding, and beading their long hair, which was a source of great pride to each warrior. They also spent a great deal of time in the painstaking process of plucking their facial and body hair, so that they could oil their perfectly smooth skin. Lisa thought about Nakon and realized that his hair was short, barely shoulder length, and was completely unadorned except for the leather band he wore around his forehead. She had also noticed that he often had the shadow of a beard, and she assumed that he must have kept a razor somewhere. For some unknown reason, she was glad that he didn't indulge in the foolish habit of plucking his facial and body hair.

Another favorite pastime of the men was gambling, which they did with buffalo-bone dice. According to Raytahnee, they wagered on everything, using their much-beloved horses, rifles, robes, and sometimes even their wives, instead of money. They used any excuse to gamble and would pass hours sitting in circles rolling the dice, wagering on anything they could possibly think of.

The one thing that Lisa truly missed was riding, and except for the times when Nakon took her with him, she wasn't allowed to go riding with anyone. He suspected, and rightly at the time, that she would try to escape if she were allowed to ride by herself. A day never went by that Lisa didn't think of escape. She thought it might be easier to get access to a horse when Nakon was gone, but she was so closely watched, that she never had a chance. That, plus the fact that Raytahnee was intensely loyal to Nakon and would never cross him, thwarted any plans she had of escape.

She still enjoyed her evening baths in the river, even more than the ones in the morning. She would completely relax and sometimes overlook the time that had passed. One evening while taking a long swim, Lisa looked up into the sky and noticed that it was almost dark. She remembered Nakon's words of warning and quickly scrambled out of the water and slipped on her dress. As she bent over to put on her moccasins, she saw a slight movement in the bushes. Thinking that it was just Osolo back from chasing a rabbit, she turned in the direction of the movement. She strained her eyes to see and suddenly a hand grabbed her arm and pulled her back, another hand covering her mouth so she couldn't scream. He turned her around and to her horror, she saw that it was Kowano, the first warrior who had raped her. She tried to free herself, but he held her tightly.

"No," she said desperately. "I am Nakon's woman."

Kowano laughed deeply, with no hint of humor.

"Nakon is a woman," he said in Spanish. "I hear he keeps you in his tipi and yet he does not fill you with his manhood."

Lisa struggled again but to no avail. He dragged her to the ground behind the bushes and threw himself on her helpless body.

"I think it's time you had the feel of a man inside of you again. Perhaps then you'll leave Nakon's tipi and come to mine as I had intended before he bought you."

"Never!" she screamed as Kowano slapped her face violently. She wrestled with him frantically until she managed to get a hand loose. She searched the ground for something with which to hit him but could find nothing, so she scratched his face as hard as she could with her fingernails. He hit her face again and again until she ceased her struggling. She could taste the blood from her mouth and nose. Where is Osolo, she wondered, why isn't he here?

Kowano ripped her dress open and began to fondle her breasts in a rough way, bruising and pinching them as he had done that very first time. In the hopes that someone from camp would hear her, Lisa screamed loudly, but Kowano quickly clamped his hand over her mouth. He held it there so tightly that Lisa felt she would suffocate from the lack of air. She ceased struggling and felt him shove her dress up and force her legs apart. And then she felt it again—the searing pain, as if her flesh were being ripped apart. She ceased to fight after a while and she shut her eyes waiting for it to be over. When he was finished, Kowano held her head tightly between his hands and spoke to her in a low voice through clenched teeth.

"If you tell Nakon about this, I'll kill you. I mean what I say."

When she looked at him blankly, he hit her on the side of the head and in the chest and stomach.

"That's just an example of what you'll get if you tell

Nakon. Do you understand?"

She nodded her head feebly.

"Good. And don't think you will be safe from me. I'll have you again anytime I wish, and there is nothing you can do about it. Nakon is my friend. If he should find out about this, he would believe me over you. I will tell him that you came to me, that you desired the feel of a man. After that, he might even kill you himself. A man may do whatever he wishes with an adulterous wife. So I'd think twice before I told him anything about this."

He stood up to go but stopped to say something more.

"You are nothing but a whore, a white whore," he said coldly. He then spit on her and left.

Lisa lay still for a while waiting to be sure Kowano was gone and then she pulled her bruised and shaking body to the riverbank. She leaned over to the water to splash some on her face and she began to vomit violently, the spasms racking her thin body. It was then she heard Raytahnee's voice behind her.

"Lisa, where are you? Lisa?" Finally, Raytahnee saw Lisa and ran to her. "My God, what's happened to you?" She pulled Lisa back from the water and sitting down, put her head in her lap. She gently dabbed the blood that ran from Lisa's nose and mouth and washed her face.

"Lisa, what happened? I saw Kowano as I walked here . . ." She stopped suddenly. "Kowano, did he do this to you?" she shouted angrily.

Lisa pulled herself up to face Raytahnee.

"Please, don't tell anyone about this. He'll kill me if I tell anyone. Please, Raytahnee." She fell sobbing into Raytahnee's arms.

"Lisa, you must listen to me. You must tell Nakon what Kowano has done to you. This is not only a crime against you, it's a crime against Nakon. You are his wife now, not the property of Kowano or any other brave."

"I'm not Nakon's wife. I'm only a piece of property to him, a white slave who sleeps in his tipi and cooks his meals," she said bitterly.

Raytahnee took Lisa firmly by the shoulders.

"When a Comanche brave takes a woman into his tipi, that means he's taken her for his wife, unless he states otherwise. You are Nakon's wife, and you must tell him the truth."

"No, I can't. Kowano will swear that I seduced him; he says that Nakon will kill me himself if he finds out. Please, don't tell him. By the time Nakon gets back here, the bruises will be gone and he'll never have to know. You must promise me, Raytahnee."

"I will promise you nothing. I am your friend and sworn to help you if I can. Kowano is a pig and should be punished for what he's done. Now, let me clean you up and then we'll go back to camp. You can sleep in my family's tipi tonight."

"No, they mustn't know what's happened. I'll be fine. Kowano wouldn't dare enter Nakon's tipi."

"All right, but you take my knife. And you're not to go anywhere without me or Osolo." Raytahnee looked around her. "Where is Osolo? He never leaves your side."

"I don't know. I was bathing and he went off after a rabbit and didn't come back. He always comes back before I'm through. I'm afraid something has happened to him."

"Don't worry about Osolo; he can take care of himself. Let's get you back to camp. I'll look for Osolo tomorrow."

Raytahnee cleaned Lisa as well as she could and helped her back to camp. They walked behind the camp so Lisa wouldn't be seen by anyone. Raytahnee helped her to Nakon's robes and gave her her knife.

"I'll be back early in the morning. You use this knife if you have to. Sleep well, my friend."

But Lisa didn't sleep well that night. She kept seeing Kowano and the look on his face. She kept Raytahnee's knife close to her. She wondered about Osolo and worried that something had happened to him. She knew how much safer she would feel if he were with her.

Lisa didn't leave the tipi the next day; she was much too sick and sore. Raytahnee came early as she had said she would. She was disgusted by what Kowano had done to Lisa and wasted no time in telling her so. Lisa looked worse the next day—her face was swollen and bruised, her lips cracked and discolored. There were large bruises from her shoulders to her waist where Kowano had beaten her, and she felt constantly nauseous from the blows he had struck her in the stomach. Raytahnee made Lisa drink some special broth she had prepared and applied herbal poultices on her face. She repaired Lisa's torn dress while Lisa slept, and then she went to look for Osolo.

As Raytahnee walked by the riverbank where Lisa had taken her swim, she heard a low moan and went into the bushes. It was Osolo, a knife wound in his shoulder. Raytahnee walked to him and looked at the wound. She ran back to camp and gathered some of her herbs to tend him. She cleaned the wound and then dressed it. Thankfully, because of his thick fur, the wound did not go as deep as was obviously intended. She brought Osolo some water and then decided to leave him where he was until he was better. She figured he would walk when he was able. She returned to Lisa and told her she had found Osolo.

"I'm sure he'll be as strong as ever. Don't worry about him. He walks with the Wolf Spirit."

"A knife wound? Do you think it was Kowano?"

"I am sure of it. He's the only man in this camp low enough to do such a thing. He wanted to make sure there would be no interference while he had his way with you. The pig!" Raytahnee spit on the ground.

"Well, at least Osolo is alive and will be well soon. Perhaps later I can go and see him."

"No," Raytahnee exclaimed with authority. "I won't have you running around in your condition. Why do you worry so about that dog and not about yourself?" When Lisa didn't answer, Raytahnee continued, "Anyway, Osolo will be fine and will come to you when he's well enough. Better to worry about yourself now."

When Raytahnee left to do some of her own chores, Lisa grabbed her arm and pulled her back.

"Raytahnee, I don't know how to thank you. You're such a good friend. I don't know what I'd do without you."

Lisa broke down again and cried until she tired herself out. As before, Raytahnee held her friend in her arms until the crying stopped, then she helped lay her back down and covered her with the warm robes.

"Don't thank me, Lisa. I'm happy to help you. I think of you as my sister now, and I love you even as I did my own sisters. I just want you to get well, in your mind and your body."

Lisa slept off and on during the day and by evening she felt well enough to get up, but Raytahnee insisted she

56

stay in bed and rest until she was stronger. She made a large fire and talked Lisa into eating some stew made of rabbit and vegetables. Then Raytahnee stayed with her friend until she fell asleep. Before she went to her own tipi, she checked to see if the knife was next to Lisa.

Sometime later Lisa was awakened by the sound of voices outside the tipi, and she instantly grabbed the knife. If it was Kowano, she decided, she would kill him before she let him touch her again. When the flap opened, however, it was Nakon who entered the tipi. Lisa quickly turned on her side and put the knife under the robes. She heard him as he walked to the fire and then to the robes and sat down next to her.

"You are not asleep, green eyes. I saw you turn away as I entered. Are you not glad to see me?"

"I am glad you are back, Nakon, and safe," she said, keeping her back turned to him.

"Did you miss me?" She could imagine the grin that was on his face as he talked.

It was some time before Lisa answered.

"Yes, Nakon, I missed you very much."

"What's wrong? Why do you turn away from me?"

"It's nothing; I'm just tired."

Suddenly his hand was on her shoulder pulling her to him. She tried to cover her face but he pinioned her arms above her head, and with his other hand he pulled the robe down to her waist. She heard his indrawn breath as he looked at her and then covered her up again. He gently pulled her chin toward him, and she shut her eyes under his close scrutiny. The beautiful face he remembered in detail was now marred beyond belief by ugly bruises and marks so that she looked very little like the woman he had left. He longed to hold and comfort her, but he was so

57

enraged he had to find out what had happened.

Lisa opened her eyes to find him staring at her, the muscle in his cheek twitching violently, as it always did when he was upset. He let go of her hands.

"Who did this?" he asked in a low and menacing voice. When she turned her head and didn't answer, he placed his hand on her chin and jerked it toward him.

"Open your eyes and look at me, damn it!" Lisa had never heard him so angry, and she instantly opened her eyes. "Now, I ask you again, who did this to you?"

Again Lisa was silent. Nakon got up and walked to the other side of the tipi. He was silent for a few minutes, but when he spoke his voice boomed furiously across the tipi.

"If you don't tell me who did this to you, I swear I'll go outside and wake up the whole camp until I find out who did." When Lisa still didn't answer, Nakon moved the flap of the tipi to go out, but her voice stopped him.

"No!" She hesitated before speaking, as if gathering her thoughts. "I fell. Raytahnee and I were collecting herbs out in the woods and I got lost and fell down a hill, But I'm all right now, really I am."

Nakon walked over and squatted in front of Lisa, taking both her hands in his. His light eyes bored into hers, as though seeking the real truth.

"Do you think I'm a fool, Lisa? Don't you think I know what a man's fists can do to a woman? I think you'd better tell me right now what has happened."

It was the first time he had ever called her by her name and it unnerved Lisa. She wanted to tell him the truth so that he could punish Kowano, but she was afraid of what his reaction might be. He had warned her not to stay by the river after dark, so he might blame her for what had happened. She looked up finally, and met his eyes, and

58

she knew she couldn't keep it from him any longer. No matter what the consequences, she wanted him to know the truth from her own lips.

As calmly as she could, she told him what happened, how she heard the movement in the bushes and went to see what it was, what Kowano had done to her, and the threats he had made against her. She began to shake as she related the details, going over in her own mind the whole dirty scene, but she refused to break down in front of him again.

Nakon sat very still while she related her story to him, not moving, not saying anything. When she was through, she sat, waiting for him to say something to her. It was awhile before he spoke.

"Why did you feel you had to lie to me? Did you really believe I'd punish you for what that bastard did?"

She nodded her head silently.

"You haven't learned very much about me then if you think that," he said softly. "Kowano will pay for this. I promise you, he will pay."

Lisa reached for his arm.

"Please, Nakon, don't fight over me. I'll be all right and we can forget that it ever happened," she said with a pleading note in her voice.

He shook his arm free and stood up.

"I'll fight him because it's my honor that's involved, too. I won't fight him here because I don't wish to bring dishonor upon his family. But there will be a time when we are on a raid together . . ." His mind seemed to dwell on the time when he would avenge his honor. "You're not to go anywhere alone; understand?"

Lisa nodded and laid back down.

"Where was Osolo when this happened?" Nakon

asked suddenly.

"He went after a rabbit and didn't come back as he usually does. Raytahnee found him in the bushes by the river today. He'd been stabbed."

He nodded absently and walked out without another word. Lisa turned on her side and to her dismay, began to cry. It seemed that he did blame her for what had happened, even though he didn't come right out and say so. He wasn't concerned with her feelings or the damage that had been done to her; he was only concerned with his own honor. She felt cheated somehow; she had expected him to comfort her, to hold her and tell her she wasn't to blame. He had done none of these things and she felt terribly hurt. She wondered where he had gone but had been too frightened to ask him. She closed her eyes and before long sleep overcame her; her last waking thoughts were of Nakon's handsome face and his wonderful blue eyes.

Nakon barely spoke to Lisa the next day except to tell her not to leave the tipi until Raytahnee came for her. She was still sore and slightly weak but she and Raytahnee made their morning walk to the river. Lisa didn't bathe completely, only washing her face and hands. She was solemn and said very little. She told Raytahnee she was not up to practicing her daily lessons. She was anxious to see Osolo but when they went to the spot where Raytahnee had found him, he was gone. Lisa was worried that some wolves might have come and taken him, but Raytahnee assured her that he was safe. He was, after all, part wolf himself. She told Lisa he was off tending his own wounds until he was better. They walked back to the woods to try some practice with the bow and arrow, but Lisa wasn't able to do anything right.

"I'm sorry, Raytahnee, my heart isn't in it today."

Raytahnee spoke while shooting at her target.

"Perhaps if you thought of the target as that pig, Kowano, it might be easier for you to hit."

In spite of her bad mood, Lisa laughed. When it came time for her to shoot again, she hit the target squarely in the middle, and they both laughed heartily. After a while, they sat down so Lisa could rest.

"I told Nakon everything last night. I think he's angry with me."

"He's not angry with you. He's angry with himself. He's angry because he wasn't here to help you when you needed him. His pride has been hurt—he was unable to protect his woman."

"But it wasn't his fault," Lisa said defensively.

"We know that, but he still blames himself. I hope he kills Kowano."

"Don't be bitter toward Kowano because of me. I'll be fine."

"It's not just because of what he did to you that I'm bitter toward him." Raytahnee went on to tell Lisa that when she was fourteen years old, Kowano tried to rape her. She fought him and was able to stab him with her knife. "Notice the scar he has on his left arm? Well, I gave it to him. I'm very proud of that. He hasn't bothered me since, although he's tried to force himself on the other young girls of the camp at one time or another. His captives suffer greatly at his hands, as you well know, but you were one of the lucky ones. He's beaten and abused most of them until they died from the abuse. Some, when he was tired of them, he traded to other tribes, but by then they were half dead anyway. You don't know how lucky you are that Nakon chose you for his wife."

"You're wise for your age and you know many things. Have you ever had any education?"

Raytahnee's young face lit up.

"Yes, from the time I was five years old until I was taken captive, I was educated at a mission school in Mexico. I was the best pupil in my whole class. The thing I miss most is reading, but I have some books that Nakon brought back for me from some of his raids. I keep them hidden under my robes. My family wouldn't understand. I read them only when I'm away from the tipi."

"Oh, Raytahnee, that's wonderful. I wish you and I could escape from here; we could go California together," Lisa said thoughtfully, staring at the ground.

"What about you? You're very smart and you speak Spanish as well as I. How did one from the East learn Spanish?"

"Though French was the language all girls took because it was the fashionable thing, I took Spanish. You see, I knew I'd be going to California to see my brother someday, and I wanted to be prepared."

The two girls found another thing in common to bind them closer together. As they walked back to camp that afternoon, Raytahnee told Lisa how successful the men had been on their raid and that Nakon had counted many coups.

"Coups? What are coups?" Lisa asked.

"A coup is when a warrior touches or lands a blow on a living enemy. He may use a spear, knife, or hand ax, but he must be close enough to touch the enemy himself. It must be witnessed by another warrior. When a warrior lands a coup he will scream, 'Aaa-hey' so that he will be recognized. Nakon has never looked to count coups, but his men are loyal. They are the ones who bear witness to the many times he has landed blows. That's why he is so popular with his men. He is not proud and boastful, yet he is fearless in battle and keeps very little for himself."

By the time Lisa got to the tipi she was so tired that she immediately lay down to sleep. When she awoke, she found Nakon preparing their dinner. She started to get up to help but he waved her back.

"It doesn't make me feel less of a man to cook. I have some fresh rabbit here. It should bring back your appetite."

Lisa ate her rabbit with relish and even had a second helping. She noticed that Nakon ate with her, telling her not to wait. She was too hungry to object. When they finished, she cleaned up and went back to the robes.

"You're not going to the river this evening?" he asked.

"No."

"I'll go with you."

"No, I don't want to go," she said finally.

"Are you so afraid of Kowano then? Has he cowed you that much?"

Lisa looked up at him, her green eyes aflame with anger.

"What do you know about fear? How do you have the right to sit there and judge me? You have no idea of the torment I have been through since I met your people—nothing but hatred and fear and abuse. Do you know what it's like to be taken against your will, not by one man but four; and when you try to fight them, to be beaten for your efforts. Do you know what it's like to be made a prisoner when all of your life you have been free to do as you please? You honorable people are not so honorable, I think. You are so self-righteous about your lands, about the way the Texans are taking them away from you. You keep saying these are your lands and you want to be free. Yet you take captives and make prisoners and slaves of them with no thought of their freedom.

"Yes," she continued, "I am afraid of Kowano. I don't like to be beaten. Everytime I think of him, I think of the threats he made against me, and I shiver at the thought of him touching me again. If you think me a coward, then that's what I am. But don't sit there in judgment of me when you have no idea what it's like."

Nakon sat silently through Lisa's long speech and stared at her. He looked at the brilliant green eyes sparkling with anger, the color in her cheeks, her long, shiny hair streaming around her shoulders. In spite of the bruises and marks on her face, he realized she was the most beautiful and alive woman he had ever known. He knew he had to be careful what he said to her.

"I don't sit in judgment on you, Lisa. I was afraid that this man had broken you completely, had broken the spirit which I so admire. If I judge anyone, it is myself, but never you. You've been through too much already, and I only hope that your spirit will carry you through this. But don't give Kowano the satisfaction of breaking that spirit, of changing your life, of making you constantly afraid that he will do this to you again. I promise you, he will pay for this, and until he does, he will not touch you again." He reached over as if to touch her, but pulled back and got up and left.

Lisa went to bed immediately after that, feeling much better. He did care, after all. Raytahnee had been right, as usual. Nakon blamed himself, not her. She fell asleep and awoke in the middle of the night with a start, sensing a presence near her. She tried to see who it was. Then she

64

felt a furry nose nuzzling her, whimpering for a little pat.

"Oh, Osolo, he brought you back." She put her arms around the big dog and hugged him, sensing that there was not much damage. She lay back down to sleep, feeling secure with her dog beside her, and the man with whom she was falling in love holding her in his arms.

CHAPTER IV

The next morning, while waiting for Raytahnee to come to take her to the river, Lisa was surprised by Nakon's return to the tipi. He seldom came back during the day so she was quite surprised to see him. He had a small, leather-bound bundle in his hand.

"Do you feel well enough to ride today?" he asked.

"Yes, I think so," she said with growing excitement.

"Good, then I've made plans for us today. I'll go and prepare your horse and pack some food for us. We'll go after you come back from the river." He handed her the small bundle. "I thought you might like these."

When he left, Lisa sat down and opened the bundle. Inside was a hand-carved, wooden box containing a beautifully inlaid mother-of-pearl brush, comb, and mirror. Also, tucked in a tiny piece of blue silk, were ten gold hairpins. Lisa was delighted. She had dreamed of a real brush since she had been taken captive. The porcupine-quill brush that Raytahnee had given her served its purpose, but it didn't make her hair as soft and shiny as a real brush did. For a fleeting moment, she wondered where they had come from but she remembered Raytahnee telling her that Nakon never killed unless it was necessary, and that he seldom kept anything for himself. That made the gift all the more special to Lisa.

She immediately began to brush her hair, then decided to wait until she had washed it at the river. After her bath, she asked Raytahnee to brush it until it was soft and shiny and then asked her to fix it for her. Raytahnee pulled back the sides and braided them, weaving colored beads throughout the braids. She then placed a gold pin on each side to hold back the stray hairs. The effect was lovely and Lisa felt really pretty for the first time in months. When she first looked into the mirror, she was shocked by the sight of her bruised face, but she quickly recovered. She decided to do the best with what she had. She also put on a new buckskin dress which she and Raytahnee had been making, and which she had designed. It was straight and simple, with very little fringe, and short sleeves to make it cooler. There was a tie around the waist to draw it close rather than let it hang loose as had her other one. When Nakon came back to the tipi for her, he didn't say anything about her appearance, but she could tell by the look in his eyes that she pleased him.

It was a beautiful day, clear and warm, and it was a glorious feeling for Lisa to be riding again. She had been riding since she was seven years old; and although she was taught to ride sidesaddle, she very often threw off the saddle and rode bareback when she was away from the stables. She was always driving her mother into fits by her unladylike behavior.

They rode for miles through a deep canyon, which Nakon told her was the Palo Duro Canyon. The band always stayed here in the spring and summer, he said, until it was time to break camp for the hunt. He told her that their particular band were the Kwerhar-rehnuhs, the fiercest and most aloof of all the bands of Comanche. There were four other major bands, besides theirs, and seven or eight lesser known bands, all of which ranged throughout Texas and Mexico in an area known as the Comancheria. The Comancheria ranged from the southern parts of Colorado and Kansas, to the mideastern parts of Oklahoma and Texas, to the southern part of Texas, and occasionally into Mexico, and on the west, eastern New Mexico. The Comanche shared parts of the Comancheria with their allies, the Kiowa and Wichita, but the land was strictly theirs to have and to hold. The Comanche did not tolerate outsiders—red or white.

He told her of the other Indian tribes that bordered the Comancheria. The Cheyenne, Ute, Arapaho, and Pawnee ranged north of the Arkansas River; the Wichita, Caddo, and Waco ranged in the eastern part of Texas; the Osages the southeastern part; the Lipan Apache, the southern part of Texas; and the Kiowa and Kiowa-Apache, the western part of Texas. All of these tribes resided in and ranged into various parts of Texas, but none of them ever dared go deeply into the Comancheria, unless by consent of the Comanche. Even other tribes were awed by the fierceness of the Comanche.

After a couple of hours, Nakon drew up his mount and jumped off.

"Since you're so fond of water, I have a little surprise for you. We'll tie the horses here. We have to walk the rest of the way."

They tied the horses to some nearby brush and Lisa followed Nakon as he led the way through some thick brush and trees. Finally clearing the brush, they came into a small clearing, lush and green, with a small lake in the middle. The lake was clear and light blue in color, and as Lisa looked around, she was reminded of a setting in a fairy tale she had heard as a child. She looked back at Nakon and found him staring at her, waiting for a reaction.

"It's beautiful!" she said enthusiastically. "It's the most beautiful place I've ever seen. It's so secluded and peaceful. I almost feel as if . . ." She stopped suddenly.

"As if what, Lisa?"

She looked up and met his clear eyes.

"As if I were someplace else, as if I could forget everything that has happened."

He reached down and rubbed her cheek with his hand, as was his habit of late.

"I hope that for one day you can forget, Lisa. This day is yours."

She didn't move but remained standing next to him, looking into his eyes. Her name had never sounded so beautiful as when he said it. Reluctantly she moved away from him and walked to the water's edge. She took off her moccasins and tested the water, wading into it a little ways. Then, without hesitation, she pulled off her dress. She felt his eyes on her, but she didn't care.

She swam more than she ever had in her life that day. When she got tired, she would lie on the bank, basking in the warmth of the sun. For a long time, Nakon just sat on the bank and watched her swim. Lisa wondered if he were able to swim, but soon found out that he was a very strong swimmer when he shed his clothes and swam to her in strong, even strokes. He swam around her, disappearing at times, and coming up underneath her to lift her up out of the water. She loved the feel of his wet, naked body holding hers, and for the first time since her rape, she felt something other than disgust for a man.

They explored the land around the lake and collected wild berries which they ate as part of their lunch. After lunch, Nakon sat and watched as Lisa went back into the

69

water to swim. He liked seeing her so free and happy, and secretly wished that he could always make her so.

All too soon the day ended, and it was time to go back to camp. When they were ready to walk back to the horses, Lisa impulsively threw her arms around Nakon's neck. She kissed him lightly on the lips. When she started to pull away, he held her against him and he kissed her back, softly, slowly, letting his tongue lightly probe the inside of her mouth. Their bodies melted together and Lisa felt a slight stirring in the pit of her stomach. She rested her head against his shoulder while he held her. They stayed that way for a long time, then he lifted her chin and looked at her.

"You see, Lisa, not all men are savages." She nodded her head slightly and watched as a deep frown appeared on Nakon's face. "I will never forget what he did to your face. I blame myself because I wasn't there to protect you. He will pay for it." When she started to answer, he took her hand and they walked back to their horses. Soon, they were on their way back to camp. They rode in silence, but once in a while, Lisa could feel Nakon's eyes on her.

They got back to camp after dark, and as they were walking along, Lisa saw Kowano ahead of them, walking in their direction. Involuntarily she stopped, but Nakon pulled her along with him. She pressed close to Nakon as Kowano came near. Nakon stopped and she felt his arm tense, but his voice remained calm as he talked in Comanche to Kowano. She saw Kowano smile and nod his head and felt his eyes bore into hers, but before long, they were on their way to their tipi. As they walked toward the tipi, she turned to see if Kowano had gone, and she found him staring at her, a look of intense hatred on his face. By the time they got to the tipi, Lisa was trembling.

70

"I told you not to worry; I will not let him hurt you again. Why do you tremble so?"

"The memory is still clear," she said softly.

He came to stand close to her.

"Don't be afraid of him; he won't touch you again. Soon, he will not touch anyone again."

Lisa shivered at the tone of his voice, and in spite of her hatred for Kowano, she did not want Nakon to kill because of her. She also knew that it would do no good to try to dissuade him. He left the tipi shortly after that and did not return until late. When he came back, Lisa was sitting huddled in her blanket by the fire, thinking of the wonderful day they had had together, and wondering what the future held for her.

When he asked if she was ready for bed, she said she wanted to stay up for a while, and she watched as he undressed and lay down, and then, as he slept. She was in awe of his beauty and his strength. As she watched him, she wondered why he had not used her as the others had. As her husband, he had the right to do anything he pleased with her, but he had never been anything but gentle with her.

She walked over to his sleeping form and knelt down next to him, transfixed by his handsome face in repose. She looked at his mouth—a beautiful, full mouth, and she reached out to touch it, her fingers resting gently on his lips. Suddenly, he opened his eyes. She started to take her hand away, but he grabbed her wrist.

"I have felt your eyes on me for a long time, green eyes. I wondered what you were going to do."

He held her hand to his mouth and kissed her fingers, one by one, and then the palm of her hand. When he took her other hand, she was forced to lay against his bare

71

chest, her face close to his. He looked at her intently and she felt his warm breath against her face. She felt almost hypnotized by his eyes. He reached up and traced the outline of her mouth, her lips trembling under his touch. When his lips touched hers, she struggled to get free, but he held her close to him, her lips giving way to his demanding kiss.

Lisa was beginning to feel something she had never felt before. She began to respond to Nakon as she never thought she could respond to any man, and he turned her onto her back and untied the leather straps that held her dress together. He moved his hand gently on her face and then down her neck to her bruised breasts. He stroked them lightly and then lowered his mouth to them. His lips traveled up and down her neck and shoulders and down again to her firm, young breasts. He teased her nipples with his tongue until they became erect and he sucked at them gently. It was so unlike what Lisa had experienced with Kowano and the others, that she couldn't compare the two experiences.

He pulled her dress off and she lay completely naked in front of him, feeling no shame. He kissed her again and she immediately responded. She put her arms around his neck and drew his body close to hers. She felt the warmth of his chest next to hers and the rapid beating of his heart. His hands traveled down the length of her firm body, eliciting responses from Lisa she didn't know existed. His touch was so soft, so gentle, she felt absolutely no fear of him. When his hand moved between her thighs, however, she felt herself automatically stiffen. All the bad memories came flooding back. She tried to pull away from him, closing her legs against his probing hand.

"Please, don't, Nakon. I can't. I just can't," she said fearfully. He pulled her back toward him, holding her and stroking her hair. He turned her face so that it was close to his.

"Face your fear, green eyes. You want me, I can feel it. Let me show you how a man really loves a woman. Let me show you how good it can be." She felt his hands on her again. She cringed at the thought of his manhood piercing her and the terrible pain it would bring.

His hands moved slowly, expertly, forcing her to relax against her will. To her surprise, Lisa found that there was no pain when his fingers found their way to the softness between her legs. It was very pleasing and she found the sensation kept building in intensity. After a while, she reached out for him, knowing she was ready for the rest. He gently spread her thighs apart and entered her. She tensed herself for the pain but it didn't come. He had entered slowly, and equally as slowly, he almost withdrew but entered her again. He kept up this slow, rhythmic pace until Lisa felt she could take no more. She kept hearing little moans and cries and realized they were coming from her.

Finally Nakon began to thrust faster and faster, until Lisa felt herself rising to meet him, her hips pressed close to his. They climaxed together, their bodies as one in a tumultuous release of passion. Lisa screamed out, not in pain, but in the most exquisite sensation she had ever experienced.

Afterward, when she lay in his arms weak and tired, she couldn't prevent the tears from flowing. She knew what she had just experienced was the ultimate fulfillment for a woman, but she couldn't prevent the guilt and shame that went along with having been shown this by an Indian. Her emotions were atumble. In just a few months, she had traveled the road from inexperienced virgin to fulfilled woman. There was none of the humiliation that she had experienced with the others, only a strange fullness. He had loved her so gently and sweetly, that it had been the most wondrous thing she had ever experienced. But the thought that a savage, a man who killed without conscience, had shown her how to love, made her feel terribly confused inside.

Nakon was a paradox: he was a savage, yet he was, without a doubt, the most gentle and loving man she had ever known in her life. More importantly, he treated her with great respect and understanding. She knew she was powerless to fight him. Powerless because she had responded to him as any woman would to the man she loved. Nakon pulled her closer to him, kissing her lightly on the cheek.

"Why do you weep? Wasn't I gentle with you?"

She nodded, but still she couldn't speak her thoughts.

"Please, tell me what is wrong. This is a time for happiness not sadness."

She wiped her eyes and looked at him, reaching out to caress his cheek.

"I'm so confused. You're my captor and yet you've treated me so well and with such kindness. I'm a used woman and you have treated me as if I were untouched. I cannot understand an Indian, especially a Comanche, who thinks as you do. You are an unusual man."

Nakon smiled.

"I am many things which you do not know. It's not difficult for me to treat you well. You're a beautiful woman, full of love and life. You care for others and you haven't become hardened by your experiences. I've been

74

alone a long time, but when I saw you, I knew it was time to end my lonely and wifeless state." He sat up and pulled her to him. "And as far as I am concerned, you were untouched when I made love to you. My braves did not take you as men would, they only used you as a receptacle for their lusts and their hatred of the white man. I made you feel as no other man will ever be able to make you feel. Now, you belong only to me." He kissed her possessively and they lay back down on the robes.

He was right, she thought. As far as she was concerned, no man had ever taken her before Nakon. He made her feel loved and she would always respond to his touch, as she was doing now, as she would always do. Abandoning herself once again to him and forgetting the terrible thoughts that had been plaguing her, she locked her arms around his neck and let the glorious sensations flow over and consume her once again.

The weeks passed more quickly for Lisa, now that she felt she belonged to someone. Her life with Nakon was good and with every passing day, she became more and more a part of the Comanche way of life, something she swore she'd never do. She seldom thought of escape these days; and only if she and Nakon had fought about something. With Raytahnee's help, she learned all the duties of a Comanche's wife. She learned not only how to prepare various meals and foods, but how to cure and tan deer hides, and how to sew buckskin dresses and shirts, something she had watched the other women do. The band was preparing to leave for the winter buffalo hunt soon, and Raytahnee was trying to teach Lisa how to slaughter larger animals, such as elk and deer, so that she'd know how to help with the buffalo.

Lisa spent parts of her days watching as some of the young boys were instructed in the use of the bow and arrow and the knife. Their hunting skills were honed from an early age, four or five, as were their riding skills, and they practiced daily at each. Lisa was intrigued by their skill at hunting and riding, and watched for hours as the young boys tracked small game.

Boys and girls both were put astride a horse as early as four years old, and were all excellent at handling and riding horses by the time they reached their teens. The boys in particular drilled daily. At first they traveled at full speed on their mounts and picked up small objects from the ground, then later, larger and heavier objects. Eventually, a boy was able to swoop down from the flank of his mount and pick up the body of a full-grown man, a skill which could later be utilized by the boy in battle to pick up a wounded comrade.

The horse, Lisa had already learned, was all-important to the Comanche warrior, and the animals were noted for their agility, speed, alertness, and endurance, and were trained to respond instantly to touch or word. The Comanche were also skilled horse breeders, and they used only the most responsive and fleetest stallions as studs. The horse wasn't only indispensable for combat and hunting, but also as a source of wealth. Although breeding was a source of new horseflesh, stealing was the preferred method of obtaining new horses. The Comanche loved the challenge of stealing horses from enemy camps and it also served to enhance their reputation as horse thieves, and the dominant equestrian people of the plains.

Many times Lisa watched as the men staged mock battles and she was enthralled to see one of them hook one of his heels over the horse's back and hang down under the horse's neck in order to shoot at the enemy from under the horse's neck or over its back.

Although she found she was accepting the Comanche way of life for the most part, there were many of their ways which Lisa could and would not follow. She was told by Raytahnee that during her menstrual cycle she would have to be confined in another smaller tipi away from Nakon so she wouldn't bring bad medicine on him, but she refused to leave Nakon's tipi. Rather than get angry with her, Nakon only laughed at her stubborn and head-strong ways and let her stay. He explained to her that it was the Comanche belief that bleeding women were unclean and cursed and they nullified all magic. When her time had passed and a woman wanted to enter her husband's tipi again, she had to go through purification rites and bathe in the river. Because Nakon permitted Lisa to stay with him during her time, the other warriors came to believe that his magic was indeed strong.

Once, when a raiding party came back to camp with the dead body of one of the young braves, his widow went into public mourning. She proceeded to maim herself, as was the custom. She wailed, moaned, howled, and tore off her clothes, only to replace them with filthy rags. She then gashed herself across the face, arms, legs, and breasts with a knife and cut off all of her hair. This mourning continued for days and in some cases, for months, and Lisa found this custom difficult to understand. Often, Raytahnee told her, the self-inflicted wounds proved to be fatal to the women because infection would set in. Usually the Comanche was stoical and unemotional about killing, but when it came to the death of a loved one, they went to the opposite extreme.

Nakon explained that the reason for the self-imposed torture was that the pain was supposed to divert the mourner's thoughts from her grief. He told her that in the old days, wives of warriors were sacrificed on the graves of their husbands, but as years passed, the practice was replaced with the self-torture.

The longest days for Lisa were those when Nakon was away leading a raid and she was unsure whether he would come back. She looked forward to the times when he returned safely because it seemed their lovemaking was always more ardent at those times, as if it were their last time together. One particular time Lisa was not so enthusiastic, however. While Nakon was gone, she learned she was pregnant. She had suspected it before he left, but she had been unsure then. When she woke up sick every morning and grew more so at the sight of food, her suspicions were confirmed.

Lisa was afraid to tell Nakon for fear he did not want children. They had never talked of children before and she herself was not quite sure how she felt about being pregnant, being only eighteen years old. When Nakon entered the tipi upon his return from the latest raid, Lisa smiled at him but continued with her work.

"Aren't you happy to see me, green eyes?" He came up and put his arms around her.

"You know that I am, Nakon, but I must prepare some food for you. You must be very hungry after your long ride." Lisa quickly withdrew from his arms. She wasn't yet sure how to tell him her news of the child.

After dinner, Lisa gathered up her things, and with Osolo behind her, she went to the river. She undressed and stepped into the cool water, and as she leaned her head back to wet her hair, she heard a movement in the bushes by the bank. Instinctively she reached for the knife that she always wore strapped to her thigh since Kowano's attack. When she stood up to look, she saw Nakon, completely naked, his lean, brown body entering the water. The sight of his naked maleness aroused her so that she forgot what she was doing. He always affected her this way—every time was like the first time. Nakon smiled as he watched her face.

"Do you need some help, green eyes? You seem to forget how to wash your hair." He reached out for the soap and lathered her hair. He leaned her back across his arms so she could easily rinse off her hair. While she was still in that position, he pressed his mouth to one of her breasts and she quivered.

"Your breasts seem larger, fuller. Why do you suppose this is?" His blue eyes probed hers for an answer. Lisa looked at him, not answering. "Could it be that you carry my child and you do not wish me to know about it?" He pulled her upright so that he could look at her. She could not return his steady gaze and she stared into the rippling water.

"Yes, Nakon, I am with child." She pulled away and started for the riverbank, but Nakon grabbed her arm and pulled her back to him.

"Don't you want my child? Does it make you unhappy to carry it?"

"Oh, no," she said softly. "It's just that I wasn't sure how you'd feel about having a child that would be half white." She watched as a slight frown appeared on his face and quickly disappeared.

"It doesn't matter, Lisa. You and I are the parents and it doesn't matter whether you're white and I am Comanche. It was conceived in love and it will be reared

79

in love. I'm proud that you carry my child." She laid her head against his chest in happiness. Nakon picked her up and carried her to the bank, where he placed her on their clothes. He made love to her there on the riverbank, their passions boundless.

A few weeks after Nakon learned that she was pregnant, Lisa learned that Nakon was to lead another raid. They were becoming more and more frequent, and Lisa constantly worried about him. She never asked him exactly what he did on these raids—she wasn't sure she really wanted to know. She had some idea from the things Raytahnee had told her but she refused to accept the fact that Nakon could possibly be like the others and do the things they did. She still hadn't accepted the fact that Nakon was a true Comanche and that his first loyalty lay with the tribe. She just couldn't convince herself that he was full-blooded Comanche. Not only did he look different from all of the other men in camp, he acted differently. He didn't seem to be bothered by "bad medicine" which was so much a part of the other warriors' lives, and superstitions held no meaning for him. He was clean and his habits were neat. When they talked at great length about things outside of the Comanche camp, Lisa found him to be very articulate and knowledgeable on subjects that an Indian would have no knowledge of. And there were the times when she heard him speak English in his sleep. She never told him of this, but it only confirmed her own suspicions that he wasn't entirely of Comanche blood.

This particular time before the raid, Lisa did something she had never done before—she asked Nakon not to go on the raid. She knew he would be angry at her interference, but she had a terrible sense of foreboding about this trip.

"Please, Nakon, for me, don't go this time," she asked as they sat around the fire.

"You know that I can't do that, so why do you keep badgering me like an old woman? It will be months before the child is born. I will be back here long before then. Why do you ask me to stay now?" He was growing very impatient with her, but Lisa wouldn't give up.

"I don't know; I just have a feeling. Please, just this time, don't go. I feel that something bad is going to happen." She was pleading with him now. It was the wrong thing to do. He turned to her, the anger showing in his eyes.

"You know I don't believe in silly superstitions. Your being with child has made you light-headed. I'm glad to be getting away from you for a while." He left without another parting gesture. It was the first time he had ever left without some sign of affection. She thought that perhaps he was growing tired of her. The party left after the war dance, and two weeks later they returned without Nakon.

Lisa had known something would happen; she had felt it. When she questioned some of his braves, they told her that he was probably dead by now, as the white man did not keep Comanche prisoners.

Lisa couldn't believe that Nakon was dead—she refused to believe it. Even though she felt something bad would happen, she never dreamed he would be killed. She waited patiently for some word or some news of his whereabouts, but none came. Raytahnee tried to comfort Lisa, but she refused to be comforted. Each day was agony for her, a living hell, but Lisa did not give up hope. She wouldn't go into public mourning as everyone

81

expected the wife of a great warrior to do because she was so sure he would return. But time was growing short. The camp was preparing to leave for the plains to hunt buffalo and she would have to pack up and go with them.

When, after a long month of waiting, Nakon did not return, Lisa finally realized he never would. She also knew that she could not go on without him here in the Comanche camp, but she was equally afraid of the humiliation that would be cast on her and her half-breed child if she returned to her own people. It seemed that there was no place for her in either world now.

One evening after dinner Lisa made her usual walk to the river for her bath. She walked upstream a little way to the place where she and Nakon had bathed together, to the place he made love to her when he found out she was carrying his child. She knelt down on the soft grass and reached out to touch it. She could not bear to think of living without Nakon—he had brought substance and meaning to her life. What she regretted most of all was that they didn't even say good-bye to each other. She didn't even have a last kiss to remember him by.

"Are you all right, Lisa?" She heard the concern in Raytahnee's voice as she approached her. As always, Raytahnee had been a faithful friend but Lisa had neglected her terribly over the past weeks.

"I just want to be alone. Do you mind?"

"I just wanted to make sure you're all right. I'll take Osolo back to camp with me."

Lisa nodded her head and kept staring at the grass, remembering. As if in a daze, she removed the long, thin knife from her thigh and looked at it. She rubbed her hand along the sharp edge and saw a thin line of blood appear on her hand. She was sitting there, deep in thought, and did not hear Kowano as he walked up. She looked up when she heard him come near.

"What do you want?" she asked coldly, the knife held high in her hand.

"I think you should come back to camp now, it is getting late."

Lisa began to laugh hysterically.

"Why, Kowano, don't tell me that you fear for my safety. Are you afraid that someone might rape and beat me?"

Kowano saw the glazed look in her eyes and did not attempt to move any closer.

"I was wrong about you. You have turned out to be a true Comanche and have earned my respect. I know of the great love Nakon had for you. I want to protect you now that he is gone."

Lisa stared at him in hatred, hating him all the more because he was alive and Nakon was dead.

"I don't believe you. If you come near me, I swear I'll plunge this knife into my heart. I would rather die than have you touch me again. Nakon was more of a man than you could ever hope to be, Kowano. If he is truly dead then I have nothing to live for anyway." She lowered her head and began looking at the knife again.

Kowano saw his chance and leaped at Lisa but she rolled away. Before he could grab the knife from her, she plunged it deeply into her chest and fell limply to the ground. She opened her eyes for a moment, wondering why it didn't hurt. There was no pain, only blessed darkness.

CHAPTER V

Nakon tossed restlessly on the feather bed. It had been a long time since he had slept in a real bed. He tried to get up but winced at the sharp pain in his side, realizing it would still be some time before he was able to leave. He watched Jenny as she puttered around the room, making sure that he was comfortable and that he had eaten all his lunch. He guessed she was about sixteen years old, about Raytahnee's age. She was a pretty girl with honey-blonde hair and large blue eyes. He felt sorry for her when he thought of what her future was destined to be in this desolate place. But he was not really interested in Jenny. Looking at her only served to remind him of Lisa. He wondered how she was, if she was now larger with the child, and if she had remained with the band when they broke camp for the winter hunt. He knew the band was probably at the plains by now. His mind kept returning to Kowano. God, he should have killed the bastard when he had the chance. Kowano might force himself on Lisa again, force her to become his wife—she would not be able to fight him in her condition—and he dreaded to think what abuses he would make her endure.

He thought of the last time he had seen her, how cruel he had been to her, the look on her face when he walked out without saying good-bye. But he had been troubled then, troubled by the fact that she was coming to mean more to him than the tribe. Troubled because he had actually thought of taking her and their child and leaving the band. He was constantly plagued by these doubts. It made him angry to think that he had so little control over his emotions. And although he hadn't meant to, he had taken his anger out on Lisa. God, if only he could be with her now, hold her, tell her . . . It was no use thinking about it now. He could only hope that she would be safe until he could get back to her.

He had been lucky. When he and his band were ambushed by a small group of rangers, he had been one of the first to be wounded. He fell from his horse and during the ensuing melee, he dragged himself to some nearby rocks where he lost consciousness. When he came to, the fight was over. Both the rangers and his men were gone. He staggered out and dragged the bodies of three of his men into the rocks. He then found a dead ranger and stripped him of his clothes. The man wasn't quite his size, but the fit was good enough. He ripped a hole in the shirt where he had been shot and rubbed some blood on it so it looked as if he had been shot with the shirt on. He knew that in these clothes, with his hair as short as it was and his blue eyes, he would have no trouble passing for a white man. And he needed help. The wound in his side was bleeding profusely, and he was growing progressively weaker. He knew his only chance of getting back to the band alive was to get the bullet out of his side.

He set out on foot, unaccustomed to the feel of the restricting boots on his feet. He stumbled and fell many times, but he kept on walking. He didn't know how much time had passed when he saw the smoke from a chimney in the distance. He headed toward the small ranch. By the time he reached the door, he nearly collapsed in the arms of the man who opened the door. They took him in without question. They cared for his wound and fed him. He felt obliged to tell them something, so he told them he had been riding with a group of rangers who had been ambushed by a band of Comanche. As far as he knew, he was the only survivor. His English was excellent. There was no way they could contradict his story. He only hoped they wouldn't ask why a Texas Ranger had a bullet from a Colt pistol in his side when the rangers were the ones who carried Colts.

He figured he had been here two, maybe three weeks, and he was anxious to be on his way. More than five weeks had passed since he left the Comanche camp and he wanted to find Lisa. Even though he tried not to, he thought a great deal about her while he was lying in bed for so long. He admired the way she had adapted so well to Comanche life and still maintained her spirit. She was so beautiful it made him ache inside for want of her. He hated to see what the hard life of an Indian squaw was doing to her. However well she was adapting to the life, it was not adapting well to her. Her hands were growing rough and callused, her legs almost constantly cut and bruised from foraging for food and hunting in the woods. Her bright green eyes always had dark circles underneath them, and he worried that the child was taking too much out of her.

Another worry that constantly plagued him was the birth of their child. He had heard too many screams from dying women in camp, women who died from complications of a birth or a hard labor. The mortality rate of women and newborns in the Comanche camp was extremely high. Nakon didn't want his wife and child to

86

be part of that. It was now that he thought of taking her back to her own people to have the child. There she could have the best care with a doctor to look after her and the child, and she could go back to a way of life to which she was accustomed.

As Nakon sat there in bed thinking objectively what should be done and why, he realized how difficult it would actually be for him willingly to give her up. She had become so much a part of his life that the thought of not having her around seemed unbelievable. But he had to do what was best for her and the child, and there was no doubt in his mind that sending her back to her own people was the right thing.

By the end of that week Nakon was on his way back to the Comanche camp in the Palo Duro Canyon. The money he found in the ranger's shirt, he gave to the people who had taken him in and cared for him. He felt it was the least he could do to return their kindness to him. Heading toward the Palo Duro, he hoped that the tribe had not yet broken camp. He knew that it was probably fruitless, but he had to see for himself that Lisa was not there.

Two days later Nakon rode into the empty camp by the river. He knew immediately that something was wrong when he saw his tipi and another smaller one next to it. He jumped from his horse and ran to the tipi, meeting Raytahnee as he went inside. He felt a sharp pain in the pit of his stomach as he saw Lisa lying on the robes. It was stuffy and gloomy in the tipi, as if death were lurking nearby. Raytahnee pulled him outside, away from the gloom of the tipi.

"What happened to her?"

"She went to the river to be alone, to think. A month

had passed since the warriors came back without you. Kowano tried to speak to her. She thought he was trying to harm her again and she warned him that if he came near her, she would kill herself. He tried to get her knife away from her, but she was too quick and she knifed herself in the chest. She told him she would rather die than have him touch her again. Kowano swears that he was only trying to protect her until you came back, but Lisa didn't believe him. I think she wanted to die anyway, Nakon, thinking you were dead."

"How bad is it?"

"It's very bad. The knife missed her heart and entered the ribs below. She lost so much blood from the wound that we thought she would never make it through the first night. But she did; she is stubborn. She's very strong and has a good chance. There's something else." Raytahnee watched with great sadness as Nakon looked at her. "The child, Nakon, it is dead. She bled and we couldn't stop it. The child didn't have a chance. It was a male child. The wound seems to be healing but she continues to bleed slightly from the loss of the child. We've done everything we can for her. We don't know what else to do."

Nakon looked at Raytahnee, and taking her hands in his, thanked her and entered the tipi. He walked over to Lisa and knelt beside her. Her face was thin and very pale. He pulled down the robe covering her and removed the poultice over her wound. It was an ugly wound, wide and deep, but it did look as though it was beginning to heal. He pulled the robe down even farther to reveal the bright red stains that showed on the layers of cloth that the women had put beneath Lisa. The bleeding still had not stopped. He covered her up again and walked to the old woman, Matay, who was the best healer in the band. Raytahnee had always trusted her because she had once saved her life. The old woman used no magic in her medicine, only herbal and grass poultices and broths which had much more effect on her patients than magic.

"Matay, is there anything I can do? Can I do something to help her?"

The old woman reached out and touched the young chief's shoulder. She saw the anguish in his blue eyes as he looked at her. She had always been fond of him, ever since he had come to them as a child. He had been one of the few who had defended her against charges by the puhakuts, the medicine men. They said she was a witch because she did not use magic in her medicine. They called her an alien spirit. Because of Nakon's defense, she had become a respected healer in the band. She chose her words carefully.

"There is always a chance, my son. We have done all we can for her. Perhaps what she needs now is you. If you talk to her and stay with her, perhaps she will hear you and know that you live. You may be the only cure for her now."

Matay and Raytahnee went to their own tipi, leaving Nakon alone with Lisa. He stared at her still form, taking her limp hand and pressing it to his mouth. He leaned close to her, his lips next to her face.

"Green eyes, you must try to live, you must try to get well. You must live for me. I love you with all my soul. I would trade my life for yours this second if only you would live." He laid his head on her chest and could not stop the tears that came to his eyes. He cried as he had not done since he was a child, when he learned of his father's death. It wasn't fair. Two of the people he loved most in

89

the world to be taken from him so soon . . . He felt a slight movement on his head and looked up to find Lisa's hand touching his hair. He looked at her face for some sign of recognition, but her eyes were closed. Had he imagined it? No, it had been real and she had heard him. He kissed her lightly and again rested his head on her chest, each beat of her heart reassuring him that she was still alive.

Lisa knew she was in heaven. She was asleep and her beloved was sleeping with his head on her breasts. She smiled. This was how it should be. He would be with her always now. She tried to move and cried out in pain. Pain? Was one supposed to feel pain in heaven?

Lisa's cry immediately awoke Nakon.

"Lisa, can you open your eyes?"

Slowly, Lisa opened her eyes and looked at his face. Oh, God, what a face. It was a sin for a man to have such a wonderful face, she thought. She reached up to touch it, stroking the smooth skin, making sure it was real.

"You're alive?" she asked very softly.

"Yes, I'm alive. Did you really think I'd ever leave you?" He bent down and kissed her gently on the lips and then cradled her head in his large hands. "I knew you wouldn't leave me. I'm helpless without you."

This brought a smile to Lisa's lips. Nothing could have been farther from the truth, but at that moment she didn't care. She was just happy to hear his voice.

"I don't know about your being helpless, but they're nice words to hear. What happened? Where were you all this time? I thought you were dead," she said in a trembling voice, her eyes filling with tears.

"I'm very much alive, as you can see, my love. I will

tell you about it later. Now, I want you to try to eat something and then rest. There'll be plenty of time for talk later."

"Nakon . . ." Lisa started to talk but choked on the tears. "The baby . . ."

"I know, Lisa, I know. But there will be more children. We'll have the rest of our lives to plan for and to live. Now you concentrate on getting well." He got up to leave, but Lisa called him back.

"Don't go yet. Please, stay with me awhile. I need to feel you next to me." She patted the robe on her side.

He lay down next to her on the robes, trying not to hurt her. He held her and she laid her head on his shoulder. When he looked at her he saw that she had fallen asleep, a slight smile on her lips.

Lisa grew stronger with every passing day. Matay had been right; Nakon was the cure she had really needed. A week after he came, Nakon suggested that the other two women go to the band, but they insisted on staying until Lisa was well enough to ride and they could all go back together.

Once Nakon walked to the place where Lisa had tried to take her life, where they had made love. He sat down, staring at the clear water, running his hands through his hair. Never in all his life had he expected to feel so strongly for another person. He didn't know how he would tell her he was going to take her back to her own people, but he was convinced, now more than ever, that he had to take her back. He could not bear for her to suffer anymore; she would always suffer if she stayed with him here. She was not made for this kind of life. He would tell her when she was completely well, when she could take the shock. It was hard enough for him now, listening to her plans for the future, having more children, loving them, raising them. He tried to discourage such talk, but it seemed to give her hope for the future, a future she didn't know would be without him.

After a few more days of rest, Lisa asked if she could go outside. Nakon carried her, keeping her bundled in a robe. The fall air was growing crisp, but the day was clear and Lisa rejoiced in its beauty. He allowed her to stay out a little longer each day, and when another week had passed, they walked to the river and back. The fresh air did wonders for Lisa—her skin glowed as it had before and there was color in her cheeks. Her eyes were clear and sparkling and she longed for a bath, a sure sign that she was getting well.

Lisa's strength surprised even Nakon. She seemed to accept the loss of their child and took hope in knowing it would not be long before she had another. Nakon seldom left her side during this time, and even when she was well enough to walk by herself, he was always with her. Soon she was her old self again, eating normally with the wound almost completely healed. They decided that in a few days they would leave and travel at a slow pace for the lower plains. Lisa was excited about the buffalo hunt and couldn't wait to be a part of it.

One day when they walked to the river, Lisa undressed and stepped into the cool water before Nakon could stop her. She had soap in her hand and she began washing herself all over. She smiled invitingly at him until he too undressed and joined her. He didn't know if she were well enough to make love, and he didn't want to force her, but being to close to her lovely, naked body, made it extremely difficult for him. When Lisa first saw the scar under her breast she was horrified and tried to cover it with her hands, but nothing could hide the ugly red gash that marred the once-perfect flesh. Nakon took her hands away and lowered his mouth to the scar. She tried to pull away, but he wouldn't let her and he pressed his mouth to the scar.

"Oh, don't, it's so ugly."

He held her near, raising his head to stare into her clear, green eyes.

"You think the scar is ugly and mars your skin, but it only serves to remind me how much you love me. It was my fault that you did this. It is something that will weigh heavily on my heart until the day I die." He picked her up and carried her to their place on the bank. He kissed her gently, his mouth moving to her ear. "God, how I love you. Always remember that." He made love to her gently at first, and then with such intensity that he cried out and held onto her, so as to never let her go.

On their ride to the lower plains, Nakon explained a little about the hunt to Lisa. The best hunting season was in late summer or early fall after the molting season. The buffalo grew a dark-brown pelt in the fall, the best for robes, and also put on its winter fat. They would kill buffalo until early December or until the first deep snow came. He explained that the hunt was a cooperative venture; every man, woman, and child went along and took part, each performing a role suited to strength and sex.

The hunter scouts would ride out to locate the biggest herds of buffalo, the main body of hunters following, with the entire camp, mounted, close behind. Flocks of ravens usually pointed out the herds, as these birds ate

93

the parasites from the buffalo. The hunt was loosely organized so that the riders were allowed to ride alone and shot buffalo at random since there was no shortage of the buffalo. Nakon said the lance was the favorite way to kill the buffalo. Since they were such excellent horsemen, the Comanche found the lance more of a challenge. More strength and daring were needed to spear a buffalo than to kill one with a bow and arrow. To carry a lance on the hunt was a mark of pride. He explained, however, that no matter how skilled the hunter, any type of mounted hunting was dangerous. Riders running through a herd could be thrown or their horses horned, or their mounts could easily break a leg in one of the numerous prairie-dog holes and throw the rider.

Lisa asked what the women did in the hunt. Nakon was rather evasive about it, but when Lisa persisted, he told her a little. Many of the women liked to chase after a wounded buffalo with bow and arrow. Some of the women were almost as skilled with bows as the warriors; they lacked only the great arm strength. The children were kept far from the hunt so they could not be hurt, but could still scream and yell encouragement to their favorite hunters. Some of the older children helped the women carry the fresh meat to camp. Nakon really had not answered Lisa's questions about the work. He wanted to discourage her as much as possible from helping out. This was exactly the kind of thing he didn't want her doing. It was hard, grueling work for the women, and it usually didn't end until they went to bed at night.

The little group reached the band in less than a week. Nakon had wanted to take their time but Lisa insisted that she was well enough to ride at a normal pace. The camp was a bustle of activity as they rode in during the early afternoon. They set up the tipi, and Nakon went to join the hunt. Lisa went with Raytahnee who told her to stay out of the way and watch. She had strict orders from Nakon to keep Lisa away from any hard work.

Lisa walked to a higher spot so she could have a good view of the hunt. It was easy to spot Nakon, his large form practically blending into his horse. It came as no surprise to her that he carried a lance. She looked at the women among the scattered carcasses and noticed that they descended upon the animals before they were dead. The carcass belonged to the hunter who had killed it. It was easily identifiable by the markings on the shaft of his lance or arrow.

The skinning and butchering were a community affair, families pitching in to help with each carcass. The men did the hard work first, skinning and quartering the animal, then the rest was left up to the women and girls. When this was done, the hunt leader always set aside meat and hides for the aged, the ailing, or the orphaned. The hunters always killed a few extra buffalo; no one starved.

Lisa watched with great interest as the women battled to be the first to a fresh carcass. They cut out the liver smeared with the salty juices of the gall bladder, cracked the raw brains from the skull, and stripped the marrow from the bones. These were all eaten on the spot and Lisa came close to vomiting the first time she watched this ritual. They also drank the blood from the animal, and the milk from any nursing mothers. All these things were considered delicacies but Lisa knew she would never consider them so. Raytahnee explained that it was really not so barbaric as it seemed. By eating the fresh entrails of the animal, they could get the badly needed nutrients that they lacked in the other foods they ate. It was one of the few ways they had of getting the essential foods needed to keep them healthy.

Later, while buffalo steaks were roasting on sticks over fires, the long, drawn-out, laborious work of tanning hides began. Lisa had some idea of what was involved from what she and Raytahnee had done to the deer hides, but it was nowhere as difficult as tanning the huge buffalo hides. The total process took about six weeks. They were first laid out on a flat log, and all the flesh was cut away from the hide until it presented a uniform thickness all over. It was then stretched upon a large wooden frame and rubbed with a kind of pumice stone until the surface became fuzzy. To prevent it from drying hard, they used a preparation composed of basswood bark pounded very fine and mixed with the brains of the buffalo, which was then applied day after day until the skin was thoroughly saturated and became soft and flexible. Sometimes, if the hide was particularly brittle, the women would chew on it until it became soft enough to make into shirts, leggings, moccasins, dresses, and gloves. The thicker skins served as blankets and robes, the tails as fly whisks. Rawhide was made into strings and lassos, and, when shrunk, fastened stone heads to war clubs and arrow points to their shafts. Buffalo hair had myriad uses. Woven, it became rope; loose, it stuffed cradle boards, gloves, moccasins, saddle pads, and pillows; tightly rolled, it was an excellent ball for games. The horns of the animal were made into spoons and drinking vessels; the bones into saddletrees and various tools; the ribs, when tied together with rawhide, became sleds; while small bones were made into knives and awls. Rattles were also made out of the buffalo's hooves and its scrotum.

The meat from the animal was cooked on sticks over hot coals or on an open fire, emerging charred on the outside, raw on the inside. This meat provided breakfast, lunch, and dinner as the women had little time to prepare meals during the hunt. They also boiled the meat in the metal pots they had acquired from the Mexicans. This way they provided a stew of sorts with a tasty broth. Many of the women liked to stew the whole buffalo paunch as this, too, was considered a delicacy. For winter use, they dried vast quantities of meat which hung from poles and racks to dry in the sun and then made into jerky or pounded together with berries and fat and made into pemmican, a high-protein food carried by the warriors on the trail.

After a few days, in spite of Nakon's insistence that she not do any of the hard work, Lisa began to help Raytahnee and the other women. She never ate any of the raw entrails, but she helped to butcher the animal and to tan the hides. The days went quickly but the work was hard and tiresome. The band could soon feel that winter was close—the air and the wind became more chill each day. Nakon and Lisa did not talk much during these days because they were usually too tired from the work. But their relationship was such that words weren't needed. Their love was enough for them.

Nakon knew it was time to tell Lisa of his plan to take her back to her own people. He talked to some Comancheros who came to their camp to trade for buffalo robes and hides. They told him of a white man who was looking for a white woman captive who fit Lisa's description. Nakon suspected that the man was Josh Wade, the man of whom Lisa had spoken. Nakon told the Comancheros that he would be willing to trade her only if this man, Josh Wade, came himself to take her out. He told them the Comanche would be leaving for their winter camp soon and that the traders would have to get Wade here in less than a month if he wanted to trade for her. He disliked deceiving Lisa, but he knew this was the only way he would be able to get her to go. He kept telling himself that it was the best thing for her, but he was finding it more and more difficult to accept.

One evening while they were going for a walk, Nakon decided it was time to tell Lisa the truth. He knew he couldn't keep it from her any longer.

"Green eyes, I have something of great importance to talk to you about." He took her hands and set her down on the ground. He sat next to her. "I have thought about it a long time, even before you were so ill and lost the child. I have decided that you should return to your own people."

Lisa was astounded.

"I will not go without you. If you plan to come with me, then I'll go. We can go west together."

"You know I can't leave here. But you must go; this life isn't for you. You were made for a different life; you were born to a different life. You weren't raised to live as a Comanche and it's not fair for you to stay here and live as we do." He paused for a moment, thinking back to an earlier time. "I remember a time when you would have given anything to get out of here."

She looked at him earnestly, taking one of his hands and kissing it softly.

"That was before you, my love. Now I have no reason to leave, and I won't go. You can't make me."

They argued and argued, and still Nakon could not convince Lisa that it was the best thing for her. She stubbornly refused to go without him, and the subject was dropped for the time being.

Three weeks later, Josh Wade and a small group of Comancheros rode into camp to trade for Lisa.

Lisa went to the flap of the tipi to see what all the commotion was about. She was preparing dinner when she heard shouts and noises outside. When she started out, she found a brave barring her exit.

"What's going on, Kwektay? Why can't I leave the tipi?"

"Nakon say you stay. He not tell me why." Gently he pushed her back inside.

Nakon returned to the tipi sometime later and Lisa knew immediately that something was wrong. He walked to the fire and squatted in front of it, warming his hands. He didn't look at her when he spoke.

"Tomorrow you will return with the white scout to your own people. Your friend Wade is here. It has been decided."

Lisa walked over to him. She couldn't believe what she'd just heard.

"What has been decided? Surely, you're playing a child's game with me? You wouldn't send me back against my will. I am your woman, your wife."

"I said you will leave tomorrow with Wade. It is best. My people need the guns and ammunition your trade will bring. I must do what is best for my people." He refused to look at her, but continued to stare into the fire.

Lisa knelt beside him, pulling at his shoulder.

"Your people, your people! I am one of your people, but you don't seem to care what's best for me. No! I won't go. I won't leave you. I refuse to be traded for some guns and ammunition. Surely, I am more important to you than these things?" she asked him in desperation.

"Do not argue with me, woman. I have told you what must be. I've thought long on it and I think it's best for you to go. You are not Comanche, after all." His voice was cold and emotionless. Lisa couldn't believe this was the same man who had loved and cared for her so gently.

"Don't make me go. Please, let me stay. I'll do anything you ask. I'll tell the white man I don't wish to go with him. Let me stay with you." She held onto his arm tightly. Roughly, he pulled his arm away.

"Enough! Do not shame me so, woman. Do not grovel at my feet like a shameless bitch in heat. I tell you you must go. Do not argue with me; it is not your place to argue. You do what I tell you to do. I tell you this, if you don't leave here, I'll divorce you and take another wife. Would you be able to stay then?" He got up and walked to the robes. "Get ready for bed now, I grow weary of all this chatter."

Very slowly, Lisa stood up, tears streaming down her face. She walked to him, standing over him until he looked up at her. Finally, his eyes met hers. He had never seen such a look of hatred and contempt.

"I will not spend my last night with you on these robes, knowing you would trade me, our love, for a few guns. You've grown tired of me so you toss me aside like a used piece of clothing. I thought our love was sacred to you, but I can see that it has no meaning for you. You're not Nakon, you're some stranger I don't know and don't wish to know. I have no love for you." She reached up to wipe the tears from her eyes. "I will do as you say, but only because I don't wish to further humiliate myself. I did not mean to shame you, please believe that. I only meant to show you that I would rather stay with you forever than return to my own people. I was wrong." She started to leave, but stopped. She turned to look at him once more. "I'm glad I didn't bear your child."

She ran out of the tipi without looking back. Nakon's eyes followed her as she went out. When she was gone he covered his face with his hands. Well, he had done it and now she hated him. But perhaps her hatred would carry her through. But what, in God's name, would carry him through.

Lisa walked to the river and sat down. It reminded her of their camp in the Palo Duro Canyon except this river wasn't quite so large. Osolo followed her, sitting down next to her, his head in her lap. She petted him unconsciously, her eyes staring up at the sky. It was dark now, with only a trace of moon stirring behind the clouds. She laid her head against Osolo's and shut her eyes. She felt so tired and so alone. She sat for a long time not even able to cry; she felt empty inside. Empty and bitter and betrayed. She would never understand why he had done this to her. Perhaps he blamed her for the death of their child, after all. She was suddenly very ashamed of the way she had given herself to him all those times, so freely and openly. And now it seemed he was tired of her and ready for another wife.

She spoke out loud to herself.

"Nakon, do you forsake everything I have ever given you? Have our lives not met and become as one? Do you hold me in so little regard that you can trade me for so little in return?"

"I told you once before I love you more than life itself." Lisa was startled by the sound of Nakon's deep voice. She looked up and found him standing behind her.

He pulled her up to him.

"I did not lie to you then; I do not lie to you now. What I do, I do for your own good. You don't belong here. You must return to your own people. I don't want to see you dead from smallpox, pneumonia, or childbirth. Even the rangers could find our camp. They get closer all the time. It won't be long before they track us to every camp we have. They've already penetrated the Comancheria and they're not afraid to fight us all. They won't stop at killing defenseless women and children."

Lisa spoke, forgetting her anger.

"But they wouldn't kill a white woman?"

"Do you think you look like a white woman the way you're dressed, the way your skin is brown from the sun? They won't take the time to ask."

"Then come with me. We can leave together. We go someplace far away, to the west, to California. No one will know you are Comanche there. You have blue eyes and with your hair cut shorter, you could pass for white. And you can speak English, I've heard you many times." He looked surprised at this and he took her by the shoulders.

"Did someone tell you this? I've never spoken English in front of you."

"No one told me." She shrugged off his hands. "I heard you speak it many times in your sleep. When I was sick, you thought I was asleep, and you spoke to me in English."

He let go of her and walked to the edge of the water. He bent down and picked up some stones, tossing them into the water.

"There is much I should tell you, but can't. At least not now. Why don't you just do as I say? You know I

102

can't go with you. I am a chief and I am Comanche, no matter what you think, and I must remain with my people. You are white and must return to yours."

"You keep saying you are Comanche, Nakon. Who are you trying to convince, me or yourself?"

Nakon looked at her, a tired expression on his face.

"We will talk no more about it. You have no choice in the matter. You will leave in the morning. I have tried to explain my reasons to you, but you refuse to listen."

"Then go back to your tipi and leave me alone," Lisa cried angrily. "I don't want to see you before I leave. You're a coward, Nakon, for you can't even tell me the truth. The truth is you're tired of me. You can't tell me so you find it easier to trade me off to the white man. Is there another woman? One who is younger or prettier, perhaps? You said if I stayed you would marry someone else." She stopped for a moment, trying to gather her thoughts. "Before you go, I want you to know what it'll be like for me when I go back. Do you know how white women who have been Indian captives are treated? They are treated no better than common whores. But then that's what I've become anyway, so it shouldn't be too difficult for me to sell myself to men. I'm sure there are many who would pay highly to learn the tricks of a Comanche squaw."

She didn't see the blow coming, and it struck her with such force that it knocked her to her knees. She felt blood drip from the corner of her mouth and when she raised her hand to touch it, she felt the swollen bruise on her mouth. She began to cry hysterically, unable to stop the sobs which racked her body. Nakon knelt down and pulled her into his arms. She tried to fight him.

"Let me go. I hate you, I hate you!" She screamed and

fought him but he held her tightly. She wasn't physically or emotionally strong enough to fight him, and she fell into his strong arms until she stopped crying. He raised her face and reached into the water and washed the blood from her mouth. He held her face between his large hands, staring intently into her eyes.

"I'm sorry I hit you, but I won't allow you to speak of yourself in that way. I do hold our love to be sacred. I know that I will never again share with a woman what I shared with you. But it's because of this love that I must send you back. Wade will take you to California to your brother. You will have a new life there." He stopped once more to wipe the blood from her mouth. "I was almost the cause of your death once, I won't be again. You are young and beautiful; there will be many men who will be proud to make you their own. You must make a new life for yourself and forget about the time you've spent here with me."

"Can you let me go, knowing that another man may know me the way you have, or will love me in the many ways you have?"

"Stop it, Lisa, it's hard enough without your saying these things."

Lisa sat quietly for a moment, watching the muscle in Nakon's cheek twitch violently. He did love her, but he was still sending her away. She still didn't completely understand his reasons, but she didn't want to leave him in anger.

She reached up and touched his mouth the way she had done the very first time they made love. She felt no anger now, only a deep love and a fierce need to be with him on their last night together.

She pressed her lips softly against his then pulled away

104

and stood up. She looked at him and then slowly, seductively, took off her dress, letting it slide down across her hips and legs. She shook her hair free and let it hang loosely around her shoulders. Nakon's eyes watched her every movement and she felt confident in her naked beauty. She walked to him and knelt down, leaning forward. She kissed him slowly, her tongue probing the warm softness of his mouth.

"You will never forget me, Nakon, I won't let you. There will never be another woman who will please you as I do, who will love you as I do. Never." She pressed her soft, pliant body against his, reminding him of the many times he had loved her. He responded eagerly and she pressed him down on the soft grass. He was so fiercely possessive that Lisa was almost afraid, but she knew it was his way of saying that no matter what happened, no man would ever possess her the way he had. She gave herself to him completely, unashamedly, with all of her being.

In the early-morning hours when the sun was about to rise, they made love for the last time. She clung to him tenaciously and cried out for him not to send her away, but he only looked into her eyes and said in English, "I love you, Lisa—forever." He too gave himself totally and completely to her. Before they went back to camp, Nakon took the silver necklace from his neck and placed it around Lisa's.

"This was given to me in love, and so I give it to you. Wear it always so you will never doubt my love for you."

Later, when Nakon took Lisa to Josh, he could barely stand to look at her. He no longer felt like a brave Comanche warrior. He was surprised at Lisa's strength. She hugged Raytahnee and clung to her friend for a long time before letting go. They both had tears in their eyes. Then she hugged Osolo, her huge friend. She didn't want to leave him behind, but knew it wouldn't be right to take him from his home. She went back to Nakon.

"Please, don't forget to do what I asked you to do this morning. If ever there's a chance of trading Raytahnee to some good people, try to do it. She wants to leave, she always has. You will do that?" He nodded and she pressed herself against him. She looked into his eyes and felt her own fill with tears. She kissed him softly and whispered something in his ear and then turned to leave. She wanted him to be proud of her so she mounted her horse and rode away. She didn't look back, fearing she'd break down if she saw him. She wondered if it was as difficult for him.

Nakon watched as Lisa rode away, her back straight, her long chestnut hair falling to her waist. "Forever, my love," she had said to him. His last view of her was obscured by the tears that filled his clear, blue eyes.

CHAPTER VI

Josh decided to follow the Canadian River into New Mexico and take Lisa to Santa Fe. He figured they could make it in less than a week. The weather was already cold and small snow flurries appeared now and again. He thought they would stay in Santa Fe until the worst of the winter snows were over. Josh had some friends there, Will and Rebecca Stiles. They had a small ranch and could put Josh and Lisa up for the winter.

Josh and Will had fought together for Texas independence under General Sam Houston. They had been among the group of Houston's men at Gonzales when word reached them of the fall of the Alamo. After that, they left Texas, Will to marry and settle down with Rebecca outside of Santa Fe, and Josh to go back to Missouri to become a scout for westward wagon trains. Will and Rebecca were good, hardworking people, and Josh felt that they might help Lisa forget what had happened to her. They would show her that not all people were savages like the Comanche.

Lisa puzzled Josh. She had hardly spoken a word since leaving the Comanche camp two days earlier. He wished she would talk about the experience, get it out in the open; but she kept silent. She was very unlike the girl he had known on the wagon train; but still she looked to be in good health and even radiant, he thought.

When Josh went into the camp with the Comancheros to trade for Lisa, he had been prepared for the worst. In fact, he was not even sure he really wanted to find Lisa. The Comancheros told him that the few white women they had seen who had been captives of the Comanche, hardly resembled women any longer; they were more like dirty animals. But instead of finding a wretchedly used and humiliated woman, Josh found Lisa to be even more beautiful than before. Her tall frame was slimmer but tanned dark from days in the sun, her bright green eyes stood out even more in her thin face. Her chestnut hair was shot through with streaks of red and was pinned back on the sides with gold hairpins. She was dressed in a long buckskin dress with a buffalo robe wrapped around her shoulders. When Josh first saw her his breath caught in his throat—he had never seen so beautiful a woman in all his life. He wondered how a woman who supposedly should have been broken, could look that way.

She had changed in other ways, too. He couldn't imagine all she had been through, but she seemed overly thoughtful and pensive, almost sad. If only she would say something to him, anything at all. He had hoped for too much when he thought she'd be glad to see him. She had changed and Josh was loathe to find out all she had endured during her months of captivity; he only hoped it had not made her a bitter, empty woman.

Suddenly Josh remembered the look on Nakon's face when he had come to trade for Lisa. He had been surprised that the young chief sent for him personally. Nakon seemed almost unconcerned about the number of guns and ammunition being traded for Lisa, and that was very unusual for a Comanche. They were known to be very hard to deal with. Nakon's only concern seemed to be with Lisa's safety. He had taken Josh aside after the bargaining and asked him to take Lisa to her brother in California, and to make sure she got there safely. He had even given Josh money to help pay her way.

"She has talked highly of you. I trust you to look after her and see that she gets there safely," Nakon had told Josh.

Josh was unable to see Lisa until they left the next morning, but he knew from asking around the camp that Nakon had taken Lisa for his wife. When Nakon and Lisa came out that morning, she hadn't even looked at Josh. She hugged a young girl and a huge dog; then she turned to Nakon. She kissed him and whispered something in his ear, then mounted her horse without looking back. Josh knew then there was a great love between the two. He didn't ask Lisa about it, but he would never forget the tortured look on Nakon's face when they rode away—he was a man who had lost a part of himself.

"Josh."

Josh's reverie was disturbed by Lisa's voice.

"Where are we headed?"

It was the first time she had asked him anything since they had been on the trail.

"Thought we'd head into New Mexico—Santa Fe. It's dead of winter now, and we're not gonna get far in this kinda weather. I got some friends who've got a little spread there, and they'll put us up. Besides, we could use a little rest."

Lisa regarded him seriously for the first time.

"Oh, Josh, I'm sorry. I've been so wrapped up in myself I haven't even thanked you for coming to get me. It was very brave of you to come into the Comanche camp

109

to trade for me. Why did you do it? You didn't even know me that well. And why, in God's name, did you come into a Comanche camp after you had just recently escaped from them? How did you escape them anyway?"

"Me and some of the kids hid under one of the overturned wagons. Good thing for us, the Comanche didn't wait around long enough to search everything. And I think you know why I came in there after you. I ain't known you a long time, Lisa, but the time we spent together on the train—well, it was a special time for me. Hoped it was for you, too."

Lisa looked at Josh and touched his hand gently.

"You'll always mean something to me, Josh. I'll never forget what you tried to do for me on the train."

"Yeah, but it wasn't enough; the bastards got you anyway." He looked at her, the question he had been waiting to ask her, poised on his lips. "You don't feel the same way about me, do you? Didn't even know I was alive until a few minutes ago."

Lisa looked at Josh guiltily.

"Someday I'll tell you about it, but not now. Not now."

Josh saw the tears fill her eyes and he didn't press her.

They reached Santa Fe about a week later. Josh rented a room for Lisa so she could bathe and change into a dress before meeting the Stileses.

Will and Rebecca Stiles were warm, friendly people who welcomed Lisa with open arms. Lisa couldn't resist Rebecca's frail charm and her cornflower-blue eyes. Lisa thought Rebecca hardly looked old enough to be the mother of four. Will was much older than Rebecca and very rugged looking, with piercing black eyes and a knack for telling a good story. Lisa liked them instantly and an easy friendship developed between Lisa and the Stileses, one which she would never forget. The time she spent with them helped to give her hope that one day she could again be happy and live without Nakon.

Lisa didn't know what Josh had told Rebecca and Will, and they never asked her any questions. Lisa told them she had been captured by the Comanche and lived with them for almost seven months, but neither Will nor Rebecca seemed to care—they still treated her as an honored guest. Lisa knew that few people would be as kind and accepting as Will and Rebecca. They were helping to give her a secure start back in the white world.

Lisa helped Rebecca with the daily chores and with the children. She was growing very attached to the youngest, the baby, Will. He had black hair and Rebecca's blue eyes, and every time she looked at him, Lisa wondered if their son might have looked like him.

It was getting close to Christmas so Lisa helped Rebecca make presents for the children. They made ornaments for the tree and baked lots of little pies and cakes. Lisa asked Josh to go into town to buy her some materials so she could make her own presents. She was given the room of Rachel, the eldest girl; and there Lisa worked on her presents each night when everyone else was in bed. For the three girls, she made rag dolls, all with different colored yarn hair and dresses. For baby Will, she made a stuffed horse with large button eyes. For Josh and Will, she made winter shirts embroidered in colorful stitching; and for Rebecca, she made a nightdress of light-blue silk with lace cuffs and collar, and tiny pearl buttons down the front. When she was finished with all of her gifts, she wrapped them up in colored pieces of leftover material.

The next day, Josh and Will and the two oldest girls

went out to look for a tree. They came back happily with a gigantic pine that barely fit through the door. After they set it up, the women and children spent the day trimming it with their homemade decorations and strings of nuts and berries. On the very top of the tree was a small wooden angel that Will had carved the first year of their marriage.

Christmas day was a beautiful and memorable day for Lisa, full of love and warmth. They all rose at dawn and had hot chocolate while they sat around and opened presents. Everyone was pleased with Lisa's gifts, but she hadn't expected to get so many of her own. Rebecca had made her a lovely dress of dark-green silk, and they both laughed at the gifts they had made for each other—each made a gift to match the other's eyes. The girls made Lisa a hat for the snow; Will made her a carving he had done of baby Will. Lisa couldn't believe the intricateness of the carving—it was a perfect likeness of the child. Josh gave her a delicate gold bracelet which she put on. She tried to thank everyone when they were through, but she ran into the kitchen, fearing she'd break into tears. Josh started after her, but Rebecca waved him back and she went instead. She put her arms around Lisa.

"Sorry, Becca, it's just I'm so overwhelmed. You've all been so wonderful to me."

"It's all right. We feel the same way about you. We're not doing it to be nice; we love you. You're like part of the family now."

When Lisa composed herself, she and Rebecca prepared breakfast. After breakfast, Will and Josh took the girls outside to play in the snow and Rebecca put Will down for a nap. Then she and Lisa settled themselves by the fire and talked. Rebecca talked Lisa into trying on the green dress. When she came out in it, Rebecca cried out in delight.

"You're so lovely. Don't think I've ever seen a prettier woman."

"It's a bit daring, don't you think?" Lisa asked, while trying to pull up the low-cut bodice. It barely covered the swell of her breasts. "I've never worn anything like this in my life. Why, I look like a . . ."

Rebecca laughed.

"Listen, you look like an enticing woman, that's all. But I want you to save the dress for a very special occasion. When you go to California, I want you to show those provincials out there what it's like to be really elegant." Rebecca jumped up. "Wait a minute, there's something I want to get." When Rebecca came back, she made Lisa sit down and she arranged her hair. She brushed it up and pinned it on top of her head so that loose curls fell around her face and neck. When she was through, she handed Lisa a small hand mirror. Lisa looked into the mirror and was amazed at the transformation. Suddenly she looked elegant and mature. She waltzed around the room with an imaginary partner while Rebecca clapped her hands in delight. They didn't hear the door open and see Josh and Will enter. Lisa twirled around and ran into Josh and they both stumbled backward into the door. He held her in his arms and stared down at her barely concealed breasts.

"I was just trying on the dress Becca made for me," Lisa said breathlessly, a blush spreading over her cheeks.

"You look real pretty," Josh said softly, his eyes drilling into hers.

"Thank you," Lisa said excitedly. "I'll change now." She excused herself and ran from the room to change.

113

There was no mistaking the look in Josh's face—he desired her and he wasn't hiding it any longer. Rebecca followed Lisa into her room.

"Did you see the look on Josh's face when he saw you. I swear his mouth went dry. Thought his eyes would fall out."

Lisa changed into another dress and took her hair down. While she brushed it out, Rebecca told her about the hacendados in California.

"Most all of them are of Spanish ancestry. They were given land grants when they came to this country, and many were given grants by the Mexican government when the missions were secularized in the thirties. They don't do anything but have fiestas and entertain their friends and neighbors. Their ranchos are run by majordomos, who manage the Indian labor and Mexican vaqueros. What a life. I envy you, Lisa. It all sounds terribly romantic to me."

"How do you know so much about California? Have you been there?"

"No. Will and I thought about moving out there when we were first married, so we found out as much about it as we could. As it happened, I was pregnant with Rachel, and Will didn't want me traveling in my condition. We were going to go after the first child was born, but you can see how that turned out." She took Lisa's hands in hers. "It can be so different for you, Lisa. You're young and beautiful. I bet all the men out there will go crazy when they get a look at you. They're used to their plump, dark women. When they see you, they'll all fall over their feet to get to you."

"I doubt that," Lisa said laughingly.

"And then there'll be that one special man. He'll look

114

at you and you at him and then . . ." Rebecca stopped when she saw the look on Lisa's face.

"I'm sorry. Did I say something wrong?"

Lisa shook her head.

"No. It's just that there was a man like that once, and I don't think anyone can ever replace him. He was my husband in the Comanche camp."

If Rebecca was surprised by Lisa's admission, Lisa couldn't tell by the look on Rebecca's face.

"The necklace you wear all the time, he gave it to you?"

"Yes, the morning we parted." Lisa went on to tell Rebecca the story of her captivity and her life with Nakon. She eliminated nothing except the details of her rape. "I still don't think I can ever understand why he sent me back. I know he loved me as much as I did him, but still he made me go."

"From what you've told me, it sounds like he loved you very much to do that. He knew the life was too hard for you and he didn't want to see you suffer anymore. I think he must've been a wonderful man. Was he very handsome? I've heard so much about Indian men."

Lisa smiled.

"He was the most handsome man I've ever seen. Very tall and brown, hair not quite as dark as Will's, and the bluest eyes in the world. But it wasn't just his looks that made me love him, it was his gentleness and understanding."

Rebecca nodded.

"Baby Will—is that why you're so attached to him? Perhaps your child may have looked like him?"

"He may have, but I'll never know. It's just that I often wonder what he would have been like. They told me he was a boy. I don't think I'll ever be able to forgive myself for what I did. If I hadn't used that knife on myself, our child would probably be alive right now. Then I'd have a part of Nakon with me."

Rebecca reached out to Lisa.

"Listen to me. I know this may sound trite coming from me, but you must try to be happy. What you had with Nakon in that short time, most women will never have in their entire lifetimes. You must rejoice in the love you had for each other. Stop blaming yourself for the death of your child. You had no idea what Kowano was going to do. Just be thankful for what you had with Nakon."

"I'm sure you're right, but having known such a love, I don't think I can settle for anything less than that. The rest of my life I'll be searching for something as fulfilling."

"You may feel that way now, but things will change, believe me. When you came here a month ago, you were sad and withdrawn and already you're a changed person. Give yourself a little time, Lisa."

Lisa leaned over and kissed Rebecca on the cheek.

"You remind me so much of my friend, Raytahnee. You're kind and understanding, just as she was. A person has to be lucky to have two such friends in one lifetime."

The two women spent the rest of the day preparing a Christmas feast. When Will and Josh and the girls came back from playing in the snow, they were all cold. The girls' cheeks were red and their noses runny. Rebecca gave strict orders that they all were not to go outside again, and the rest of the day was spent indoors playing games with the children, reading, and telling stories.

Dinner was a lavish spread consisting of roast turkey;

chestnut dressing; baked pumpkin and squash; potatoes; fresh, wild berries; and biscuits with butter. For dessert, Rebecca made hot apple pie with cream poured over the top, and Lisa made English raisin pudding, a recipe she had acquired from the English cook in her mother's home.

After dinner, they sat around and sang songs and talked and drank the wine Will brought from town. It had been a lovely and full day but it soon came to an end. They said good night to one another and Josh and Lisa were left alone. Lisa walked over to Josh.

"Josh, I don't know how to thank you for all you've done for me. You brought me out of the camp to this wonderful place. It was what I needed to feel human again. You're such a wonderful friend, I'll never forget what you've done for me." She looked up at the blond man, his face partially covered by the thick, blond-red beard, the soft brown eyes looking back at her. He was such an attractive man and she had thought herself in love with him once. If only she hadn't known and loved Nakon . . .

Before she knew what was happening, Josh took her into his arms and kissed her. He kissed her passionately and held her tightly against him. She felt the hard muscles of his chest and thighs as he pressed against her. She pulled away.

"Please, Josh."

"Sorry, Lisa, it's just you looked so beautiful standing there in the firelight. I guess I couldn't help myself."

"It's all right. I guess I'm just a little jumpy these days. I want to thank you again for the lovely bracelet and the most wonderful Christmas I've ever had. Good night."

"'Night," Josh said thoughtfully. He watched her as

117

she walked from the room and then sat down by the fire, absently rubbing his beard. A smile spread across his face. She was coming around, he thought. She had responded to his kiss, if only for a moment. Underneath her cool exterior a fire was smoldering. All it needed was to be rekindled. He shut his eyes and dreamed of what it would be like to have her when that fire was really blazing.

During the next few days, a howling blizzard kept them all indoors. The only time anyone went outside, was to feed the animals. Tempers began to flare as they were all cooped up for almost a week. Everyone snapped at everyone else; they all found it difficult to occupy themselves. Lisa and Rebecca were the only ones who didn't have a problem getting along. They used the time to sew new dresses for themselves and the girls. Rebecca also used the time to tell Lisa a little about herself.

She had been educated in the East, but her father had always had a romantic vision of the West. When her mother died, she and her father came west and settled in Santa Fe. Rebecca found it boring and unstimulating after her busy life in the East. Her only diversions were the books which she brought with her and the soldiers who came to call from the fort.

Then a man came along, the most exciting man she'd ever known, and he completely swept her off her feet. They fell deeply in love and were to be married, but he got involved in Houston's war against the Mexicans. It was after he left from one of his infrequent visits to her, that Rebecca found out she was pregnant.

"Rachel is not Will's child. She is Josh's."

"The man you were in love with was Josh?" Lisa

asked, astonished.

"Yes, and he doesn't know about Rachel. He thinks she's Will's. Couldn't you tell? She looks a lot like Josh, really. She has his sandy-blond hair and his soft brown eyes."

"But why didn't he marry you? I can't believe he wouldn't have if he'd known you were carrying his child."

"Yes, I'm sure he would have, but I couldn't tell him. When he came back from the war, he brought Will to meet me. It was plain enough for me to see that he was trying to get me interested in Will. He obviously had found someone else, or," she shrugged, "he just fell out of love with me."

"Oh, Becca, I had no idea. And here I've been feeling sorry for myself. I feel so foolish."

"Don't feel sorry for me. I have a good life now and you know what a wonderful man Will is. He's completely devoted to me and the children. Just wanted you to know I really do understand what it's like to be so in love with a man you think you can't go on without him. But you can; I'm proof of that. Oh, every once in a while when I look at Josh or when he comes up and puts his arms around me, I wish things could've been different, but you can't change the course of things."

There was now a new bond between the women, and Lisa felt even closer to Rebecca. She resolved never to talk about Nakon again.

It was shortly after the blizzard stopped and the snow started to clear, that Josh announced he and Lisa would try to make their way to California. Will thought him crazy and tried to dissuade him, but Josh wouldn't be swayed. He wanted to get Lisa to California so he could

119

get back to Missouri and find out if his farm was still running. They were to leave as soon as the skies cleared completely.

Lisa packed all of her things and tried to take in the buckskin pants that Josh bought for her. He wanted her prepared to leave on the spur of the moment.

Their departure was postponed, however, when Rebecca came down with a bad cold. Lisa would not leave Will alone to care for the children while Rebecca was ill. She insisted that they stay until Rebecca was on her feet again. But Rebecca didn't recover in a few days as was expected; her cold developed into pneumonia. To make matters worse, she was also pregnant with their fifth child. The doctor from Santa Fe estimated that she was about three months along; he was very concerned for her and the baby. He felt the combination of the pneumonia and the baby were too much for Rebecca's frail body. Every day, it seemed, Rebecca found it harder and harder to breathe.

Lisa did all of the chores during the day and took care of the children and nursed Rebecca at night. The ordeal was taking its toll on Will—Lisa thought that he looked ready to break down at any time. She made sure that Josh kept him occupied when he wasn't at Rebecca's bedside. A week later, Rebecca miscarried; she grew even weaker from the loss of blood. The doctor said if she made it through the miscarriage, she would probably survive the pneumonia, as there would be no child to sap her strength. Lisa knew how strong Rebecca was, in spite of the doctor's insistence that she was frail, and she began to show signs of improvement in just a few days. Her breathing wasn't quite so labored and her fever was going down. Josh relieved Lisa every night at midnight so that she could get some rest. He was afraid that the long days of work and the nights nursing Rebecca would make her ill, too.

After three long weeks, the doctor said that Rebecca would get well, but she would still need complete bed rest. She was to stay in bed for at least another month or a relapse could occur. Lisa said that she would stay as long as she was needed, but she suggested that Josh go back to Missouri and check on his farm and his job with the train. Josh decided to leave as soon as possible; and when he was through with his business in Missouri, he would return for Lisa. He would be back by the end of March, he told them.

When Josh left, Lisa felt sadder than she thought she would. He was a wonderful friend to her and had filled a great void in her life. When she walked him to his horse the morning he left, she felt like crying and she threw herself into his arms.

"You've been so good to me, I can't believe it. I'll miss you terribly." He held her back and brushed the hair from her face.

"Not as much as I'm gonna miss you, I wager. But I'll be back in a couple of months, and then we'll be on our way to California.

"What about your farm and your job? You can't just drop everything to take me to California. I can get there on my own."

"No way, darlin'. Made a promise to someone that I'd take you to your brother in California, and I mean to keep that promise. Now, you just hold the fort till I get back. And don't worry about my job. Good scouts are hard to find and my bosses know that." He lifted her face up to his and kissed her. This time she didn't fight him. She put her arms around his neck and pressed her body closer to his, their kiss growing deeper, more intense. When they broke apart, Josh found it very difficult to leave. Of all the times for her to start responding to him.

"We got a lot to talk about when I get back, girl."

She nodded.

"I know. Just come back, all right?"

He smiled, kissed her good-bye and rode off, turning to look at her once more. The memory of those large green eyes and that long chestnut hair would be forever fixed in his mind. God, but it was hard to leave her, especially after she'd kissed him like that. He wondered how she'd like Missouri and he smiled when he thought of holding her in his arms every night, loving her, making a life with her. He wondered if their children would have green eyes.

CHAPTER VII

The time that Lisa spent taking care of Rebecca and the children passed quickly. During this time, she wrote a letter to her brother in California, telling him about her captivity, how Josh came in and got her, her stay at the Stileses', and why she would be delayed. She said that she hoped to be there by late spring or early summer and she couldn't wait to see him.

Lisa received an answer from Tom only three weeks later. It was dropped off by a friend who was passing through Santa Fe. Her brother told her that, of course, she was still welcome and that he was deliriously happy to know that she was alive and well. He told her that he had looked for her himself but had had no luck. He never lost faith, he told her, that she would be found; he knew they would be together again someday. After reading Tom's letter, Lisa was more anxious than ever to get to California to see him. It seemed that at last, things were looking up.

A month after Josh left, Rebecca was almost her old self again. The doctor warned her against overdoing it, so Lisa still did the heavy work, the cooking, and made sure the children stayed out of Rebecca's way. It was early March now and Lisa felt the beginnings of spring in the air. The weather was getting warmer and the snow on the flatlands was beginning to melt. Lisa saw wildflowers popping up in the more sheltered areas. As much as Lisa loved Rebecca and Will, she was eager to see Josh and to get on to California. She was ready to get on with her own life now.

Lisa had changed since coming to the Stileses' in early December. She had been scared and timid and insecure then, but now she was strong and ready to face whatever life held in store for her. And Nakon, she could sleep at nights now without constantly seeing his face. She would never forget him nor what he had been to her, but she felt that the pain was not quite so bad now. She felt, too, that it was time to let Will and Rebecca get on with their lives.

She planted a flower and vegetable garden for Rebecca and tended it lovingly each day. She spent as much time as she could outdoors in the hopes that she would see Josh ride up. Rebecca noticed Lisa's uneasiness of late, and she thought she knew what was causing it.

"Are you in love with Josh?" she asked one day at lunch.

Lisa felt slightly embarrassed by the question because of the way Rebecca had once felt for Josh.

"Don't worry, I'm not in love with Josh anymore, so you won't hurt my feelings," Rebecca said reassuringly.

"I honestly don't know. I know that I feel very deeply for him, and lately, I can't seem to wait for him to come back. And when he left he kissed me and I kissed him back. Becca, I actually threw myself in his arms and kissed him back!"

Rebecca laughed good-heartedly.

"Sometimes I'm truly amazed at how naive you really are. I'm sure you didn't throw yourself at him; you probably just responded to his kiss as any normal woman would do. That's a good sign. It means you're beginning to forget."

"I suppose, but I don't want to jump into anything new right away. I still need time. I need to spend time with my brother, to think, and to enjoy life for a while without any serious commitments. I hope Josh will give me that time."

"I'm sure he will. Josh is a patient man. He's waited for you this long, hasn't he?"

Still more weeks passed and Josh didn't come. Lisa was beginning to worry that something had happened to him. She hadn't heard from him in almost two months. She tried to keep herself busy during the days, but she found them going much too slowly of late. She was pulling weeds in the garden one day when she heard Rachel screaming.

"Uncle Josh, it's Uncle Josh."

Lisa stood up, wiping her hands on her apron and trying to push her disheveled hair from her face. She ran into the yard. She saw Josh smile as he rode up. He jumped from his horse and walked to her.

"You've come back," she said almost unbelievingly.

"Did you think I wouldn't?" He looked at her for a moment before taking her in his arms and kissing her. She buried her face in his broad chest.

"Why're you hidin'?"

"I'm not hiding, I'm just glad to see you. It's been so long." She looked up at him, tendrils of hair in her face, her large eyes misty. He cupped her chin in his hand and kissed her softly, and then with such intensity, that Lisa felt embarrassed. She heard Rachel giggle. Josh smiled and took her arm.

"Think you really did miss me, girl. You'll have to

show me just how much later." Lisa blushed slightly as they walked into the house.

Will and Rebecca were almost as glad to see Josh as Lisa was, and they had a happy reunion, especially since Rebecca was recovered. Josh said they'd stay another week so he could help Will with some repairs on the barn and fences. Lisa packed her things and made ready for their journey.

The day after Josh returned, Will went into town to buy some things he needed to make repairs. When Will came back from town, he always brought the latest news. This time he talked about what was going on back east in Washington and New York; the Indian problem seemed to be getting worse and there were plans for more forts along the southwestern frontier; California was still in a mess, with all the gold miners and foreigners causing unrest and forcing land takeovers from the Californios.

"This bit of news should interest you, Lisa honey. Seems a few months back a Comanche war chief was killed down in southern Texas. There's been a bounty out on him for quite a while now. Guess every soldier and Texas Ranger in the area was tryin' to get him. Well, seems they got lucky and they captured him. He and his band were ambushed along the Concho River some-where—they even brought his scalp back for proof."

"What was his name?" Josh asked, glancing over at Lisa.

"Let me see . . . It was Nakon. Yeah, that's it, Nakon."

Lisa dropped the cup she was holding on the table where it fell with a loud crash. Everyone at the table looked at her, startled.

"You're sure, Will? You're sure his name was Nakon?

How long ago did it happen?"

"Oh, yeah, sure as can be. Like I said, they brought his scalp back, and his horse, a big ol' paint. Guess it happened about three months ago. Seems he was gettin' mighty reckless, like he was tryin' to get himself caught or something."

With a smothered cry, Lisa got up from the table.

"Excuse me," she said and ran from the house. Her nerves had been worn to a frazzle during the last weeks while taking care of Rebecca and her family. The news of Nakon's death was shattering.

"What's wrong with her?" Will asked in dismay. "Did I say somethin' wrong?"

"I'll take care of her; you folks just go on with your dinner," Josh said, following Lisa out of the house.

"Well, hell, I sure don't understand what that's all about. Just thought she'd be interested in a little news about the Comanche. Didn't think she'd be so damned touchy about it."

Rebecca's eyes followed Josh as he left the house, knowing why Lisa was so upset. Lisa's husband had been killed. Although she was getting over him, the news of his death was too much for her to take. She still loved him.

Josh looked for Lisa and found her by the stream in back of the house. She was on her knees, sobbing into her hands, her shoulders shaking. It was the first real emotional response Josh had seen from her since they came here. He knelt down next to her and pulled her into his arms. He knew the reason for her behavior—she was still in love with Nakon.

"It's all right, darlin', let it all out. It's not good for you to keep it all in." He stroked her hair and held her for a long time until she finally pulled away from him. She sat back on the ground and stared down at the stream.

"I loved him, Josh. I loved him more than I'll ever be able to love anyone again. I wanted to stay with him, but he made me go. He said it wasn't safe for me there anymore. Oh, God . . ." The tears welled up in her eyes again.

Josh reached out and wiped the tears from her cheeks.

"Thought so. When I went into the camp to trade, he didn't seem much interested in the ransom—and that's not like a Comanche. He took me aside and asked me to watch out for you."

Lisa managed a slight smile.

"He was good to me. He never hurt me and he treated me with great respect. He never took another wife either; said I was all he needed."

"You have to know Nakon knew this was going to happen. He didn't want you around when it did. He did the right thing. Now it's time for you to forget him and get on with you life."

Lisa reached up and toyed with the necklace Nakon had given her.

"Forget him? I'll never forget him. How could I forget someone who is such a part of me and who meant everything in the world to me?" She sighed and looked back at the stream, remembering the times Nakon had made love to her by the river.

Josh was stung by Lisa's frank admission, more than she could imagine. He had hoped that she was forgetting Nakon and the past and learning to accept him as part of her future. Now, it seemed as though she'd be a long time forgetting.

"I guess you're right," Lisa said suddenly.

Josh was surprised by her voice.

"What'd you say?"

"I said I guess you're right, about getting on with my life, I mean. It's about time I thought of the future."

"But I thought you just said . . ."

"I said I'd never forget Nakon and I won't. But I've got to start living again. He wouldn't want me to give up like this; he'd want me to go on. I've been stuck away here in my safe little hideaway for much too long now. I'm anxious to get to California." She smiled. "Nakon always liked my spirit—he said I was like a wild horse that could never be tamed."

"I guess I'd have to agree with that statement," Josh said laughingly.

"Well, I guess we'd better be getting back to the house. They'll all be worried." Lisa stood up and turned to Josh. "Thanks again, Josh, it seems like you're always helping me."

"My pleasure, little lady. I'm always at your service."

The week went quickly and the night before Josh and Lisa were to leave Rebecca made a special dinner for them, and Will had brought some champagne from Santa Fe to have with it. After dinner they listened while Will told them many of his favorite stories, and he and Josh went over many of the adventures they had had together. They all decided to leave their final good-byes for the morning, and Lisa and Josh were left alone to say their good nights.

Lisa was growing increasingly uncomfortable around Josh. She often caught him looking at her and he took every opportunity to be close to her. While she felt a great affection for Josh, she was not ready for an intimate relationship with him. So when she and Josh were left alone, Lisa quickly excused herself and went to her room.

When she went to her bedside table to turn up her lamp, she had no idea that Josh had followed her, and she turned when she heard the door close behind her. Josh walked to her and pulled her to him, covering her mouth with his. He kissed her deeply, arousing sensations in Lisa that she thought were dead. She remembered how she had felt about Josh on the train and how he had kissed her good-bye. She had wanted him to make love to her then.

Josh led Lisa to the bed. She felt curiously detached, as if she were someone else watching her and Josh. Josh pulled her down on the bed and his kisses touched her face and neck. His fingers reached for the buttons of her bodice and quickly undid them and slipped the dress from her shoulders. She felt the familiar burning sensation in her loins as Josh pressed his weight down against her, and she could feel his hardness against the thin material of her chemise. She wanted Josh but she was suddenly afraid. Her mind went back to other times and she saw Nakon. She remembered the times he had made love to her, how gentle he had been with her, how wonderful it had been with him. She realized she didn't even know if she loved Josh and she felt disloyal to Nakon. No matter how much her body cried out for Josh, her mind wouldn't accept him. She managed to push him away and stand up.

"What in hell are you doing?" he asked angrily.

"Please leave. We can't do this in Rebecca and Will's house."

"Are you plumb crazy, woman? Will and Rebecca would be the first to congratulate us. Now come back here and let's finish what we started." He reached out for her.

"No," Lisa said as she backed up. "I want you to leave."

Josh stood up, running his hands through his thick, blond hair.

"Jesus Christ, woman, I think you must be deranged. You respond to me so much that you're moaning like a whore and I'm about ready to bust my breeches, and then you tell me to get out, as if nothing happened. No wonder that Indian sent you back!" Lisa grabbed for his arm as he walked to the door, but he shook it free and stomped out. She sighed deeply and sat down. She wasn't looking forward to the trip with him after what she'd just done. She couldn't blame him; it had been an awful thing to do. But she just wasn't ready for another man yet, not so soon, not with the memory of Nakon still fresh in her mind. She closed the door and climbed into bed, unable to still the trembling of her traitorous body.

Lisa was up and packed before dawn the following morning and already had breakfast started by the time Rebecca was up.

"How you spoil me. I don't know what I'm going to do when you're gone," Rebecca said sadly.

"Live your life with some privacy for a change," Lisa said seriously.

After a very quiet breakfast, Lisa and Josh walked to their horses, followed by the entire Stiles family. Josh hadn't spoken to Lisa and she wondered if he ever would again.

They all said their good-byes quickly and vowed to visit each other whenever they could. Lisa held baby Will for a long time before giving him up to Rebecca, and then she held her dear friend in her arms.

"I'll never forget what you've done for me, Becca. You and Will have helped to make me a whole, strong person

131

again. I might never have done it without you two." The two women clung to each other, and Lisa was surprised to see Rebecca more upset than she herself was. Finally Will pulled them apart and gave Lisa a giant bear hug, almost cracking her ribs.

"You come back and see us again, girl. You're part of the family now. I'll never forget what you done for Rebecca, never." He looked at her a long moment, tears clouding over his dark eyes, and then gave her a kiss on the cheek.

Lisa and Josh mounted their horses, and before she knew it, they were riding off. It was with a heavy heart that Lisa said good-bye to these good people, but it was with a building sense of excitement she hadn't felt since leaving Boston, that she began, at last, the final part of her trip west.

Josh decided to take the Old Spanish Trail out of Sante Fe into Los Angeles, and from there, the El Camino Real northward to Monterey. They would keep to the southern trails in case any of the northern trails still had snow on them.

They rose early each day and rode until noon, when they'd rest the horses for a short while, eat, and then continue on until they found a place to camp before sunset. They were good, full days for Lisa, full of excitement in knowing her final destination was so close, and in the anticipation that every day brought her closer to that destination and Tom.

After their first day out, Josh seemed to forget he was angry with Lisa, but he still kept his distance. He talked only when she asked him a question or when he was giving orders. She knew that she'd hurt his pride terribly and she felt sorry about that. She knew she would have to try to make it up to him somehow.

When they reached Needles, California, they camped along the great Colorado River. Josh told Lisa that this was where the Yuma and Cahuilla Indians roamed, two of the few hostile tribes in California. But he figured they'd be safe enough where they were. He found a shallow place where Lisa could bathe and where water was easily obtainable for them and the animals.

Even though this was desert, the water was cool and Lisa wasn't able to stay in as long as she usually did for a bath. After she took a quick bath and rinsed the trail dust from her hair, Lisa stepped out onto the sandy bank, only to face Josh. He had been at the water's edge watching her, completely entranced with her long, graceful beauty, unable to take his eyes away, unable to hide his fierce desire.

The sun was setting and it cast a firelike glow over Lisa's brown body, and standing there in the cool evening air, Josh thought she looked like some kind of a goddess. He walked toward her, his desire showing in his eyes.

"Josh," Lisa said in a small voice, trying to cover herself. "Josh, please."

She reached for her clothes on the bank, but Josh stilled her movement, encircling her with his husky arms. He pushed back the wet hair that hung in her face and then kissed her on the mouth, traveling down to the hollow of her throat.

"God, but you're beautiful," he murmured huskily against her throat. He held her tightly, so that she was unable to move, slowly running his hands along the smooth skin of her back and down to her firm buttocks. She started to pull away, but he held her fast.

"Do you know what you're doin' to me? Seein' you everyday; I can't touch you, can't hold you. You're drivin' me crazy." Josh sank to his knees, pulling Lisa with him. He forced her onto her back, and moved his lips lightly over her neck and breasts.

Lisa tried to push him from her, but he held her firmly beneath him, her arms crushed to her sides. She squirmed beneath him, evoking memories not of Nakon, but of those first nights in the Comanche camp when she had been so brutalized.

"Not like this, don't take me like this. It's too soon, it's too soon." The anguish in Lisa's voice made Josh stop. He got up, raking her body with his eyes, having again been cut short of his desire.

"You sure seem to get pleasure outta humiliatin' me," he said gruffly. "Well, lady, I hope you have a lotta fun makin' love to a memory." He stood up and stomped off toward camp.

"Wait, you don't understand. Damn it, you don't understand," Lisa said despondently.

"Damn men," she yelled. Why was it they always took it as a personal rebuke if you said no to them? Couldn't they understand that it was difficult for a woman sometimes, especially if the memory of rape was still fresh in her mind.

"If only he'd been gentle with me, like Nakon. Nakon . . ." she thought, and picked up a handful of sand and threw it in the direction Josh had gone.

She sat on the bank for a while, thinking about what to say to Josh. It was the first time she'd looked at Josh as a possible lover. Even after the two times that Josh tried to make love to her, she really hadn't accepted the fact that he wanted her as a woman, as Nakon had wanted her.

It wasn't as though Josh wasn't attractive; on the contrary, Lisa thought him to be extremely so. He was taller than Nakon and stockier of build, but every inch of him was muscle, hardened from endless days in the saddle. His blond hair was streaked red in parts, his full beard and mustache slightly darker than his hair. He was dark skinned from being constantly in the sun, and those soft brown eyes, which were so kind and understanding, stood out in his kind face. Indeed, he was very attractive and she would have cared for him if it hadn't been for Nakon. She had to talk to Josh.

She sighed deeply, slipped into her clothing, and strode back into camp with a determined effort to make it up with Josh. When she got back to camp, however, Josh was nowhere around. She thought he probably needed some time to himself so she boiled some water for coffee and took out some hardtack and jerky and ate. After an hour or so when Josh still hadn't returned, Lisa picked up the extra rifle and set out to look for him. She hadn't gone far when she spotted him perched atop a rock, staring out at the river.

She walked slowly up to him, speaking tentatively.

"Are you all right?" she asked softly.

When he didn't answer, Lisa walked close to the rock, looking up at him.

"Please don't ignore me, Josh; I've got to explain something to you. Please don't make it more difficult for me than it already is."

Josh finally relented, putting out a hand to help Lisa up onto the rock next to him. He still refused to look at her, and they both sat there for some time before Lisa got up enough courage to speak. She spoke slowly, trying to put into the right words some of her most private thoughts.

"The fault's not yours, Josh, it's mine."

He looked at her now, trying to see her meaning.

"You're such an attractive man, a girl would be crazy not to fall for you. I didn't mean to make you think I was ready for an involvement. I'm sorry if you thought that. It's not that I don't find you attractive because I think you're one of the handsomest, most wonderful men I've ever known, and I'm sorry I couldn't let you make love to me. It wasn't Nakon I was thinking about down there; I was thinking about my first few nights in the Comanche camp with the four braves who took me from the train. I was raped by all of them, every one of them, every night, until Nakon came and made me his woman. When I tried to fight them I was beaten until I couldn't fight. I just lay there while they had their fun with me." She lowered her head, trying to blot out the disgusting memories.

Josh started to reach out to her, but thought better of it; she didn't need his pity, not when she was learning to be strong again.

"I think that's why my love for Nakon was so strong because he was gentle and patient with me; he made me feel as if I had never been touched by a man before, let alone four men. Do you realize how that made me feel, Josh? He brought me out of my despair and made me believe in myself again—he made me feel needed and loved."

"Back down at the river, I saw a scar under your breast, looked like it'd been done with a knife. Did he do that?"

"No, I did it. I tried to kill myself."

"You tried to kill yourself? I don't believe it," Josh said, as though trying to reassure himself.

"Believe me, I tried and almost succeeded. I did

136

succeed in killing our unborn child." Lisa stopped for a moment, trying to gain a measure of self-control before continuing.

"Nakon went out on a raid and didn't return with his band. I waited, for over a month, but there was no word from him. I was at the river thinking of using a knife on myself, thinking that there was no other way out for me. I really don't know if I would've used it but Kowano came and made the decision for me. He was the first brave who raped me, and he raped and beat me once after Nakon had taken me for his wife. I hated him. I told him if he came near me, I'd kill myself. He tried to take the knife from me, but I stuck it into my chest. I still cringe when I think of Kowano.

"Anyway, two of the women stayed behind to take care of me when the rest of the band broke for winter camp. Nakon came back and helped nurse me until I was well again. When I was recovered, we returned to the band. It was during the buffalo hunt that he told me he was going to send me back to my people. I didn't believe him, of course. He said he wouldn't stand by and see me die from a life I wasn't used to. I told him I'd never leave him. He didn't argue with me at the time so I thought he'd given up on the idea. When he told me you'd come to take me back, I was incredulous at first, and I was angry. I said some horrible things to him and called him a coward. I loved him so much; couldn't he see that?" She covered her face with her hands and turned her back on Josh.

"I'm sorry," she mumbled.

Josh reached out and put his arm around her and she laid her head on his shoulder. Josh felt almost jealous of the man, even though Nakon was dead. To have a woman like Lisa so much in love with you must be an incredible

137

feeling, he thought.

"The man was anything but a coward, Lisa. Do you know the courage it took for him to send you back at all? I'm sure he would've wanted to keep you there, but he couldn't." He turned her face toward him. "He made me promise to get you safely to your brother in California. Said to look out for you."

"He was the one you made the promise to?"

Josh nodded.

"He loved you, that's for sure. But he was right. There was no future for you there. You wouldn't have survived many more years as a Comanche squaw."

"I know, but if he really loved me, he would've let me make the decision, or he would've come with me." She stopped for a moment, as if pondering what she'd just said. "But that's all over now. Nakon's dead and I'm alive, and I've got to go on living and forget the past. I'm stronger now. I'm not the same naive, idealistic girl I was on the train, or the same weak-willed woman who tried to kill herself in the Comanche camp. But I need time. I need to think things through. After a while with my brother, I should be able to sort out my feelings better. Please, Josh, can you give me the time I need to get myself straight?" She smiled at him and Josh couldn't resist her smile. He took her hand and held it to his lips.

"The way I figure it, little lady, what's really worth havin', is worth waitin' for. Guess my damned pride got in the way back there." He nodded back at the river. "I'll take you to Monterey, and I'll give you the time you need with your brother; but I'll be back. And when I am, I expect an answer from you. We could have a good life together, you know?"

Lisa reached up and touched his face.

138

"Thank you. Thank you for your understanding and your friendship—a girl couldn't ask for more."

As they packed up to leave the next morning, Lisa had a sense of well-being that she hadn't felt since living with Nakon. She was fairly content. She had resolved a few things in her mind and in her heart. She now felt she was ready to begin a new chapter in her life. As she had told Josh, she would never forget Nakon, but she would no longer mourn him. She would live for the present and take each day as it came.

CHAPTER VIII

The small camp fire crackled and sizzled as the juices from the rabbit dripped into it. The man reached down and took the stick with the plump rabbit speared on it from the fire and began to tear pieces from it. It tasted good, and after he had had his fill, he leaned back against the saddle, thinking of the past few weeks, to a time when his life had been vastly different. He looked over at the young girl and the big dog who slept beside each other close to the fire. They belonged to him now; they were his responsibility.

To any outsider, the man looked like a white man, dark skinned, but a white man, nevertheless. He had thick, black hair that curled about his ears and neck, and clear, light-blue eyes that seemed almost transparent. He was dressed in buckskin pants and shirt, and he had his hat pulled low over his eyes. His gun belt was slung low on his right hip, and on his right thigh was strapped a long knife. He was tall and lean, and he moved with an animal-like grace that deceived many a man. He appeared to be a white man, but to Lisa Jordan, he would be known as Nakon—her lover, her husband, the man for whom she had wanted to die, the man she thought was dead.

After Lisa had left the camp, Nakon began leading more and more raids further south. He didn't raid strictly for the booty, but more to be a thorn in the sides of the army and the Texas Rangers. The rangers, together with the governor, were trying to eradicate all Comanche.

Nakon was fearless as a leader. His warriors followed him wherever he planned a raid. On their raids, they always brought back horses, rifles, and liquor. The spoils were divided among the men—Nakon never took anything for himself. The only thing that the young chief desired, and he was explicit about this, was that his men should not kill, rape, or steal any white women. They all knew why—such was the respect he had for his white wife that he wanted no other white woman to be harmed. They all heeded his wish gladly, especially when he took no booty for himself.

While to the younger men Nakon seemed fearless, to the older, more wise men of the tribe, he appeared to be reckless, bringing undue attention to their band. It seemed that no matter where they made camp, the rangers kept getting closer. The elders suggested that Nakon hide out for a while and let up on his raids, but he would not. He was a driven man.

On one of these raids, Nakon took Kowano with him. They camped, ready to raid a small town in the morning. Nakon's thoughts never veered far from Lisa; and whenever he thought of her, he thought of what Kowano had done to her. Nakon sat, alone, drinking from a cheap bottle of mescal, looking over at Kowano. Kowano was sitting with a group of young braves, regaling them with his tales of valor and his many female conquests. Kowano picked the wrong night to talk of his many female captives. Nakon walked over to him, the muscle in his cheek twitching violently.

"Kowano, why don't you tell the youngsters about the

white female captive you took last spring—the beautiful one, the spirited one. The one you continually raped and tried to beat into submission." He took a long swig from his bottle. "And even when she was chosen by another, you raped and beat her again. But that didn't work either, did it? She was not the weakling you thought her to be. Well, I told you your time would come, you bastard, and it's now," he said harshly, flinging the bottle away.

Kowano stood up, looking around him at the other braves for support, but he received none.

"Nakon, surely you wouldn't choose to fight me the night before a raid. You need every man you have."

"One less man won't make any difference; we will fight. I challenge you, right here, right now. How do you wish to fight?"

Kowano saw there was no way out. The only way to save his honor was to fight Nakon.

"Knives," he said softly.

Nakon nodded his assent. He gave orders to one of the other men to assume command should he be killed, and the other men moved back to form a circle around the two combatants. They removed their knives and slowly circled each other. Kowano attacked first, taking Nakon off guard and slashing his right forearm. They both recovered quickly and were back facing each other in the circle. The look of intense hatred that emanated from Nakon's light eyes nearly mesmerized Kowano. For a small moment he forgot where he was and that was all Nakon needed. He leaped forward, his knife finding the flesh in Kowano's side. They both fell to the ground, struggling in earnest. Kowano was not as tall as Nakon, but he was heavier and stockier, so he was an equal match in strength.

The two men grunted and struggled for some time, neither able to gain the advantage over the other. Kowano, who was on the bottom, managed to bend one of his legs and push Nakon off. When Nakon fell backward his knife fell from his hand. He reached for it, but felt instead Kowano's knife stab into his shoulder. They struggled again, this time for Kowano's knife. Kowano forced the knife toward Nakon's throat, narrowly missing it and sticking the weapon into the ground. It gave Nakon the time he needed to reach his knife. By the time Kowano had retrieved his knife, Nakon stood ready to face him again. This time, however, Nakon did not hesitate; he ran forward and plunged his knife deeply into Kowano's heart. While Nakon stood catching his breath, the other braves came to congratulate him on his victory, and it was in this undefended position that they were attacked.

The rangers had moved in silently, not willing to risk being anticipated. They saw their chance as they watched the fight betwen the two braves. When they saw the other braves circle around the winner, they rode into the small camp, shouting and screaming, their pistols firing at the Comanche. The warriors didn't have a chance and the rangers knew it. Nakon looked up in time to see a ranger aiming at him, and he instinctively threw his knife, striking the ranger in the chest. When the dead man fell from his horse, Nakon picked up his pistol and began shooting at the other rangers, trying to give his own men enough time to gather weapons or retreat.

It was then that everyone's attention was diverted by a bloodcurdling scream. It was Sewak, the youngest member of the warrior group, astride Nakon's paint. He was a magnificent sight—a young warrior astride a reared stallion. They all stopped to look for a moment. He wielded his lance and, holding it high in the air, as if in a salute he yelled, "Nakon!"

He was acknowledging Nakon as his leader, saluting him. Then the horse came down on all fours. He charged through the camp, lancing two of the rangers before he was shot.

Seeing there was no way to beat the armed men, Nakon signaled for his remaining men to flee for the nearby rocks. To a Comanche, it was no disgrace to run when there was no way for them to fight. Indeed, they would have gladly stood their ground and fought to the death had they not been so completely surprised by the armed men.

Nakon grabbed one of his injured men and set off for the woods. His last sight was of two rangers standing over Sewak, scalping him, and holding Nakon's horse. He wondered why they would take Sewak's scalp and none of the others.

He made his way deep into the woods, knowing that he would have the advantage there. The rangers were excellent trackers but even they couldn't keep up with a Comanche when he wanted to get lost. He carried the wounded man over his shoulder, fighting his way through the dense trees and bushes. When he found a small tree, he stopped and slowly began to climb, holding his man as best he could. It was a cumbersome way to climb, but eventually he made his way to the top where they sat on a thick branch. Nakon only hoped that the brave hadn't lost enough blood to leave a trail for the rangers to follow.

When he was settled, he listened for any sound of approaching rangers. But aside from some distant shouts and some beating of brush, the rangers didn't attempt to follow him into the forest. He was sure that after a quick search of the area, they would leave as quickly as they had come.

Nakon waited for what seemed like hours before he made his way down the tree and back to the camp. He was right, the rangers were long gone. They were not known to linger long in an area after an ambush, in case some of the escaped Indians might make their way back.

Nakon walked around the camp eyeing the dead, Comanche and rangers alike. In spite of his hatred of them, he had great respect for the rangers. Not only were they fearless fighters and excellent trackers, they seldom tortured or maimed their enemies, unlike his own people. That was why he was puzzled about Sewak—he had never before seen or heard of a ranger scalping an Indian. It didn't make sense, but as he thought of the scene that took place before Sewak's death, it occurred to him that the rangers may have thought Sewak was he, Nakon. There had been a bounty out on him for a long time, and maybe because Sewak screamed, "Nakon," they thought he was screaming his own name. Maybe they were taking the scalp back to their people to prove they had killed the notorious war chief.

He picked up the bodies of his dead men and pulled them to the middle of the camp. Having no utensils with which to dig a grave, he gathered brush and fallen wood to make a circle around the men; then he set it on fire. He felt it was better to burn them than to let their bodies be torn to bits by wolves or coyotes.

When he was finished, he gathered what supplies he could and set out in search of a horse. Finding one not far from camp, he tethered it to a tree and went back for his wounded man. When he got to the tree and climbed to

145

the top, he found the man had died from his wound. Nakon left him in the top of the tree. He made his way back to the horse, mounted, and rode off.

When Nakon returned to the main camp, everyone was surprised to see him. They all had heard he was dead from the few survivors who had made it back before him. Nakon didn't listen to their talk but wished only to talk to the tribal council as soon as possible. He believed he should be punished for what had happened—many of his men had died because he had pursued a personal vendetta.

That night a meeting was held by the council, which included all the tribal elders, the war chiefs, the head peace chief, and the puhakut. All were there at Nakon's request. They sat in a circle in the tipi of Shomaton, the wisest and most knowledgeable peace chief. Shomaton sat facing the east with Nakon sitting across from him; the rest formed the circle. The pipe was brought out. First, Shomaton puffed and offered smoke to the sky, the earth, the four directions, and the guardian spirit. All the others did the same and the meeting began.

Shomaton was the one who would speak. He addressed Nakon.

"Do you remember, my son, when we first found you? You were sick and weak. You were young then. We brought you to our camp. You recovered and became strong. Then you said you wanted to stay with the Comanche, that you had no other home. We adopted you. You made your vision quest. You went to the great mountain; you smoked, you prayed for power, and you lay facing the east. You stayed there alone for four days and nights. And you found your medicine. An eagle landed next to you on the mountain just as the sun was

146

rising. You came back and painted the eagle on your tipi with the rising sun. That was long ago, and we accepted you as our son and brother.

"Then you got older. You became strong and knowledgeable in our ways. We were proud. We were even prouder when you counted many coups on the enemy, and you showed yourself to be a fearless warrior in battle. You were one of our finest young warriors.

"We have loved you, my son. There was no question but that you were one of us. You were one of us until the white woman came—and you changed after you had her. She made you realize you were not Comanche, that you did not belong in our world any longer. She knew that you belonged with her in the white world, but you would not listen to her. You would not accept her truths, so you sent her away, thinking you could hide from these truths. When you sent her away, you became bitter because you had sent away a part of yourself."

Nakon lowered his eyes. It was difficult for him to listen to what old Shomaton was saying because these were things that he had been trying to cope with himself in the last few weeks.

Shomaton continued.

"You thought to forget this white woman by leading many raids and fighting many battles with the enemy. But you could not forget because she reminded you of the life you once had in the white world; she showed you the kind of life you could have had together. You think, because you have been so long in the Comanche world, that you cannot go back to your old life. You are wrong, Nakon. You can go back. You must go back. Your heart is no longer with the Nemenuh, the People. It is with the white woman. You are caught between two worlds and it

147

is tearing you apart. Do not stay with us out of gratitude—you owe us nothing. You belong where your heart is, and your heart is with the white woman. Go to her."

Shomaton was finished. Nakon looked around him at the men, young and old alike, whom he had known for almost ten years. He was being sent away and that was his punishment. But somehow it was a weight off his mind. The decision had been made for him. His gaze returned to rest on Shomaton.

"Thank you, Shomaton, for speaking so well. You are wise; I know that you speak the truth. You have shown me much over the years and your wisdom has always guided me along the right path. I hope I have not brought shame to you and to the others. I will go but it will be with a heavy heart. You have all given me love and warmth when I most needed it; you were my family. But I am a man now and I must face up to my past. I do not wish any long good-byes. I want to leave as a man. I will remember you all."

Nakon stood up and looked at the small group once more, then left the tipi. He went to the tipi of Raytah-nee's parents and spoke to them. He told them he was leaving the band and he wished to take Raytahnee with him. He gave them two hundred horses for her and it elevated their status in the tribe, although they lost Raytahnee. He split up the rest of his horses and belongings among the old and needy in the camp, and before dawn the next morning, he and Raytahnee, followed closely by Osolo, were packed and riding west to California, to the Rancho del Sol.

Nakon sat staring at the fire, thinking of that day, less than a week before. Shomaton had been gracious with his

148

words—much more so than he should have been, Nakon felt. He really felt he should have been punished. It had happened so fast he hadn't had time to think about it before now. It was easier than he thought it would be. He had packed a few meager belongings, and he and Raytahnee rode from camp, he on one of his best paints, she on her own horse. Shomaton was right; Nakon's heart was no longer with the Comanche. Lisa had taken it with her when he sent her away.

Lisa—it had been over two months since he last saw her. Still, the memory of that lovely face, the large green eyes and the chestnut hair, was branded in his memory for all time. The way she had of touching his mouth, of smiling that beguiling smile, he could never forget her. He had to find her. All he knew was that she was going somewhere in Alta California, but he'd search all of California if he had to until he found her.

A feeling which had been gnawing at him for some time finally came to the surface. What if Lisa hadn't gone to California at all? What if she had settled someplace else, with Josh Wade? Nakon couldn't believe she would do that—she loved him. Still, he had sent her away when she had begged to stay—that was something she was not likely to forget. But he'd find her and he'd make it up to her. But first he had to return to the del Sol and face his mother.

"Mother, you bitch," he thought bitterly. He hated her and all she stood for. It would be no easy task going back there, especially after all this time. It was something he dreaded. But he had to go back because the del Sol was his; he was determined to claim it. He would get it back from his mother at any cost.

Suddenly he thought of his grandfather, Don Alfredo

de Vargas, and he smiled. He dearly hoped Don Alfredo was still alive. He loved the old man who had always represented a safe haven to him when he was a child. Don Alfredo had been the only reason Nakon regretted leaving California. Whenever he had felt troubled about anything as a child, he rode to his grandfather's rancho. The Rancho del Mar was situated on a towering bluff that overlooked the Pacific Ocean. It was much smaller than the del Sol, but Nakon had always considered it more of a home.

That's what he would do now; he would go straight to his grandfather's to sort things out, as he had done so many times in the past. He needed time to talk to Don Alfredo about the many years that had passed and the things that had happened to each of them. He needed this time before he faced his mother.

When Nakon came within a few hundred yards of the Rancho del Mar he reined in his horse and stopped to look. He was amazed at how well the hacienda had been kept up through the years. The adobe was sparkling white, and the frames of the French windows and doors were painted black to contrast with the color of the house. The hacienda was built in an L-shape, and in the center was a beautiful courtyard which was surrounded by a black wrought-iron fence. All of the shrubs and bushes and trees had grown over the years: the gardenias, the camellias, the fuchsias, acacias, and honeysuckle had all grown larger and more luxuriant. The citrus trees growing around the courtyard were now as tall as the hacienda itself.

Nakon remembered that his grandmother had loved flowers and the smell of orange blossoms. His grandfather had planted as many flowers and trees as possible to please her. He wanted his wife to feel at home in her new country.

Don Alfredo had built the Rancho del Mar for his wife, Amparo, in the early 1800's, just after they arrived from Madrid, Spain. The climate was much the same as it had been in Spain, so Don Alfredo had little trouble in planting and growing the flowers and fruit trees that his wife had loved so much.

The Rancho del Mar had always attracted attention in the small population of Monterey because of its design and the fact that it had glass windows. Don Alfredo had been shocked when he saw that most of the ranchos had no glass for their windows, but pieces of hide tacked down instead. He also built fireplaces in every room in his home, wanting each person in his family to be always warm and comfortable.

Don Alfredo grew all of his own fruits and vegetables which served the needs of his family and the workers' families. He raised over a thousand head of cattle, and he had his own vineyard, cultivated by his own hands, which was used to make some fine wines and champagnes.

When Don Alfredo first came to Monterey, his plans were to build only the Rancho del Mar, even though he owned upward of twenty-five thousand acres. But when his young daughter, Mariz Elena, married a New England shipping captain, he thought of building a home for them further inland.

Upon the birth of his grandson, Alejandro Esteban de Vargas, Don Alfredo decided to build the great two-story rancho that would later become the Rancho del Sol. It would become his grandson's when the youth attained the age of twenty-one years.

Now, that grandson, Nakon, Alejandro de Vargas, was home to claim his inheritance, to claim the land which was his by his grandfather's bequest, the Rancho del Sol.

Don Alfredo de Vargas was a tall man in his late sixties, with silver-gray hair and dark-brown eyes. For all of his years, he was still a very handsome man. He had found it difficult to go on after the death of his beloved wife, Amparo, fifteen years earlier, but he thrived on the love of his grandson, Sandro. Except for the light-blue eyes, Sandro looked very much like his grandfather, and Don Alfredo had always been proud of this fact. Now, looking at the grandson he had not seen for almost ten years, he was prouder than he had ever dreamed possible.

The two men, grandfather and grandson, stood facing each other for some time, then Don Alfredo reached out and hugged his beloved Sandro to his chest. They held each other in this mutual embrace until Don Alfredo pulled away, still leaving his hands on Sandro's shoulders.

"I knew you would return, Sandro. I always felt that you couldn't get this land out of your blood." He held on to his grandson a moment longer before letting go.

"There is much I have to tell you, mi abuelo. You should sit down, it is a long story."

"I received your letter, let's see—it was almost nine years ago, sí? You have lived with the Comanche all these years? Was your hate for your mother so strong to make you stay away this long?"

Alejandro walked over to a small table in the corner, and poured himself a large brandy from the decanter.

"Abuelo, I've chosen to go by my father's name, Eric

Anderson. It was the one he gave me, the one my mother would never call me. It's my name."

"But Sandro, I have never called you by that name, yet you do not get angry with me."

"You know the reason for that. You didn't try to change me or make me into something I am not. That was my mother's mistake—she tried to make my father into an old-country Spanish aristocrat, and when she couldn't do that, she tried to make me into one. Then when she saw that I wanted to go to sea with my father more than anything else in the world, it became an obsession with her."

He took a sip of the brandy and then laughed.

"You know, I think it always bothered her that I have blue eyes like my father, instead of dark Spanish eyes. It was like a personal affront to her."

He stopped for a moment when he saw Raytahnee enter the room. He had sent her to the kitchen when he arrived so that she could have a real Mexican meal for the first time in years. He walked to her, a smile on his face, and took her to his grandfather.

"Abuelo, this is Raytahnee. I brought her from the Comanche camp with me."

Raytahnee smiled and extended her hand. Don Alfredo returned the smile and got up and kissed her hand.

"I am very pleased to meet you, Raytahnee."

"I think that Raytahnee is probably very tired, abuelo. May we send her up to her room so she can rest?"

"Certainly. I will send for Enrique." Don Alfredo picked up a little bell and rang it. In seconds, an elderly man appeared and, upon Don Alfredo's orders, took Raytahnee from the room. Don Alfredo looked at his grandson, a quizzical expression on his face.

153

"Isn't she a little young?" Don Alfredo asked sarcastically.

Eric laughed and walked over and sat back down next to his grandfather.

"It's not what you think, abuelo. I will explain it all to you." He looked absently ahead of him. "Where do I begin?"

"At the beginning, Sandro, at the beginning."

The young man walked to the window and looked out into the courtyard, which was surrounded by the orange trees and all the flowers. The fragrance of the orange blossoms mixed with that of the gardenias took him back to a time when he had played in this courtyard as a child and looked through the windows and waved to his parents. Those were happy times, such sheltered times, when he actually believed his parents were in love and happy.

"What are you thinking, Sandro?"

"Of other times," he said softly, "happier times." His thoughts turned to Lisa and an incredible weight settled on him. He walked back across the room and sat down in the chair opposite Don Alfredo. He put his glass down and, leaning forward, running his fingers through his hair, he told his grandfather what had occurred in the past nine years of his life.

When he left Monterey at the age of sixteen, he traveled south into Mexico, where he met some Comancheros, who, learning of his bitter hatred toward the Spanish, took him into their fold. He rode with them across the Rio Grande into central Texas where they went into several Comanche camps to trade for goods and white captives. It was on their way back from one of these trips that they were attacked by a band of Apache. All were left for dead but Eric, who had been hit in the chest with an arrow, but had not been fatally wounded. He was found a day later by some of the Comanche with whom they had just traded. They recognized him and took him back to their camp where he was cared for and treated as a guest. When he was well, he was given the chance to decide whether he wanted to stay or leave. He decided to stay and after a while, was adopted into the tribe.

It was at this time that he wrote a letter to his grandfather explaining what had happened and why he had made the decision to stay. He sent the letter with some traders hoping it would eventually get to his grandfather. He had elected to stay with the Comanche forever or for as long as they would have him.

He stayed and proved himself in battle many times and became a respected warrior. By the time he was twenty years old, he was a war chief, one of the youngest and most respected in the tribe.

He had not yet taken a wife, but he hadn't yet met anyone about whom he felt strongly enough. There were enough willing maidens in the camp with whom he could sate his desires, but he had lived in the white world long enough to know that he couldn't take a wife unless he had some deep affection for her. He wouldn't make the same mistake his parents had.

Then Lisa entered the story, and for the first time, Eric's voice faltered. He told his grandfather everything about her, of the love they felt for each other and of how he sent her away. At this point in the story, he stopped.

"You loved this woman very much?" Don Alfredo asked.

"Sí, more than I thought it possible to love someone. I'm going to try to find her. I am going to find her."

"Do you know where in California she is going?"

"No, just someplace in Alta California. There can't be too many white women who fit her description in these parts. Somehow I'll find her."

"You forget you've been gone for almost ten years, Sandro. Monterey is a large city and Yerba Buena is now called San Francisco and is a booming town. Since the gold rush . . ."

"The what?" Eric asked incredulously.

"Gold was discovered in '49 at Sutter's Mill. Since then, every nationality you can think of has come here to seek their fortunes. Yankees, French, English, Mexican, Portuguese, Australians, Hilos—practically any kind you can name. They are all here now. It will be harder than you think to find your woman."

"Jesus," Eric muttered. "When I left, there were less than a hundred foreigners in all of California. These foreigners, they will force a change in the lifestyle, sí?"

"I'm afraid so, but that is the way of life. Things change and we can't stop the changes or the people from coming." Don Alfredo sighed heavily. "What about the girl, Raytahnee? What is she to you?"

"She and Lisa were very close in the camp, like sisters. When Lisa left, she asked me to get Raytahnee out somehow if I could. Raytahnee is really Mexican. She was captured when she was ten years old. I traded for her when I left."

"Sandro . . ." Don Alfred paused for a few moments. "Have you thought about the possibility that she may not have come to California?"

"Why wouldn't she?"

"You said that this man, the scout, took her from your camp. He must have cared deeply for her if he came into a

156

Comanche camp and traded for her."

Don Alfredo watched Eric and saw the muscle in his cheek twitch as it had when he was bothered as a small boy. There were some things about him which hadn't changed.

"Are you saying she may have settled with Wade somewhere else?"

"It's a possibility."

"No, she wouldn't do that. I know how much she loved me. She wouldn't—couldn't fall in love with someone else so soon after leaving me. She'll come to California to visit her brother. Here's where I'll find her."

"As you say, but I just don't want you to be disappointed if you don't find her."

"I will find her," Eric said harshly. He got up and walked to the table and refilled his glass. "This is better than mescal." He downed the brandy and poured another. "I don't want anyone to know I was a Comanche. You can tell anyone who asks that I lived with a plains tribe for a few years. No one needs to know anything more."

"And Raytahnee?"

"I'll say she's the daughter of a friend in Mexico who was killed. I'll say I'm her guardian."

"All right. There's something else I think we should talk about."

Eric looked at Don Alfredo, a frown creasing his handsome face.

"Mother?"

"Sí, what about your mother and the Rancho del Sol?"

"You haven't changed anything since I've been gone? the del Sol is still mine?"

"It's still yours, but your mother won't give it up

157

easily. There's something else. A young man has been running the del Sol for the last five years. He and your mother are very close, if you know what I mean. So, you will have to contend with both of them."

"I don't care about my mother or her lovers. The del Sol is mine. You and father built it for me and I intend to take it over. But there's so much for me to learn."

"Yes, many things have changed."

"Has this man done a good job of running the del Sol?"

"Sí, Tom Jordan is a good man. He is also a lawyer and has helped many of our neighbors with their land claims and titles. Since the gold rush, many of the Yankees are trying to take over our land and destroy the ranchos. There are even professional squatters who stay on the land and refuse to move. They have shot many of the vaqueros who have tried to move them. I'm afraid that in ten years there will be few ranchos left."

"But why? There's enough land here for everyone."

"Ah, but the Yankees are greedy and they want the land that has already been farmed and is rich for grazing. They want to drive us from our own land and take it for themselves after we have put our life's blood into it. You more than most people can understand how we feel about it, Sandro. The Comanche and the other plains Indians are having to fight the same battle. The army is trying to drive them from their land and move them onto reservations. Well, they are trying to hold on to their land just as hard as we are trying to hold on to ours."

Eric paced the room, his eyes darting back and forth across the room and out the window.

"Must it always be this way, abuelo? Do the natives always have to fight the outsiders to keep what's theirs?"

"Unfortunately, the 'outsiders,' as you call them, are

the future of California. Eventually, we Californios will be the exception and the Yankees and others, will be the real Californians. All we can do is try to keep what is ours. We can do no more."

"We could go somewhere else where there are not outsiders."

"There comes a time in a man's life when he has to stop running and accept his fate, Sandro."

Eric stopped pacing and looked at his grandfather. The old man reminded him of Shomaton—wise and good. He was suddenly overwhelmed by his love for don Alfredo and he walked over to him and pulled him to his feet.

"You always knew best when I was small. You always seemed to point out the logical way in the midst of my confusion. Things haven't changed in ten years—you still seem to be able to guide me in the right direction. I feel lost abuelo. I'm not Comanche and I'm not a Californio. I am a man who is unsure."

Don Alfredo looked at his grandson, tears clouding his dark eyes at the young man's confession.

"A man isn't completely lost if he's loved, Sandro. When you find this woman you love so much, you will find a place to begin building your future. And you know you always have a place with me here. You are my blood, nieto," he said tearfully and hugged Eric. Eric wrapped his arms tightly around Don Alfredo. He had come home.

CHAPTER IX

At age forty-three, Mariz Elena de Vargas y Anderson was still a very beautiful woman, full of life and vitality. Her hair was a lustrous black, with just a few streaks of gray in it, and her almond-shaped, dark-brown eyes sparkled like onyx. She was small in stature, but she exuded such a presence that she appeared to be taller than she was. Unlike most Spanish matrons of her position and age, she was still very trim and always meticulously well dressed in the latest styles. In overall appearance, Mariz looked like a woman almost half her age.

Mariz was confident of her appearance and in the power it wielded. At the moment, she was particularly aware of her special power over Tom Jordan, the young man who took care of her finances and ran the del Sol. He was also her lover.

As she got up from her morning toilette she looked at Tom, still asleep in bed. He had attracted her from the first, his tall, lean good looks, the gleaming smile that was so captivating and disarming, and the hazel eyes, which changed from yellow to green depending on his moods.

Mariz and Tom had met five years earlier in New York. She had stopped there on her way home from Europe to do some shopping, and Tom was there visiting some friends from law school. He had gotten his degree from Harvard Law School and rather than stay and practice law in the East, he decided to go west and practice. He was intrigued with California and felt it would have a need for lawyers in the future.

Tom and Mariz had met when he inadvertently bumped into her, knocking the packages from her arms, while coming out of the lobby of their hotel. He apologized profusely and asked her to dinner. She accepted. They dined that evening, had lunch the next day, dinner again the next evening, and by the morning of the third day, they had become lovers. It had never entered Mariz's mind that Tom Jordan was young enough to be her son.

Mariz suggested that Tom return with her to the del Sol and at first he declined, feeling insulted.

"I refuse to be a paid companion to a middle-aged woman, no matter how rich and beautiful she is," he said, his eyes growing dark in anger.

Mariz's first response was one of anger and then she smiled—she liked a man who stood his ground. Men who catered to a woman's every whim were so boring.

"I have no intention of paying you unless you work for it, señor. I have been running my rancho alone for the past five years and it is becoming too much for me. I could use a strong man to help me run it and help me with my financial investments. You, being a lawyer, should have some good ideas. Surely, a man of your obvious intelligence must have an endless supply of money-making schemes. I want to make the Rancho del Sol one of the richest ranchos in all of Alta California. If you succeed in helping me do this, you can share in the

161

profits." Tom agreed to give it a try and had been there ever since. That had been five years ago.

Mariz smiled and walked over to the bedside, stooping down to place a kiss on Tom's mouth. He stirred slightly, but didn't wake up. She brushed the chestnut hair from his face, thinking what a lovely child he must have been. Silently she remembered her own son, Alejandro, and wondered if he would ever return. She knew the hatred he had for her and over the years, his absence had caused her to hate him in return. It was her defense for being shunned by her only son. But it hadn't always been that way; it had been different when he was a child.

He had always been her pride and joy and never had she seen a more handsome or spirited child. Even the blue eyes, which sometimes held the same contemptuous look as his father's, did not detract from his dark handsomeness. Rather, they seemed to enhance his looks. Mariz knew from the time Alejandro was old enough to walk and talk, that he was drawn to his father, and she always bitterly resented the fact. She had wanted to make him her son, to mold him into the kind of man she thought was proper for his station in life. But he rebelled against this.

It seemed that from the time of Alejandro's birth, Mariz and her husband started to grow apart. Her husband had wanted to name his son after him and in fact, had demanded it. But Mariz insisted that he be christened Alejandro Esteban de Vargas, in the tradition of her Spanish heritage. It had caused a breech between them when Eric didn't change his name and accept her faith when they married, as most all the other Yankees had done who had married Californio women. So, Eric called his son Eric, and Mariz called him Alejandro. From the beginning the child had to choose between his parents.

As the boy grew older, Mariz could see the growing attachment the boy had for his father. When Captain Anderson was at sea, Alejandro would grow sullen and morose, and when the captain returned, the child again turned into the charming, vibrant boy he normally was. During his father's absences, Mariz tried everything to take Alejandro's mind from his father, but all attempts failed save one—his grandfather. Alejandro was very close to his grandfather and Mariz resented their closeness. She wasn't used to being second best and it was difficult to accept the fact that her own son seemed to love his father more than her. It had never dawned on Mariz that had she not pushed her son so much, he would have gladly returned her love.

Mariz remembered the last time she had seen her son, and the hatred that blazed from the blue eyes. She would never forget that look as long as she lived. His eyes were overflowing with tears and the dark lashes were stuck together in small points. He had walked up to her, already towering over her at his young age. He glared down at her.

"It's your fault that my father is dead. I will never forgive you for it. I hate you, mother." He turned to walk away but stopped and turned back to her.

"With the exception of my grandfather, I spit on you and all the Spanish people and all they stand for. You and your Spanish heritage can go straight to hell." He spit on the floor and walked out.

"What were you thinking about?" Tom's voice startled Mariz from her thoughts. She started to get up but was stopped by his hand on hers.

"I just couldn't believe I have you all to myself."

"I'm yours completely, señora." He pulled her mouth down and kissed her. Mariz kissed him back then drew away.

"I must get dressed or Marta will be in here clucking like a mother hen over me. You sleep in darling, you deserve it."

Tom stretched out, placing his hands behind his head, and stared at the woman in front of him. He wondered how he had made her fall in love with him or when it had happened. This strong, intelligent, enigmatic woman was in love with him. At first it had been a game with him, a challenge. But now that she was really in love with him, he didn't feel so smug. He liked Mariz and enjoyed her company. She had treated him well and offered him many opportunities to better himself, and had introduced him to many of her friends and neighbors. He was grateful to her, but he wasn't in love with her. He often wondered where the relationship would end and how, if ever, he would break off with Mariz. But for now, the relationship was satisfactory to both of them. As long as Mariz didn't push him. He didn't like to be pushed by anyone, least of all, by a woman.

As Tom lay in bed thinking, a picture of Lisa entered his mind—Lisa, his beautiful, vivacious, little sister. He remembered her laughing, as she always was, running after him, trying to keep up, screaming his name at the top of her lungs. It had never mattered that he was eight years older than she, it just made him all the more protective of her. When he left Boston five years earlier, she had been only fourteen, but even then, the flower of her beauty was beginning to blossom. He hated leaving her, but he promised to send for her when he was financially able. He knew how unhappy she was living in the big mansion with their mother and rich stepfather. Lisa and Tom had always been especially close to their father, and it was he who had filled their heads with visions of California and the opportunities to be had there. When he died, they became even closer. Thus it was, that Tom had sent for Lisa over a year ago, and still he had yet to see her.

Tom blamed himself for Lisa's capture. He knew he should've insisted that she come by ship around the Horn rather than by wagon train as she had wanted to do. She had wanted the excitement of the overland trip. Tom couldn't believe it when he received a letter from Josh Wade, the wagon scout, telling him Lisa had been captured by a Comanche raiding party. Tom immediately went to Texas to look for her.

After hiring a scout who had traded with the Comanche for white slaves, they rode into various parts of the Comancheria tracing all leads but not finding Lisa. It seemed that no one had heard of or seen a woman fitting Lisa's description. Tom finally gave up after two months of searching and returned to California. It had come as something of a shock, when, months later, he received a letter from Lisa explaining that she was alive and well and briefly what had happened to her. His first impulse had been to go to Santa Fe and get her, but Mariz had persuaded him against it.

"She needs time alone, Tom. She would have asked you to come if she wanted you to be there. She will come when she is ready," Mariz told him.

Tom saw the logic in this and agreed to wait until Lisa came to California on her own. But he couldn't keep his thoughts from returning to Lisa and her capture. He couldn't imagine what she had suffered at the hands of the Comanche. His scout had made sure to supply him with all the grisly details of what other white captive women had gone through and every time Tom thought of the humiliation and degradation Lisa must have endured, he burned inside. He was almost afraid to see her, afraid of what they had done to destroy her innocent beauty. But all he could do was wait and pray, that at the age of nineteen, she wasn't just the bitter shell of a woman.

CHAPTER X

The next few weeks were busy ones for Eric. The first thing he did was to make some contacts among his old friends and neighbors and let them know he was back. It was strange seeing some of the people after so long. Many were happy to see him, some were angry with him for leaving his mother, the rancho, and California. Everyone seemed to be genuinely surprised by his appearance—his long, shaggy hair, buckskins and moccasins. It certainly wasn't the type of dress befitting a hacendado.

Eric also made inquiries about Lisa. He gave her description to everyone he saw and asked them to contact him if they saw her. He even hired two men to search some of the ranchos farther south for her. He figured he would find her eventually if she were anywhere in the area.

He was amazed at the growth in the area and of Monterey itself. There were many more buildings, including wealthy homes, and Don Alfredo told him that many of the rancheros divided their time between their ranchos and their pueblo dwellings. Since the gold rush, however, the population had dwindled. Many of the buildings had fallen into disrepair and some of the stores had closed and there was a local scarcity of supplies. Everything that could be used to mine gold: trays, pans, bowls—anything that could hold sand and water—was taken and sold to the miners.

The state of the government, Eric learned from Don Alfredo, was mass confusion. Since 1847, they had been under military rule, but the local alcaldes still administered civil law. On May 20, 1848, the Treaty of Guadalupe Hidalgo concluded the Mexican War and resulted in the cession of California to the United States. Many of the Americans and Californios had hoped that Congress would then confer upon Californians their constitutional rights as United States citizens, but the territorial government was slow to be authorized. The political future of the territory was left undecided. Eventually, a constitutional convention was held in Monterey on September 3, 1849, to discuss how the state would be run and the likelihood that it would be admitted to the union as the nation's thirty-first state. The convention discussed many matters, among them: separate property rights for women; the unanimous vote against slavery; public education; taxes; and California's boundaries. As a result of the convention, it was hoped that the United States Congress would soon debate on California's prospective statehood.

"We now have two state senators, Mr. Fremont and Mr. Gwin. They have been to Washington and presented copies of our new constitution before the Congress and requested that we be admitted to the union. The news is that we will be the thirty-first state of the United States by the end of the year."

"How do you feel about that, abuelo? The life of the hacendado won't last forever."

"As I told you before, I cannot stop the tide of change, none of us can. The population of California now consists

168

mostly of foreigners who want to change our way of life, and maybe they are partly right. As you know, I've never fully agreed with the rancheros' philosophy of life. I have always worked hard, as did my father before me, and his father before him. I built this rancho with the help of my vaqueros and Indios; I never believed in sitting around drinking and gambling. Even your father, although he wasn't a hacendado, believed in working hard, and he was always away on his ship. But I have earned the right after all these years to be able to relax and enjoy my life, and pass on what I have built to you and your children. That's what I resent most—the fact that I may not be able to pass it all on to you because some Yankee or foreigner has taken over the land."

"Don't worry, abuelo, we will fight to keep this land and the del Sol. Just because we become part of the United States, doesn't mean we have to give up what is ours."

After a few weeks' stay at the del Mar, Eric decided it was time to go to the del Sol. The morning he left the del Mar, he was filled with mixed emotions. He knew the del Sol was legally his and that according to the way it was set up, his parents were to leave the del Sol when he became of age. It was intended for him and his future wife and family, and his parents were to move back to the del Mar and take it over. But he wondered if he really had a right to it after all this time. He knew that his main motivation for going back was to hurt his mother. But, he wondered, had she suffered enough in the last ten years? Then there was Lisa. He didn't want to bring her into this kind of family conflict when she had already been through so much. He didn't have any answers. The only thing he knew for sure was that he had to go to the del Sol to face his mother once again and see if anything had changed between them.

Eric left Raytahnee with Don Alfredo. She had accepted the story about her background without question and she seemed very content, except she continually asked about Lisa. Unfortunately, he had heard nothing from any of his contacts.

Riding the distance from the del Mar to the del Sol, something Eric had done constantly as a child, he took notice of the changes that had occurred during his absence. Trees that before had been small were now larger and filled out, and many of the orchards were now bearing fruit. Watering holes and feeding troughs dotted the landscape at different intervals. The land was covered by wild yellow mustard and was rich and productive, and the cattle and horses that grazed on it were healthy.

It wasn't long before Eric saw the red-tiled roof of the del Sol. For a brief time, thoughts of his childhood invaded his head. He saw the figure of a young boy running and laughing, his mother and father smiling after him.

A small bouquet of wildflowers. "For you, mama."

A bright smile and a curtsy. "Muchas gracias, hijo."

A ship on the horizon. Tears. Arms to hold and comfort him. Love and security. There wasn't always the hate. There was a time . . .

Eric was fast approaching the front of the hacienda. His mind snapped back to the present. He looked around him. The orchards surrounding the hacienda were bigger, full of orange, avocado, lime, lemon, and peach trees, and they were all meticulously well kept. The different gardens, full of flowers and fruits and vegetables, scattered around the grounds, were for the inhabitants of the ranchos and the vaqueros and workers. There were also the field crops, such as wheat and corn. Even the small vineyard with the neatly painted white trellises, was still there. The small huts for the vaqueros and the Indios—it was all the same. Then there was the enormous two-story structure of the hacienda itself, built in a squared-off U-shape with a courtyard in the center, much like the del Mar but on a grander scale. Each of the upper bedrooms opened onto a small balcony which overlooked the courtyard, and like the del Mar, each bedroom had a fireplace. It was a beautifully designed place, designed entirely by his father and grandfather, and Eric was surprised at the effect it had on him after all these years. He had been a Comanche for ten years of his life, but he had lived here for even longer and he realized that the Rancho del Sol was still a part of him.

He rode up to the front, dismounted, and walked through the wrought-iron gate to the courtyard. No one recognized him; they assumed that he was a stranger. He walked up the stairs of the veranda and through the heavy oak door to the hallway and into the dining room and kitchen. That had been another marvel about the Ranchos del Mar and Sol—the kitchens had been attached to the haciendas rather than being separate rooms outside of the hacienda.

Eric stood at the door of the kitchen, watching the old Indian woman who was baking fresh rolls and making tortillas. He walked up behind her and wrapped his arms around her. It was Marta, the cook and housekeeper, and she had been his favorite as a child. "Hola, Marta, cómo, está?"

Marta screamed and stepped back. When she got a

good look at him she almost collapsed. She walked closer to him, staring up into the familiar blue eyes.

"Madre de Dios," she said dramatically as she crossed herself. "Is it really you, Alejandro? Is it true?" She touched him as if to see if he were real.

Eric laughed and, taking off his dusty hat, bowed deeply.

Sí, Marta, it is I. I am here and I am real. Have I changed so much in ten years?"

Marta smiled, her brown eyes filling with tears.

"No, you are still my guapo—very handsome, mi patrón. But those clothes, your hair. You look so different."

"I am different and I've been to a lot of different places. Now, are you still the best cook in all of Alta California?"

"Por supuesto! You still know how to say the right things, eh? I'm sure you have set many young hearts aflutter." She grew suddenly serious. "What of the patrona; have you seen her yet?"

Eric's smile immediately changed to a deep frown.

"No, I haven't seen her yet. Has she been down?"

"No, but she will be shortly. She will be in for her coffee and roll soon."

Eric walked over to the adobe oven and took out a hot roll, talking while he ate.

"Tell me about this Tom Jordan. What's he like?"

"Oh, Señor Jordan, he is a good man. Very kind. He helps the hacendados to keep their land."

"Ah, Marta, you still make the best rolls in the world. Has this Jordan done a good job around here?"

"Sí. He is good and fair to all the workers. I think the rancho has made much money since he has been here because he and the patrona have lent money to other hacendados who have gambled theirs away. I think they have a partnership."

"I bet they do," Eric muttered wryly.

"What did you say, patrón?"

"Nothing. And does this Jordan plan to stay on here for very long?"

"I don't know for sure but I'm sure he will stay awhile. He has a sister coming to visit."

"A sister? How does my mother feel about having to share her young man? I wouldn't think she'd be very happy about having to compete with another woman."

"The patrona is very happy for Señor Jordan. She knows how much he cares for his sister. The patrona says Señorita Jordan is welcome to stay here for as long as she wishes."

"Kind of her," Eric said dryly, "but that doesn't sound like my mother."

Marta glared at Eric.

"You may own this hacienda and this land, but I am much older than you and I have been with this family since before you were born. The patrona has been good to me and my own. Please do not belittle her in front of me."

Eric was taken aback, but he respected Marta's loyalty to his mother.

"Perdóname, Marta, my tongue is still much too quick. I have grown taller and bigger, but my mouth is still that of a young boy."

Marta laughed and kissed Eric on the cheek.

"I cannot stay mad at you for long, Alejandro, I never could. You are so big and handsome now. And your eyes, they are still so blue, like the ocean."

"Did you expect me to have brown eyes when I came back?"

Marta looked at him seriously and then burst into laughter. It had always bothered Mariz that Eric had inherited his father's blue eyes, rather than her black ones.

"Here, have another roll and leave me alone. I have things to do. Go see your mama; I think she will be happy to see you."

"You are as persuasive as ever, Marta. But I will see you later and I'll expect a freshly baked pie for dessert tonight." He leaned over and kissed her wrinkled brown cheek, grabbed another roll, and walked out.

Marta's eyes followed Eric as he left the kitchen. Like Don Alfredo, she too, had known he would return.

"There will be much trouble around here," she muttered to herself. "The patrona won't change and neither will Alejandro. They both hurt inside yet neither one will give in. It will be very interesting now that the young patrón is back." She clucked, a grin appearing on her old brown face.

Eric stood at the bottom of the stairs and waited for his mother to come down. He had no idea what he was going to say to her. He wondered if he could forget the past and apologize to her. Maybe they could learn to love each other again. A movement caught his eye and he looked at the top of the stairs. Mariz stood at the top pinning a brooch to the bodice of her dress. He couldn't believe that she could look so young, still be so beautiful. It would have been easier if she had grown old and fat.

As Mariz started down the stairs she looked up and saw Eric. For a short moment she felt her knees buckle, and she had to grab hold of the banister for support. Her son was a grown man now, a very handsome man, like his father. She continued down the staircase as calm and composed as if Eric always waited for her there. When she got to the bottom stair she extended her hand, and automatically Eric kissed it.

"Well, Alejandro, it is good to see that wherever you have been all these years, you haven't forgotten your manners."

Eric flinched. She hadn't changed. She was still arrogant and disdainful of others. They could never be friends.

"You look lovely as ever, mother. What keeps you so young? Must be the young man you keep company with."

"Well, I see I was wrong, after all. You have forgotten your manners. And those clothes and your hair, you are filthy. How dare you come into my home looking like that. My vaqueros are cleaner than you are."

"Don't worry, mother, I didn't touch anything on my way in," Eric said sarcastically.

"Well, what brings you back after all this time, or need I ask?"

Eric glared at her, turning to walk into the study.

"You know what brought me back here—the del Sol. It's mine."

Mariz followed him.

"It isn't yours and you know it. While you were gone to God knows where, I have been right here, working hard to make the del Sol what it is today. You don't care for this land, you only care about getting back at me for something you think I did. I won't give up the del Sol, Alejandro."

Eric walked around the room, looking at the familiar

books and objects. He was glad that Mariz hadn't changed anything in the room. She must have cared for his father a little to leave everything as it was. He walked over to the bookcase and picked up the model of the *Adventurer*, the last ship his father had captained. He ran his hand along the smooth lines of the little ship then put it down.

"You're right about one thing, I do want to get back at you. But you're wrong about the land—I want the land. This rancho is something my father and grandfather planned for me and I refuse to let you have it. I bet this land means more to me than it does to you. You don't fool me. I've had a lot of time to think and I know the kind of selfish and self-serving person you really are. You don't do anything unless your best interests are at stake."

"My, my, you have become philosophical in your travels, Alejandro," Mariz said sarcastically. "By the way, where have you been? You talk like a Cholo or a savage, and you look even worse. You expect to become patrón of this rancho looking and acting like that? You make me laugh; you may look like a man but you still think and act like a boy."

"My name is Eric Anderson," Eric shouted angrily, "and I lived with some Indians who are more civilized than you could ever hope to be. They may look and act differently from you, but at least they are real and warm, not a cold imitation like you."

"Stop it!" Mariz screamed furiously. "Can't you even act civilly toward your own mother?"

"You're being a bit overdramatic, aren't you, mother?"

"I made a mistake and you found out I was less than perfect. You couldn't accept that. It was your fault for believing I was perfect."

"Perhaps you're right. But what a mistake you made—you killed my father. That's something a young boy isn't likely to forget, no matter how much time passes. And it wasn't one mistake you made, there were many, and they led to my father's death."

"All right, I see that it doesn't matter what I say, you will persisit in believing what you will. This constant bickering is getting us nowhere, and I haven't yet had my coffee and roll. Tom will be down shortly; you can discuss any business matters with him. He is completely in charge of all my legal and financial matters."

Eric watched her as she left the room. She still had that damnable way of dismissing a person, as if one was no more than a mere servant.

Tom Jordan—Eric had already formed his opinion of the man. He knew he wouldn't like him. He held very little respect for a man, especially a young one, who lived off an older woman. He could imagine the type of man he was.

"Alejandro, I'm Tom Jordan," Tom said suddenly, startling Eric from his secret thoughts.

Eric turned around and his earlier resolve began to melt when he saw Tom's smile and his proffered hand. He was tall and lean with chestnut-colored hair and hazel eyes, and when he smiled it reminded him of someone else, but for the life of him, Eric couldn't.think who. All he knew was this was the kind of man who could disarm an enemy in seconds. Eric liked him without even speaking to him.

"Call me Eric," he said, extending his hand to shake with Tom. "I was named after my father and his name was Eric Anderson. He was a Yankee sea captain."

"Okay, Eric," Tom said amiably.

"There're a lot of things I want to talk to you about." He walked to the fireplace and leaned against it. "I don't know if you know, but I'm the legal owner of the Rancho del Sol, even though I've been away."

"Yes, I know, I've read the papers."

"Well, as a lawyer, you should know that there is nothing my mother can do to contest the fact."

"Yes, I know," Tom said, nodding.

"I'm going to take over the del Sol now that I'm back, and I want to know exactly what it is you do here. Do you run the del Sol or do you serve as my mother's . . ."

"As your mother's what?" Tom asked coldly, taking a step forward. The smile suddenly faded from his face.

"My mother's legal counsel," Eric replied lightly. He noticed the change in Tom's manner when he had even tried to infer that he was Mariz's kept man.

"I've been handling your mother's legal investments and the selling of the beef and crops. I've also been kept busy with land titles. I've secured those of the del Sol and the del Mar, and I've been trying to secure those of the others in the area. Since the gold rush, many of the foreigners have been trying to prove that the land that the rancheros hold isn't theirs and that the titles are false. Lawyers have been hired from the East to work for the Yankees against the rancheros. The Californios know little about the new land claims and titles and they're being cheated out of what has always been theirs. I'm afraid that in a few years, if things continue as they are, there will be few ranchos left in Alta California."

"My grandfather told me the same thing."

"Then did he also tell you that the Californios are defeating themselves. I can only do so much to help them, but they still persist in their old ways. They gamble

178

away much of their land to miners who expect land as payment. The Californios still want to live as kings and they refuse to believe that they will lose everything they covet if they aren't careful."

"They're stupid. It has always been the way of the Californios to live the easy life. They have lived rich, soft, pampered lives, with the vaqueros, Cholos, and the Indios to do all their work for them. Their idea of work has been to have rodeos, hunts, races, fiestas, and to gamble all their money away. They'll never change."

"They must if they want their land. But there're other troubles, too. The government supports the Yankees in their efforts to gain control of the land. If the Yankees can't get the land through the courts or through gambling debts, they squat on it. There have been raids— horses and cattle have been rustled and killed, and even some of the vaqueros have been killed trying to stop them. We've been forced to create our own private army to patrol the del Sol and the del Mar."

"But there's too much land to watch all the time."

"Exactly. And that's not all; there've been raids by bandidos. Mexicans and Indians have been raiding ranchos for stock and entering some of the haciendas and stealing anything they can get their hands on. Some of the women and girls have been raped, the men killed. They mean business. One of the worst is a mestizo called Chuka."

"Chuka? You're sure?" Eric asked in surprise.

"Yeah, why?"

"I knew him once a long time ago."

"Well, he's notorious now, a killer."

"I feel like I've been gone for a hundred years instead of ten," Eric said sadly. "So much has changed since I've been gone."

"Yeah, and it's not all for the good."

"Well, what about the beef and horses? What kind of prices are you getting for them?"

"The beef are the most profitable right now because the miners are in constant need of fresh beef. We drive them to different camps along some established trails, along with some of the horses. We're getting up to seventy dollars a head for them. The miners pay highly to have fresh beef."

Eric breathed deeply. Ten years ago they had barely been able to get two dollars a head. Seventy dollars a head was almost inconceivable to him.

"We can also salt the beef and sell it to the ships, along with the hides and tallow. We trade them for spices, sugar, tea, cocoa, tools, cutlery, and Chinese silk and china. And we have a good market for the citrus. The ships buy it in bulk to take on their voyages to prevent scurvy among the crew. And many of the sailors buy our wine. I guess they get tired of drinking rum all the time. So, as you can see, the del Sol is one of the richest, most productive ranchos in Alta California."

"And the del Mar? Have you helped my grandfather as you have helped my mother?"

Tom smiled.

"Don Alfredo is a very stubborn man, but I have given him my advice on some things. He does well enough without my help it seems."

"That sounds like my grandfather," Eric agreed. In spite of himself, Eric was impressed with Tom. It seemed that the man had worked hard at using every resource on the del Sol in order to prevent any waste and to make it productive. And he was direct and honest.

"I'll need your help, Tom. I have a lot to catch up on and learn, and you can teach me. You better than anyone can teach me." Eric stopped for a moment, and walked to the bookcase, absently picking up the *Adventurer* once again. "I don't know what my mother has told you about me, but I'm going to be here from now on. I've been gone long enough. Anyway, will you stay and help me?"

"Sure, I'd be glad to help you. Then when you feel you're ready to take over, I'll leave. I have some plans of my own anyway."

"Do they include your sister? Marta told me your sister is coming to visit."

"Yes, she is. She should be here anytime now. I have some property north of here and I'd like to build a place for me and Lisa to live. It certainly won't be on the same scale as the del Sol, but it'll be mine."

Eric turned, his face very pale.

"What did you say your sister's name was?"

"Lisa, Lisa Jordan." Tom reached into his pocket and took out a watch, snapping it open as he did so. "Here's a picture of her. 'Course, she was only about fourteen then but I bet she's a real beauty now."

Eric took the watch from Tom and stared at it. A lump formed in his throat as he looked at the small daguerreotype of Lisa. She was much younger then, but the promise of beauty to come was already there. Her dark-chestnut curls were pulled back by a ribbon and she was dressed in a simple, white dress. Even the copper color of the picture couldn't detract from the sparkling eyes and smile. The smile, of course. No wonder he had recognized Tom's smile—it was exactly like Lisa's. He handed the watch back to Tom.

"She's very pretty. How old is she now?"

"Nineteen." Tom looked at the watch once more then snapped it shut and put it back in his pocket. "She has the most incredible green eyes. Never seen anything like them."

"Yes," Eric answered absently.

"What?"

"I said I'm sure she does," Eric said and turned away, embarrassed that he'd made such a slip. "Is your sister from the East?"

"Boston, but she left there over a year ago. She was coming to visit me, but she was captured by some Comanche. Don't know how long she was with them before the wagon-train scout found the Comanche camp and traded for her. She's in Santa Fe now with some friends of the scout. Seems she's pretty grateful to this guy. Most of her letter was about him."

"Oh," Eric muttered, thinking back to what his grandfather had said. What if she had fallen in love with Josh Wade? "When will she be here?"

"Should be here by summer. It's been a helluva long time; I can't wait to see her. You don't mind if she stays here, do you?"

"No. You both stay as long as you like," Eric said, his mind wandering to Josh and Lisa. By the time they got to California, they would have been together six months or so, almost the amount of time she had spent with him. He didn't want to believe that she could fall in love with another man, but the thought plagued him.

"Hard to believe I haven't seen her in over five years. I bet she's changed a lot." Tom laughed. "Jesus, but she was a little wildcat when we were younger. She could outcurse and outride just about any boy her age and older. Our mother was in a constant state of the vapors over Lisa's unladylike behavior. I just hope her experience with the Comanche hasn't changed her too much. She's only nineteen years old—too young to have gone through what she has."

Nineteen—Eric hadn't even known Lisa's age. She had endured far too much for her age, he thought. He wanted to make it all up to her. He turned to Tom. "I hope you'll stay, Tom, I really need your help. I've been out of touch with this life for a long time."

"Sure, I'll stay for a while, but I'm about ready for a place of my own—a place where I can be my own man." The eyes of the two men locked for a moment, and Eric couldn't be sure what Tom was thinking. He thought Tom's voice had held a touch of bitterness, but he couldn't be sure. One thing he was sure of, Tom Jordan wasn't the type of man that could be kept by a woman. Even if that woman was his mother.

CHAPTER XI

Eric spent every day of the next few weeks riding around the del Sol with Tom, and getting used to the changes that had been made. He met all the vaqueros, many of whom he had known when he left. Hector, the majordomo when he left, was still the majordomo and the best man with a horse Eric had ever known. Hector was pleased to see Eric back at the rancho because he had always felt a fondness for the boy. He showed Eric some of the horses, especially some of their prized palomino stock, and explained how they had been breaking some of the stock and then herding them to some of the mining camps. Eric rode out with the vaqueros each day to check on the cattle and horses, and make sure that squatters hadn't stolen or killed any more.

In a couple months Eric was beginning to feel at home on the del Sol again. He got along well with Tom and found him to be invaluable in matters concerning the rancho. He had to admit his mother had been wise to hire Tom to run it. During this time, Eric and his mother maintained a polite indifference toward each other, more for their mutual liking of Tom than for their love for each other.

It was during this time that Eric also reacquainted himself with another old friend, Consuelo de la Morena.

They had been childhood friends and had experienced their first sexual encounters with each other's young, inexperienced bodies. As soon as she heard he was back, Consuelo went to the del Sol. She had often wondered what kind of man he had turned into, and during the years, had had many fantasies about him.

When Eric saw Consuelo for the first time, he was genuinely happy to see her. She reminded him of some of the good times they had had as children, when both their lives were happy and uncomplicated. In the ten years since Eric had seen her, Consuelo had matured into a woman. She was very small and petite, with black hair and eyes. Her olive complexion was flawless and she had a beauty mark at the corner of her mouth, which gave her a very provocative look. The changes weren't only in her appearance. Outwardly, she was still the same compliant, sweet girl that Eric had known, but inwardly, she had a fierceness that rivaled Mariz's in intensity. Over the years she had built up a picture of Eric in her mind—a picture with whom no other man could compare. In her heart, she knew he would return and when he did, she knew it wouldn't be long before they were together again as they had been as children. She had already decided she was going to marry Eric.

Mariz liked Consuelo and she encouraged the relationship. She felt it would be good if Eric married Consuelo. Not only would it tie in all the Morena ranchland, but it would raise Eric's position in the area again. There were still some rancheros who were skeptical about Eric's return, and Mariz knew that a marriage to a wealthy Spaniard would again gain Eric a respected position. As much as she tried to act as though she didn't care, Mariz was happy that Eric was back, and proud of the way he

185

was taking over the rancho. It was what she had always wanted, and now, even after all this time, it looked as though she would get what she had dreamed of. Her son would marry a Spaniard and be the patrón of the del Sol.

Consuelo ordered trunks of clothes brought from her rancho and she stayed at the del Sol. Eric was so happy to have some female company that he didn't notice the possessive way Consuelo began to regard him. Whenever he was free, Consuelo was always with him, walking or talking to him, holding on to him, reaching out to touch him whenever she could. Eric was the culmination of all Consuelo's childhood dreams. She was sure that he was the right man for her and in her blindness, she didn't notice that Eric didn't return her affection. In the few days they had been together, Consuelo adopted an unreal devotion toward Eric.

On the night before Consuelo was to return home to receive guests, she and Eric dined alone. Tom and Mariz went out to visit friends; Mariz arranged for Eric and Consuelo to be alone as much as possible. They had dinner and then walked in the gardens, sipping wine in the courtyard.

"Why do you wear those strange clothes all the time, Alejandro?"

Eric laughed. "They're not strange to me."

"But you don't look like a hacendado. You should make other men respect you, Sandro."

"If men are going to respect me, Consuelo, it'll be because of the kind of man I am, not because of the clothes I wear."

"Well, I suppose so. But you are going to be an important man around here and . . ."

"Let's drop it," Eric said in annoyance and stood up.

"I think we'd better go in now. It's getting late."

Consuelo got up and walked to Eric.

"Are you angry with me, Sandro? I only want to help."

"I know. Let's go in now."

"California is growing and you could be an important man. Would you like that? I could help you, I know a lot of people."

Eric turned to Consuelo, clearly irritated now.

"Consuelo, I don't need your help to introduce me to people or to make me respected. All I want to do is run the del Sol and keep it out of the hands of any Yankees or foreigners who want it."

"But . . ."

"Don't push me," Eric shouted angrily. "I'm going in now."

Consuelo watched as Eric walked up the steps of the veranda and went into the hacienda. His attitude perplexed her. She hadn't expected him to react so violently. She was sure he'd want her help, but she'd been wrong. Maybe she'd misjudged him. Well, she thought mischievously, there's more than one way to reach a man like Eric. She picked up her wine glass and followed him into the house.

Eric was dreaming. He was lying on his bed, covered only by a sheet, a cool breeze blowing in through the window. The combination of the wine and brandy had made him fairly drunk. The door opened and Lisa walked in, dressed in a sheer, white nightgown. He couldn't move; he could only watch. She walked to his bed and stood there while the breeze whipped the sheer cloth around her slender frame. She looked into his eyes and then slowly took off the gown. Beams of moonlight fell on

187

her long, brown body, illuminating it against the dark room. She pulled back the sheet and slid into bed beside Eric, rubbing her body against his. Her hands touched him all over, they seemed to have a mind of their own. Her lips touched him in places that excited him to the core, and still, all he could do was lie there and watch. She lay on top of him, moving her silken body against his, murmuring in his ear. Funny, but her body didn't seem so long and slim as usual, her skin not quite so soft, her lips . . . Eric sat up suddenly, jarred into reality by the woman next to him. He had hoped that it was Lisa, but he knew that it couldn't be. He saw the dark skin and eyes and he knew it was Consuelo in bed with him. He grabbed her shoulders and tried to move her away, but she wrapped her arms around him.

"Consuelo, you can't do this. You don't understand."

"I understand, querido. You desire me as much as I desire you. Even after all these years the fire has not gone out." She moved against him again and draped her leg over his thigh.

"I don't love you, Consuelo. If you want love, I can't give it to you."

"I have love enough for both of us, querido. I have so much love. . . ." she murmured huskily into his ear and reached down and ran her hand over the hard muscles of his stomach and still lower. Eric moaned involuntarily, and in spite of himself, he found himself responding to Consuelo's experienced touch. He had been months without a woman, much too long.

Eric turned Consuelo onto her back and took her with incredible force and longing. He heard her cry out and he felt her nails dig into his back. He couldn't believe that this fiercely passionate woman was the same sweet, little

Consuelo, who only hours before, had let him kiss her on the cheek. He felt slightly guilty about making love to her like this, but he found himself unable to resist her luscious little body. And she had wanted it. It was she who had found her way into his bed and forced herself on him. And he had been honest with her and told her he didn't love her. No, there was no reason to feel guilty. If a man wanted a woman, why shouldn't he take her if she was willing? That's how it should be, he thought. If a man and a woman wanted to be together, they should just be together. There didn't have to be any other attachments. Like the Comanche.

Eric looked over at Consuelo and he turned on his side. He was tired and he felt good. He shut his eyes and felt his muscles relax. A faint vision of deep-green, tear-filled eyes came into his head. He remembered the way they had looked the first time he had seen them—full of defiance and pain. He had been taken captive by those eyes and even now, he was still a prisoner of them. He wished that it had been Lisa he had made love to, and that it was she lying next to him. But soon, very soon, she would be lying next to him, and nothing would ever separate them again.

Consuelo left the next morning after breakfast and Eric was relieved to see her go. All through the night she had murmured words of love which he couldn't return. She had begged him again and again to tell her he loved her, but he couldn't. She had made much more out of their night of lovemaking than she should have, and Eric was afraid she would continue to do so. He realized, too late, that he'd made a mistake making love to her. Consuelo was the kind of woman who demanded

189

commitment, and when she didn't get it, there was no telling how she'd react.

It was the time of the matanza, the spring slaughter of the beef. The cattle were rounded up, slaughtered, and their carcasses stripped of the hides and meat. The meat was salted and sun dried to make jerky, and the fat was boiled into tallow for soap. It was tiresome work to most, but to Eric, who had participated in countless buffalo hunts, the work was not bad. The vaqueros were astonished by the patrón's stamina and they held him in high regard for even taking part in the matanza. The fact that he had been gone for so long and had suddenly come back to take control of the rancho was no concern of theirs. All they knew was that the patrón dressed like them and worked alongside them; any other details of his life didn't interest them.

The matanza was barely over when Tom received a letter from Lisa. She and Josh were in Los Angeles and she sent the letter by messenger, stating that they would arrive at the Rancho del Sol at any time. Eric couldn't take a chance on being seen by Josh, so he told Tom that he wanted to visit with his grandfather for a few days, and he went to the del Mar. Lisa arrived the next day.

Lisa and Josh stopped to dismount by a little stream fed by the nearby mountains. Josh looked around him and up at the Santa Lucia Mountains. It was the fifth time he'd been to California, but each time he came it felt like the first. It was an incredibly beautiful country, young and unspoiled, a virtual paradise. It's too bad that gold's been discovered, he thought. Now, it'll never be the same. People will come, and more people, and then it'll be crowded like the cities in the East. He looked over at Lisa.

This country reminded him of a young girl—like Lisa had been before the Comanche had raped her. It was so raw before the miners came, but it'd soon be spoiled.

Josh watched Lisa as she bent down to pick some wildflowers. He thought that this was an appropriate place for someone like her. It was a place where she could forget the past and start fresh, without any reminders of what had happened. She was like this land, he thought, young and unspoiled, no matter what happened to her. She looked up at him and smiled.

"Aren't these beautiful? Have you ever seen so many colors?" she asked, smelling the different flowers.

Josh looked at her and smiled, hardly noticing the flowers she held in her hand. Ever since the time by the river when he'd forced himself on her, he found it difficult to be around her. Every time he looked at her, he remembered the way she had looked when she stepped out of the water—he had never seen such perfection in his life. He watched her as she walked around the field and it occured to him that he would do anything to have this woman. He'd sell his farm in Missouri and quit his job as a scout, anything, if she'd just say the word. He'd never known a woman quite like her and he'd known many. She was so lovely, yet so totally unaware of the effect she had on men.

Josh walked over to her.

"You done yet, girl? Where in hell are you goin' to put all them things?" he said, pointing to the flowers.

"I just thought it'd be nice to bring some flowers to the patrona of the rancho; don't you think so, Josh?"

When Lisa looked at Josh so imploringly with her large, green eyes, he wasn't altogether sure she was unaware of the effect she had on men. In fact, he had the funny feeling she knew exactly what she was doing.

"Don't you think the flowers are a good idea? Why do you have such a serious look on your face?"

"Yeah, the flowers'll be real nice, but if you don't get your butt up on that horse, we'll never reach that rancho before dark. We still got a ways to go."

"All right, I'm ready to go." She swung herself up onto her horse's back. She looked over at Josh and smiled. She couldn't believe that her long journey was finally coming to an end.

Lisa's first sight of the Rancho del Sol was partially obscured by the tall rows of wheat and corn. She thought it must be a large structure from what she could see of the red-tile roof which seemed to stretch for yards. Indian and Mexican workers looked up at them as they rode past and a few smiled. Lisa smiled back and waved. She wondered how people who labored in the fields all day in the hot sun could be so cheery. Then she remembered how she and the other women of the Comanche camp had worked all day, day in and day out, making clothes, hunting small game, preserving fruits and vegetables, tanning hides, gathering the wood and water. It too had been hard work, but they had done it because it was their job, just as working in the fields was the work these people did.

When they left the fields, Lisa got her first real look at the Rancho del Sol. It was different from the way she had imagined it. She had pictured a crude, adobe structure like many of the ones she'd already seen, but this rancho was nothing like the others. It was certainly different from any style she'd ever seen in the East, but she thought it was quite earthy and stylish.

The hacienda was constructed of wood and adobe and it had French windows and doors which gave the appearance of a European style. It had two stories and all the windows on the second story faced out to a balcony which overlooked the courtyard. In front of the courtyard, there was a high wrought-iron gate, through which Lisa could see a fountain in the courtyard. Beyond that, was the main part of the building, the hacienda itself.

As they rode up to the railing, Lisa saw Tom come through the courtyard. He'd evidently been waiting for any sign of her and Josh. Lisa jumped from her horse and ran into Tom's outstretched arms.

"Lisa, Lisa," Tom murmured into her hair. He cradled her in his arms and stroked her long hair. "My God, but you're beautiful, even in those dirty clothes. You were just a little girl when I left and now you're a woman." He crushed her to his chest and they both began to cry. "You can't know how glad I am that you're finally here, alive and well."

"Probably about as glad as I am to be here," Lisa replied. "Oh, Tom, you look wonderful." They both began talking excitedly about old times and the tricks they used to play on their mother. They were oblivious to Mariz and the obvious stares of disapproval she was giving them.

Mariz had been apprehensive about Lisa's visit from the start, but she was sure she could undermine any influence Tom's sister might have. Now, after looking at the girl and the way Tom held on to her, she wasn't so sure. She was a beauty and she had Tom wrapped around her finger. She didn't like the idea of sharing Tom with anyone, and that included his own sister. She'd have to be very careful where this girl was concerned, she thought.

Mariz cleared her throat impatiently, hoping to get Tom's attention. Tom turned around, remembering Mariz. He brought her forward to Lisa, just as Josh dismounted and walked to the group.

"Tom, this is Josh Wade. He is the one who brought me here. He came into the Comanche camp and traded for me." Lisa took Josh's large hand into hers.

Tom reached out and grasped Josh's free hand with both of his, shaking his hand vigorously.

"How can I ever thank you? If there's ever anything I can do for you . . ."

"You don't have to thank me," Josh interrupted. "I didn't do it for any reward. Your sister just happens to have a way about her and I just got used to havin' her around. I was glad to do it."

Tom nodded his thanks and he put his arm around Mariz. She stared at Lisa, a smile on her face, a building resentment growing inside her. She seemed to have this man in her power, too.

"Lisa, Josh, may I present Mariz Elena de Vargas y Anderson. Mariz's son owns the Rancho del Sol." Mariz scowled at Tom's reference to the owner of the del Sol, but extended her hand to Lisa and smiled.

"I'm so pleased to meet you, my dear. I've heard so much about you and your terrible tragedy. I hope you are well now," she said with a trace of sarcasm in her voice.

"Very well, thank you, señora," Lisa replied. She hadn't missed the way Mariz had looked at her and Tom and she immediately suspected that Mariz resented her intrusion into their lives. "I hope I won't be imposing on you too much."

"No, not at all. We are glad to have you and your friend." Mariz put deliberate emphasis on the word "friend."

Lisa introduced Josh to Mariz and then Tom led them all inside. When Lisa saw the lovely flower gardens in the courtyard, she decided to leave her flowers in her pack. A woman like Mariz wouldn't be impressed with wildflowers.

They walked up the steps of the veranda and through a heavy oak door, which was elaborately carved. Tom led them down a hallway and into the dining area. The room was filled with polished pine furniture, very heavy and durable. It was an open, cheery room, with a high-beamed ceiling of polished wood, and French windows which looked out on the courtyard.

They barely sat down when Marta came in carrying trays of food. The meal consisted of beef cooked in a spicy barbecue sauce, ears of fresh corn, potatoes, carrots, and onions; a steaming bowl of frijoles, and a large stack of fresh tortillas. Lisa and Josh devoured the food while Marta looked on in satisfaction. Their glasses were constantly filled with a sweet, red wine, which, Tom told them, came from the rancho's own vineyard.

"My God, you two look as if you haven't eaten in weeks," Tom said jokingly.

"If you'd lived on hardtack, jerky, and coffee for almost a month, this food would look pretty good to you, too," Lisa replied. "Thank you for the excellent meal, Marta," Lisa said, turning to the older woman. "I can't remember when I've enjoyed a meal so much," she said in Spanish.

"Por nada señorita," Marta said, clearly flattered by Lisa's attempt to speak in Marta's own language.

195

"Where did you learn to speak Spanish so well, dear? In the Comanche camp?" Mariz asked, ignoring the cold stare she received from Tom.

"I learned it back in Boston, señora. Not many of the Comanche spoke Spanish. They don't need to speak the same language to be understood." She stared at Mariz, her green eyes grown cold. She had understood Mariz's attempt to belittle her, but she refused to back down.

"Now that your stomach's full, I've got something to ask you," Tom said, trying to change the direction of the conversation. "How'd you like to see Mexico City?" He ignored the cold look Mariz was giving him and continued to look at his sister. He had promised Mariz a trip to Mexico City after the matanza, but he hadn't said anything about inviting Lisa to go along.

"Mexico City? Really? I'd love to see it, of course," Lisa replied enthusiastically.

"Good. Mariz and I plan to leave day after tomorrow, and we want you to come with us. I'd say you're in line for some new clothes anyway. Will you be rested and ready to go by then?"

Lisa looked over at Mariz and met the black eyes, cold as stone. She knew Mariz didn't want her along. Then she looked at Josh. She couldn't leave him after he'd brought her all the way to California. Mexico City would have to wait. She reached over and took Tom's hand.

"Could I go another time? I'm really tired from our ride. I really think I'd like to stay here and catch up on my rest. We could go another time, couldn't we?"

"But I want you to come," Tom said sincerely. "You don't have to stay here all alone when you could be with us in Mexico City living it up. You won't be interfering, Lisa."

"I know I won't be interfering, but I'd really prefer to go another time when I'm rested and can enjoy it more. Please, you and the señora go and have a good time. I'm sure Marta will take good care of me."

"Excuse me, darling, but your sister is right. She would enjoy it more another time. We can take her measurements and buy some clothes for her. After what she's been through with those savages, I'm sure staying at the rancho alone won't bother her."

"That's enough, Mariz," Tom shouted angrily. "I don't need you to tell me what's best for my sister."

Josh and Lisa exchanged silent looks, both embarrassed at being present during their exchange.

"It's all right, Tom, really," Lisa insisted.

Tom finally relented.

"Okay, sis, but as soon as you feel up to it, I'm going to take you on a tour of Mexico City you'll never forget."

Lisa got up and walked over to Tom. She bent down and wrapped her arms around his neck.

"I love you, Tom. You're the only family I have now," she said sadly.

Tom reached up and pulled her hands down, kissing them softly.

"We have a lot of years to make up for, little sister. We'll begin as soon as I get back from Mexico."

Neither Tom nor Lisa noticed the intense look of hatred which suddenly appeared on Mariz's face as she watched them both, but it didn't go unnoticed by Josh. He didn't like Mariz. He hadn't from the moment he'd met her. He'd have to tell Lisa to watch out for her. He was sure that Mariz Elena de Vargas y Anderson was a dangerous woman.

*   *   *

197

Lisa couldn't believe her room. She was tired but she leaned against the door, looking around her. There was a four-poster in the center of the room with ornate carvings on the headboard and posts. There was a tapestried coverlet on the bed which matched the floor-length curtains which were at the windows. A trastero, or armoire, was on one side of the door, while on the other stood a huge gilded mirror in a carved pine frame. A pine chest rested at the foot of the bed and in the corner by the windows, there was an escritorio, or writing desk with chair. The polished hardwood floor was covered with different colored rugs which matched the deep blues, reds, and golds of the tapestries. Lisa loved the room, and she felt comfortable in it immediately.

She walked over to the windows that looked out on the courtyard and breathed in the fragrance of the flowers. She was interrupted by a knock on the door. It was Rosa.

"Señorita, your brother says that he is sending up a tub so that you can take a bath before you go to bed. I have some of the water here." She walked over to the fireplace and placed the bucket in front of it. A moment later, two boys came in with a brass tub and Rosa began filling it with hot water. Before long the tub was full and Rosa handed Lisa some towels and a bar of sweetly scented rose soap.

Lisa quickly undressed and lowered herself into the steamy water. Her tired, sore body immediately felt the soothing sensation of the water. She had not taken a hot bath since leaving Boston. Even at Rebecca's and Will's, they bathed in the stream behind the house.

She leaned her head back against the rim of the tub and unwillingly her thoughts drifted backward in time. She closed her eyes and thought of the baths she and Nakon

198

had taken together and the many times they had made love along the riverbank. She felt the tears run down her cheeks, and reached up to wipe them away.

"Will I never forget you, my love? Will I never again know what it is like to be held by arms that love me, to be loved by a man such as you?" After sitting a long while in the tub, Lisa got up and dried herself and her hair. She changed into one of the nightgowns Rebecca had made for her and brushed her hair with the brush Nakon had given her. Finally, she got into the soft bed, luxuriating in its feel. It wasn't long before she fell into a deep sleep, untroubled by nightmares this night, but with a strange feeling that something was about to happen to her that would change her life forever.

CHAPTER XII

The next day Tom showed Lisa and Josh around the rancho. They rode along the coast and into Monterey. Tom pointed out the ships in the bay that were from different countries and told them about the various cargoes that they carried. They rode through the streets of Monterey. Lisa was impressed by the fact that the ocean could be seen from almost anywhere in the pueblo. It had a principal square around which the homes were built. Most of them were built in the old style with an outside stairway leading to a second-story balcony. In the afternoon, the three of them picnicked on a bluff overlooking the Pacific and they watched as some of the ships entered or left Monterey Bay.

Dinner that night was fairly congenial, but Lisa felt completely out of place in the gingham dress she wore, especially next to the rich red-satin gown which Mariz wore.

"My dear, Tom and I will certainly have to buy you some pretty new dresses while we're in Mexico City. You're much too young and pretty to wear things like that," Mariz said, nodding at Lisa's dress.

Lisa blushed at Mariz's pointed insult, but she refused to be cowed by the woman.

"I'm sorry if the dress displeases you, señora, but it

was made for me by a dear friend. It has a lot of sentimental value to me." She looked at Josh and he smiled, acknowledging her defense of Rebecca.

After dinner they all went into what Mariz called the "sitting room," although Tom never could figure out why she called it that. He couldn't stand the room for more than a few minutes at a time. It was done with such feminine tastes in mind that Tom always felt out of place there. After a short while, he excused Lisa and himself and they went into the study, his favorite room in the hacienda.

"I had to get out of there," he said while pouring wine for Lisa and himself. "I hate that room. Reminds me of a whorehouse I once visited." He looked up at Lisa and saw her laughing. "Sorry, sis. I keep forgetting that you're my little sister. I never was able to watch my tongue in front of you."

"It's all right, I'm not a child anymore. I don't think you could say much of anything that would shock me." Lisa paused for a moment, swirling the wine around in her glass. "Are you in love with Mariz?"

Tom looked at Lisa and then down at the floor.

"Well, I see you're still as direct as always. Hell, I don't know, Lisa. She's a difficult woman to understand. Most of the time she drives me crazy she's so self-centered and domineering, then other times she can be so . . ." He stopped, not sure of what he wanted to say. "I know one thing for sure, there's no future for Mariz and me."

"Tell me about her son," Lisa said, trying to change the subject.

"His name's Eric."

"Eric? That's not very Spanish sounding."

"His father was from New England, a sea captain. Eric goes by his father's name, rather than by the one Mariz gave him."

"He sounds like he's as strong willed as his mother."

"That's an understatement," Tom said with a laugh.

"Well, where is this patrón of the Rancho del Sol? I want to meet him."

"He's visiting his grandfather for a few days. He'll be back soon. He said you're to make yourself at home here. You'll like him, sis, he's a good, fair man."

"I don't understand. When you wrote me, you said Mariz was the owner of the del Sol. Now you tell me her son is."

"I don't quite understand it all myself. From what I understand, Eric and Mariz had a falling out a few years ago and he left. She hadn't heard from him in almost ten years until he turned up here a few months ago. He's the legal owner of the rancho even though Mariz has been running it all this time. Needless to say, it's caused some friction between the two, but I think it'll be resolved in time. Mariz is already showing signs of giving up and letting Eric run the rancho, and she has visions of him being a great hacendado. She even has a future wife picked out for him."

"Well, it sounds like his future is all laid out for him."

"Only problem is Eric does what Eric wants to do and not what Mariz wants him to do."

"So where does that leave you?"

"Eric still needs me to show him everything. Don't forget, he's been gone for almost ten years and a lot of things have changed in that time. And I'm kept very busy with helping other rancheros settle their land claims in court. I'd like to open up a law office in Monterey or San Francisco."

"How do you feel about it? I mean, if this Eric has been gone all these years, do you think he has a right to come back and take over, especially if the rancho means so much to his mother?"

"It's not up to me to judge, Lisa. But I think I agree with Eric. I could tell right away the land meant something more to him than wealth and power. It's in his blood. His grandfather and father built the rancho for him when he was a child so that when he came of age, he would have a place for his wife and family. It's sort of a legacy, I guess. Mariz knew all along that it really wasn't hers. I guess she just assumed that her son wouldn't come back after he'd been gone so long and now that he has, she doesn't want to give it up. Mariz prizes the rancho because it gives her wealth and power—she thrives on those things." He sighed deeply. "Enough about them. What about you? How are you really?"

Lisa looked at Tom, suddenly overwhelmed by the warmth and love in his eyes.

"Oh, I'm all right. So much has happened to me in the last year, even I can't believe it. I just need some time to sort it all out. I'll tell you about it someday, I promise."

"Sure, sis. I won't push you, you know that. But I'll be ready to listen whenever you need to talk. There's something else. I'm sorry about Mexico; Mariz can be so damned possessive at times. I still think you should come. I hate the thought of leaving you here alone for almost two months."

"Don't worry about me. Besides, I can't run off and leave Josh after he brought me all this way. I'll spend some time with him and when he leaves, I'll get to know the del Sol. And before you know it, you'll be back and we'll be together again." The smile suddenly faded from her face. "Have you heard from mother lately? Does she know what happened to me?"

"She knows; I wrote her about it. I haven't heard from her yet. She never was one for writing letters."

"She doesn't give a damn, is what you meant to say. I should've gone back there. She would've had a hell of a time explaining her Comanche-squaw daughter to all her society friends," she said bitterly, the tears welling up in her eyes.

"Don't, Lisa, it's not worth getting yourself upset over. You know she was never the same after dad killed himself."

"I know, but she is our mother. Doesn't she care at all about us?"

"I think she must in her own way. But she has a new life for herself now, and you and I just don't fit in."

"You're telling me. Do you know where she wanted to send me this year? Miss Babcock's School for Girls. Can you imagine? It was either that or get married to one of her eligible rich young men. She almost wouldn't let me come out here, except that I threatened to embarrass her in front of all her friends and say I'd been having an affair with a married man. She almost fainted, couldn't get me out of there quick enough. I still think she believes I was actually telling the truth!"

"Oh, God it's good having you around again, sis. I haven't laughed like that in a long time. I hate to leave you so soon."

"It won't be for long. Just go and have a good time."

"What about Josh? Is there anything there more than friendship?"

"Besides you, he's probably the best friend I've ever

had. He risked his life to take me out of the camp and he left his home and job."

"He's in love with you. I can see it every time he looks at you."

"I know, he wants to marry me. But I told him I need time to think things out. After he leaves here, he'll go back to Missouri and check on his farm. Then he'll probably lead another train through to Oregon and come here. I told him I'd have my answer by then. He's such a good man, I hope I can learn to love him."

" Okay, enough serious talk for tonight. Finish up your wine and let's go up to bed." Tom got up and went to Lisa. He pulled her close to him and lifted her face up. "I'm going to take good care of you now. I see things in that pretty face that shouldn't be there. I hope someday you'll be able to talk to me about what happened and then forget about it." Tom put his arm around Lisa and they walked up the stairs together. He had no way of knowing that Lisa would never forget what had happened to her, or that the man who had made it happen, was Mariz's son.

Tom and Mariz left for Mexico the third day after Lisa arrived. Josh and Lisa rode to the harbor with them and then spent the day exploring the rancho. After they lunched, they rested under an old oak tree, watching the cattle graze peacefully.

"I've decided to leave in the morning," Josh said.

"But you can't, you've only been here two days. Please, don't leave yet."

"I have to get back to Missouri and check on my farm. I also want to collect some money that's due me." Josh reached over and took Lisa's hands in his. "I want you to marry me, Lisa. I love you. I know you don't feel the

205

same way about me, but you might in time. I said I'd give you the time you need to sort things out, but I want an answer when I get back. I'll even sell my farm in Missouri and move out here if California's where you want to live. I just want us to be together."

"Josh, I . . ."

"Don't answer now, just think about it while I'm gone. I should be back in seven or eight months. Give me your answer then."

They didn't talk about it again and Lisa felt a strange sense of loss when she saw Josh preparing to leave the next morning. She felt as though she were losing her dearest friend. When Josh kissed her good-bye and started to mount up, Lisa reached for his arm.

"I want you to have something," she said softly, and reached up and removed the necklace Nakon had given her. She fastened it around Josh's neck. "This was given to me in love and so I give it to you," she repeated Nakon's words. "This is the only thing of value I have to show you how grateful I am. I truly hope I feel differently when you come back. Vaya con Dios."

She stood and watched as Josh rode off, his large form fading quickly until he was just a speck in the distance. It was strange watching him leave when they had been together for so long. Now that Tom and Josh both were gone, she felt terribly lonely. She turned and went back into the hacienda and went into the study to look for something to read.

She walked around the room and looked through the many volumes of books. She decided on Miguel de Cervantes' *Don Quijote*, which she hadn't read since she was in school, and then it was in English. She was surprised by the vast amount of literature on the shelves.

She supposed Mariz had ordered them from the east coast and Europe.

She curled up in one of the chairs and began to read, but she couldn't concentrate for long. Her eyes roamed around the room until they rested on a portrait which hung over the fireplace. She put the book down and walked over to get a closer look at the portrait. It was of a young boy, about ten or eleven, standing by a pony. He had curly black hair and olive-colored skin, and his mouth was set in a slight smile, almost a mocking expression. The astonishing thing about the boy was his eyes—they were almost a transparent blue color. They contrasted strongly with his dark skin and hair. Lisa wondered if this was Eric, Mariz's son. She left the study and ran to the kitchen to talk with Marta.

"Marta, there is a picture in the study of a boy. Who is he?"

"That is the patrón, señorita."

"It was painted many years ago, I take it."

"Sí, when the patrón was a very young boy. Now he is all grown up and muy guapo," she said with a slight giggle and she rolled her eyes.

"Are the patrón's eyes really so blue? In the picture they look so light. Did the artist make them lighter so they would stand out in the picture?"

"Oh, no, señorita, the patrón's eyes, they are very blue, like the sky."

"Gracias, Marta," Lisa said absently and walked back to the study. She walked back over to the picture and stared at it, a thoughtful expression on her face. She wondered if it were possible for two people to have such eyes.

"I wonder if Nakon looked like that as a child," she

said, talking to herself. "I want to meet this Eric. If he looks anything like this picture . . ."

Eric was pacing the room when Don Alfredo came in.

"What's the matter, Sandro? You've been acting like a caged-up bull for the last two days."

"Why haven't I heard from Hector yet? I told him to let me know as soon as Wade left. Lisa is so close and I can't even go to her."

"Perhaps Señor Wade hasn't left yet. Maybe he's going to stay for a while. You must be patient."

"Patient? I can't be patient, abuelo. It's been too damned long already. I've a mind to ride over there anyway."

"Now you're being foolish. You know you can't take the chance of being seen by the man. If he finds out you're here, there's no telling what he'll do, especially if he cares for Lisa. Why don't you go for a ride with Consuelo and forget about the señorita for the time being."

"I don't want to go for a ride with Consuelo. She's driving me crazy. She thinks I'm in love with her, abuelo, and I can't convince her that I'm not. I don't want to encourage her."

"Is it encouraging her to ride with her? I know that she can drive you crazy and that she is self-centered and demanding, but remember that she is all alone now, Sandro. She has lost her entire family, and she feels close to us now. Just be kind to her."

Consuelo rushed into the room, just as Don Alfredo finished speaking.

"Are you ready, Sandro? I have a picnic lunch and some wine for us. It's such a beautiful day for a ride.

Please say you'll come."

Eric started to object and then saw the look on Don Alfredo's face. He nodded to Consuelo and turned and walked out, Consuelo hanging on to his arm. Don Alfredo went to the window and watched as they rode away. They wouldn't be a bad match, he thought. They had been betrothed as children, but so many things had changed. He knew Sandro didn't care for Consuelo, that he was in love with this other woman. He wondered what type of woman this Lisa was. He wondered if she came from a good family, if she was a good person, and he wondered if his grandson felt more guilt than love for what he had done to her. He had mixed feelings. He knew Consuelo was from a good family, a Spanish one, and she loved Sandro. Yet he could see by the way she acted toward Sandro, that she wasn't his type of woman. She was too dependent and clinging for him. He needed a woman who was much more independent, and his mind seemed to be set on Lisa.

He walked back to his chair and sat down. It wasn't his decision anyway, it was Sandro's. And maybe he'd decide on Consuelo. He closed his eyes and laid his head back, and he thought of the time so many years ago when he'd first seen Amparo. She was the most beautiful creature he'd ever seen. Why was it now, whenever he was tired, he always thought of her? Even though she was no longer with him, she had a way of calming him and helping him to cope with his emotions. As long as he could feel that way, she'd never be dead to him.

"My own true love," he said softly, and his head dropped to his chest as he fell into a peaceful sleep.

Lisa had been riding for over an hour when she saw

riders coming toward her. Marta had warned her to take one of the vaqueros with her, but Lisa refused. The threats of bandidos didn't frighten her as they might have before she had been captured by the Comanche. She pulled up as the riders approached and she saw that they were dressed like the vaqueros on the del Sol.

"Buenas tardes, señorita. May I ask where you are going?" one of the riders asked in Spanish.

"I don't know, I was just riding. I'm staying at the Rancho del Sol as a guest of Señor de Vargas."

"Well, you're on Don Alfredo de Vargas' land now and I'm afraid we'll have to take you with us."

"I don't understand. I'm a guest. I was told I could ride anywhere."

"You are on the Rancho del Mar now, señorita, and we must make sure you are who you say you are. I have my orders."

"I want to go back to the Rancho del Sol; they'll tell you who I am."

"After you talk with Don Alfredo, we will be glad to escort you back to the Rancho del Sol. Now please, ride along with us now."

Lisa looked at the group of men and she knew it was useless arguing with them, so she rode with them to the rancho. She remembered what Tom had said about Eric's grandfather, and the fact that he built the Rancho del Sol for Eric, and she assumed that he was a rich, doting grandfather. But when she saw the Rancho del Mar she quickly changed her opinion. It was much smaller than the del Sol but it somehow seemed warmer, homier. Everywhere she looked she saw flowers and trees. The lead vaquero told her that Don Alfredo had built the hacienda for his wife when they came from Spain and he planted everything she liked, no matter what it was. He had wanted his wife to have everything she wanted in the new world.

When they reached the hacienda, the lead vaquero helped her from her horse and then led her through a courtyard and into a small sitting room. She was suddenly acutely aware of her disheveled appearance—she was wearing a shirt and buckskin pants which Josh had bought her for their ride to California—and she tried brushing the dust from her pants and face. It wasn't long before a tall, gray-haired man appeared, meticulously well-groomed. She thought he looked like an aristocrat.

"Yes, Pedro?" he asked in a rich, deep voice.

"Perdóname, patrón, but we caught the señorita riding on de Vargas land. Our orders were to pick up any strangers."

Don Alfredo's gaze rested on Lisa for a moment, a puzzled expression appearing on his face.

"You may leave us, Pedro. You did well. Gracias."

"Por nada, patrón."

Don Alfredo walked to the small table which held the liquor and began to pour out of one of the decanters.

"Some wine, Señorita Jordan, is it? It's a rather warm day out, sí?"

"Muchas gracias, Señor de Vargas." She reached for the glass of wine. "How did you know my name, señor?"

"I guessed by your description. I heard you were a very beautiful young lady."

"I'm afraid I'm not very beautiful at the moment, señor. I didn't anticipate visiting anyone today. I hope you'll excuse my appearance."

"On the contrary, señorita, even dressed as you are, you are very attractive. That is the sign of a very

211

beautiful woman."

"And I think you are full of flattery, señor, but thank you. Your wine is excellent."

"And you too, know how to flatter. So, you are visiting your brother?"

"Yes, but unfortunately he's in Mexico with your daughter right now, so we'll have to wait for a while for our visit."

"Weren't you invited to go along?"

"Yes, but . . . well, I was very tired from my journey."

"I see. In other words, my daughter didn't want you to go along?"

Lisa looked at Don Alfredo, her mouth agape.

"I know my daughter well, señorita, and she is very possessive. She does not want to share your brother with anyone, even you."

"You're very direct, Don Alfredo. Not many parents can speak so honestly about their children."

"Not many parents know their children as I know my daughter," he said softly, a sad note to his voice.

"Perdóname, patrón, lunch is ready," Enrique said, suddenly appearing in the room.

"Have you eaten lunch yet, señorita?"

"No, but . . ."

"Good, then it would please me if you would dine with me. We have much to talk about." Don Alfredo stood up, holding his arm out to Lisa.

"Gracias, Don Alfredo."

"Tell me more about yourself, Señorita Jordan," Don Alfredo said, as they walked to the dining room. He wanted to find out as much about Lisa as he could before Sandro returned and found her. He especially wanted to find out what kind of woman could make his grandson learn the meaning of love again.

Eric lay on the grassy knoll, chewing on a piece of grass, feeling the hot sun beat down on his bare chest. He watched Consuelo as she struggled into her abundance of petticoats. Since she had discovered he was at his grandfather's, she had come to visit as quickly as she could. She seemed to know his every move. She also had found her way into his bed every night, proclaiming she couldn't exist without him. He liked Consuelo; he even found her to be an extremely accommodating bed partner, but he couldn't put up with her constant proclamations of love and suggestions of marriage. He had absolutely no thought of marriage. In his mind, he was already married to Lisa.

When Eric thought of Lisa, he felt slightly guilty about his relationship with Consuelo. He knew that Lisa would look upon it as a breach of faith, but he didn't feel that way. He knew that he loved Lisa and that he wanted her in all ways, but Consuelo was available and he couldn't deny the urges which he had denied for so long already. And that was all he felt for Consuelo, a purely physical desire. But even that paled next to his desire for Lisa. He remembered the last time they had made love, when she had seduced him so artfully. He remembered the slim, lithe body pressed against his and he groaned involuntarily.

"Did you say something, querido?"

"What?" Eric asked in an annoyed tone.

"You sounded like you said something, you made some kind of a noise." She smiled, showing little white teeth. "Maybe you were just remembering our love-making."

"You finished yet? I want to get back to the rancho," Eric said impatiently. He stood up and hurriedly put on his shirt and moccasins.

"Why are you in such a hurry? Don't you want some more wine?"

"No. I just want to get back." He held out his hand to help Consuelo up.

"Always in such a hurry. You aren't that way when we make love, querido," she said seductively moving her body against his. "Oh, Sandro, I could make you so happy."

"Don't, Consuelo. I told you before, I don't want to get married." He pulled her arms from around his neck. "I also told you I don't love you. I make love to you, I like your body, but I don't love you. Do you understand that, Consuelo?"

"Sí, I understand. But I think you care for me more than you say. When I left your rancho you were very cold toward me, but you are not that way now. I think your feelings will change in time."

Eric looked at Consuelo's dark-brown eyes and sighed. He had been stupid to get involved with her in the first place—she wouldn't let it go as just a physical involvement. He was already beginning to lose some of the discipline he had learned as a Comanche. They had taught him he could control any urge he had if he were strong enough, but he hadn't done that with Consuelo. He had given in to his physical desires. He helped her onto her horse. Well, he'd have to learn how to control his desire for her. Lisa would be here soon and there would only be room for her in his life. He looked over at Consuelo. How would she react when he told her there was another woman in his life and that other woman was

214

the reason he could never love Consuelo. He shook his head and sighed. How had being in the white world for so short a time disoriented him so quickly? He didn't like the feeling of not being in control of the situation; it made him uneasy. He wondered if he would ever be able to fully fit into this world, or if he would always be a man living in two worlds.

CHAPTER XIII

Eric walked toward the garden room, intent on speaking to his grandfather. He had decided that he was going to the del Sol, no matter what the outcome. He had to see Lisa. He opened the door and started to walk in but stopped. He saw Lisa sitting next to his grandfather on the couch. Lisa looked up and without realizing it, dropped the cupful of hot tea on her lap.

"Oh, my dear, let me help you. Are you all right?" Don Alfredo wiped the tea from her lap with his handkerchief. Lisa ignored him and slowly, as if in a dream, she stood up and walked toward Eric. He was dressed differently and his hair was shorter, but he was the same man she had left so many months before. She stood in front of him and reached out to touch his face. Her fingertips had barely touched his cheek when Consuelo burst into the room.

"Querido, why do you always walk so fast? You know I can't keep up with you and your long legs." She grabbed Eric's arm and held on to him while she adjusted one of her boots.

Lisa pulled her hand back when she saw the other woman, unsure of what to do. Don Alfredo walked over to the small group.

"Lisa, this is Consuelo de la Morena, one of our neighbors. Consuelo, this is Lisa Jordan. She is visiting

216

her brother at the del Sol."

"Pleased to meet you, señorita," Lisa said absently, still staring at Eric.

"Yes," Consuelo said dryly, watching the looks that passed between Eric and Lisa. She held on to Eric possessively. "Have you met my fiancé before, señorita?"

"Your fiancé?" Lisa stammered. "No, I . . ." She turned to look at Don Alfredo. "If you'll excuse me . . ." She ran from the room.

"Why the hell didn't you tell me she was coming here today?" Eric shouted at his grandfather.

"I didn't know until just a few hours ago. Some of my vaqueros picked her up riding on my land."

"Damn," Eric muttered and hurried out.

"Who is that woman," Consuelo demanded, "and where is Sandro going?"

"She is a guest at the del Sol; she is Tom Jordan's sister. And as to where Sandro is going, I have no idea. You of all people should know that Sandro does as he pleases." Don Alfredo walked to the French windows and looked out at the garden. He saw Lisa standing by the fountain, and he could tell by the way her shoulders were shaking that she was crying. He had wanted to tell her about Sandro but he hadn't known how. Now, he wished he had told her.

Lisa heard the footsteps behind her and she knew it was Nakon. Or Eric or Sandro. She didn't even know anymore who he was. She had wanted to run away when she saw the other woman and the way she held on to Eric, but she couldn't run away knowing he was alive and so close to her. She had to see him, to touch him. Her hand covered her mouth as she tried to stifle the sobs which rose in her throat. Her body shook and she felt faint. She felt his arms around her shoulders and he turned her around to face him. He looked at her for a moment and then pulled her close. She buried her face in his chest.

"You're alive," she mumbled tearfully.

"Of course I'm alive." He tilted her chin up. "You're even more beautiful than I remembered." He lowered his mouth to hers and kissed her softly. "Come, we have to talk." He took her arm and led her into the house and up to his room. She didn't resist him—she couldn't. When they got to his room, he closed and bolted the door. He stood looking down at her and he ran his fingers over her face, wiping the tears from her eyes. He picked her up and carried her to the bed and his mouth covered hers as he lay down next to her.

"No," she muttered in protest, but he ignored her pleas and continued to kiss and touch her. Lisa was in a whirlwind of confusion. She wanted Eric, was happy he was alive, but she wanted to know about the woman, Consuelo. She summoned all her strength and pushed Eric away from her.

"Tell me about Consuelo. Is she your fiancée?"

"We haven't seen each other in seven months and all you want to do is talk. Well, I have other things in mind." He stood up and quickly picked Lisa and the quilt up, depositing them on the floor. "That's better, I don't like the bed." He stripped and Lisa watched in mesmerized silence. Her body ached for his. How many times had she dreamed of being loved by him again? He knelt over her.

"You're my wife," he said deeply and ripped the dress from her body.

"No, you said we'd talk."

"We can talk later." His mouth ravaged hers. She

218

moved her head away and pushed at his shoulders. She resented the fact that he assumed she'd fall into his arms no matter what. And she resented the fact that he wouldn't tell her about Consuelo.

"Why are you fighting me?" he asked in a surprised voice. He had expected her to fall into his arms.

"I want to know about Consuelo and I want to know what you're doing here."

"Well, I don't care what you want right now. All I care about is what I want," he said angrily, and rolled on top of her. Before Lisa could protest, he drove himself into her. She bit her lip to keep from crying out. He was trying to hurt her. There were no soft words or gentle caresses, just a brutal assault on her body. She was angry, but at the same time, she wanted him to love her. She wrapped her arms around his neck, and for the moment she forgot about Consuelo.

"You're mine," he whispered. "Open your eyes and look at me."

Lisa complied and looked into the light-blue depths which she had memorized. It seemed so right to be in his arms and to be loved by him. For now she was his. Now was all she could count on.

"Yes, I'm yours. I'll always be yours," she said gently, surrendering her body to his. Her senses drank in the feel of him, his smell, the taste of his mouth on hers. Nothing else mattered but him.

She began to cry when their lovemaking was over. She didn't know if it was from her overwhelming happiness at being with Eric again, or from her fear of the future with him. She felt his arms tighten around her.

"You cried the first time we made love; do you remember?" She nodded. "Why are you crying now?

You should be as happy as I am."

She sat up, pulling the quilt around her.

"You can't know how happy I am to see you. I thought you were dead."

"Dead?"

"Yes. I was staying with some friends of Josh's in Santa Fe and they heard you were killed and your scalp had been brought in as proof."

"I'm sorry. No wonder you were so shocked to see me."

"It wasn't just the shock of seeing you alive. It was the shock of seeing you here in Monterey, engaged to another woman."

"I told you before, you're my wife. Consuelo has nothing to do with us."

"But she does. Have you made love to her?" Lisa demanded angrily.

"Just leave it alone, Lisa. I told you Consuelo doesn't matter."

"Have you made love to her?" she repeated coldly.

He looked at her, his blue eyes cold.

"Yes, and she knows how to keep quiet when we're finished."

Lisa stood up and reached for her clothes.

"Do you love this woman?"

"No, and she knows I don't. She accepts the situation the way it is," he lied. "No questions asked."

"It was a mistake my staying here with you," she said tearfully. "I don't belong here; I don't belong with you." She walked to the door and unbolted it. "Will you please go while I get dressed."

Eric didn't move. He watched Lisa as she struggled into her clothes.

"Please go. I still have some pride left. I won't beg for your love."

Eric stood up and slipped on his pants and shirt.

"All right. I'll give you time to cool off. I'll see you later."

Lisa closed the door after him and leaned against it. The moment of love had passed, and she wondered if they'd ever get it back.

Don Alfredo knocked lightly and then opened the door to Eric's room. Lisa was standing in the corner by the windows, looking out at the courtyard. He walked over to her and put his arm around her. Lisa turned around and he could tell by her red, swollen eyes, that she had been crying.

"I'm so sorry, my dear, I . . ."

"You knew, didn't you? You knew and yet you let me be humiliated. How could you do such a thing, Don Alfredo?"

"I'm sorry it happened this way. I didn't mean for you to get hurt. I guess I'm just an interfering old man. You see, when Sandro came back, all he could talk about was you and how he had to find you. When he found out you were Tom's sister, he knew it was just a matter of time before you came here. When you wrote Tom that you'd be coming any day, Sandro came here to wait until the scout left. Then when my vaqueros brought you here, I felt it was my chance to see what you were like without Sandro around."

"Why didn't you tell me he was here? At least you could have prepared me for the shock, and spared me the humiliation of meeting his fiancée." She walked across the room. "I thought he was dead. I was told months ago

221

that he was killed in a skirmish with the Texas Rangers. Do you know what a shock it was for me to see him standing there, not only alive, but looking so well?"

"I had no idea. If I'd known that, I most certainly would have told you he was here. I didn't mean to toy with your emotions. I tried to tell you several times, but I didn't know how. I thought it was something that was between you and Sandro. I hope you'll forgive a foolish old man."

She looked at Don Alfredo, seeing the sadness in his eyes.

"It's all right; I guess I was just feeling a little sorry for myself. There's so much I don't understand. He sent me away on the pretext that he loved me, and then I came here and found him alive and heir to a large rancho and engaged to another woman. I don't know what to believe."

"There's much about Sandro which you don't know, I'm sure, much of which he'll have to tell you himself. But I'm going to tell you enough so that you will at least give him a chance to explain." Don Alfredo got up and walked to the window. "He was christened Alejandro Esteban de Vargas by his mother, but his father named him Eric Stephen Anderson, after himself. Mariz and I have always called him Sandro, but he chose to go by Eric. He idolized his father and wanted to please him in every way possible."

"Did he know it was his rancho I was coming to?"

"How could he? He didn't even know your last name. He looked everywhere for you. Then he found out you were Tom's sister and he knew it was only a matter of time before you came here. He was quite worried that you had gone off and married that Wade fellow."

222

"He obviously wasn't too worried."

"What do you mean?"

"Consuelo. He can't have been too upset about me if he got engaged to another woman."

Don Alfredo laughed.

"I don't think it's funny," Lisa said angrily.

"I wasn't laughing at you, my dear. How can you believe Sandro loves Consuelo after the way he looked at you? Even I, an old man, saw the love in his eyes when he looked at you. As for Consuelo, it is she who says they're engaged; Sandro has never said so. He puts up with her out of boredom, I think. I must admit, I myself thought they would make a good match when I saw them together, but I soon saw that Consuelo wasn't Sandro's type of woman. And when I met you today, I could see why he was so in love with you. There is something very special about you, Lisa."

"Thank you, but I still don't feel any better about Consuelo."

"Even if you hadn't come back here, Sandro wouldn't have married Consuelo. It is you he loves."

"When I heard he was dead, I thought my life was over too. But I went on. I adjusted to the fact that he was dead, I accepted it. Now . . ."

"I can imagine how difficult it is for you, but you two belong together. It's obvious to me; why do you fight it when it's what you both want?"

Lisa turned abruptly.

"Don Alfredo, you can't possibly understand all that's happened to me in the last year. Sometimes I can't even believe it myself. Right now, more than anything, I need time to think it all out. That's what I came to California for, to think things through before I make any decisions.

You can understand that, can't you?"

"Certainly. You'll stay here, of course. No one will bother you." He got up and started for the door but stopped. "He'll want to see you. You can't hide forever."

"I don't want to see him now. If you don't mind I'll just have my dinner up here and retire early."

"Of course, Come, I'll show you to your room."

Lisa lay down on the bed in her room, suddenly very tired. She shut her eyes and tried to sleep, but thoughts of Eric kept invading her mind. She didn't hear the door as it opened.

"Are you going to sleep the rest of the evening away when we have so much to talk about?"

"Raytahnee?" Lisa jumped off the bed.

"Who did you think?" Raytahnee hugged Lisa and they both sat down on the bed.

"I can't believe it. How did you get here?"

"Can't you guess?"

"Nakon."

"Yes. When he was sent away from the tribe he brought me with him. He said we would all be together again. He never doubted it."

We're all together again, Lisa thought, but it's not the same. Everything has changed.

"Let's go for a ride. There're some beautiful places around here. It will do you good to get out instead of staying in here. Besides, Osolo needs a good run."

"Osolo?"

"We brought him too. The family wouldn't be complete without him."

"I can't go riding; I don't want to see Eric."

"Ay de mí! You're being silly again. I won't ask you what happened between you two, but we can go without

224

being seen. C'mon, let's go."

Raytahnee led Lisa down the stairs and out through the kitchen, where Osolo was waiting by the door. He was fully accustomed by now to small gifts from the kitchen. His ears pricked up immediately when he saw Lisa, and he ran to her. He smelled her familiar odor and rubbed his head against her hand. Lisa bent down and hugged him, talking to him in a soft voice.

"Let's hurry," Raytahnee said, "there isn't too much daylight left."

They rode for a ways in silence, both of the girls just happy to be together again, and Osolo content to trot along after them. It was awhile before Lisa spoke.

"Where were you today when I came here? Why didn't you come see me sooner?"

"I was riding with a friend the whole day. I just came back awhile ago and saw Sandro, and he told me you were here. He was angry. Did you two fight?"

Lisa nodded.

"Tell me about him, Raytahnee. Why did he send me away if he was coming back here?"

"He didn't know he was coming back here. He told you the truth when he said he'd stay with the Comanche forever; he thought he would. But after you left, he led more and more raids until his band was ambushed. He was one of the few survivors. Everyone thought he was killed, but he came into camp a few days later. He asked for a meeting of the high council because he felt that the ambush was his fault. He had been fighting with Kowano at the time, and all of the men, including the guards, were watching. That was when they were ambushed. They didn't have a chance. Sandro felt his men died because of him.

"The high council met and decided that he should leave because his heart was no longer with the Comanche but with the white woman who had been his wife. They told him to go back to you and to his old life."

"I hope he didn't leave in disgrace."

"No. He had been too good a warrior. He left because he knew the council was right—he was never the same after he sent you away."

"I know it must've been hard for him to leave. He was a loyal Comanche."

"Yes, but he's more loyal to you."

Lisa looked at her and stopped her horse and dismounted. They were both quiet for a while and then sat down on a grassy knoll overlooking the Pacific.

"Sandro thought it best to tell everyone that I am the daughter of an old friend of his who had been killed," Raytahnee said, trying to change Lisa's mood. "He thought it would be best if I lived with Don Alfredo so no one would talk. I love it here. Don Alfredo treats me like a daughter and gives me everything I want."

"And how do we explain the fact that we all know each other?"

"We don't. Sandro and I aren't supposed to know you, as far as other people are concerned. You and I just happen to be fast friends."

Lisa smiled and then a frown appeared suddenly.

"Is Eric in love with Consuelo? I have to know, Raytahnee."

"He's not in love with her. I've watched them together and she is like a spider, always reaching out for Sandro. He just puts up with her because they were childhood friends and he feels sorry for her because she lost her family. I think she's a silly, empty-headed woman. Not at all like you and I."

Lisa looked at Raytahnee and started to laugh.

"Oh, Raytahnee, it's so good to be with you again. And you look so lovely. You're letting your hair grow."

"Yes, I decided it's time I start to look and act like a woman. Don Alfredo is teaching me many things, and you haven't even noticed how much my English has improved since we last spoke."

Lisa hadn't even realized they were speaking in English.

"I'm so proud of you," she said, reaching over and hugging Raytahnee. "You know, it's strange speaking to Eric in English instead of Spanish. It's all so strange. I don't even know who he is, a Comanche, a Spaniard, or a Yankee."

"He's your husband; that will never change."

"He's made love to Consuelo; he told me so."

"So? It is natural with men, no? It doesn't mean he loves her. Men have certain urges, so I'm told."

"That's ridiculous. Women have urges too. Does that mean they should go out and make love to any man who comes along?"

"I don't know. I guess that's what makes the difference between us and the other kind of women."

"What other kind of women?"

"You know what I'm talking about, Lisa. We had them in the Comanche camp. Whores."

"Well then, I suppose I could be called a whore. I've known more than one man."

"Don't talk like that about yourself," Raytahnee shouted angrily, echoing Eric's earlier words to Lisa. "You know what happened to you wasn't your fault. Now, let's talk about something different. Don Alfredo is having a fiesta tomorrow night. It's to celebrate one of the saints' days. He had a beautiful dress made for me and we must find one for you. I'm so excited—it's my first fiesta since I was a little girl."

"I know you'll look lovely and you'll have a wonderful time. But I can't go. I'm not ready to face Eric again, and I'm certainly not ready to see him with Consuelo."

"I didn't realize you were such a coward, Lisa. I remember a woman who would've done anything to keep her man. Would you give up so easily what you worked so hard to get?"

Lisa looked at Raytahnee. The girl's wisdom had always disturbed her. She seemed so much older than her sixteen years.

"Maybe I am a coward, I don't know. All I know is that when I saw him standing there alive, looking so handsome, I wanted to throw myself into his arms and stay there forever. But Consuelo came in and ruined that moment. I'm afraid, Raytahnee. Things are so different here—not like they were in the Comanche camp."

"Of course things are different now. This is a different place and much time has passed. But there's no reason why you can't get used to the change. If you can get used to the life in a Comanche camp, then you can get used to the life on a big rancho. You're making things more difficult than they really are. All you really have to do is go to him. He loves you."

"Maybe, I don't know."

"All right, I know you've got a lot to think about right now. But promise me you'll come tomorrow night. It will be such fun. And there will be other men there besides Sandro, so you don't even have to see him if you don't want to. Please, say you'll come."

228

"All right, I'll go to your fiesta. And don't worry about a dress for me. I have just the one."

When the girls got back to the rancho they went up to Lisa's room and had dinner, and then they spent the rest of the evening catching up on the past months. Very late in the evening, Raytahnee went to her own room and Lisa was left alone. She lay on the bed thinking about Eric; she always seemed to think about him. She didn't know when she'd be ready to face him again, yet she wasn't sure how long she could stay away from him. But the most important thing was that he was alive, alive and well and so very close to her.

The evening crawled by for Eric. He had wanted to go up to Lisa, but his grandfather had forbade him to do so. When she didn't come down for dinner, he got anxious and began to drink heavily. He got tired of hearing Consuelo's whiny voice. She always managed to bring the conversation around to herself, and he was bored with the stories of her travels and all the men she had known. The only person on his mind was Lisa. His mind dwelt on the events of the afternoon, and how Lisa had looked when he walked into the garden room. She had looked so young and vulnerable. But she had made him angry with all her questions about Consuelo and then he'd been rough with her. He should've been more gentle, more loving, but he wasn't able to control himself when he was so near her. All he could think of was possessing her, and finding out if she still needed him as badly as he needed her.

"Coming, Sandro?" Don Alfredo asked.

"What?"

"Coming to bed? I'm sure we could all use a good

night's rest."

Eric glared at Don Alfredo, knowing full well what he meant. Don Alfredo's room was between his and Lisa's, and he would be able to hear if Eric entered Lisa's room.

"No. I'm staying down here," Eric said angrily and went into the study and locked the door behind him. Don Alfredo had no doubt that his grandson would try his best to drink himself into total oblivion this night.

CHAPTER XIV

Lisa and Raytahnee spent the following day helping Don Alfredo prepare for the fiesta. Lisa took out the green dress which Rebecca had made for her and steamed it so it would be fresh for the evening. They also managed to take a ride in the afternoon before the guests began to arrive.

Lisa and Raytahnee acted as hostesses for Don Alfredo and saw to it that all the guests who were spending the night got settled in. Everyone was pleased to meet Lisa, as they all knew Tom because of the court cases he had fought for them. She was accepted without question; she didn't know if they knew about her capture by the Comanche.

Late in the afternoon, Raytahnee and Lisa went up to their rooms to bathe and change. After her bath, Lisa sat at her small dressing table trying to fix her hair in a variety of ways, but nothing pleased her. As she stared at herself in the mirror she realized that it wasn't herself she was trying to please, but Eric. She wondered if he would be there, if she would see him, perhaps even dance with him. She was being silly, she knew, but she would always feel that way about him. As much as she tried, she couldn't still the rapid beating of her heart.

There was a knock on the door and Raytahnee came in,

gowned in a peach-colored silk dress. Don Alfredo had given her a string of pearls with earrings to match. Lisa sat her down and began to fix her hair. She wet her hair completely and brushed it so that as it dried, it framed Raytahnee's small, piquant face. Raytahnee was delighted with the effect.

"Now it's my turn," Raytahnee said, as she sat Lisa down in front of the mirror and began to brush her hair. She pulled back the sides and braided them with a green satin ribbon interwoven, and then pinned a gardenia on either side. It wasn't the fancy hairstyle that many of the women here wore with elaborate combs and mantillas, but on Lisa the effect was stunning. Just as Lisa had finished getting into her dress there was a knock on the door and Don Alfredo entered. He handed a box to Lisa. Inside was a diamond necklace with matching earrings.

"Raytahnee told me the color of your dress and I thought these would go nicely with it," Don Alfredo said, reaching into the box and taking out the necklace to fasten it around Lisa's neck. Lisa put on the earrings and then stepped in front of the mirror to look at herself.

"Oh, Don Alfredo, they're exquisite. Were they your wife's?"

"Yes, and I'm sure she'd want you to wear them. They look wonderful on you. You are a beautiful woman, Lisa."

Lisa looked again at the image that stared back at her. Somehow she had changed from a girl to a woman. The green dress fit her perfectly, and accentuated her small waist and hips. While she was uncomfortable with the low-cut bodice, she thought it was becoming and would definitely catch Eric's eye. She was pleased with her appearance but she was apprehensive. She felt as if she were a different woman, that Eric was a different man, and she knew it would be strange meeting him dressed as she was, rather than in Indian buckskins. But as Raytahnee had said earlier, it was a different place and time, and she and Eric were different people now. She had to remember that. She had to try to accept Eric as he was now.

"The men won't be able to keep their eyes from you," Raytahnee exclaimed excitedly.

"I don't know what you're talking about, you look absolutely stunning. Doesn't she, Don Alfredo?"

"You both will outshine all of the other ladies in attendance. Now, shall we go down?"

The fiesta was different from anything Lisa had ever been to. There were tables laid out with food and wine in the courtyard. Musicians walked around playing different Spanish songs. Some of the men and women danced the fandango, a very sensual dance done with castanets. The women, she noticed, were all dressed in bright colors with layers of jewelry and large jeweled combs in their hair. The men were similarly dressed in black-velvet charro suits, but many wore brightly colored shirts and silk sashes.

Lisa was immediately caught up in the excitement of the evening. Most of the men were overwhelmed with her beauty and appearance, and she was seldom without a dance partner or a glass of wine. At one point, she excused herself from her partner and stood by the fountain, watching all the people. She saw Raytahnee with a young man, a look of utter joy on her face, and Don Alfredo was with a group of older men, talking animatedly about something. She was ready to sit down

233

by the fountain and rest her feet, when another young man asked her to dance. He whirled her around the courtyard until she felt almost dizzy from the excitement and the wine. It was at that moment that she saw Eric standing by the French doors. He was dressed less elegantly than the other men, in buckskin pants and a brightly colored peasant shirt, but to Lisa he was the most handsome man there. She watched him as he stood talking to some men, his tall muscular form towering over everyone else. As her partner moved her around the courtyard, she looked over his shoulder to see if Eric was dancing with anyone, but he still stood on the perimeter of the courtyard. The dance seemed to drag on forever and when it was finally over, the same man asked her to dance again. When she declined, he swept her into his arms, assuming she was just being coquettish. She tried to pull away from the man, but he held her firmly and swirled her around the courtyard. Just as she was about to say something rude to the man, she felt him stop.

"I believe this is our dance, señorita?" She turned and met Eric's clear blue eyes.

"The señorita is dancing with me, Don Alejandro," the young man objected. He started to dance off with Lisa, but was stopped by Eric's hand on his arm.

"Señorita?" Eric said coolly, looking at Lisa.

"Yes, yes it is our dance, Señor Anderson. I had forgotten." Before the young man could object further, Eric swept Lisa into his arms and moved her deftly around the courtyard.

"How is it you are able to dance so well after all these years?"

"There are some things a man never forgets how to do," Eric said in a low voice, pulling her closer. "I didn't realize it would be so difficult to dance with my wife," he said playfully.

Lisa looked up at him, a puzzled expression on her face. "Your wife?"

"Of course, you are my wife. I have no other."

"I'm not your wife. I was only a white slave you kept for your entertainment, and when you grew tired of me . . ."

"You won't even give me a chance to explain, will you? You just want to believe what you think is true—that I'm a cold-blooded bastard who threw you out when I was tired of you." Lisa looked away, but he continued. "You at least owe me the courtesy of listening to my side of the story."

"I don't owe you anything. You sent me away saying you would stay with the Comanche forever. Then I come here and find you alive, the owner of a rancho, and engaged to another woman. Just how do you expect me to feel?"

As Eric looked at her bright-green eyes, he couldn't keep from smiling. Every time she got angry, she looked like a defiant little girl, who was trying to look grown-up.

"What are you laughing at?" Lisa demanded angrily.

"You. I can't help thinking how young you look when you're angry." She lowered her eyes. She always did that when she didn't want to confront him. "We have to talk, Lisa. Let's go into the garden."

"No, I don't want to talk. Why don't you just leave me alone or go ask your fiancée to dance?"

"Why, green eyes, I believe you're jealous," he said with a mocking grin.

"It's not funny," she said angrily and tried to pull away. "Let me go!"

"Why? Are you afraid of your feelings for me? I know you and you desire me as much as I do you. I can see it in those glorious eyes. And I felt it yesterday."

"Don't," Lisa cried. "I can't be with you knowing how you feel about another woman."

"But you don't know how I feel about Consuelo. That's why we have to talk." He took her arm and started to walk into the garden, but Lisa stopped.

"I don't want to go with you," she said desperately.

"Either you come with me right now, or I'll tell this whole group of people that you're my wife and that I was a Comanche warrior. They should be quite interested."

"You wouldn't dare."

"You still don't know me very well, do you?" he said, walking to the middle of the courtyard. Lisa followed after him and pulled at his arm.

"Don't. I'll walk with you." With a satisfied grin, Eric took her arm and led her into the garden. Lisa turned to him abruptly.

"Why would you do such a stupid thing? You know there's a price on your head in Texas."

"There was a price on my head. I'm dead, remember?"

"Don't play with me. When I heard you were killed, a part of me died too."

"Again, I'm sorry. I always seem to cause you pain, don't I, green eyes?" He pulled her to him and held her tightly. "I have so much to tell you, to explain to you, but the most important thing for you to know right now is that I love you. I'll always love you," he said huskily, lifting her chin and covering her mouth with his. She threw her arms around his neck and pressed herself against him. He felt the tension leave her body. "I was in agony watching you with those other men," he murmured against her ear. "I can't stand the thought of anyone else touching you. Let's go upstairs."

Lisa nodded and Eric took her by the arm.

"Ah, there you are, my dear. I've been looking all over for you," Don Alfredo said loudly, walking into the garden. "I want to introduce you to some friends of mine."

"Abuelo, Lisa and I have other plans."

"But Sandro, I only want to borrow her for a few minutes."

"No," Eric shouted angrily.

Lisa looked from Eric to Don Alfredo, and pulled her arm free from Eric's.

"It's all right, we can talk later," she said looking at Eric. "I'd love to meet your friends, Don Alfredo." She offered the old man her hand and they walked off toward the courtyard. She turned to smile back at Eric, but he was gone.

The rest of the evening was interminably slow for Lisa. She almost wished she hadn't tried to please Don Alfredo by meeting his friends, because she couldn't find Eric anywhere afterward. She had seen Consuelo come in in a flourish of petticoats and red satin and had later seen her leave. She wondered if Consuelo and Eric were together somewhere, and if he were whispering the same words of love to Consuelo that he had whispered to her earlier in the evening.

After what seemed like an eternity, the evening came to an end. There were still a few people dancing and drinking, and the musicians continued to play, but Lisa had had enough. She said good night to Don Alfredo and went to her room. She almost knocked on Eric's door, but she was afraid he might be with Consuelo, so she went into her room.

She undressed in front of the fire that Rosa had lit for her, and she stood next to the flames, staring into them. She was tired and she undid her hair and slipped into bed in her chemise. It wasn't long before she slipped into a deep sleep, oblivious of everything around her.

They were back again—the Comanche braves— laughing at her, tearing at her clothes, touching her body. She could smell their rotten breaths and their dirty bodies. They held her down so she couldn't move, spread-eagled and helpless. The pain—she couldn't take the pain again. Not again. She started to scream, but was hit again and again until she stopped. She thought her heart would burst; she couldn't breathe. Why didn't someone help her?

Then his face appeared, soft and reassuring, blue eyes comforting. But he started to go away.

"No, Nakon, don't leave me. I need you; please don't leave me!"

Eric heard Lisa's screams and ran to her room. He knew she was probably having her nightmares again—it seemed they'd never stop plaguing her. He started to sit down on the bed but stopped. She was quiet now and he thought that perhaps it was over. He turned to go when he heard her voice.

"Don't go," she uttered almost in a whimper.

He sat down on the bed and pulled her limp form into his arms. She felt so much slimmer than he remembered, almost frail.

"All right, I'm here now. I won't leave you. I'll never leave you again." He held her gently as he would have a child, stroking her hair. "You're all right now. There's

238

nothing to worry about. You go back to sleep now. If you need me, I'll be in the next room." He was surprised at his own solicitousness toward her, especially when he ached for the feel of her. But he wouldn't take her like this, not when she was so vulnerable. He got up to leave but felt her hand on his arm, pulling him back.

"Don't go; I don't want to be alone."

"Are you sure?"

She nodded.

"I don't seem to be able to think clearly when I'm with you. The only thing I know for sure is that I need you and want you. Please stay with me, Eric."

He lay down next to her and pulled her against him. She reached out and touched his face, and ran her fingers through his thick hair. She pulled his face close to her breasts, and he buried his face in them. He felt her nipples harden and he pulled down the straps of her chemise and kissed them softly. He pulled the chemise the rest of the way off until she was completely naked. He stood up and took off his pants and then lay next to her again. They lay still for a long time, basking in the warmth and feel of each other's bodies. Then he began his reacquaintance with her body.

His mouth began at her face and moved downward. Her skin was soft and silky and smelled faintly of roses. Her stomach was flat and firm and he moved his lips across it. He kissed her inner thighs and then moved to the softness between her thighs, kissing and probing her with his tongue. He heard her soft moans of pleasure and he moved back upward, across her stomach and breasts and back to her mouth. He kissed her softly while his fingers moved over her body. Lisa felt the familiar pressure building in her stomach. She ran her fingers down the taut muscles of his back to the firmness of his buttocks, and then she reached out for him. She gasped when she felt the erect member. It had been so long since she'd been with him and she'd forgotten. He took her gasp as one of fear.

"Don't be afraid; I won't hurt you this time. I'll be gentle."

"I'm not afraid of you—never afraid of you," she said softly.

He climbed on top of her and thrust himself deeply inside her. She cried out at first but he moved slowly and gently, until she moved with him. He moved faster and he felt her hips thrust up against his; her nails dug into his back and her long legs wrapped around his back. She arched her back, rising to meet him each time, until finally, they both climaxed in a thunderous explosion of love. They lay unmoving, completely exhausted. Lisa felt too content to even talk, and before she drifted off to sleep she heard Eric's voice whisper in her ear.

"I've come home," he said softly, and Lisa let the sweet thoughts of their lovemaking lull her into a dreamless sleep.

Lisa woke up the next morning Eric was gone. She got up and went to the window. It was a beautiful, clear day. She felt incredibly happy. She looked at the tousled bed and thought of the passionate night she and Eric had spent together. It had been wonderful for her and completely fulfilling—so much better than the previous afternoon.

She quickly cleaned up and dressed and went downstairs to find Eric. She couldn't find him in the kitchen or dining room, but she found Don Alfredo in the sitting room. He smiled when he saw her come in.

"Good morning, my dear, you look lovely today. I trust you slept well?"

"Very well, thank you," Lisa said, a blush spreading over her cheeks.

"Good. Would you like some tea or hot chocolate before breakfast?"

"Tea, thank you." She walked over to the French doors, opening them and breathing in the fragrance of the flowers.

"It's a beautiful day, Don Alfredo, full of light and hope and . . ."

"And love?"

"Yes, and love." She walked over to sit next to him. "Where's Eric? I couldn't find him anywhere."

"He's out with my vaqueros checking on some squatters. He said to tell you he'd be back by early afternoon so you could take a ride together."

"Good. I'm so hungry this morning, I think I could eat a dozen eggs by myself. Aren't any of the guests up yet?"

Don Alfredo laughed.

"One thing you'll learn very quickly around here is that Californios like to enjoy themselves. When they stay up late at a fiesta, you can be sure that very few of them will appear before the noon hour."

"But you're always up early. So is Eric."

"I have always ridden with my vaqueros in the morning and I'm used to getting up early. As for Sandro, he was raised the same way, and I suppose he wasn't a lazy man in the Comanche camp."

"You know, it's funny. In all the time I spent there, I never saw what he and the other men did most of the time. I saw them break horses, and have races, and work

241

on their arms, but many times the men would go into a sweat lodge and stay there for hours. Half the time I never saw Eric during the day."

"Well, now that he is back, he is an early riser who likes to ride with the vaqueros. He will be a good patrón."

"He was a good chief, too," Lisa said with obvious pride.

"Well, shall we go into breakfast? Since it will only be the two of us, I'm sure you can have all the food you want."

After breakfast Lisa went up to see if Raytahnee was still asleep. She knocked at the door and when she didn't receive an answer, she walked in. She found Raytahnee lying in bed, her arms thrown up over her head, a dreamy expression on her face.

"Are you feeling all right?" Lisa asked.

"Quite all right. In fact, I've never felt so well in my whole life." She sat up, patting the bed next to her for Lisa to sit down. "I think I'm in love."

"In love?"

"Yes. He's the son of one of the hacendados. He'll inherit his father's rancho someday."

"Who is he?"

"Miguel Figueroa. He has relatives all over California and in Mexico. He says the richest ones live in Los Angeles, in Baja California."

"How old is he?"

Raytahnee laughed.

"You sound like a stuffy old duenna. I'm sixteen years old, you know. In the Comanche camp I would've been married and carrying my first child by now."

"Well, this isn't the Comanche camp and I want you to be careful. I don't want you to get hurt; you're still so young. You have so many years ahead of you."

"I didn't say I was going to marry Miguel. I just enjoy his company and I think he likes me. Last night wasn't the first time we met. He and his father have been here a few times and we have gone riding before. He is such a gentleman."

"Well, I'm glad for that at least," Lisa said dryly. "Will you be seeing him again?"

"Yes, we're going riding today. He wants to show me some of his land."

"I'm happy for you, Raytahnee, but please be careful. Men have a tendency to take advantage of young, innocent girls."

Again Raytahnee laughed and she reached for Lisa's hand.

"You're so funny. Here you are lecturing me and I think you're more naive about love than I am. You're only nineteen years old yourself, remember?"

"I know, but I'm not quite as innocent as you," Lisa said sadly. Sometimes she felt as if she were twice her age.

"Don't, Lisa. I told you before that what happened to you doesn't change what you are inside. You must learn to respect yourself again. And don't worry about me. It's just such a nice feeling to know that someone cares for me and he wasn't chosen by someone else because of how many horses he could bring my family."

"All right, I'll go now and let you get back to your dreams. I don't know what I'm worried about you for, you can handle your life much better than I can my own. I'll see you later."

Lisa decided to go for a ride rather than wait around for Eric. She rode along the coastline, never tiring of looking at the magnificent Pacific Ocean. She saw a ship on the horizon and watched until it became a tiny speck in the distance. She rode hard and fast, enjoying the freedom of the open land. When she rode back to the hacienda, she hoped that Eric would be back. She was looking forward to seeing him. She went through the courtyard and into the garden room, knowing that's where she'd find Don Alfredo. As she approached she heard Consuelo's voice. She had forgotten about Consuelo after last night.

"Ah, you are back. Did you have a nice ride?" Don Alfredo waved Lisa to sit next to him.

"Yes, thank you. But I'm going to go up and change before lunch."

"Yes, I think that would be an excellent idea," Consuelo cut in. "Tell me, Señorita Jordan, do you enjoy dressing like a man? I suppose you even ride a horse astride?"

Lisa turned to Consuelo, her green eyes aflame.

"As a matter of fact, I do ride my horse astride, señorita. And I dress like this because it's much more pratical than layers of burdensome petticoats. I have always felt that riding sidesaddle is for old women and ladies who don't know how to ride. I've always thought it looked perfectly ridiculous."

A red flush suffused Consuelo's face. She turned to Don Alfredo.

"Would you be so kind as to leave the señorita and me alone, Don Alfredo? We have a few things to talk about."

"Lisa?" Don Alfredo looked at Lisa questioningly.

"Certainly, Don Alfredo. We'll be in for lunch soon."

Don Alfredo walked out of the room, closing the doors behind him. He knew what Consuelo would say to Lisa; he knew how she felt about her. She had just been berating him about inviting the girl into his house to

244

tempt Alejandro. It had taken everything in his power not to slap the impudent girl's face. She had changed far too much since the death of her parents.

Consuelo got up from her chair and paced around the room.

"Where were you last night?" She turned to Lisa suddenly.

"It's really none of your business where I was last night," Lisa replied coldly.

"I asked you where you were, but I already know— you were with him."

"With whom?" Lisa asked calmly, brushing the dust from her pants.

"With my fiancé," Consuelo screamed.

"I beg your pardon, señorita, but from what I understand, you are the only one who thinks Señor Anderson is your fiancé. He doesn't seem to agree with you."

"Then I was right, you were with him last night!"

"As I said before, it's none of your business where I was last night."

"I know you were together because Sandro wasn't in his room."

"You checked his room?" Lisa asked incredulously.

A sly smile spread over Consuelo's face.

"I wasn't checking his room, I was waiting for him as I always do. He prefers that I come to his room."

Lisa felt the blood drain from her face and Consuelo saw that she had gained the advantage and she pressed her attack.

"Oh, he didn't tell you that he and I have been lovers since his return? Yes, you aren't the first and most certainly not the last. A man like Sandro, he must have

245

many women. But I can forgive his little indiscretions because I know he'll always come back to me. He and I are the same kind. We belong together."

Lisa couldn't talk. Eric had told her that he and Consuelo had been lovers, but it was a different thing entirely hearing it from Consuelo. She just couldn't accept the fact that he had been as intimate with Consuelo as he had been with her.

"What's the matter, don't you believe me? I can assure you that I'm telling the truth. Sandro's a magnificent lover, he . . ."

Lisa ran from the room; she couldn't stand to hear any more. She went to Raytahnee's room but found her gone. She knew she had to get away. She ran down the stairs and straight into Don Alfredo.

"Where are you going in such a hurry?"

"I'm going back to the del Sol. I have to get away from here."

"What did Consuelo say to you? You can't leave without speaking with Sandro."

"I can't stay here knowing that she and Eric are lovers. I'm not that strong, Don Alfredo."

"Don't you see, that's what Consuelo wants you to do. She's trying her best to scare you away. Please, stay until Sandro returns."

"No. Everything is happening too fast. Maybe you're wrong, maybe he really does love Consuelo. Maybe he doesn't even know how he feels. I just have to get away from that vicious woman. Forgive me for being such a coward." She kissed him on the cheek and ran out the door.

Don Alfredo walked outside and watched as she rode away. He wished he hadn't left her alone with Consuelo.

Too much was happening to her too quickly, and she wasn't able to deal with it. She'd only been here less than a week. Well, the ride would do her good and when Sandro got back, he'd go after her. And hopefully, she'd give him a chance to become a part of her life again.

CHAPTER XV

When Lisa got back to the del Sol, she noticed a commotion in the main corral. She dismounted and walked over to see what was going on. She spotted Vicente, Hector's son, and she spoke to him in Spanish.

"What's all the commotion about, Vicente?"

"Ah, señorita, look at the stallion they are bringing into the corral—is he not magnifico?"

Lisa walked over and stepped up on one of the rails so she could look over the top. A large golden horse was running around the corral, his long white mane and tail flying.

"I've never seen such a horse before. What breed is he?"

"He is a palomino, señorita. The Californios have been breeding them for a long time now, but unfortunately, not all the offspring turn out like this one. He is a beauty and he has the devil's own temper, this one."

Lisa watched as the palomino snorted and bucked his way around the corral. Two of the vaqueros attempted to get a bridle on him, but the horse wouldn't allow either of the men near his head.

"Look señorita, the men are trying to bridle break him first. When he gets used to the bridle, they will lead him around and then the patrón will try to break this one for himself."

"How could anyone break a horse like that?" Lisa asked, awed by the magnificence of the animal.

"The patrón is the best horseman I have ever seen. He has a way with animals. He talks to them first; then, if they do not listen, he finds a way to break them."

Just like women, Lisa thought bitterly. She had seen Eric and the other Comanche break horses in the Comanche camp, but never in a corral. They lassoed the wild horse, hobbled its front feet, and fastened a noose around its jaw. The warrior then slowly advanced toward the snorting animal and placed a hand over its eyes and breathed into its nostrils, actions which usually helped to calm the animal. The other way she had seen them try to break wild horses was by taking them ino a deeper part of the river so that when they bucked, the water would tire them out quickly. She wondered, though, how good Eric would be at pitting his strength against this animal's in a corral.

"When will the patrón try to break him?"

"When he returns from Don Alfredo's. It will be something worth watching, señorita."

Lisa noticed the pride in the young man's voice when he talked about Eric; all the vaqueros seemed to feel that way about him, just as he had been greatly respected in the Comanche camp.

She left the corral and went into the hacienda, telling Marta she was back, and then went up to her room and threw herself on the bed. She was tired, but try as she would she couldn't sleep. She couldn't get the memory of the previous night out of her head. Their lovemaking had been passionate and tender; she had been sure Eric loved her. Now she wasn't so sure. She wondered if he had said the same things to Consuelo.

She tossed on the bed and covered her eyes with her arm to blot out the sun. A soft moan escaped her lips as she thought of the intensity of their lovemaking and how she had responded so wantonly to Eric. She wondered if it were the same with all men and women. God, she thought how he could excite her, and when he had come into her room to comfort her, she had been the one to ask him to stay. Even after the way he had treated her that first afternoon, she knew she'd give in to him again. It seemed as though she had no will of her own where he was concerned.

There was a knock on the door and Rosa entered.

"Señorita, it is time for your bath. I will have the boys bring up the water now."

Lisa sat up, rubbing her eyes.

"What time is it? I didn't think I slept that long."

"It's almost time for dinner. The patrón requests that you dine with him as soon as you are bathed and dressed."

"The patrón? He's here?"

"Sí, señorita. He got back a short while ago."

Lisa got up off the bed.

"Tell the patrón that I don't wish to dine with him this evening. Tell him that I'm not hungry and that I prefer to stay in my room."

"But señorita . . ."

"Please, Rosa. Just tell the patrón what I said. Thank you."

"As you wish, señorita," Rosa said quietly and left the room.

Minutes later the tub and buckets of water were brought in and Lisa undressed and stepped into the tub.

As she started to sink down into the tub she caught sight of herself in the mirror and stopped. She was tall and lean, her skin brown from hours in the sun. Her breasts weren't large but were well formed and firm. Her eyes rested on the large red gash underneath her left breast and she touched it. It didn't seem real—was it really Eric whom she had tried to kill herself for? She couldn't believe she'd done such a thing but the scar was there to prove it. She continued the cool appraisal of her body, seeing her flat stomach and long, slim legs. She unknotted her hair and it fell in a tangled mass almost to her waist. She wondered if she presented a desirable picture to a man. She had always thought of herself as being too tall and skinny, "not enough curves," her mother had once told her. But Nakon—Eric—had told her how beautiful she was; he had told her that again last night. If she were so beautiful, she thought, why didn't she feel it? Why did she feel so inferior to women like Mariz and Consuelo, and why didn't she feel confident enough to try to hold on to the man she loved? She had no answers and she lowered herself into the steamy water. She luxuriated in the feel of the soothing water. Lost in thought, her eyes closed, she was taken completely by surprise when the bedroom door crashed open and Eric walked in, slamming it behind him.

"What're you doing?" Lisa cried indignantly.

Eric walked over to the tub and looked down at her, his eyes dark and brooding.

"Isn't it nice that my mother saw fit to order a tub from the East so that she and people like you can take baths in it? Well, if you're not careful you're going to be taking your baths outside."

"What do you mean?"

"I mean, I don't want you acting like a goddamned princess. What is between us is a private matter and I won't have you taking your anger out on the servants. I don't give a damn how you feel about me, but the servants are another thing. They've always been treated with respect here. You won't be rude to them and you won't involve them in our private quarrels; do you understand?" He walked over and sat down on the bed, and watched as Lisa shifted nervously in the tub. "Another thing, you're a guest here and when I ask you to have dinner with me, I expect you to be there. If you don't learn how to act properly, I'll have to teach you some manners."

"Well, you're certainly learning quickly how to play the role of the patrón, aren't you? You never cease to amaze me. One week you're a devoted Comanche warrior, the next, a rich Spanish don. You're lucky you have so many choices," she said contemptuously.

"We all have choices, Lisa, it's just a matter of what we do with them."

"Well, it seems to me I've had little choice in the way my life has gone in the last year. You gave me very little choice when you sent me away; you're giving me little choice now."

He got up and walked to the tub, an angry scowl on his face.

"Oh, there's a choice. Either you come downstairs and eat or you don't eat at all."

She slapped her hands down on the water, spilling most of it on the floor.

"You're a bastard!"

"I told you once before that dirty mouth of yours was going to get you into trouble someday. I can't understand

252

it, I thought you were a lady of proper breeding. Must've been all the time you spent with those savage Comanche."

The bar of soap hit the door just as Eric closed it. Lisa heard his deep laughter from outside the door.

"Damn you, Eric," she screamed, "oh, damn you!"

When Lisa walked into the dining room, Eric stood up to help her to her seat. He couldn't hide the look of amusement on his face. Lisa was dressed in a long, colorful peasant skirt, which was too short and fell well above her ankles; a loose white blouse, which kept falling from her shoulders; and a pair of leather sandals. Her hair was pulled back in a thick braid, like many of the Indian women wore it. He didn't know where she'd gotten the clothes, but he suspected she'd dressed that way in an attempt to make him angry. As he pushed in her seat he leaned down and placed a kiss on her bare shoulder.

"Would you please stop that?"

"Perdóname, señorita, it's just that when you walk into a room dressed like a peasant girl, I expect that you're probably going to act like one. Most of them give freely of their attentions to the patrón, you know."

"Well, why don't you pick one of them? Or do your tastes run higher, patrón?" she asked angrily.

"Ah, Lisa, it's only you I desire. Your long, slim brown body, your . . ."

"Stop it. Don't you have any sense of propriety?"

"I have quite a sense of propriety, but when I get near you my blood gets hot. You excite me more than any other woman has. That never embarrassed you before."

"Things were different before," she said coolly.

253

"Were they? I guess they were. And last night, in your room, was it so different then, too?"

Lisa looked up and met his penetrating gaze. Those pale-blue eyes could mesmerize a person. They stared at each other and it was Lisa who lowered her head first. He reached out and took her hand in his.

"It's all right, I don't expect you to accept things right away. I just want us to quit battling each other and live in peace." His voice was so gentle and understanding that Lisa looked up and smiled.

"Thank you, I . . ." She never finished her sentence because Marta came in with dinner. Lisa was quiet throughout dinner and Eric wondered what she had been going to say when Marta entered.

After dinner they went to the study for coffee and brandy. Lisa sat on the chair which faced the fireplace and looked at the portrait of Eric. Eric poured himself a brandy and walked around the room, watching Lisa.

"I should've known," she said softly.

"What'd you say?"

"I said I should've known that painting was of you. There couldn't be two people in the world with eyes like yours," she said proudly. Eric walked over and pulled her up to him.

"We have to talk. Come over here to the couch."

She followed him over to the couch and sat down next to him. He took the cup she was holding from her hand, placed it on the table and cupped his large hands around her smaller ones.

"First of all, I didn't tell you how charming you look in those clothes."

She smiled, realizing how silly she'd been.

"It's good to see you smiling again. When I first met

your brother, I was prepared to dislike him. Then he came in here, holding his hand out and smiling, a smile just like yours. I couldn't dislike him. He's a good man."

"I think so, too. He still tends to be a little overprotective of me though."

"I don't blame him; I'm the same way about you."

She held his gaze for a moment and tried to pull her hands away, but he held them tightly.

"Don't pull away from me. You have to let me explain to you."

"What purpose will it serve? What will it change?"

"You're my wife, and that hasn't changed. I can't believe you don't love me."

"I never said I didn't love you. But your wife? I'm not your wife and I never have been."

"As far as I'm concerned, you were my wife under Comanche law and that's enough for me. I love you and want to be with you. Why do you have to fight me?"

"Because I'm so confused." She finally managed to pull her hands free and she clasped them together on her lap. "I'm still not sure I understand why you sent me away; I feel as though I've been betrayed by you. You say I'm your wife and that you love me, yet you didn't seem to mind making love to another woman when I wasn't around. I think you take the word 'wife' too lightly. I'm not your wife, Eric; we aren't married under the white man's law or in the eyes of God. The only position I would hold in this house if I stayed would be as your mistress."

Eric got up and walked to the fireplace, an irritated look on his face. He leaned against it for a few moments, and then turned to Lisa.

"Does it matter so much to you? What could we do

after the vows are said that we haven't already done?" He saw her blush slightly, and her eyes grow dark. "Lisa, it doesn't have to be all that complicated."

She got up and walked over to him, placing a tentative hand on his arm.

"Is it so much to ask? To be married, to have a real wedding?"

"Damn it, I don't even believe in God! And why the hell would being married guarantee that I'd never leave you?"

"It wouldn't," she said softly, her voice sad, "nor would it prevent you from sending me away again. But I'd be able to share your name and so would our child, if we ever have one again." She walked to the other side of the room and turned back to face him. "Maybe you're just afraid to choose between me and Consuelo. After all, she can offer you much more than I."

Eric walked over to her and grabbed her by the shoulders.

"She has nothing to do with us."

"She has everything to do with us!" Lisa cried angrily.

"All right, what did she tell you? My grandfather said that you and she had words."

"No, she had words. She told me that you two have been lovers since you've been back, and that you're going to marry her."

"So we were lovers, I already told you that. I didn't know when I'd see you again and she made herself available to me. I've never said I was a saint. A man does have certain urges, if you'll remember. I wasn't about to become a monk until I saw you again."

"That's obvious," Lisa said hotly and she started for the door.

"Will you wait, damn it! I don't love Consuelo and she knows it. I've been more than honest with her from the beginning."

"Then why does she think you're going to marry her?"

"I don't know; I never told her I would." He shut the door again and pulled Lisa to him. "Damn, you're a stubborn woman. Just exactly what do you want from me?"

She looked up at him, her green eyes softly shining.

"I just want you to marry me and for us to be together." She took a deep breath and continued. "If you can't give this to me, then we have nothing more to say to each other."

Eric's eyes met her direct scrutiny and he held her gaze. It was some moments before he spoke.

"I won't be pushed," he said coldly, and turned back to the fireplace. This time he couldn't look into her eyes. "I guess we have nothing more to say to each other." He watched as the tears welled up in her eyes and rolled down her cheeks. He longed to reach out to her but she suddenly ran from the room.

"What the hell's the matter with me?" he yelled angrily. "Why can't I keep from hurting her?" He walked back over to the desk and poured himself another brandy. He started to drink it, but turned and threw it against the fireplace, where it broke into a hundred tiny pieces.

CHAPTER XVI

Lisa arose in the quiet glow of the predawn sky. She dressed in her buckskins and went out to get a horse. On her way to the stables, she stopped by the main corral and climbed onto the rail and looked at the palomino. He sensed her presence immediately and snorted loudly. She talked to him softly in a soothing voice so he quieted down somewhat. But when she walked around the corral to get closer to him, he galloped away to the other side. She shrugged her shoulders and went into the stables, grabbed a blanket and hackamore from the tackle room, and led her horse outside. Living with the Comanche, she had learned to ride bareback and found that she liked it better than riding with a saddle. She threw the blanket on the horse's back and led him a little ways from the rancho before she swung up and rode off.

It was a cool, foggy morning and Lisa thoroughly enjoyed the feel of the wet air against her face. She tried to keep her mind from the events of the previous evening, but she kept hearing Eric's cold voice when he said, "I guess we have nothing more to say to each other."

She heard waves crashing and she realized she had already ridden the two miles to the ocean. She reined in her horse and stopped. She looked around, but she couldn't see anything, not even the cliffs. Struck with a sudden overwhelming fear she dismounted and walked slowly forward, and nearly walked over the edge of the cliff. She jumped back quickly, her heart pounding. Had she kept riding, she realized, she would've ridden off the edge. Still shaky, she led her horse back until she felt a safe distance away from the cliffs. She knew she'd have to wait until the fog lifted before she attempted to find her way back to the rancho.

She pulled the blanket from the horse, wrapped it around herself, and lay down on the damp ground. In spite of her fright, the sound of the waves pounding on the beach lulled her to sleep.

Eric was angry. He got up to go downstairs and found Lisa's door open and her gone. He was certain she had done something stupid. Marta hadn't seen her, and when he went out to the stables, Hector told him a horse was gone.

"Little idiot," he yelled, "she should know better than to go riding in this stuff," he said, gesturing at the thick fog. He was angry, but at the same time, worried—he'd known people who had ridden right off the cliffs in dense fog. The sound of the waves was deceiving, and a person might think he was farther away from the edge than he actually was.

He guessed she had ridden toward the ocean because of her love of water. He rode the distance quickly and when he thought he was near enough to the cliffs, he dismounted and walked on foot carefully. By now, the sun was up and he was able to see more clearly. He called Lisa's name but received no answer. He was about to give up and wait until the fog cleared completely, when he heard a horse whinny in the distance and his horse answer. He followed the direction of the animal's sound and found Lisa's horse grazing peacefully. He walked a little farther and found Lisa curled up on the ground in the horse blanket. His first reaction was one of anger, but when he saw her lying there, his anger subsided. He sat down and pulled her sleeping form into his arms. He wrapped the blanket more tightly around her and held her closely.

"Why can't it be simple, Lisa? Why can't it be like it used to be? We love each other yet we fight each other." He leaned over and kissed her forehead, gently touching the thick, sooty lashes that were silhouetted against her face. Eric cradled Lisa in his arms until the sun was completely up and she began to stir. When she opened her eyes, she found Eric staring down at her, his arms around her.

"What're you doing? Where am I?" Then she remembered what had almost happened. She sat up and pulled the blanket from around her shoulders, and pushed the damp strands of hair from her face. She looked at him and had an urge to touch his mouth, but the memory of his last words the evening before made her stop. She stood up. "I'm sorry you had to come all the way out here; I would've been fine," she said haughtily, her voice cool and distant.

"That's why you almost rode off the edge of the cliffs, I suppose. You little fool, you could've killed yourself. What in hell possessed you to go riding in weather like this?" He walked over and grabbed her shoulders. She shook free and stalked to her horse.

"I'm sorry I ruined your morning, patrón. I won't do it again!"

Eric grabbed her and pulled her back.

"Damn it, Lisa, it's very dangerous riding in a fog like this. People who've lived here all their lives don't go riding until the sun comes up and the fog clears. Please, don't do it again. Wait till the fog clears next time." The note of genuine concern in his voice made Lisa soften.

"I'm sorry, I promise I won't do it again." She walked to her horse and swung up, heading in the direction of the rancho. They both rode back to the rancho in silence, neither knowing what to say, each remembering the words they had spoken the night before.

The rest of the week continued much the same. Lisa rode in the mornings after waiting for the fog to clear. She had breakfast after her ride and then went to the corral to watch the men break horses. She started taking an apple or some sugar to the palomino each day. The first day he refused to take the apple from her hand so she left it on the ground. He slowly came up and took it. The next morning she held out her hand, palm open, talking to him all the while, and he very tentatively took the apple from her hand then raced to the other side of the corral. On the third morning, he came over when she appeared at the corral. She named him Vida, meaning "life" in Spanish.

Lisa watched each day as Eric tried methodically to break Vida; but each day the stallion held out. Just when Eric felt he had won the battle of wills, Vida bucked a few more times to let him know there was still fight left in him. Eric could see Lisa at these times, sitting on the edge of the corral, a look of triumph on her face. It made him more determined than ever to break the horse.

After her morning ride and watching Eric and the men

in the corral, Lisa would read or help Marta in the kitchen, learning recipes from her. In the afternoons, she rode again and then came back and cleaned up for dinner. Dinners were quiet affairs, Lisa speaking only when spoken to. Afterward, she excused herself and went up to her room to read. She tried to keep busy because it was the only way to keep her mind from Eric. She knew she couldn't avoid him forever, but she wanted to keep her distance from him until she had a chance to think things over.

The nights were lonely for Lisa but even more so for Eric. Knowing that he'd put the breach between them made him angry with himself, but even more so with Lisa. He felt she had no right to give him an ultimatum, when she should've been happy that he was alive and they were together again. But they weren't together again, not really. Lisa was there in body but not spirit. Everything she did around him, she did mechanically. She smiled, said thank you, ate, and excused herself to go off and be alone. He knew she acted that way to make him feel guilty, and it was driving him crazy. He'd had enough of being treated like a criminal in his own home. He decided to have it out with her, no matter what the outcome. He couldn't take the silent treatment from her any longer; a week of it had been enough. After having five full glasses of brandy, he had thoroughly convinced himself that he had been wronged by her, and he stumbled upstairs to Lisa's room.

Lisa was sitting in bed reading when she heard Eric on the stairs. She was used to hearing his steps at night, but when they stopped by her door instead of going down the hall, she looked up. Eric threw open the door and came in. They stared at each other and without hesitation Eric walked to the bed, pulled back the covers, and lifted her in his arms.

"What're you doing? Put me down!"

"Come along, wife," he said coldly, and walked down the hall to his room and threw her on his bed, where she landed in a heap with her nightdress pulled up to her thighs. She watched as he took off his shirt and moccasins, then walked over to the bed.

"Take that thing off," he said, pointing to the nightdress.

"No. I have no intention of taking this off or of staying in this room." She jumped off the opposite side of the bed and ran to the door. He grabbed her from behind, holding on to her hair.

"Ouch, let go," she screamed loudly.

"I told you to take that damned thing off. Most mistresses don't have to be told how to please their men; they usually know what to do."

Her hand lashed out to slap his face, but he caught it in an iron grip, pinning her against the door.

"I've decided you're going to earn your keep around here. Everyone else works on this rancho, there's no reason why you shouldn't, too." He bent down and pressed his lips to hers, leaning his weight against her body. She pulled her head away.

"You're drunk!"

"Only on you, green eyes. You say you want marriage, but all you really want is love. Let me love you," he whispered huskily, picking her up and laying her on the bed. When he reached to unbutton her nightdress, she rolled to the other side of the bed and stood up.

"I won't be your whore, Eric. I'm not the weak, dependent woman I once was. I'll fight you if you make me."

263

Eric smiled, a mocking grin, and advanced around the bed to stand in front of her.

"Good, I like my women with some fight. You were always too easy for me, anyway." This time her hand struck home, sending a crashing sound across the room. He grabbed her arms, forcing her backward onto the bed.

"You'll pay for that," he said coldly, while straddling her on the bed.

Lisa looked up at him and couldn't believe that this was the same man who, only a week before, had made such gentle, sweet love to her. His eyes were glazed over and there was a light-beaded sweat on his face and chest. He was much too strong for her, but she was still determined to make it hard for him. As much as she loved him and wanted him, she refused to be taken like a cheap whore.

When Eric rolled to his side to take off his pants, Lisa lunged across the bed. She ran across the room to the desk and picked up a book and threw it at him. He easily ducked the flying book and continued to walk across the room. She ran to the fireplace and picked up a piece of wood from the box, holding it in front of her.

"C'm on, Lisa, I know you won't hurt me. It's not as though we've never made love before. Now put the wood down and come here." He reached out for her, but she threw the rough piece of wood and it struck him in the shoulder. She hadn't meant to hurt him, and she knew as soon as she saw the look on his face, that she had made a mistake. He was to her in a second, ripping the nightdress from her completely, and dragging her to the bed.

She looked up at him, her eyes wide with fright, as he climbed on top of her. But instead of the force she'd expected, he gently took her head in his hands and began to kiss her, moving down her throat to her breasts. She felt her breath quicken and she knew his ploy. She could fight him all she wanted, but he'd arouse her until she responded to him. It was worse, she thought, than being taken by force. Her body betrayed her and there was nothing she could do about it. Even as she thought this, she felt her hips move underneath him, her hands stroke his back. As his lips teased her nipples, she felt that lost. She was able to fight him in every way but this. For the first time since she'd known him, she felt ashamed of the feelings he evoked in her, and she knew her mind could never accept what her body had so willingly.

If the gap between them had been difficult to breach before, it was now almost impossible. Eric looked over at the empty space where Lisa had lain only a short while before. He ran his hand over the place—it was still warm.

His mind went back to the night before. He was astonished at his behavior; he'd been like a wild man. All his years as a Comanche had taught him tremendous control, but after only a few glasses of brandy, he'd literally gone crazy. His desire for Lisa had overcome his common sense. He didn't like the kind of man he was becoming since his return to California. He was constantly at odds with himself. He tried to fit into the life at the rancho, tried to change his ways, but it was harder than he thought. He wasn't adapting as well as he led Lisa to believe.

Lisa said she wouldn't be his whore, but he'd made her feel like one in forcing himself on her. She had responded to him, as he knew she would, but he'd forced her in the beginning until she did give in. He had belittled and humiliated her in the worst possible way. He'd been no better than the braves who had raped her.

When it was over she had rolled away and sobbed into her pillow. He tried to hold and comfort her, but she shrugged him away. He watched her for a long time as she cried, her shoulders heaving, until she fell into an exhausted sleep. He had done that to her.

He tried to assuage his guilt by telling himself that she had provoked him by her silence all that week, and by the ultimatum she had given him, but he knew he was lying to himself. In reality, it was he who was to blame. All she wanted was some assurance that they'd be together.

He thought back to the times when they had lived so peacefully as husband and wife in the Comanche camp. Those were such tranquil, harmonious times, in spite of the constant threats of war and death which lurked over them. He hadn't minded being married to Lisa then. In fact, he had often wondered how he'd ever lived his life before she came to the camp. And always during that time, she'd given herself freely to him, in love. How much better it had been then. He got up and slipped on his pants. He walked to the window and looked out at the swirling, gray clouds of fog.

"There's only one thing to do," he said out loud. "I'll marry her. I'll do as she wishes and we'll get married. But it'll be my way." He walked back and put on the rest of his clothes. He knew he'd have to be patient in order to win her all over again, to earn her trust again. He smiled to himself as he put on his moccasins and left his room. He'd always liked a challenge—it'd been that way when Lisa first came to the Comanche camp. But he had one thing in his favor this time—she was already in love with him. Now all he needed to do was reinforce that love and make it strong again.

"Well, if I'm going to court her like a gentleman, I may as well start looking like one," he said decidedly. She'd be his again, the way it used to be, the way it was meant to be.

On his way to the stables, Eric saw Lisa sitting on the top rail of the corral, the palomino's head resting in her lap, Osolo at her feet. The stallion was chewing on an apple and Lisa was talking to him and petting his nose. It was just like her to have the brute eating out of her hand when he'd been busting his butt all week to try and break him.

He walked up behind her. When Vida saw him, he snorted and ran around the corral, his tail flying high in the air. Lisa turned and gave Eric a cold look.

"You shouldn't be up there, it's dangerous," he said, reaching up to help her down. She pulled away and jumped down by herself.

"I see you've made friends with the brute," he said in a friendly tone, meaning to compliment her.

"I've found he responds more quickly to love than to force," she said harshly, her meaning clear to Eric. "I want to ask you a favor," she said suddenly, her voice changing to a conciliatory tone. "I'd like to work with Vida, the palomino, I mean. He seems to be responding to me. I think I can ride him bareback in a few days. Please, will you let me try? I'm afraid if you continue to try to break him every day, you'll break his spirit."

She was right, of course, and Eric knew it. The horse wouldn't be worth anything if he continued to try to break him when he wouldn't be broken. Besides, it would make Lisa happy.

"I don't want you to be . . ." He had started to say,

"alone with him," but Lisa didn't let him finish.

"All right then, break him. Break him your way and there'll be nothing left of that magnificent animal but a shell. Is that what you want, to prove to me how all-powerful you are?" She stood before him, defiant, her hands on her hips, her loose hair streaming around her shoulders and arms. He couldn't believe any woman could be so exciting.

"Lisa, I think . . ." Again she interrupted him.

"I know what you think of me, you made that perfectly clear last night," she screamed, her voice reaching a fevered pitch. "I'm too easy for you, isn't that what you said? Well, as soon as Tom gets back we'll be leaving and I'll be out of your life forever." She started to walk away but stopped. "I don't think you know who you are anymore; I certainly don't know you. When I was in the Comanche camp, I fell in love with a gentle, kind, and understanding man who was supposed to be a savage. Now, here we are, back in civilization, and I find you're more of a savage than you ever were when you were a Comanche."

He reached for her but she pulled away violently.

"Let go of me; I don't want you ever to touch me again. Why don't you go to your rich Spanish doña, I'm sure she's one person who's even easier than I am. I'm sure she'll be most happy to please you in any way possible!" She stalked off, her hair flowing out behind her, her tall, slim form enhanced by the tight buckskins. He leaned against the railing and watched her until she disappeared into the courtyard.

"Hell," he said thoughtfully, "it's going to be harder than I thought. She won't forget last night very easily, or that Consuelo and I were lovers." He shook his head and walked into the stables, where Hector was feeding the horses.

"Hector, come here."

"Sí, patrón."

"I've given the señorita permission to work with the palomino. You'll tell her this, please. But I don't want her to be alone with him. I want you to be around at all times; do you understand?"

"Sí, patrón. This will make her very happy. I've seen her with him in the mornings; he warms to her. I think she'll be able to bring him around."

"So do I, but remember not to leave her alone with him. I won't be here all day, I have something to do. You'll be in charge while I'm gone. Está bien?"

"Sí. When will you return?"

"I should be back by this evening. Where is Vicente? I have an errand for him to do."

"I'll find him, patrón."

"Send him up to the hacienda. Gracias, Hector," he said, slapping the older man on the shoulder. He went back to the hacienda and into the study. He took out pen and ink and some paper, and scribbled a note to his grandfather. He told him that he and Lisa would be coming the next day for a short stay. After folding the note, he summoned Vicente.

"Ah, Vicente, have you eaten breakfast yet?"

"Sí, patrón."

"All right then. I want you to take a note to my grandfather. You know the way?"

"Sí, I have ridden it many times with my father."

"Good. Then you go and saddle a horse and be on your way. And be sure to get something to eat and drink while you're there."

"Sí, patrón."

He walked back out to the stables and got his paint. He led him outside, put on a blanket and hackamore, swung up, and rode off. He hadn't seen Lisa again, but he thought it better to avoid her until he returned. He hoped that by the time he got back that evening, she'd be in a better mood or would at least talk to him. He had to earn her trust again, and he'd start that night. He hoped she was ready to begin by then.

CHAPTER XVII

From her bedroom window, Lisa watched Eric ride out of the yard. She hated fighting with him but she had no choice. She had lived with respect as his wife among the Comanche, but here it was different. She couldn't live as his mistress and have respect for herself. He had made it clear that he still wanted her, but not enough to marry her. He'd probably save marriage for another woman, probably Consuelo. If that happened she would leave. She couldn't bear to see him married to another woman. But where could she go? Not back to Boston, certainly not now. Her mother would never again be able to hold up her head among her society friends if it were known that her daughter had lived with Indians. Her mother would never understand anyway—her sense of propriety would make her kill herself rather than be touched by savages. She would never understand why Lisa had wanted to live afterward. No, she definitely couldn't go back to Boston.

Suddenly a picture of Josh came to mind. He loved her; he'd said as much. She knew she could never love Josh the way she loved Eric, but there was something solid and dependable about Josh. She could learn to love him, surely. He desired her and she was attracted to him, so that part of their life wouldn't be forced. And she would find other ways to please him, too. She was sure she could make him happy. She would seek refuge in Josh's love, and eventually she would grow to love him back.

She got up, feeling a little better about having made a decision, and she went outside to the corral. She saw Hector by Vida's corral and she went over to him. He told her what Eric had said about Vida and she was incredulous but excited. She tried to remember their conversation of that morning and she realized she hadn't let Eric finish what he was going to say; she'd been too busy yelling at him. She'd make a point of apologizing to him when he returned, and thank him for letting her work with Vida. There was no point in causing more friction. It was better to make the best of the time she had left here.

She spent the better part of the day with Vida. By evening, she was leading him around by a hackamore with a blanket on his back. He was beginning to trust her, and she was sure that in a few days she'd be able to ride him. Vida also let Hector near him, and both he and Lisa found Vida to be a very responsive animal. He had a mind of his own, yet he wasn't averse to a little pat on the nose or a fresh apple.

Lisa was pleased with the day's work and before she went into the hacienda to clean up, she talked with Hector. She wanted to know how other hacendados broke their horses. Hector told her of the cruel way in which some of the Spanish and Mexicans broke their horses and he mentioned the different types of bits which were used—the half-breed, spade, and ring bits being the most cruel. All were designed to injure the roof of the horse's mouth if he didn't respond to a command.

"I have learned, señorita, as have most of the rancheros, that a good horse seldom gives its best when it's in pain. Better to have patience and have a good, loyal horse. The Indians of the plains have the best horses around. They don't mistreat them, but show them love and respect. That's what we try to do here."

On her way back to the hacienda, Lisa decided she'd never put a bit into Vida's mouth, no matter what kind. She'd train him with a hackamore and teach him to respond to her by voice and leg pressure, just as the Comanche did.

After a quick bath, she dressed in one of the dresses Rebecca had made for her. It wasn't fancy, but it was serviceable and much better than her buckskins. She decided to be cordial to Eric at dinner, but when she went down, he wasn't there. He still hadn't returned from wherever he'd gone that morning. Fleetingly, she wondered if he were with Consuelo, but quickly dismissed it from her mind. What Eric did or whom he saw was no longer any concern of hers. In a few months she'd probably be gone from the del Sol and married to Josh, living on his farm in Missouri. But for some reason, the thought of being married to Josh and living in Missouri wasn't very comforting. Dinner was lonely for her without Eric, and no matter how much she tried to convince herself otherwise, she missed his company. It was easy for her to tell herself that she was going to forget him and marry Josh, but in reality, it was Eric who dominated her thoughts.

She sat idly and toyed with her food, trying to pass the time. She refilled her wine glass numerous times, but it didn't seem to alleviate the loneliness she felt without Eric. She was fussing with a piece of beef when she heard the front door open and Eric scream for Marta. In an instant, Marta flew out of the kitchen and past Lisa. Lisa started to get up, but remained seated; he had called for Marta, not her. She heard Marta's and Rosa's voices and wondered what all the excitement was about. Finally, after what seemed like an eternity and no one came to get her, she got up and wandered out to the entryway and on up the stairs to her room. She heard the excited voices of the two women chattering away in Spanish and giggling, and when she entered her room she saw what all the commotion was about. There were dozens of boxes and bolts of material scattered all over the bed and room.

"What's all of this?" she asked, walking up beside Marta.

"Clothes, señorita, and many pretty things. All for you. From the patrón." She and Rosa began to giggle.

"But there must be some mistake. I didn't ask for these things." But in spite of her protests, she was already looking with interest at some of the boxes.

"No mistake, señorita, the patrón says they are all for you." Marta and Rosa left, admiring the beautiful scarves Eric had brought back for them.

Lisa was enthralled by everything: dresses, gowns, nightgowns, underclothes, and shoes. There were even two riding outfits and bolts of cloth of different colored silks and satins. There was one box which stood out among the others. She opened it and drew in a deep breath—inside was a dark-green velvet cloak. She pressed the soft cloth to her cheek, luxuriating in its richness.

"Here, let me," Eric said, walking up behind her and taking the cloak from her hands. He placed it around her shoulders and turned her around to fasten the frogs at her throat. He pulled her hair out from beneath the cloak so that it fell caressingly down the length of the

274

green velvet.

"Beautiful," he said softly and led her to the mirror.

Lisa stared at her reflection, marveling at the difference in her appearance. For a long time now, except for the green dress, it seemed the only things she wore were her buckskins, moccasins, and gingham dresses. The cloak made her feel elegant and pampered.

"Even this velvet can't compare to the color of your eyes. That's a color that can never be matched," Eric said gently behind her. Lisa looked up and their eyes met in the glass, and for a small second, she could still believe it was the same between them. Their small moment of reverie was broken by Marta, who wanted to know if Eric wanted dinner.

"Yes, thank you, Marta. I'll be down as soon as I wash up." He turned back to Lisa. "Will you join me in the study for brandy after dinner?" She nodded her assent and set herself to the task of putting away her new clothes. When she went down to the study, Eric was already there, pouring the brandy.

"Where did you get so many beautiful clothes out here?" Lisa asked incredulously.

"I rode up to the harbor. There're always a lot of different ships in port. Many of them have come from New York, or Paris, or the Orient, anxious to sell or trade the latest clothing they have with them. They know they can command a high price because the wives and daughters of all the rich hacendados must have the latest styles."

"How did you get it all here?"

"One of the sailors from the ship followed me in a cart. He was paid well and didn't mind leaving the ship for a few hours." He handed her a glass. "Well, tell me about the palomino. Were you able to work with him?"

"Oh, yes, he's wonderful, and very smart. I think I'll be able to ride him soon."

"It seems there's more Indian in you than in me," he said with amusement.

Awhile later, Lisa got up to go to her room, and Eric walked her to the door. She looked up at him and then raised herself up on tiptoes and kissed him on the cheek.

"Thank you for all the lovely clothes. I've never had so many beautiful things in my life. And thank you for letting me work with Vida—it means a lot to me." She started to walk away, but Eric took her hands and held them against his chest.

"It's the least I can do after last night. I promise you, Lisa, that will never happen again. I'm sorry I hurt you." He lifted her chin up gently and kissed her lingeringly on the mouth, then he pulled away and walked back into the study.

Lisa went up to her room and changed into one of the nightgowns Eric had bought for her. She rubbed her hands along the smooth material and then reached up and touched her mouth where he had kissed her. Was it possible that he really did love her? And the clothes—they had been his way of telling her he was sorry. Still, there was a difference between desire and love, and she wasn't really sure Eric knew the difference. She'd made the right decision when she decided to marry Josh, she told herself. With him, at least, there would never be any doubts.

But it wasn't Josh that Lisa thought of when she fell asleep that night. Her last waking thoughts were of a sensuous, warm mouth, and light-blue eyes.

*   *   *

The next morning at breakfast, Eric told Lisa that Don Alfredo had invited them to spend a few days with him and Raytahnee.

"Will we be the only ones there?"

"The only ones. It seems my grandfather misses you, and Raytahnee is angry with you for leaving so soon."

"All right. I'd enjoy being with Don Alfredo and Raytahnee again."

They left after breakfast, loaded down with some of Lisa's new clothes and a basket filled with fruit, wine, and a lunch which Marta packed for them. They rode at a leisurely pace, taking in the beauty of the warm, summer day.

Lisa asked about the missions, and Eric took her to the Mission San Carlos. Lisa was amazed at the intricate workings of the mission—it looked like a city in itself. Eric explained to her that up until 1834, the missions actually were self-contained cities. Until that time, they had been the mainstay of social and political life in California. There were twenty-one missions in all, all of them founded by Fathers Serra and Lasuen. The southernmost mission was San Diego de Alcala; the northernmost, San Francisco Solano in Sonoma.

In the early days of California, the missions alone were supplied with enough land and labor for large-scale operations. Each mission had its own farms and ranchos embracing many thousands of acres. Cattle raising was of prime importance and it gave the province its first major export products in the form of hides and tallow.

By the early 1830's, the few hundred cattle brought from Mexico had increased to herds totaling nearly forty thousand head at the twenty-one missions. They also had herds of sheep and horses, flourishing vineyards, and broad **fields** of wheat and corn. In addition, the friars designed irrigation systems and taught their neophytes such arts as tanning, leather working, flour milling, soap making, weaving, and masonry. The missions approached self-sufficiency, but never fully attained it.

"But I don't understand how they could fail if they were so powerful and controlled so much land and manpower."

"Their main problem was that they were reliant on the outside world for luxury items and some necessities. They were supported by the Spanish government until the Mexican government took control in the 1820's; and when secularization was ordered by the Mexican government in 1834, most all of the missions were abandoned. Many have already fallen to ruin. Suddenly, they weren't so powerful anymore."

"What's happened to all the Indians?"

"Most of them fled and many have fallen into pitiful degradation. They were subjugated for so long, they forgot how to fend for themselves. My grandfather and many like him hired many of them for good wages and gave them land of their own. The original plan of secularization was for the padres to hold the land in trust for the Indians until they were ready to run it themselves, but it hasn't worked. They are so used to being told what to do, they don't have any idea of how to run a rancho or take care of the land. Except for small groups who've tried to lead others in revolt against local government, or have joined in with bandits, the majority are mindless souls wandering around without a purpose. They lost sight of their heritage. Before the Franciscans came here, these Indians were a proud, contented people. Their life was simple and leisurely. They collected nuts, berries, killed small game, and fished. It was a good life until the missions were built on their lands and they were forced to work. Actually, their existence bordered on slavery. They were forced to convert to Catholicism and forsake their old way of life and settle down at the missions into a routine of labor and religious ritual under the iron rule of the padres. If they ran away they were brought back, whipped, and put into irons."

"But the padres were men of God. Why would they have used such punishment on those poor people?" Lisa asked incredulously.

Eric laughed bitterly.

"It's time you grew up and saw things as they really are, Lisa. These Franciscans may've been men of God, but they governed their Indians with iron fists. Do you know that before these 'men of God' came to California, these Indians were actually a physically different race? Originally, they were a tall, muscular, and very handsome people. Look at them now, does this short, hump-shouldered, spiritless group of people even slightly resemble a once-proud race? So you see another example of why I have no great belief in God."

Lisa looked at Eric and at some of the Indians she saw around her. They looked so sad and hopeless, so different from the ones she's seen on the del Sol and del Mar. She thought of the Comanche, a fierce, proud people, who were constantly fighting for their land and their very existence. She could never imagine them subjugated the way these people had been. It made her sad to think that all this land belonged to the Indians before the missionaries came. But it was the same all over the country now. In the southwest and midwest, the government was trying to run the Indians from their land

and relocate them on reservations in order to make room for more whites who were migrating westward. It was as if the government and white people felt the Indians had no right to their own land. It made her understand a little better the tenacity of the Comanche and others when it came to their land. It would be a hideous fate for them to wind up like these people.

"What're you thinking?" Eric asked Lisa as they walked back to their horses.

"I was thinking about the Comanche. I think I understand them a little better now. I can't imagine them living an existence like this."

"Before the Spanish came to this country, the Pomo, Modoc, Patwin, Miwok, and Maidu couldn't imagine living an existence like this either," he said bitterly.

"How is it you know so much when you've been gone for almost ten years? You sound like a history book."

"My grandfather told me everything that's happened since I've been gone, but most everything has remained the same, particularly the treatment of the Indians. I had a best friend who was a Pomo, and I saw how he and his family were treated. I guess that's part of the reason I stayed with the Comanche so long. I think I felt guilty for having been brought up in a big hacienda with lots of money and servants. Somehow it didn't seem quite right, when I saw the Indians laboring in the fields or working at the mission. Maybe I was trying to ease my conscience a little."

"But it wasn't your fault you were born into a wealthy family."

"I know that, but still I felt guilty about it. I could never understand why we Spanish were supposed to be better than the Indians who were here long before us. It's never made sense to me. Neither has the way most of the rancheros have lived for so long. Most of them are rich, lazy bastards, living a life that is ready to pass them by. I'm beginning to think the gold rush was a good thing."

"But why? I've heard you say you don't want any foreigners here."

"I'm not sure how I feel. I don't think the Americanos and the foreigners have the right to come here and take land away from us that's been ours for years and years, but I think they do have a right to make a life for themselves. California is a vast land with room for lots of people."

"That doesn't sound like you. I thought you'd fight to the death for your land."

"I will. I'll fight anyone who tries to take the del Sol or the del Mar. But there is plenty of other land, and we can't stop the people from coming. All we can do is try to make a good life ourselves."

Lisa looked over at Eric as they rode away. He seemed to be changing in ways she hadn't noticed before. He was an intelligent man, knowledgeable on many subjects, but what surprised her the most was his acceptance of the way things were changing. As Nakon, he had fought fiercely against any change, but as Eric Anderson, he was a man capable of dealing with the changes wrought by time, people, and a new environment. He was completely different now, from the way he dressed to the way he spoke in English, and if their love was ever going to work, Lisa had to try to forget the past and accept Eric for the man he was now.

CHAPTER XVIII

"How would you like to have lunch on the beach?" Eric asked, pointing down a steep cliff.

"All the way down there?"

"Why not? You're the one who's so crazy about water. I thought maybe you'd like to see it up close."

"Isn't there a way we can ride down on the beach?"

"Farther on, but I'm hungry; I don't think I can wait another two miles. It's that hard to climb down. C'mon, we'll leave the horses here. Just follow me and we'll be down in no time.,"

"All right," Lisa said dubiously, and followed Eric's lead.

The path that led down to the beach was precarious in parts, but Lisa found it wasn't as bad as it looked from the top, and she made it with little trouble. Climbing back up would be the hard part. When they reached the shore they spread out a blanket and unpacked the lunch which Marta had packed for them. It was a warm, pleasant day, and after a filling lunch and a couple glasses of wine, Lisa felt very relaxed. She took off her shoes and stockings and went to wade in the water.

"Better be careful; don't go out too far. This isn't like swimming in a lake, the waves are stronger than they look. They can knock you down in a second."

"I'll be fine," Lisa yelled happily, running down to the water.

Eric watched as she picked up her skirt and ran along the water's edge. She looked like a child at play. One time, when she went out a little too far and turned to wave up at him, she was struck from behind by a large wave which knocked her face forward into the sand. She got up, completely soaked, her hair and dress sticking to her body. She walked up the beach to the blanket and looked at Eric, and he burst out laughing.

"Well, I just met the Pacific Ocean up close. Think I like it better from a distance—like way up that cliff! What am I going to do? I wanted to look so nice when I saw Don Alfredo. I knew I should've worn my buckskins."

"Well, you either walk up to your horse and get another dress from your bag or you take that one off and let it dry. It's a warm day, it shouldn't take too long," he said with a lazy smile. He was enjoying her discomfiture and he lay back in the sand watching her.

Lisa stared back at Eric, knowing by the amused look on his face that he was daring her, and feeling a bit reckless after the wine, she took the dare. Very slowly, she unbuttoned the tiny buttons on the bodice of the dress, slipping it off each shoulder and down the length of her body. She stood before him in her chemise and slips and looked directly at him, a challenge in her eyes. She removed each thing until she was clad only in her thin, satin chemise. For once, she appreciated her body and how it could arouse a man, especially Eric. She told herself it was just a game, that she was just playing with him, teasing him, but deep inside herself she knew the truth—she wanted him more than ever. She could see the desire in his face but he didn't do anything; he was fighting to control himself. She knew he was trying for her sake to control himself, especially after what had happened a few nights before, but she didn't care. She wanted him now; nothing else mattered. She knelt down next to him and pushed him back on the blanket, and she lay on top of him, molding the length of her body next to his. It was suddenly all-important to her to know that she excited him more than any other woman, that he desired her more than any other.

"Don't be foolish, Lisa. You know what'll happen." He tried to push her from him, but she wouldn't move.

She continued to move her body against his, kissing his face, throat, and chest. She unbuttoned his shirt and moved her fingers over his chest and down his hard stomach. She was intent on proving only one thing—that he couldn't find another woman anywhere who was as passionate and loving as she. She seemed to forget her resolve to forget Eric and marry Josh—there was only room for Eric in her life now.

He lay there passively, trying to ignore her, trying to pull away, but he felt himself responding to her lips and her touch. It wasn't like her to play the aggressive wanton.

"What do you want, Lisa? To bring me to the point of no control until I make love to you and then you can hate me all over again?" He sat up, holding her firmly by the shoulders. "Don't play games with me," he said firmly.

"I'm not playing games," Lisa responded, wrapping her arms around his neck. This time, Eric didn't fight her and he lay back down, pulling her down with him. He kissed her deeply, not understanding this sudden change in her, but not wanting to question it. He started to roll her over onto her back but he sat up suddenly.

"What's the matter?" Lisa asked incredulously.

"Be quiet," he said harshly, and laid his ear against the sand. "Get dressed, I think some riders are coming."

"But I didn't hear anything."

"Get dressed, damn it! I felt the vibration when I was lying down."

Lisa knew better than to doubt his word when he had lived with the Comanche for so long. She jumped up and quickly dressed in the cold, wet dress. Just as she started to button the bodice of her dress, she saw some riders in the distance. They were riding hard and fast. Eric, shielding his eyes from the sun, looked and counted six riders. He turned to Lisa.

"Sit down on the blanket and put this gun under your dress. Use it if you have to."

"But who are they?"

"I don't know. They could be friendly or they could be bandidos. We'll have to wait and see. Now do as I say." Lisa sensed trouble in his voice and did as she was told. He was reacting like a Comanche now, entirely on instinct.

The riders approached rapidly as Eric and Lisa sat watching. Eric was tense by Lisa's side, his hand on his knife. Before long, six men rode up to them, the man in front the obvious leader, in spite of his youth. He and Eric stared at each other for a long time before either spoke.

"Well, well, if it isn't Don Alejandro de Vargas come back from the dead. I thought as much when I saw the brand on the horse up there." He motioned up to the cliffs. "Back to claim your inheritance, eh bastardo?"

285

The man's glance shifted from Eric to Lisa, his dark eyes raking over the dress which clung so tightly to her breasts. "It looks like we have interrupted something, eh compadres?" They all laughed boisterously.

Lisa felt Eric's arm tense, but he showed no sign of emotion.

"Hello, Chuka, I heard you were around here. What's the matter, not enough people to steal from down in Mexico?"

Lisa looked at this man called Chuka. He was young, about Eric's age, with brown skin and black eyes. He wore a long-sleeved muslin shirt with buckskins and a kind of moccasin. He wore a type of gun belt slung across his chest and back, and he wore two pistols and a knife. When he turned his dark eyes to Lisa, she detected a terrible menace in them. She felt herself move closer to Eric. The man Chuka was cruel.

"I see your grandfather has told you about me. I've been leading some Indios and Mexicanos in raids against some of the bigger ranchos. I'm trying to get back what is ours in the first place. So far, I haven't raided the del Sol or the del Mar, but now you're back, I'll make it a point to do so."

"You're a pig, Chuka, and not much smarter than one. If you want to lead your people, why not do it civilly, without bloodshed? What're you accomplishing this way? The land is yours, the government has given it back. What good will all this do?"

"If I were you, de Vargas, I'd be careful what you say to me. After all, there are six of us and only one of you. And as for the land, how can we fight both the rancheros and the Americano squatters, eh? We find it easier to take the cattle and horses we need, or any other supplies we want from the haciendas, including women." His eyes moved to Lisa. "Ah, such a lovely señorita. It has been a long time since I or my men have seen so lovely a woman. It wouldn't be difficult for us to hold you while we had our pleasure with her." Lisa looked at the man in front of her and for the first time, sensed his power. She wasn't sure what Eric could do against six men.

"Do you think I'd be so stupid as to ride out alone?" Eric lied. "There are ten vaqueros following us not fifteen minutes behind. I told them we were stopping here for lunch and to keep a lookout for bandidos. You wouldn't get very far."

Chuka laughed.

"Ah, de Vargas, you always had all the answers, didn't you? Always so smart and handsome and rich. Always first at everything, and very big with the women. I'm surprised you're with one so young, I thought you liked the older ones." Chuka spat bitterly.

Lisa looked over at Eric, watching the muscle twitch in his cheek. He was getting angry and she was afraid he'd do something rash.

"Don't expect me to feel sorry for you, Chuka; you had plenty of chances to change your life, but you always messed up. You were too stupid to see things as they really are."

"Too stupid, eh? Too stupid because I found out you and my mother were lovers? And when your mother found out she sent our family away from the only home we ever knew? I think it was you who was stupid, cabrón, because I will get my revenge yet."

"I thought you did that when you raped Consuelo."

"Ah, yes, sweet little Consuelo with the loving eyes. Well, I figured I could at least teach her a few things before you took her to your marriage bed." Chuka laughed loudly.

Lisa was engrossed by the conversation between the two men. It was obvious that they hated each other and that Eric had been Chuka's mother's lover. How old had he been? And was he also in love with Consuelo then? There were still so many unanswered questions. She listened again to the conversation.

"She was so young and sweet then," Chuka continued, "like a frightened little doe. She kept calling your name, you know."

Eric got up and walked to Chuka's horse, grabbing it by the bridle.

"You're a bastard, Chuka, and you're also a coward. Why didn't you take it out on me rather than on an innocent girl?"

"Are you challenging me, de Vargas?"

Eric wanted to say yes, but he thought of Lisa. If something happened to him and he lost the fight, there was no way he could keep these wolves from her.

"Not now, but someday. We'll meet again, I'm sure. And you won't have these five men to back you up then."

"I won't need five men to back me up, cabrón. When we meet again, it will be for the last time." His look passed to Lisa and again his eyes raked her body in a crude manner. "And when I'm finished with you, I'll be sure to look after your lovely señorita here. I will teach her what it's like to have a real man."

His words struck home, and Eric reached up and grabbed Chuka's arm.

"Listen, you son of a bitch," he said, his voice low and menacing, "if you ever go near her or even touch her, I'll kill you. I swear I'll track you down and I'll find you,

Chuka. And when I do, you'll wish I hadn't.''

Chuka reined in his horse, pulling his arm free from Eric's iron grip.

"Your threats don't bother me, de Vargas. It's you who should be careful; you're the one who has so much to lose. And as for you, señorita, we shall meet again. I promise you that." He looked at Lisa once more, then he and his men were off as quickly as they had come.

Eric turned around and looked glaringly at Lisa.

"Get your things," he barked angrily. Lisa felt that part of his anger was directed at her, although she couldn't understand why. She quickly gathered up the rest of her things and repacked the basket. Eric had the blanket and was halfway up the path before he stopped. Lisa was having difficulty making it up the steep embankment, but she wouldn't ask him for help. Finally, seeing that she was in some trouble, he walked back and extended his hand to help her up the rest of the way. In a few minutes, they were mounted and riding toward the Rancho del Mar.

Lisa knew better than to question Eric when he was in such a foul temper, but her curiosity was getting the better of her. What was it that connected Eric, Chuka, and Consuelo? A slight shiver ran through her when she thought of the way Chuka had looked at her. He had such cruel eyes, the kind that belonged to a man who was capable of inflicting great pain on others. She hoped to God that she never met him again, and especially that he and Eric didn't meet again. She knew that if they did, it would be a fatal meeting for one or the other. The thought of Chuka taking his pleasure with her made her stomach turn and she thought of the Comanche who had raped her. She hadn't thought about it in a long time, she realized, but it was still as terrifyingly clear to her as if it had happened yesterday. If it hadn't been for Nakon . . .

She looked over at Eric riding so straight on his paint, his jaw clenched tightly, not willing to open himself to her as he had earlier in the day. She wondered why he and Chuka hated each other so much. There were still so many things she didn't know about him. She had only known him for such a short period of time in the Comanche camp, but Consuelo had known him as a child; they had grown up together. And had they been lovers even then? Despair settled over her. She had really hoped, had even thought for a while that day that things were going to change between them, but things were still the same; they would always be the same. The desire was there but there was no love. And after the desire was gone there would be nothing left without love.

She saw the familiar outline of the Rancho del Mar in the distance and she had a sudden sense of well-being and warmth. It would be good to see Don Alfredo and Raytahnee again and perhaps here, she and Eric could resolve something of their future together. She needed to know once and for all how he really felt about her.

CHAPTER XIX

Don Alfredo hadn't seemed surprised when he had received his grandson's note, and was extremely glad to see him and Lisa when they rode up. Eric was still in a bad mood and after a few terse words to his grandfather, he excused himself saying he wanted to go for a swim. Don Alfredo went into the garden room and sat down.

"Are things any better between you two?" Don Alfredo asked Lisa directly.

"Not much."

"You know, my dear, there was a time when my daughter and my grandson were very loving to each other, a typical mother and son. But as Sandro grew older and more independent, they began to clash with each other. The boy idolized his father and wanted to go to sea with him, but Mariz absolutely refused to let a son of hers become a common seaman. He was to be educated by the Franciscans and then sent to Spain or Mexico for a formal education. On this Sandro's father agreed—he wanted his son to have a good education. But he said that when the boy was old enough to decide for himself, he would have his father's permission to go to sea. Mariz still kept trying to mold Sandro into a true Spanish aristocrat, but Sandro rebelled. He did his lessons, but his free time was spent with his father on his ship in the harbor. If his father was at sea, Sandro spent his time with his friends roaming around the countryside, or with me. One of his friends was an Indian boy, a son of one of Mariz's servants. Mariz felt that the boy was a bad influence on Sandro and not the type of company he should be keeping. She forbade them to see each other."

"What was the boy's name."

"His name was Chukando, but Sandro always called him Chuka."

"Chuka," Lisa said pensively.

"Yes. The boy was rebellious and wild, but no more so than was Sandro. They were great friends all of their young lives until something happened which split them apart, I fear, forever." Don Alfredo sighed deeply, as if reliving the whole experience over again.

"While Sandro was going through this bad time with his mother, his father came home for a short time before leaving again on a trip to the Orient and Hawaii. Sandro was very excited about it and he had talked his father into taking him on the trip with him. He told his father that the trip would be an education in itself. But Mariz refused and as always, she got her way. She told her husband that if he took Sandro on the trip, she would tell the boy about all the other women he had had for years. Not willing to be belittled in his son's eyes, Eric gave in to his wife. Sandro remained here. It was on this trip that Eric was killed. Sandro blamed his mother. Had his father delayed his departure for a week, as he had planned to do if Sandro had joined him, the *Adventurer* would have missed the violent hurricane which dismasted and sank her off the coast of Mexico. Quién sabe? But Sandro felt that Mariz had killed his father as surely as if she had killed him with her own hands."

"Was it then that he left and joined the Comanche?"

"No, that was a little later. He stayed for a while, delighting in punishing his mother in every way he could. He was in terrible pain and the only way he could excise it was by lashing out at the person he thought caused it, and by seeking solace elsewhere."

"With you?"

"No, with a woman—an older woman." Here Don Alfredo paused, clearing his throat, as though embarrassed to tell Lisa the rest of the story.

"The older woman was Chuka's mother. She was still a fairly young and beautiful woman, though older than Sandro, and the mother of his best friend. Sandro was always at their hut, and so, it had been a natural place to go when he was hurting. At the age of sixteen, Sandro was very mature and physically he looked like a man of twenty. The night he found out about his father's death he went to the hut, intending to talk with Chuka, but Chuka was off somewhere and he visited with Nora, Chuka's mother. They talked, drank some wine, and before long, Nora was comforting Sandro in the only way she knew how—by making love to him. He was young, hurting, and seeking comfort from this woman because he couldn't seek it from his own mother. It was while they were asleep together on the bed that Chuka came back. He went into a rage, calling his mother a whore and trying to kill Sandro with the knife Sandro had given him for his eleventh birthday. They struggled and Nora's screams were heard by some of the vaqueros who came in and broke up the fight. Somehow Mariz found out about it and Nora and Chuka and the rest of the children were immediately sent away to Mexico, to some distant relatives of ours. It was the excuse Mariz needed to have

Chuka out of Sandro's life. Chuka swore revenge on Sandro, saying that if it took the rest of his life, he would get back at Sandro for what he had done." Don Alfredo stopped again, wiping his forehead with a handkerchief. "Chuka got his revenge before he left. He raped the young girl to whom Sandro was betrothed. They were to marry when Sandro turned eighteen."

"The girl, who was she?" Lisa asked tentatively.

"Consuelo," Don Alfredo said sadly. "In those days she was such a sweet girl, not at all like the woman she is now. She idolized Sandro when they were children and dreamed only of becoming his wife and the patrona of the Rancho del Sol. But after what Chuka did to her she was totally shamed and humiliated, and her parents sent her away to a convent in Mexico. She was only thirteen at the time. While she was in Mexico, both of her parents and her two older brothers were killed. She has been all alone since then."

"My God," Lisa said in a surprised voice, "I think perhaps I've judged Consuelo too harshly. It seems she's been through more than I realized."

Don Alfredo reached out and took Lisa's hand.

"And what of you, my dear, have you not also been through too much for a young girl? Yet, it doesn't seem to have jaded you the way it has Consuelo. You are a very forgiving person, Lisa."

"Please, Don Alfredo, don't give me undue credit. I only feel sorry for Consuelo; it doesn't mean I like her. But I know what it's like to be all alone in the world. It's a terribly frightening thing." She stopped, thinking back to the time in the Comanche camp before Eric helped her. It had been frightening, degrading, and humiliating, and she had felt such futility. She turned back to Don

Alfredo. "But what of Eric? What did he do when he found out what Chuka had done to Consuelo?"

"Sandro wanted to kill Chuka, but he and his mother had already left for Mexico; there was nothing he could do. And Consuelo was being sent away without being allowed to say good-bye to Sandro. His young life was falling apart, and he blamed his mother for all of it. It was at this point that he left."

Lisa shook her head, trying to take it all in.

"No wonder there's such hatred between Chuka and Eric."

"You know of Chuka?"

"We met him on the way here. He was with a small group of men. He and Eric talked and Chuka swore he'd kill Eric. I didn't understand then what it was all about. He scared me. There was a certain look in his eyes, a certain cruelty, as if he'd stop at nothing to accomplish his goal."

"Yes, he's been back here awhile. He and some bandidos from Mexico have been raiding ranchos. Well, we shall see what happens. Chuka was not totally to blame. He was a wild boy, but he was basically good. He too, was a victim of circumstances."

"And what about Consuelo? Had she been in the convent all this time?" Lisa couldn't believe that a woman like Consuelo had been raised in a convent.

Lisa watched as a frown appeared on Don Alfredo's forehead.

"Her family was killed when she was seventeen years old. As she was the only heir to the family fortune, she returned here to clear up the financial matters. After that, she was a very rich young woman. She went back to Mexico, but not to the convent. She went to Mexico City and Monterey, and when she grew tired of it there, she went to Spain, Paris, and different parts of Europe. She came back to Monterey only a year ago. She never married, she told me, because she was waiting for Sandro to come back. She said there were never any men to compare with him, and she had known many in the past years. When I pointed out to her that she hadn't even known Sandro as a man, only as a boy, she said if he was strong as a boy then he was even more so as a man."

"After almost ten years she was still in love with him? That's incredible."

"Yes, but I don't believe it's a mature love. She still thinks of the feelings they had for each other as children; she refuses to admit that things have changed or they have grown up."

Lisa shifted nervously in her seat, finally getting up enough courage to ask Don Alfredo the question which had been troubling her.

"Don Alfredo, if they had been betrothed as children, are they still betrothed? I've heard that these marriage contracts are very binding, a matter of honor."

"The contracts are only binding if both parties agree to them when they come of age. In the olden days children always did as their parents wished and married the people whom their parents chose for them. But it is different now. Children do as they please. The betrothal was originally made to tie in all of the de Vargas and Morena land, to have one vast holding between the two families. It was thought to be an excellent match, although Sandro's father completely opposed it. But Mariz went ahead and signed the contract, betrothing the young ones. But the contract is no longer valid. Consuelo is hanging on to a dream. You see, Sandro saved her from further rape by Chuka's friends. Sandro heard Consuelo's screams coming from the small hut where the three of them had played together. Chuka had raped Consuelo and was urging some of the other boys to take their turns with her, but Sandro burst in, a rifle in his hand and chased them off. He helped Consuelo and when he went looking for Chuka later he was gone. So you see, Consuelo still thinks of Sandro as her savior, her shining knight."

Thinking of her own experiences, Lisa couldn't help but wonder what emotional scars Consuelo had. How would something like that affect a girl of thirteen. Eighteen had been bad enough, but thirteen? And Eric— he had been her savior too, just as he had been Consuelo's. Could she then blame Consuelo for the strong feelings of love and devotion she had for Eric?

"What are you thinking, my dear?"

"Oh, just that Eric saved me too. He took me out of a horrible situation and gave me back my pride. I had never met such a gentle man in my life, so ready to give of himself and ask nothing in return . . ." Lisa stopped, embarrassed by having revealed so much of her feelings to Don Alfredo.

"But you helped Sandro too. When he left here, there was no room in his heart for love—only bitterness, hatred, and revenge. You showed him how to love again."

Lisa looked up at the old man, her eyes misting over.

"It was so different then, Don Alfredo. He was such a different man then."

"Of course he was different then, my dear. It was a different time, a different place, and a different set of circumstances. Don't make the mistake of expecting him

297

to be the warrior Nakon. Part of him is Nakon and I expect will always be, but the major part of him is Eric Anderson, the man he is now. You must learn to accept him as he is now and quit comparing him to what he was. Unfortunately, he too is having to struggle with that."

Lisa considered what Don Alfredo had just said to her, something that she had thought about on the ride here. Perhaps she was making the mistake of wanting things the way they were in the Comanche camp—simple and uncomplicated. But life wasn't like that and the sooner she accepted that fact, the better. Things were different now, and she had to face up to the reality of the situation.

Don Alfredo reached out and took Lisa's hand.

"Why don't you go up and rest? You must be tired. I'll have a bath sent up before dinner. We can talk again later."

"Thank you, Don Alfredo, it's easy to see why Eric loves you so much." She leaned over and kissed him on the cheek and went up to her room.

Don Alfredo watched her as she left the room. He thought she was one of the most beautiful young women he had ever seen, yet she seemed so natural and unaffected. He liked that in a woman, especially one of beauty. He shook his head in annoyance. Why was it young people always wasted time, precious time? Now were the best times of their lives, yet they were both so stubborn.

He rested his head against the back of his chair and closed his eyes. He thought of his beautiful Amparo. If only they had had one more year together, one more month even. They had not wasted their time together. They had taken advantage of every moment, had lived life to its fullest. He reached up to brush a stray tear from his cheek. Such a shame that youth was wasted on the young.

Lisa did her best to make a good impression at dinner. She dressed with great care in a yellow silk gown that fell off the shoulders, and which had a rounded, low-cut bodice. Cream-colored lace ran across the edging of the bodice and sleeves, and encircled the hem of the rounded skirt bottom. The dress fit tightly across her small breasts and did justice to her narrow waist and flat stomach. She patted the soft material, swishing the skirt around. She didn't believe in corsets and stays and yards of petticoats, so that long skirt fell smoothly against her slim figure, enhancing its lines. She pulled her hair back loosely with a yellow ribbon, and for the first time in a long while, she wore comfortable slippers which matched the dress. When she walked into the garden room that evening, she noticed the look of surprise on Eric's face—he was still not used to seeing her in anything but buckskins. She thought he looked pleased. He walked over to her, bowed deeply, and kissed her hand.

"You look lovely tonight, Lisa. It's a good thing no other ladies are present; you would put them to shame."

She smiled, her green eyes sparkling brightly.

"Thank you, sir, and might I say how handsome you look this evening, also?"

They both turned at the sound of Don Alfredo's footsteps.

"I am sorry to interrupt you, but it is time for dinner. It is now my turn to compliment you, señorita; you are a vision of loveliness. May I escort you in to dinner?"

Lisa extended her arm to Don Alfredo.

"I would be honored, señor."

It was a leisurely dinner, Don Alfredo animatedly telling Lisa stories about Eric as a child, and the scrapes he invariably got himself into. Lisa was slightly disappointed at the news that Raytahnee would be gone for a few days; she was staying with Miguel Figueroa's family, but the evening was entirely enjoyable for her, nevertheless. It was later, while they were having their dessert, that Don Alfredo made an announcement.

"I have decided I shall have a big fiesta here, like the old days, Sandro."

"But you haven't had a fiesta like that in years, abuelo. One night is fine, but three or four days is tiring. Are you sure you're up to it?"

"Of course I am up to it. Besides, I will have help," he said mischievously, smiling at Lisa. "Lisa will be here to help me."

"Of course, Don Alfredo, I'll come over to help you plan," Lisa said cordially.

"No, my dear, I thought you might just stay here until the fiesta. It would save you the trouble of riding the distance back and forth. After all, it will only be a little over three weeks." He looked at Eric and Lisa over the rim of his wine glass and smiled. Maybe some time apart would bring them to their senses.

"There will be so many plans to make," he continued, "and I will need your help most every day. I'm sure my daughter won't attend, so I can't ask for her help. And Raytahnee is always off with Miguel. What do you say? Would you deny an old man such a small favor?" Don Alfredo studiously ignored his grandson's frown.

Lisa looked over at Eric, unable to read the expression on his face. She didn't like the thought of being away from him for so long, especially when she had decided to try to work things out with him. But she couldn't say no to Don Alfredo either, not after he had been so kind to her. She looked back at Don Alfredo.

"Of course, I'll be glad to stay. I'd enjoy spending some time with you and Raytahnee."

Don Alfredo smiled smugly, looking over at Eric.

"Good, then it is settled. And you, Sandro, will have to get back to the del Sol soon, no? It's very dangerous to be gone from it too long. There is so much going on with the squatters and such."

"You know I can't stay here very long," Eric grumbled, quickly downing his glass of wine and pouring another.

"Well, I remember how bored you were as a child when it came to planning the fiestas. You were always off somewhere else when your help was needed. I'm sure you still feel the same way, no? You would probably prefer being off with your horses and cattle," Don Alfredo said casually, enjoying watching his grandson's uneasiness. "All right then, we'll expect you three days before the ball, in time for all the games and races. You will race this year, won't you?"

"Of course I will. It's about time I showed these gentlemen how to really ride a horse. For some reason, they have the impression that they're the only people in the world who can ride a horse. I don't think they've every heard of the Comanche."

Lisa looked up excitedly.

"What kind of a race is it?"

"The one we are talking about is the long-distance race, but we also have many races in which the men show their skill and daring."

"Can anyone enter these races? A woman, I mean?"

Lisa asked, ignoring Eric's glare.

Eric shook his head and looked at her in understanding.

"Oh, no you don't, you won't enter that race."

Don Alfredo laughed.

"Women don't normally enter the races, but there is no rule against it. I myself, think it would add a touch of excitement to the race, don't you, Sandro?" he asked his grandson innocently.

"You're crazy to even think of it," Eric said angrily. "You'll get yourself killed or badly hurt. This isn't like riding out on the open plains, Lisa, it's hard, fast, and grueling. And also very dangerous." He stopped for a moment, thinking to himself, then he spoke again. "Just what horse were you planning to ride, may I ask?"

Lisa looked at him defiantly.

"You know very well that I can ride a horse almost as well as you, if not as well. And as for the horse, I will ride Vida, of course."

Eric stared at her openmouthed and then burst out laughing.

"God, you are crazy. You haven't even been on his back and you expect to ride him in this race."

"Well, I haven't exactly seen you ride him around the range, either. At least he allows me near him. which is more than I can say for you. And you have no idea of the progress I've made with him. If you'll let Hector bring him to me here, I promise you that I'll ride him in that race," she said bravely.

A wicked smile slowly spread across Eric's face.

"Would you care to make a little wager on that, sweet lady?"

"Anything you like," Lisa said confidently.

Eric thought for a moment, drumming his fingers against the tabletop.

"You make the stakes," he said suddenly.

"All right. If I win I get to keep Vida for my own. If you win, he's still yours. Willing to take a chance on the stallion?"

"Oh, I'm willing, but shouldn't we up the stakes just a little? I want them to be worthwhile. After all, you're betting with something that already belongs to me."

Lisa looked at Eric disconcertedly.

"But I haven't got anything . . ."

Eric leaned forward on the table, his white teeth showing brightly against his dark skin.

"That's where you're wrong, Lisa."

"Well, what do you propose then?" she asked hesitantly.

"Ah, a good choice of words. I propose that, if you win the race, you get the horse and marriage to me." Lisa drew her breath in sharply, but Eric continued. "But if I win, I get the horse and you. And I mean just you—no strings attached, no marriage."

Lisa looked at him silently, embarrassed that Don Alfredo was witness to the wager. She thought of Josh and his imminent arrival. What if she won the wager? Worse still, what if she lost?

"Scared?" She heard the mocking tone in Eric's voice.

"Don't be so damned arrogant, you haven't won the race yet."

"Well then, is it a bet?"

Lisa looked at Don Alfredo then back at Eric, sighing deeply.

"Yes, it's a bet," she said with more confidence than she felt.

"Good, I'll be looking forward to it," Eric said cheerfully, and raised his glass up. "Shall we drink a toast to it?"

Lisa lifted her glass, clinking it against Eric's, and meeting his inscrutable eyes. She wondered how she could have bet with anything so precious as her life. How had she let herself get talked into it? It seemed that he had disarmed her again, just as he had been doing since they had met, just as he would continue to do until . . . until what? she wondered sadly. Unfortunately, that was something she didn't know the answer to, and was almost afraid to find out.

CHAPTER XX

Next day, Eric left the del Mar, promising Lisa that he'd send Hector over with Vida the following day. He even offered to let Lisa use Hector for the next three weeks, saying laughingly, that she would need all the help she could get.

Even though they were in bantering moods, Lisa was sad watching him ride off after only a chaste kiss on the cheek. Her mind was a whirlwind of confusion. She had told him she wouldn't be his whore, yet on the way here, she'd practically seduced him on the beach. And if she lost the bet, she would be his mistress, and no backing out would be allowed by Eric. The only thing she could do was put all of her effort into making Vida an excellent mount by the time of the race.

Lisa and Don Alfredo spent the rest of that day walking in the gardens, going for a buggy ride around the rancho, and having a picnic. She asked him if her bet with Eric had offended him.

"I am too old and have lived too long to be offended by many things. On the contrary, I find your wager exciting. You are both so proud, it will be interesting to see how the loser fares, if indeed, there is a loser."

They started that day making plans for the fiesta. Lisa was to write out all the invitations herself. She noticed that Tom was on the guest list, but not Mariz.

"Don Alfredo, you said last night that Mariz probably wouldn't be coming to the fiesta? Why?"

A great sadness clouded Don Alfredo's eyes as he answered, "My daughter has not spoken to me since Sandro left ten years ago; she will probably never speak to me again. She found out that he had come to say good-bye to me before he left and that I heard from him later on. When she asked me to tell her where he had gone, I would not; I had promised Sandro. She doesn't know that he lived with the Comanche all that time. I just told her that he was well and happy in his new life. She never forgave me for not telling her where he was so she could bring him back, just as Sandro hasn't forgiven her. It is a sad legacy for our family, no? So much hatred and bitterness," he said sadly, shaking his head.

"I'm so sorry. Maybe I can understand the bitterness between Eric and Mariz, but I don't understand the way they've put you in the middle. It's not fair."

"You are very close to your family then?"

"No, and I didn't mean to judge yours. It's just that you are all alive and well and together again. It seems sad that you can't end the bitterness between you. But as I said before, I have no room to judge. Tom is my only family now, besides Raytahnee. He and I have always been close, especially since my father died. We were all a close family while papa was still alive, but when he died, mother remarried. It was never the same with my stepfather. She married into high society, and it was a place where both Tom and I felt uncomfortable. Mother is a good person and I do love her because she's my mother, but we haven't been close for years. I was always a constant source of embarrassment to her, it seems.

306

Anyway, that's why I came here after I was traded from the Comanche—I had no other choice."

"Well, at least there is no bitter hatred between you and your mother. Be thankful for that. Now, Tom and Mariz should be back from Mexico in a week or two. We can ask Tom if he'd like to stay here until the fiesta, would you like that?"

"Very much. We didn't have much of a chance to visit before he and Mariz left for Mexico. I think Tom is coming back alone. He told me Mariz planned to stay on for a while and visit friends."

"It's just as well."

"Why, would Mariz be angry with Tom for coming?"

"Tom is a very independent man, as I'm sure you know. He has come here many times to help me with the title to my land, something Mariz had him do. I think she still loves her papa, but is too proud to admit it. Ah, but about Tom. I think the reason he appeals to Mariz is because he is his own man and he doesn't ask her permission for anything. She is so used to controlling the people around her that Tom is a constant challenge to her."

"Do you think that they will ever marry, Don Alfredo?"

"I would be very surprised if they did," he replied hesitantly. "My daughter has strong opinions, not the least of which is that Spaniards shouldn't marry Americanos. And, according to law, all of her property would pass to her husband if she married and Mariz would never give up the del Sol, not for anyone. Pardon the bluntness, but Mariz may have a gringo lover but she would never marry one."

"But what of her husband, Eric's father? He was

an Americano."

"Yes, but she would never make that mistake again."

"Mistake? Did she feel it was a mistake to marry him?"

"Of course. She feels the main reason Sandro turned out the way he did was because of the mixture of Spanish and Americano blood. Unfortunately, a very narrow-minded attitude. She refuses to accept the fact that she was just as responsible for his behavior as any blood he may have inherited. My daughter is a very stubborn and bitter woman. She has the mistaken belief that because she is Spanish and wealthy, she is better than other people in the world. She is not at all like her mother was. But I suppose that is my fault. I always spoiled her because she was the only child we could have." He sighed deeply. "Shall we get on with the list?" Lisa nodded and continued to write as Don Alfredo dictated, an empty feeling in her heart because she couldn't say anything which would comfort the old man.

The days passed surprisingly fast for Lisa. She missed Eric more than she thought possible, but in getting to know Don Alfredo better, she felt she was really getting to know a part of Eric. True to his word, Eric sent Hector over with Vida the day following his departure. Lisa decided to keep Hector at the del Mar. In this at least, Eric was right—she needed Hector's expertise.

Lisa and Hector worked each morning with Vida from breakfast until lunch, and then again for a couple of hours in the afternoon. By the end of the first week, Vida was allowing Lisa to ride for short distances on his back before he became restless. Hector told her to be patient, that each day would make the stallion more trusting. The rest of Lisa's days were spent making plans with Don Alfredo for the fiesta, talking with him, and reading to him. Don Alfredo enjoyed hearing some of his favorite novels read in the original Spanish, and Lisa and Raytahnee would read to him until he fell asleep in his chair. It was after one of these times while Don Alfredo was napping, that Lisa got up and opened the doors to the garden. Now and again her thoughts wandered back to why Eric had sent her away from the camp. Raytahnee had told her a little, but she still did not understand how he could send her away and then appear here months later. She realized she had never given him a chance to explain.

"Something troubling you my dear?"

Lisa turned around at the sound of Don Alfredo's voice.

"I'm still plagued by a certain thought—why Eric came back here when he swore to me he'd never leave the Comanche. I even suggested to him at one point that we come out west together, but he got very angry with me and told me he'd never leave his people."

"Did Sandro explain to you why he left?"

Lisa dropped her eyes in embarrassment.

"I never really gave him a chance to explain. I only know what Raytahnee told me, that he'd been leading a raid and was ambushed and almost all of his men were killed. He felt responsible and asked for a meeting of the high council and then he left the tribe."

"Sandro thought he would stay with the tribe forever; he was not lying to you about that. Even though he loved you, he knew it was best for you to go to California to your brother and for him to remain with the Comanche."

"But I heard he was killed. My friend told me the chief, Nakon, had been killed."

"Sandro thinks that it was one of his young warriors.

He greatly admired his chief, Nakon, and when they were ambushed, the young warrior jumped on Nakon's horse and rode through the small camp yelling 'Nakon' as a tribute to his chief. The rangers evidently took it the wrong way, assuming the young brave was Nakon. Sandro remembers that they killed and scalped him, something the rangers don't normally do."

"It doesn't sound like the Nakon I remember, to be so careless. I can't believe he and his men were ambushed."

"He was haunted by his decision to send you away and found it wasn't as easy to live without you as he thought. The only way he had of venting his anger and frustration was through leading raids against his enemies. He was a driven man. When he knew he had failed the tribe, he expected to be punished. He would never have asked them for permission to leave because he felt he owed them too much for having saved his life and taken him into the tribe. That was why he told you he could never leave. He really felt that way at the time."

"I never gave him the chance to explain; I didn't want to listen to him."

"You felt betrayed and angry, no? But I think it is time you both put the past behind you and thought about the future. You both have so much to give each other. You are wasting so much time."

"You planned this fiesta on purpose, didn't you?" Lisa asked with a twinkle in her eye. "You wanted us to be apart so we'd be forced to think about each other. Did anyone ever tell you you're a sly old fox, Don Alfredo?" Lisa laughed along with Don Alfredo.

"You have found me out, my dear."

"Don Alfredo," Lisa said seriously, "if I should lose the race . . ."

"Don't worry yourself about it. I think you underestimate my grandson. He is a proud man, yes, but I think he is also an honorable man. I believe he will do the right thing." He put his arm around Lisa. "Come now, let's go for a walk."

Lisa smiled, but she really didn't feel as confident as Don Alfredo that Eric would do the right thing. What if Eric felt that the right thing was to keep her as his mistress and marry someone else, maybe even Consuelo. Oh, damn, she thought, will I never learn to keep my mouth shut?

Lisa looked down at the rolling valley then over at the other riders. Miguel and Raytahnee were chattering furiously, and Miguel's cousin, Francisco, was describing Santa Barbara to Lisa. This was the eighth day in a row she had gone riding with all of them and she was quickly growing tired of it. She didn't have much free time now, and in the time she did have she enjoyed taking a ride by herself or with Raytahnee. But Raytahnee had wanted her to get to know Miguel so Lisa had acquiesced. She found that it was a good opportunity to get Vida used to riding with the other horses, as he spooked so easily.

"I think you would like Santa Barbara, Señorita Jordan," Francisco said loudly.

"I beg your pardon, señor, I wasn't listening," Lisa said absentmindedly.

"I said, I think you would like Santa Barbara. It is a beautiful city, built next to the ocean like Monterey. Do you think you will ever visit there?"

"No, I don't think so. I don't know anyone there," Lisa replied uneasily.

"But you know me. I would find it a great pleasure if

311

you would visit me and my family there. We are very wealthy and would show you a most pleasurable time. Surely, one as beautiful as yourself would enjoy the attentions of all the caballeros who . . ."

"Señor, I have no intention of going to Santa Barbara," Lisa said impatiently. "And I really don't care about all the rich caballeros there either." She nudged Vida with her knees and he galloped off. Francisco watched in amazement as the huge palomino and the slim young woman took off down the valley. He wasn't sure which shocked him more, the fact that the beautiful young señorita had spurned his attentions, something which had never been done before, or the fact that she rode the stallion so well.

When Lisa got back to the hacienda, she took Vida to the stables and rubbed him down, and then went inside to her room, slamming the door behind her. The nerve of some men, she thought. What made him think that she was even interested in him? Just because he was rich and from a good family he thought he could get anything he wanted out of her. Well, she was tired of him and men like him. She needed to be around a real man for a change. She smiled suddenly, aware of what she'd just thought. Eric was a real man, in every way that counted. If only . . .

"Francisco is a little confused," Raytahnee said laughingly, as she walked into Lisa's room. "He can't understand why he hasn't won you over completely."

"Don't get me started again, Raytahnee. Damned arrogant fool if you ask me."

"You don't have to tell me, I have to spend every day with him. I can't wait for him to return to Santa Barbara." Raytahnee walked over to the bed and sat

312

down next to Lisa. "You know, Francisco finds you more of a challenge than ever now. How did he put it? You're as elusive as a butterfly." She looked over at Lisa, waiting for a reaction, then they both burst into gales of laughter.

"I miss him so much, Raytahnee," Lisa said, suddenly serious.

"I know you do. It won't be long now and you will be together. I think your wager was a foolish idea, but at least it will force you both to realize that you belong together."

"I hope you're right. I'm just so tired of waiting." She sighed deeply.

"Well, there's always Francisco to take your mind off things."

"Oh, you," Lisa laughed while throwing a pillow at Raytahnee. "What would I ever do without you?"

Eric was lonely without Lisa. He kept very busy during the day running the rancho, but his nights were almost unbearable. He'd gotten used to having Lisa around, even though they fought most of the time when they were together. The big hacienda seemed empty without her. He refused to eat in the large dining room alone, and most of the time wound up in his study with a large glass of brandy instead of dinner. He nearly rode over to the del Mar a couple of times, but decided against it at the last moment—he wanted Lisa to have to wait the time out as he had to do. He came to a certain realization in those weeks without Lisa, something his grandfather had wanted him to find out—that he couldn't lose Lisa again. They were too much a part of each other now; they had shared too much.

Consuelo visited Eric again, as always, uninvited. Eric

was cold toward her and he made no further attempts to continue their physical relationship, although Consuelo proved often enough that she was more than willing to do so. She followed him around the hacienda at night, making excuses to talk to him or be with him, but he tried to occupy his time in his study going over accounts or reading. Consuelo didn't seem to be deterred by his coolness, however.

Eric was going over some papers at his desk, trying to make some sense of the figures which he was just now getting to be familiar with again, when Consuelo walked in. She was wearing a sheer nightgown of light blue gauze. She walked in quietly, closing the door behind her, leaning sensually against it, her nakedness showing through the sheer material. Eric looked up when he heard her laugh and was shocked to see her standing there so scantily clad. He hadn't expected her to be quite so obvious.

"Hello, querido."

"What in hell do you think you're doing, Consuelo? What if one of the servants sees you?"

She walked over to him, leaning over and wrapping her arms around his neck.

"Don't be angry with me querido, I just wanted to show you the new negligee I bought. I got it especially for you. It's the latest style from Paris."

Eric stood up, taking Consuelo's arms from around his neck.

"Damn it, I don't care where it comes from or what style it is. You shouldn't be running around here like that."

"But I thought it would please you," she said sulkily.

"Don't you understand? I don't want you to please me.

314

Frankly, it doesn't matter a bit to me what you do."

Consuelo looked at him, a puzzled expression on her face.

"I don't understand. I thought we were going to be married. You do love me, don't you?"

Eric softened suddenly, watching the hurt that appeared in Consuelo's eyes. He remembered that it was because of him that Consuelo had been raped by Chuka and sent off to a convent. If it hadn't been for him maybe her life would've been different. He felt guilty for having toyed with her emotions in such a way, especially when she was vulnerable where he was concerned. He reached out and took her hands in his, his voice assuming a gentler tone.

"I never told you I loved you; I was honest with you from the beginning. You were the one who kept talking of love and marriage, not I. I don't love you, Consuelo, I love someone else. I love her very much."

Consuelo pulled her hands from Eric's and walked away from him.

"It's that girl, isn't it? That Indian whore staying with your grandfather. Has she more tricks than I when it comes to lovemaking, eh Sandro?" she screamed bitterly.

"Don't talk about her like that," he said, his voice suddenly cold. "Lisa was the victim of the Comanche, just as you were Chuka's victim years ago."

"How touching. I suppose you plan to marry her? What has she to give you? She has no dowry, no land, no family to speak of. Why, she is even too skinny to be attractive."

"I like her skinny," he said in amusement. He stepped close to Consuelo and again took her hands. "I never meant to hurt you. I cared deeply for you when we were children and I care deeply for you now but . . ."

"Then surely you can learn to love me in time, Sandro. I have love enough for both of us."

"You aren't listening to me. I don't love you. I'm in love with Lisa and that is something which will never change. I hope to make her my wife someday. I am sorry, Consuelo, but that's the way it is."

She stepped back from him, roughly pulling her hands from his.

"Well, well, I see it all very clearly now. You come back and use me terribly and then toss me aside when you find someone new. I'll not forget this very easily, Sandro. You will pay for dishonoring me. And so will she."

"Don't get dramatic, Consuelo. If I remember correctly, it was you who seduced me, not the other way around."

"And who would believe that? You are the one who left your mother and rancho and then suddenly returned to claim it all after all these years. There are many around here who who don't trust or like you. I could make it very uncomfortable for you around here." She slowly walked to the door of the study, a thoughtful expression on her face. "You know, even now I could be carrying your child. Then what would you do? Leave me and your child out in the cold?"

"Don't try to make me feel guilty because it won't work. How would I know if the child were even mine?"

Consuelo stared at him, her eyes wide with horror.

"You're a bastard; your mother was right about you. You should have never come back. You'll regret you ever did," she screamed angrily, slamming the door as she stomped out.

When Eric woke up the next morning, Consuelo was

gone. He was glad that she had finally listened to him. He was sorry that he'd hurt her, but he couldn't continue to play games with her. There was room for only one woman in his life now, and that woman was Lisa. It wouldn't be long before they were together again, and this time he would make sure nothing split them apart.

Lisa walked through the courtyard, hearing voices in the garden room. She hurried her pace, thinking that it might be Eric, but instead, to her dismay, she found Consuelo. She started to turn around, but decided not to give Consuelo the satisfaction of knowing how much she bothered Lisa.

"Well, well, if it isn't the Indian squaw. Don't you ever get tired of those filthy clothes?" Consuelo asked sarcastically.

"Bastante!" Don Alfredo yelled. "I will not have you fighting with my guest in my home, Consuelo. You go too far."

"But Don Alfredo, those clothes . . ."

Lisa walked forward, standing in front of Consuelo.

"No, señorita, I don't tire of these clothes. I told you once before I feel more comfortable in these clothes than I ever would in those." She pointed to Consuelo's frilly dress. "Clothes don't make the person, Consuelo."

Consuelo laughed harshly.

"I suppose when you've spent so much time with savages, you really don't care how you look. If indeed, you ever really did care."

Lisa's cheeks burned red and she felt her hands shake. She ached to slap the impudent girl's face.

"There's a lot I would like to say to you, señorita, but I won't insult Don Alfredo in his home., If you would care to ride with me later, I'm sure we could discuss a great deal. You do ride, don't you?" Ignoring Consuelo's confusion, Lisa walked over to Don Alfredo. "I won't be working with Vida the rest of the day; I think we can both use a rest. I'm going upstairs to clean up and then we can get on with our plans later. Till then, señor." She walked out, purposely ignoring Consuelo. She walked to her room and slammed the door behind her, throwing her gloves and hat on the bed.

"Damn that bitch!" she yelled at the empty room. "Why do I let her get to me?"

As Lisa rested in the warm bath water, she thought of the race that was now only four days away. She and Vida had come a long way and she was sure that he'd be ready for the race. He was a magnificent creature and she hadn't seen many horses faster than he. He was a horse many a Comanche warrior would pay highly to own. Hector told her that he'd seen few horses with such a great driving stride. She wasn't underestimating Eric's ability as a horseman; he was one of the best she'd ever seen. Still, on a horse like Vida, she had a good chance to win the race.

Dressing with care, to avoid more scathing remarks from Consuelo, Lisa descended the stairs to the garden room. Don Alfredo was having a glass of wine when she entered. He looked up and smiled, offering her a glass.

"Are you tired?" Don Alfredo asked. Lisa nodded slightly, gratefully accepting the glass of wine. She sat down, sighing deeply as she did so.

"It all seems so silly, such a waste of time. A man and a woman shouldn't be together because of a bet, they should be together because they love each other and they want to be together. If I win I'll have a husband, but only because I won him in a bet. And if I lose, I become his mistress and he's free to marry whom he chooses. Maybe I should leave California; that might be the best thing for everyone concerned."

"What caused this change of heart? Surely not anything Consuelo may have said?"

"Oh, I don't know. Suddenly I don't feel so sure about things anymore."

"Are you sure it doesn't have to do with Consuelo?"

"Why should it?"

"I just thought she had been saying things to you again. I wish I had the heart to tell her not to come here, but her parents were such good friends of mine and she doesn't have any other family here. I still think of her as the sweet, innocent little girl she used to be."

"Don't worry about me, I can deal with Consuelo. And I think it's wonderful that you still feel so deeply for her."

"Good evening, Don Alfredo," Consuelo said, entering the room. "I hope I haven't kept you waiting." Lisa looked at Consuelo dressed in her rich green satin gown with her satin slippers and all her jewelry, and thought her to be overly dressed. But she supposed Consuelo didn't have much to do with all her money except spend it on clothes and jewelry and trips to Europe. She felt strange being around Consuelo, especially knowing that she and Eric had been betrothed as children, and more recently, had been lovers. But she still couldn't hate the woman. Consuelo had been through so much.

"So, you decided to dress for this evening. It's nice to see that you do have some clothes," Consuelo said rudely to Lisa. "Are we ready to dine, Don Alfredo? I feel I will faint at any moment if I don't get something in my

319

stomach." She turned and walked toward the dining room, followed by an amused Lisa and angry Don Alfredo.

After dinner, they all went outside for a short walk in the courtyard and shortly thereafter, Don Alfredo excused himself and went to bed. Lisa and Consuelo went back into the garden room. Lisa walked around the room nervously, knowing that Consuelo was going to confront her with some more lies, or more truths. She wished that Raytahnee hadn't gone to Miguel's for the evening.

"Tell me, señorita, what do you think of Sandro, Señor de Vargas?" Consuelo asked Lisa while eyeing her narrowly.

Lisa turned from the table where she was pouring herself a glass of wine.

"Eric?"

"Sí, do you know him very well?"

"How could I? I've only been here a short while."

"But you must have some opinion of him by now," Consuelo persisted.

Lisa squirmed under the woman's close scrutiny.

"I think he's a charming man and he's shown me the utmost courtesy and kindness."

"Is that all?" Consuelo asked sharply.

"What do you mean, is that all?" Lisa replied angrily.

"There's no need to get upset, señorita, I merely wanted to find out if there is anything between you two. That is all."

"And if there were?"

"Then, señorita, I would have to set you straight."

"I thought you did that once before."

"Well, evidently you didn't understand. You see, Sandro and I are going to be married. I don't know when, but you can be sure it will be soon. I have just come from a stay at the Rancho del Sol and Sandro made his intentions very clear to me. He is my lover and very soon, will be my husband."

"Did Eric ask you to marry him, or have you just imagined that he did?"

"I imagine nothing!" Consuelo yelled hotly. "He will marry me because I wish it to be so." She stood up, unaccountably unnerved by Lisa's remark. "I'm growing weary of this conversation. I must get my sleep so that I can be beautiful for the fiesta. Maybe Sandro and I will have an announcement to make then." She picked up her heavy skirts and walked past Lisa, the sound of the rich cloth rustling in the air.

Lisa sat rigid, unmoving for minutes. She couldn't believe Eric would marry Consuelo, not after he'd told her that he didn't love Consuelo. She wanted to believe Eric, but there was still a nagging doubt in her mind. She hadn't been with him for over three weeks. Who knows what could've happened between Consuelo and him in three weeks?

She put her fingers up to her temples and rubbed them vigorously. She was tired of the constant bickering that went on between her and Consuelo. She got up and poured herself a glass of brandy, drinking it down in one gulp. The hot liquid burned her throat and stomach as she coughed convulsively. How did men drink the vile stuff all the time, she wondered. She walked back to the chair and sat down, feeling the warmth of the brandy already spreading through her body.

"Soon he will be my husband," Consuelo had said. Was it true? Had Eric really asked her to marry him? She felt hurt and angry, but still she couldn't blame Eric if he still felt the need for Consuelo. If she had accepted him on his own terms rather than issuing an ultimatum, perhaps they'd be together right now. And there wouldn't be that foolish wager between them.

"Well, at least I still have my pride," she said to herself, knowing even as she said it that her pride didn't compensate for the warm feel of Eric's arms around her at night.

CHAPTER XXI

In the few days left before the fiesta, Lisa and Raytahnee helped supervise all the preparations. There were decorations such as vases of flowers and colored pottery to be set up around the courtyard, and torches to be placed in the yard in front of the hacienda and in the courtyard. Long trestle tables were brought out and covered with brightly colored tablecloths, and large candelabra were set in the middle of each table. Lisa still worked with Vida in the mornings and afternoons, but now it was solely to ride him as fast as she could, trying to increase his speed and stamina. There were to be many races of skill and speed, but the longest and most arduous was to be held on the day of the ball. It would be held at noon, before the afternoon meal, so the riders would be able to talk about the race with the other guests. The course would be laid out that morning so that no one would have a chance to ride it before the race.

Lisa hadn't decided what she was going to wear on the night of the ball, and sent for a trunk of the new clothes which Eric had bought for her. She looked through them all, finding them all attractive, but she didn't find one she thought was special enough. She thought of the green dress that Rebecca had made for her, but she had already worn that to Don Alfredo's other fiesta and she wanted something really special. She wanted to look as beautiful as possible on that night, no matter what the outcome.

Three days before the fiesta, Tom arrived, as well as many of the other invited guests. True to his word, Tom brought Lisa dozens of new dresses from Mexico City, as well as other feminine articles such as jewelry, shoes, and nightclothes. Excitedly, Lisa looked through everything, astounded by Tom's good taste, and it wasn't long before she found the gown for the night of the ball. It was simple but exquisite. The bodice was cut low and off the shoulder and was trimmed in delicate Brussels lace. White satin slippers matched the satin buttons on the back of the dress, and a white lace shawl matched the lace edging. Lisa smiled as she thought of wearing white on the night she might possibly become Eric's mistress—it was an ironic situation.

After Lisa was done unpacking the new clothes, she and Tom went for a ride and she told him she was entering the big race. He tried to talk her out of it by telling her how grueling it was, but she refused to be deterred. They stopped by one of the lakes and let the horses graze while they talked. Lisa was nervous; she was afraid Tom would find out about the terms of the bet. So she told him she was in love with Eric. She didn't tell him about the Comanche camp, but that she and Eric had met back east while he was traveling through Boston, and that she had fallen madly in love with him. When she left Boston to go west, she had no idea she'd meet Eric again, and it was while Tom and Mariz were in Mexico that she discovered she was still in love with Eric. The entire time she was speaking, she was unable to look Tom in the eyes; she was afraid he would see the truth.

"I can't believe you're in love with Eric Anderson. The

324

man's been around, Lisa," Tom said harshly. "Is he in love with you?"

"I don't know, in his own way maybe. I have something else to tell you. Please don't get angry with me, Tom. Just listen." Lisa took a deep breath and continued. "Eric and I bet on the race. If I win I get to keep Vida and Eric will marry me. But if I lose, Eric keeps Vida and he gets . . ." Lisa hesitated and started to walk away from Tom. Tom walked after her and turned her around to face him.

"He gets what?"

Lisa slowly raised her head so that their eyes met. She felt more ashamed than she ever had in her life. When she spoke it was very softly, almost imperceptibly.

"Me."

She watched as Tom clenched his jaw and then walked away. He stood by the edge of the lake for a moment and then turned around and walked back to Lisa.

"What the hell has happened to you? Jesus Christ, Lisa . . ." He grabbed her by the shoulders, shaking her as he talked. "Why the hell are you so damned impetuous? Can't you see if a man won't marry you on his own accord, then he isn't worth having? Why didn't you just stay back in Boston where you belong?"

Lisa stared at her brother, tears of hurt and anger welling up in her eyes.

"Don't you tell me where I belong. I don't belong in Boston with a mother who doesn't want me, or in a Comanche camp where women are treated like slaves and whores, or with my brother whom I embarrass . . ."

"Don't sis," Tom said gently as he reached out for Lisa.

"Leave me alone. Why do you care anyway? If you'd

really cared, you would've taken me to Mexico City with you instead of leaving me here with him. Maybe he doesn't love me, but at least I know where I stand with him. Or I will know after the race." She burst into tears and Tom held her, soothing her as he had done so many times when she was a child. He had forgotten all that she'd been through in the last year and he suddenly felt like a callous fool. She needed comforting and reassurance, not chastisement.

"I am sorry, sis. I only want what's best for you but that doesn't mean that I *know* what's best for you. If you think it's Eric Anderson, then who am I to argue?"

Lisa looked up at him, wiping the tears from her eyes.

"That's just it, Tom, I don't know if Eric is the best thing for me. I only know how I feel about him—I can't seem to think straight anymore. And I'm afraid he's in love with someone else."

"He can't be, he hasn't been here that long."

"What about Consuelo de Morena? She told me he's in love with her and is going to marry her."

"I've only talked to her a few times, but I don't like her. She's a willful, spoiled little bitch who'll stop at nothing to get what she wants."

"Do you think it's true then? Do you think Eric could be in love with her?"

"More like Consuelo's in love with him, I'd say. He'd be a crazy fool to get involved with her when he can have you."

"I feel bad for her because of all she's been through; I wish I could understand her."

"Don't try. Believe me, Lisa, if she finds out you're in love with Eric she'll do everything in her power to get him away from you. In more ways than one she reminds me of Mariz."

"Why do you stay with Mariz if you feel that way about her?" Lisa asked, a puzzled expression on her face. "It can't be for the money."

"It's not the money; I have plenty of money saved. You know me well enough to know I'd never live off a woman anyway. There's something about Mariz, a certain charm and vitality . . . Oh, hell, I don't know. She drives me crazy half the time, but other times being with her is like being with no other woman. But it can never work between us; we think too differently. I'm seriously thinking of going to San Francisco and opening a law office. I've got a lot of experience with land titles and I'm sure I wouldn't have any trouble getting clients."

"Then why don't you do it?"

Tom looked at her, his face hardening for a moment, then he smiled.

"You worry too much, sis. I'd say you have too many problems of your own right now to worry about mine. Let's ride on back to the rancho."

As they rode back to the rancho in an uncomfortable silence, Lisa wondered about the true feelings Tom held for Mariz. She suspected he felt more deeply for the woman than he would admit. How strange, she thought almost bitterly, that this mother and son could have such a deep effect on both our lives.

The first day of festivities had begun and Lisa was kept so busy she didn't have time to think about anything. Guests had begun arriving the day before and she and Raytahnee were kept busy acting as hostesses. Lisa had never seen so much food in her life: wine, bowls of fresh fruit, vegetables, pastries, breads, tortillas, enchiladas, pucheros, and olives all the way from San Diego; there were chicken with rice, slabs of beef and pork roasted on iron spits over beds of coal, and wild game; butter, cheese, and milk; and sugar and chocolate were bought from some of the ships that were in the harbor. The kitchen was a bustle of activity, and Marta and some of the other women from the del Sol had been brought over to help with the preparations. Mexican musicians, with their guitars, violins, and tambourines, played constantly with only an occasional break for wine or food.

The first day, there were meriendas—picnics—in the wooded areas on the rancho, and bullfights and rodeos in the open areas, Lisa enjoyed the bullfighting immensely. Unlike Spain and Mexico, the object wasn't to kill the bull, but to tire him out. She was amazed at the dexterity and panache of the bullfighters, who inevitably drew cheers from the crowds of men, and fluttering of handkerchiefs from the ladies.

One sport which found no favor with Lisa was cockfighting, although Don Alfredo said it was very commonplace and a favorite betting sport of the vaqueros and rancheros. She saw no point in watching two birds with spikes on their talons cut each other to death, while the men cheered their favorite on. Don Alfredo told her that the cockfighting was nothing compared to a much more violent and favored diversion of many of the ranchos—bull-and-bear fights.

Vaqueros would go up into the hills and lasso grizzlies to bring back to the plaza in Monterey, or to the individual ranchos. They had to ride horses which were trained not to panic at the scent of the bear. The bear was either tied up and pulled or, still retained by the reatas, it would charge after one of the vaqueros who would race ahead of it all the way back to their destination. Once back at the plaza or corral, a hind foot of the bear was chained to a fore-foot of the bull, and they were goaded into fighting each other to a bloody and grisly death. The men gambled high stakes on which animal would win, or rather, which would kill the other first. Both animals usually died from the wounds they inflicted on each other. Lisa was glad to learn that Don Alfredo forbade this particular sport on his rancho.

There were also marksmanship contests, in which the men would shoot at a target while riding at great speeds on their horses. There were also races which demonstrated a vaquero's skill with a horse. While riding at top speed, a vaquero would lean from his saddle to one side as he swept along, and pick up a small coin from the ground, without slackening his speed. Lisa would have been more impressed except that she had seen the Comanche play a similar game, only the object that they picked up, they picked up with their teeth instead of their hands.

One thing marred Lisa's enjoyment of the first day— Eric's obvious absence. His father had asked him to come on the first day of the fiesta, but so far Lisa hadn't seen him. She hadn't seen Consuelo either; in fact, she realized she hadn't seen Consuelo in a couple of days. She wondered if she had ridden over to the Rancho del Sol to be with Eric.

Dinner that evening was served in the large dining room which hadn't been used for years. Everyone dressed formally and Lisa admired the way these supposedly uncivilized people enjoyed themselves without the typical conventions. She smiled as she thought of the look that would be on her mother's face if she saw the beautiful china and crystal place settings, not to mention silver eating utensils and platters. These Californios were far different from the uncivilized louts she had read about in the newspapers and magazines.

Lisa was so tired that night, that when she got to her room she barely had time to take off her clothes and slip into a nightgown before she fell into bed, and into a deep, exhausted sleep. No thoughts of Eric and Consuelo plagued her that night, as they had so many nights before.

The next day was practically a repetition of the first, with Lisa as busy as the previous day. There were many young men of fine families, including Francisco, who sought her company throughout the day, but she only smiled and tried to avoid contact with any of them. She always sought out Tom or Don Alfredo, but avoided Raytahnee because she was always with Miguel, and Francisco was always with them both.

The only difference between the first and second day was Consuelo's sudden reappearance, alone. She made a point of seeking out Lisa to tell her she had just left the del Sol and she was waiting for Eric to arrive at any time. But much to the consternation of both women, Eric didn't show the second day.

That evening after dinner, when almost all of the guests had retired, Lisa went into Don Alfredo's garden room for a drink of brandy before bed. Since that evening she had fought with Consuelo and drunk the brandy, Don Alfredo had showed her how to sniff the liquor and to appreciate its fragrance, and then to sip it slowly. She found she was beginning to acquire a taste for it.

"My dear," Don Alfredo said, coming up behind her, "you have been a wonderful hostess. Everyone is charmed by you, and they long to know everything about you." At the look on Lisa's face Don Alfredo smiled. "Don't worry, I have told them nothing except that you have come from Boston to visit your brother. They are very impressed by your background."

"I don't suppose it matters if you did tell them about me; Consuelo probably already told them all anyway. Brandy?" Don Alfredo nodded and Lisa handed him her glass and poured herself another. She paced around the room and then sat in the chair next to Don Alfredo, staring down at the amber-colored liquid in her glass as she swirled it around.

"Do you think he will come, Don Alfredo?" she asked suddenly, her voice sounding tired and defeated.

"If you are talking about Sandro, yes, I think he will come. I think he is trying to test you now, trying to see if you will back out of your wager. You won't, will you?"

She looked up, the familiar fire in her eyes shining.

"No, I made a bet and I intend to stick to it, no matter what the outcome."

"Are you frightened of the outcome? Does the possibility of living as Sandro's mistress make you apprehensive?"

"Of course it does," she said more sharply than she had intended. "When we lived with the Comanche, I was respected because I was his wife. I don't think I can live as his mistress and have the same respect for myself. I don't think I can do that. I'm wondering about the kind of woman who would stay with a man who doesn't really want her."

"I think you are being a bit blind, my dear. Sandro wants you; he has made that obvious enough. He loves you, too, or he would not have made that silly wager—he did that to be sure he could keep you near him. So, the question is not whether he loves you, but whether he loves you enough to marry you."

"But a man should do that if he loves a woman."

"This is different. Have you forgotten that Sandro has lived the last ten years of his life with a tribe of Comanche?" He may have come back to civilized society, but he still carries many Comanche beliefs with him. He believes that once you take a wife she is yours forever. Sandro still believes you are his wife."

"I know, he told me so. But that marriage isn't legal— at least not here."

"Does it matter if it is legal or not if you both know the truth? Does it matter so much what others think as long as you are both together?" He hugged her and then kissed her on the cheek and left the room.

Slowly, Lisa made her way up to her room. This time she didn't fall into an exhausted sleep but sat by the window looking out. She thought about the next day, and the day after the race, when her life would change forever. She thought of Eric, the man she loved but always seemed to do battle with. If the truth were known, she wanted nothing more than to be with him, whether they were married or not. She was his woman, and if all went well, she would continue to be his woman. She made a firm decision not to worry about Consuelo anymore. Now, her only thoughts were about Eric and how she would fare against him in the race the next day—and the day after.

CHAPTER XXII

The day of the fiesta dawned bright and clear, the sun smiling on the sea and mountains. Lisa was up with the sun to give Vida his morning exercise. When she came back she quickly cleaned up and changed and was down to breakfast before any of the other guests were up. After breakfast, she and Tom and Raytahnee rode out to see the course that had been marked off. In previous years Don Alfredo had done it and each year he had made the course a little different. The riders were permitted to ride on the periphery of the course but not through it until the actual race.

The course started on the south side of the hacienda and then turned abruptly west, where it ran almost to the cliffs above the beach. It ran along the cliffs for about a mile and then back eastward toward the hacienda and into the gate, where the winner would ride through a large white ribbon. The course was a total of three and a half miles, and it would take a knowledgeable rider to pace his horse so as not to tire him out. Lisa wasn't too worried about the distance because she and Vida had ridden a similar route every day for the last two weeks. She was sure Vida wouldn't have any trouble maintaining the pace—he had incredible endurance. Her trouble would come from riders like Eric, Tom, and the vaqueros who had entered the race. She knew she was an able horsewoman, but Eric had stated earlier, she wasn't used to riding in country like this. Still, she had ridden around the countryside every day, until she knew it from memory. She felt she had a good chance.

When they returned to the hacienda, many of the riders were wiping down, brushing, and exercising their mounts for the race. It evidently was the event of the day. Lisa could feel the wave of excitement going through the people in the yard. She didn't know if any of the riders knew she was riding in the race, and she supposed many would laugh or maybe even protest her participation. But they could laugh all they wanted, she thought amusedly, when they were all choking down the dust from Vida's heels.

She went into the hacienda and up to her room to change. She took out the brown-leather riding outfit which Eric had bought for her, along with a cream-colored muslin blouse. She'd never worn the outfit and she was sure it would shock most of the ladies. The pants were tight and molded themselves to her long legs. She wondered how Eric could have guessed her size so correctly. She left the blouse unbuttoned just enough to allow freedom of movement, and she rolled up the long sleeves to her elbows, then slipped on the vest. She pulled her hair back tightly with a leather thong and then appraised herself in the mirror. She smiled; she presented quite a comely sight, she thought. She hoped the men would think her too pretty to be an able rider. Just as she was getting ready to leave, Raytahnee walked in, bursting with excitement.

"You look wonderful. I think all the men will look at you instead of keeping their minds on the race. Miguel is riding in the race, too, but I am rooting for you." She hugged Lisa tightly. "I'll pray that you win and that Sandro will be your husband again. You two belong together."

"Thanks, I'll sure need all your prayers." She picked up her gloves and walked to the door. "Here goes." She smiled at Raytahnee, her hands trembling in spite of her outward composure.

The two girls walked out together and into the yard, Lisa going to the stables, Raytahnee going to Miguel. Lisa went to Vida's stall and found Hector with him. Vida had been brushed until his coat shone like spun gold, and his long white mane and tail hung like soft white silk. He wore a beautiful leather hackamore which Hector had made especially for him, and a new blanket which Don Alfredo had given Lisa as a good-luck gift for the race. Lisa stood back and looked at Vida. He snorted and pranced when he saw her and she gave him some sugar from her pocket. He nuzzled his head in her hand and she rubbed his nose, talking softly to him.

"He's the most incredible horse I've ever seen, Hector. I hope I do him justice and ride him well in the race."

"Do not worry, señorita, you will ride him well and you will be quick without the extra weight of the saddle. You both will do your best for each other; that is all you can do, no?"

Lisa kissed Hector on the cheek, much to his embarrassment, and slipped some gold coins into his hand.

"It isn't much, but I want to give you something for all the help you've given me. I wouldn't have been able to do it without you."

Hector's eyes widened at the sight of the gold pieces.

335

"It is too generous of you, señorita. I cannot accept them."

"Of course you can. It isn't much and you earned it. You can buy your family something that they want. Please, Hector, it would make me very happy if you took it."

"Thank you, señorita." He looked out into the yard. "I think it is time now." He handed the reins to Lisa. She looked around at the men in the yard and her eyes rested on the huge paint stallion and Eric. She took a deep breath.

"Wish me luck, Hector?"

Hector smiled and shook Lisa's hand.

"Mucha buena suerte, señorita, y vaya con Dios."

Lisa smiled and waved as she led Vida out to the group of men. As she got closer, she noticed that Eric was standing beside his horse talking to Consuelo. He looked up when he saw Lisa coming, gave her a faint nod, and continued talking animatedly with Consuelo. She saw him take Consuelo's scarf and tie it around his neck. She turned away abruptly, aware of the color spreading over her cheeks. She heard Don Alfredo telling everyone that there would be riders staked out at various points along the course to make sure no one took any shortcuts. Lisa swung up onto Vida's back, rubbing his neck. Tom rode up next to her and took her hand.

"Good luck, sis. For your sake, I hope either you or I win."

"Thanks. I'll talk to you after the race. Will you save me a dance for tonight?" she asked nervously, trying to maintain some equanimity.

"If I can get through the mob of men who're always surrounding you."

Vida was snorting and stamping, not used to all the other horses so close. As Lisa looked around her, she saw that many of the men were tilting their hats at her, not seeming the least bit surprised, while others pointed at her and laughed. She tried to ignore them all and concentrate on the race she was going to ride. Just before the start of the race she looked across some of the riders to find Eric staring at her, a mocking grin on his handsome face, Consuelo's bright scarf tied around his neck. She tore her eyes away from him, refusing to let him get to her. She was now more determined than ever to beat him and wipe that silly grin from his face. It seemed an eternity before all of the horses and their riders were lined up in an even line and the pistol fired, signifying the start of the race.

Lisa and Vida started at a medium pace and she was passed by more than half of the riders. But she knew that many of the horses would tire before they even reached the halfway mark. Eric, she noticed, wasn't far ahead of her. He, too, was keeping a steady pace. She felt the noonday sun beating down on her head and she wished she had thought to wear the hat Don Alfredo had given her. She felt the perspiration run down her sides and back and the hollow between her breasts, causing the thin material of her blouse to stick to her skin. She reached up to wipe her face with her leather gloves.

As they reached the cliffs, many of the horses had already slowed their pace, and Lisa was passing many who had been in the lead before. She felt light and carefree on Vida's back, and only the pressure from her knees told him when she wished to go faster. The huge horse seemed to sense that he should just keep his own pace for a while. Eric was always in her view, not far ahead of her. Once he turned back to look at her, that smile still on his face. God, how I want to beat him, she thought.

She passed a man who signaled that she was halfway through the course, and she increased her speed slightly. She saw Tom ahead of her, almost even with Eric, and there were only a few others in front of her—all the others had already tired and fallen way behind. She decided to make her move forward in the last half mile. Her thighs had begun to ache slightly from the continuous pounding, but she had ridden this way many times and she knew she could make it. Vida was still breathing evenly and was waiting for the time to give his all.

She began to press Vida faster now. He quickly picked up speed and with his long, reaching stride, soon overtook the two riders directly in front of her. She was nearly even with Tom. She looked over as she passed her brother, and for a brief second, felt a twinge of regret. But he smiled and waved her on, and she wondered if he were letting her pass him. Next, there was a young Spaniard on a black Arabian. He was an excellent horseman and the Arabian was a fast horse, but Lisa could see he was tiring rapidly, and before she had pressed Vida much harder they passed him. Now there was only Eric and a vaquero. They were even when she drew up to them and they both looked over at her. She pressed her thighs hard into Vida's sides and he began to pass the two men. Lisa was in the lead, but not by much. She looked back and saw the vaquero begin to drop back, but Eric and his paint were catching up, almost matching Vida stride for stride. It was as if it were effortless for the big horse.

The gate to the rancho was now in sight and Lisa bent low over Vida's back, talking to him, urging him faster and faster. Eric was still even with her, the two large horses side by side, their muscles bulging from their great efforts. The gate wasn't wide enough for both horses to fit through at the same time and Lisa knew she had to be the first one through. She urged Vida, hearing his breathing get heavier. For a moment she was afraid she had pushed him too hard and he would drop from the exertion, but he increased his speed and inched in front of the paint. She was sure she'd make it through the gate first when the paint made a sudden lurch forward, pushing Vida off to the side. Eric rode through the gate first, only inches before Lisa and Vida.

She heard the shouts from the crowd and was dimly aware of congratulations from many of the men for a well-ridden race. She was only conscious of the fact that she had lost and she would become Eric's mistress. She slid off Vida's back, petting and rubbing his nose, tears coming to her eyes at the thought of giving him up. He had run a great race—it had only been blind luck on Eric's part that he had won, and the fact that his horse had bumped into Vida. Hector came up, taking the reins from Lisa's hand.

"Don't feel bad, señorita, it was the closest race I have ever seen here. You only lost by inches. No one has ever come so close to the patrón, not even when he was a small boy."

Lisa tried to manage a smile which she didn't feel.

"Thank you, Hector. I lost Vida when I lost the race," she said sadly.

"With whom would you make such a bet? I know how much the stallion means to you."

"I made the bet with the patrón." She looked over in Eric's direction. "Excuse me, I'd better take him

339

his prize."

She walked over to the small circle of men and women surrounding Eric. Consuelo was at his side. He seemed preoccupied and kept looking around. When he saw Lisa he walked out of the circle to her, and took her hands in his.

"You rode beautifully. I honestly didn't think you could do it." His smile was warm, his words sincere, but Lisa couldn't bring herself to respond to his kind words. She pulled her hands away and replaced them with Vida's reins.

"Here's your horse. I hope you'll take good care of him. He's accustomed to a great deal of love and affection." In spite of her stern resolve not to break down, tears began to well up in her eyes. The smile vanished from Eric's face.

"Don't, Lisa. . . ."

"Why not? You won, didn't you? Fair and square. If you'll excuse me now." She turned to go but Eric's voice stopped her cold.

"Lisa," he said harshly, the smile gone from his face, the warmth from his voice. She turned around to face him. "I'll let you know later when I want to collect on the rest of our wager." She turned and ran from him, humiliated to the core. She didn't stop to acknowledge any of the compliments that people were giving her regarding the race, but ran straight to her room. All she knew was that she had lost, not only in the race, but in her relationship with Eric.

Eric watched Lisa as she ran into the courtyard and he smiled. He had played the game well. He untied Consuelo's scarf from around his neck and dropped it to the ground. Tonight, he thought with smug satisfaction, tonight she will be mine.

Lisa looked at herself in the gilt mirror. All signs of her crying had long since disappeared. Raytahnee had made her apply cold compresses to her face and eyes to make the swelling go down. Her cheeks glowed brightly from the sunburn she had acquired during the race, and her long hair glistened, and hung in thick waves down her back. One side was pulled back and held in place by a large gardenia. She ran her hands down the soft silk of the dress and twirled around in a circle, watching as the material clung to her. The dress was perfect, she thought. It had the effect of making her look both innocent and provocative. She almost had second thoughts about wearing white, but decided it didn't matter. It wasn't as if she were going to become a bride tonight.

As she walked into the courtyard, Lisa was greeted by many of the men with whom she had ridden that day. They all congratulated her and complimented her on how well she rode. Every time she turned around, someone was handing her a glass of champagne or asking her to dance. After numerous glasses of champagne and a few dances, she spotted Tom talking with two pretty young Spanish women. When she walked up, he excused himself and led his sister into the middle of the courtyard for a dance.

"I have to say, for a girl who lived with savages for so long, you certainly haven't lost your sense of style." He gave a long, low whistle.

"Don't you think it's a little low? Whom were you thinking of when you bought it?"

"I'm hurt," Tom said in an exaggerated tone. "I go to all the trouble of buying you a new wardrobe, and all you can do is accuse me of thinking of another woman."

"Well, even if you were thinking of someone else, I like it." Lisa looked around the courtyard, at all the young women and their duennas, the young men who were trying to court the young women, and the married couples and parents who were keeping their eyes on their daughters. She smiled.

"What are you so happy about?"

"I love it here, Tom, I don't ever want to leave. I was just thinking how warm and kind these people are, and how much love they have for each other. Their families mean everything to them." She stopped and her eyes met Tom's. She hadn't been aware that she looked so sad.

"You're everything to me, Lisa," he said softly, as he kissed her nose.

"I know that and it means everything in the world to me. I just wish . . ."

"That mom and dad were with us." Lisa nodded slightly. "Well, they're not, so we have to make the best of what we have, and that's each other. You know, I've been thinking about that bet of yours. If I went to Eric and talked to him about it, I'm sure he'd . . ."

"I don't want you to talk to him about it. A bet's a bet."

"That's crazy."

"I don't care—my pride's at stake here," she said firmly.

Tom looked as though he were about to argue, but he smiled instead.

"God you're stubborn; I feel sorry for the man who winds up with you. He'll never win a battle."

"I don't plan to battle with the man I wind up with," she said seriously. The music stopped and Tom held Lisa away from him.

"I know that, sis, I was just kidding you. God, you're a sight. Who would've ever thought that skinny, long-legged creature who used to tag along everywhere I went would turn into such a beauty. Beats me," he said jokingly, rubbing his head. "Listen, I'll see you later. I promised one of the señoritas I'd dance with her." With a kiss on the cheek and a wave of his arm, Tom was off across the room. Lisa watched until he approached one of the girls and then her arm was grabbed and she was pulled around.

"I want to congratulate you on your wonderful ride today, señorita," Francisco said incoherently. It was obvious that he'd been drinking and Lisa moved backward away from him, but his hand moved farther up her arm and he pulled her close. "You will dance with me this dance, sí?" Before she could answer, his arms were around her and they were half dancing, half stumbling across the courtyard.

"Francisco, I think we'd better sit down."

"I don't want to sit down, señorita. I want to dance with you and hold you in my arms and breathe in your wonderful fragrance."

Lisa winced as he breathed into her face, his sour breath reeking of hard liquor. His arms tightened around her waist.

"Francisco, I want to sit down. Please."

"I already told you, I don't want to sit down. Why do you argue with me?" he asked arrogantly.

Lisa looked up at him, a sly smile on her face.

"Has anyone ever told you you're an arrogant bastard, Francisco?" Francisco stopped, a look of shock on his face. "I didn't think so. Now, if you'll excuse me," she said coldly, pushing him backward and walking away with a smile on her face. She saw Don Alfredo as she approached the table, and he walked up to her, bowing low at the waist and kissing her hand.

"If I weren't such an old man, I think I would compete with my grandson for your affections."

"And I would be most honored, señor," Lisa said with a slight curtsy. "You look very handsome this evening, Don Alfredo. If I were you, I'd be careful; I see that some of these ladies can't take their eyes off you. I bet you turned quite a few heads in Madrid in your time."

Don Alfredo nodded, his eyes becoming slightly glazed at the remembrances of his youth.

"To be honest, I did turn a few heads in my time. But there was only one I really cared for—my dear, lovely Amparo. She was the loveliest, most gentle creature I have ever seen. I think she may have rivaled even you in beauty."

Lisa took Don Alfredo's arm, leading him out to the courtyard.

"I'm sure your Amparo far surpassed my beauty, Don Alfredo. Would you do a young woman the honor of dancing with her, señor?" Don Alfredo smiled deeply, the sadness disappearing from his eyes.

"My pleasure, señorita."

The musicians played a waltz and, much to Lisa's delight, it was as good as any she had heard in Boston. Don Alfredo was an accomplished dancer, and for all his years, he was still a strong and vital man. He whirled Lisa around the courtyard and she couldn't remember when she'd enjoyed a dance more. They danced again, this time to a much slower tune, a sad tune which reminded Lisa of other times. Her change of mood was apparent to the old man who was getting to know her very well.

"Don't worry, he will come. He is a proud man, but I know he will do the right thing."

Lisa looked up and Don Alfredo kissed her on the cheek. It was then that she looked over Don Alfredo's shoulder and saw Eric standing in the doorway. He was resplendent in a black-velvet charro suit, the jacket cut short and the pants cut tight and flaring out at the bottoms. He wore a ruffled white shirt and a blue sash tied around his waist. He even wore boots. She had never seen him dressed like this before and she thought, with an ache in her heart, that he had never looked more handsome. She was constantly amazed at what feeling could be aroused in her by the mere sight of him. He stood there tall and imposing, a lazy grin on his face. Many of the women and men went over to talk to him, but his gaze wasn't on them.

The music stopped and Don Alfredo looked to where Lisa had been staring for the last few minutes.

"Ah, so there he is, I thought as much. Stay here, my dear, let him come to you." Don Alfredo walked to the doorway and embraced his grandson. They exchanged a few words and then Don Alfredo patted him on the back.

Lisa stood rooted to the place where Don Alfredo had left her. Eric looked up and their eyes met. There was no one but them now. He ignored further greetings and walked across the courtyard to her. He bowed to her and took her into his arms, indicating to the musicians that they begin to play again. All eyes were on Eric and Lisa as they danced—they couldn't be ignored. Lisa thought she saw Consuelo standing by the fountain, but she wasn't sure. She was sure only of the man who was in front of her, the man who held her so possessively in his arms.

They said nothing, but continued to look at each other.

He pulled her close to him, so tightly she could hardly breathe. She felt her breasts pressed up against the soft silk of his shirt. When the music ended, she was suddenly unsure of what to do. The fairy tale had ended abruptly and she was brought sharply back to reality. But it wasn't over yet—it was just beginning.

Eric took Lisa's arm, placed it on his, and led her toward the French doors and into the garden room. He took her up to a man who was sitting on the couch, sipping a goblet of wine.

"Lisa, may I present Father Alvarado of the Mission San Carlos. Father, this is Lisa Jordan."

Father Alvarado, a balding, portly man, attempted to get up, but thought better of it. He extended his chubby hand to Lisa.

"My pleasure, señorita." Then he looked at Eric. "Are we ready, Don Alejandro?"

"Yes, we're ready, Father," he said, smiling at his grandfather and then at Lisa's puzzled face.

"Good. Now if you would be so kind as to help me up, I will make the announcement."

"What announcement?" Lisa asked curiously. Eric put his finger to her lips.

"Be quiet a minute."

Father Alvarado made his way to the center of the courtyard and raised his arms, as if in supplication.

"Please, my children. May I have silence."

When all the guests had quieted down, he began, "I am pleased to announce that in just a few moments, I shall join in holy matrimony the hands of Don Alejandro de Vargas and Señorita Lisa Jordan." Everyone turned to look at the couple, smiling and whispering. All attention was on them. Father Alvarado continued, "I realize this is unusual and I don't normally marry people outside of the church or a chapel, but Don Alejandro was in such a great hurry and wished to surprise his bride. Now, if you will all move to the outside of the courtyard, we can begin."

Lisa looked at Eric, her eyes filling with tears. He put his hand under her chin and lifted it up.

"No tears, green eyes, you are about to become a bride. Be happy."

One of the ladies gave Lisa her lace mantilla and she draped it over her head. Father Alvarado brought them into the middle of the courtyard. The ceremony was short, as Eric had requested. Tom gave Lisa away, and Don Alfredo and Raytahnee were the witnesses. At the end of the ceremony, Eric took out a small gold band with a tiny diamond in the center. He slipped it on Lisa's finger and kissed her so passionately that a hush went through the crowd. They applauded when the couple pulled apart.

"Forever," Eric said softly.

"Forever."

They danced, ate, and drank champagne. Then, as was the custom at all weddings, they danced with other partners. Lisa was so happy she felt as if she were dreaming. She looked around for Eric once and saw him dancing with Consuelo. Her throat constricted, but she stilled the doubts in her mind. He had married her, after all. When she looked at them again, Consuelo shot her a murderous glance. Lisa ignored it, but she wouldn't forget it—Consuelo wasn't one to suffer defeat easily.

As the evening grew late, Eric once again reclaimed his bride for a dance. Afterward, they bade Don Alfredo and the guests good evening and they went up to their room. They were barely inside the room when he took her in his arms and kissed her. Then he held her back and looked at her intensely.

"You are incredibly beautiful tonight. When I walked into the courtyard and saw you standing there, there wasn't a doubt in my mind—I knew I had to have you forever. There can never be anyone for me but you, green eyes."

He undressed her slowly, gently, and when she was completely naked, he took something from his pocket.

"I have a wedding present for you. It was made with you specifically in mind." Lisa opened the small box and took out a necklace. It was made of two, small, perfectly round emeralds which were spaced evenly apart on a delicate gold chain.

"It's exquisite," she said softly.

He chained it around her neck and led her to the mirror.

"I noticed you weren't wearing the Comanche necklace I gave you—I figured you lost it."

Lisa lowered her eyes, remembering her gift to Josh. "Oh, Eric . . ."

"Wait a minute, there's something else I have to show you." He took the ring from her finger. "Look inside."

There were two sets of initials: A & A—1799 and E & L—1850.

"It's your grandmother's ring. It's so wonderful." She turned to him, wrapping her arms around his neck and covering his face with kisses.

"How do I ever thank you?"

"I can think of a way," he said deeply, taking off his jacket and shirt. He was undressed in seconds and he lifted Lisa up and carried her to the bed. Lisa thought the last morning they had made love in the Comanche camp had been perfect, but her wedding night was something she would never forget. This time there was no sadness, only complete joy. They loved each other intensely and completely; they couldn't seem to get enough of each other. They searched, felt, and caressed every inch of each other's bodies, finding new areas of sensation Lisa had never known existed. When they tired they lay drowsily in each other's arms until one of them would begin to excite the other, and they would make love again. In that one night, Lisa felt that she had experienced the perfect union with another person—emotional as well as physical. She would always remember the incredible love and longing they had for each other that night.

The next morning, while they lay around in bed, Lisa asked Eric about Consuelo.

"Do you still feel strongly for Consuelo? She told me she spent some time with you and that you . . ."

Eric pulled her close, running his finger over her lips. "I'm in love with my wife."

"But before the race yesterday I saw you with her and you wore her scarf."

"Of course, because I knew you were watching. I could see the green fury blazing in your eyes." He looked at Lisa and saw there was still doubt in her eyes. "We grew up together and I'm fond of her, but I don't love her."

"She's in love with you."

He frowned, a crease appearing between his eyes.

"I'm sorry if she thinks she is, but I didn't encourage her. I told her from the beginning that there was someone else." He pulled her close, brushing his lips across her mouth. "Now, let's forget about Consuelo and everyone else in the world, and let's concentrate on more

349

important things." His mouth moved down her neck to her breasts, banishing all thoughts of Consuelo from Lisa's mind.

CHAPTER XXIII

After spending a few more days with Don Alfredo, Lisa and Eric returned to the del Sol. Mariz had not yet returned from Mexico and Tom was in San Francisco, so they had the hacienda to themselves. They decided to wait for a true honeymoon until after the summer roundup and branding.

Marta was ecstatic at the news of their marriage and she waited on them hand and foot. She wasted no time in calling Lisa, patrona, but Lisa asked her not to. She felt that that was already reserved for Mariz.

Lisa spent most of her days out on the range with Eric and the vaqueros. When Eric saw that she was serious about helping out, he let her help some of the vaqueros round up some of the cattle and horses for branding. She learned how to use a reata and soon became adept at roping strays. She reveled in each minute that they were together, still not really believing that they were married. She found the days much too long if she wasn't with him.

She had no desire to change anything in the hacienda—she didn't want to alienate Mariz any more than she already had. She wasn't looking forward to her mother-in-law's return since she knew it would bring an abrupt end to the blissful state she and Eric shared.

They spent their evenings talking, learning things

about each other, and loving each other. Lisa was amazed at how their relationship had changed. Now there was no need for secrets in their lives, no need to play games or fight, no need for lies. They even talked of starting a family so that they might be able to erase the sorrow of their lost child.

They had only a short month together before Mariz returned home from Mexico. She received the news of her son's marriage with an outward calm, but inside, she rebelled at the thought of him marrying an Americano woman. She had hoped, had even urged, that he would become involved with Consuelo and that they might marry. She couldn't understand why he would marry this girl; she had nothing to offer him, no money or family to speak of. Did he feel sorry for her because she had been an Indian captive? Mariz didn't know, but she was going to find out and, if possible, break up what was, in her view, a farcical marriage.

To compound Mariz's anger, she came home to find Tom gone. She questioned Lisa about his absence, but Lisa told her that he had gone to San Francisco for a ranchero, when in fact, he had gone there to see about opening an office for himself. Lisa sensed that Mariz was forcing herself to be cordial to her and she didn't want to give her another excuse to dislike her. She tried to help mend the breach between Mariz and Eric and for Lisa's sake, Eric tried. He was so happy in his marriage to Lisa that he didn't find it difficult to be friendly with his mother. In fact, he found her to be an extremely intelligent and articulate woman and he enjoyed really getting to know her for the first time.

Eric planned to make a trip north to some of the mining camps to deliver fresh beef to them. He insisted on accompanying his vaqueros, but he refused to let Lisa go. He said it was too dangerous for her to ride along on the trail because of the small bands of bandits, and that the men in the mining camp might not be able to control themselves when they saw her. Many of them, he said, hadn't seen a woman in months and would do anything to have one. Lisa had to agree, although reluctantly, that it was best for her to stay at the rancho. She felt strange watching him ride off, like the time she didn't want him to go on the raid, but she passed the feeling off as mere melancholy because of his departure. Still, she couldn't shake off the uneasy feeling that something was going to happen to them and that their peaceful harmony would be broken.

The day after Eric left, Consuelo arrived, loaded down with trunks and prepared for a long stay. It didn't take Lisa long to realize that the two women planned to make her as miserable as possible. Her hunch about Mariz had been right. As soon as Eric was gone, Mariz turned into a bitchy, complaining shrew, who found fault with everything Lisa did. And as she watched the two women together, Lisa realized that Consuelo was just a younger version of Mariz. They were two of a kind.

She often thought of leaving the del Sol and going to stay with Don Alfredo and Raytahnee, but she resolved to stick it out. The Rancho del Sol was her home too, and she refused to be driven away.

Most of the days she spent outdoors, away from the hacienda and Mariz and Consuelo. Eric had given orders that she wasn't allowed to ride alone because of the risk of squatters or bandits, but most of the time Hector or one of the vaqueros was too busy to accompany her, so she went off alone. She enjoyed her solitary rides on Vida because it gave her time to think about her life with Eric and what the future would hold for them. She thought of telling him the way Mariz really felt about her, but she knew she couldn't do it, not when he and his mother were getting along for the first time in years.

Although she spent the greater part of each day outdoors, it was inevitable that Lisa meet up with Mariz and Consuelo in the evenings. She tried to converse with the two women at dinner but she was almost always ignored. When they did speak to her it was in a derisive, rude manner, and they always referred to her captivity. She found it easier to eat alone and then go to Eric's study. It was the one place she found solace and neither Mariz nor Consuelo disturbed her there. She spent hours reading or going over things which belonged to Eric. For some reason, it made her feel closer to him.

One night while Lisa was reading in the study, the door opened and Consuelo walked in. Lisa looked up from where she was sitting and the two stared at each other with open hostility.

"What do you want, Consuelo?"

Consuelo walked over to the fireplace and stared up at Eric's portrait.

"I think you know what I want."

"No, maybe you'd better explain it to me."

"I want your husband. I'm a wealthy woman, as you know, and I'm prepared to pay you a handsome sum if you'll leave California and never return."

Lisa put down the book and stood up, trying to control the anger which was building up in her.

"And just what am I supposed to say to Eric?"

"Nothing. You'll be gone before he returns and I'll be here to console him. He'll realize what a mistake he made

354

in marrying you."

"Doesn't it mean anything to you that Eric married me of his own free will? Don't you understand that he loves me, not you?"

"Loves you? Ha! Maybe he married you out of a sense of duty, or pity, but love, I don't think so."

"There was no sense of duty involved. He married me because he loves me. It's that simple."

"I think not. I think he felt sorry for you because no other man would have you after you lived with the Comanche. You're filth now; no man wants a woman like you."

Lisa walked across the room to Consuelo, her green eyes ablaze, and she slapped her hard across the face, knocking her back against the fireplace. Consuelo rubbed the red mark on her face, tears stinging her eyes.

"Get out of here," Lisa screamed. "If you ever bother me in my husband's study again I'll do more than slap you."

Consuelo ran from the room without another word and Lisa slammed the door shut.

"Oh, Eric, when will you get home? I can't endure this much longer." She walked to the fireplace and looked up at his portrait. She started to reach up and touch it when the door opened again and Mariz walked in, her face livid with rage.

"How dare you insult our guest!"

"Our guest? I don't remember inviting Consuelo to stay here, Mariz."

"You are impudent and ill-mannered."

"And you, dear mother-in-law, are a hypocritical, conniving bitch!" She walked to Mariz, their faces only inches apart. "Do you think I'm an idiot? Don't you

355

think I know what you and Consuelo are up to? You think you can drive me away and split Eric and me up. But you can't. I'm not a sniveling coward who runs away from a fight. I'll stand my ground with you, Mariz—you'll never drive me away. And whether you want to believe it or not, your son loves me. So if you try to drive me away you'll only succeed in driving Eric away again."

"You're very sure of yourself, aren't you?" Mariz's dark eyes flashed.

"I'm just very sure of our love. It's something you could probably never understand."

"How dare you presume to tell me what I can understand you little . . ."

"This is the second time tonight I've been insulted in my husband's study. This is the only place in the hacienda besides my room where I can have any peace. I won't stand for any more of your or Consuelo's insults. I'm tired of both of you treating me like dirt because I lived with the Comanche. After being with you two these last weeks, I think I'd find the Comanche much better company, and certainly more civilized." She turned and walked back to her seat, picking up her book. "You know, Mariz, I'm a lot like my brother. He can only be pushed so far, too." She sat down. "You've lost Tom, you know."

"He'll be back, he's much too used to the luxuries I can give him."

"You're a fool. He won't be back; he doesn't need you. You can't manipulate him as you do everyone else in your life."

"You'll regret having crossed me, you little slut. You'll pay for this—I promise you!" Mariz stomped out, slamming the door behind her.

Lisa put the book down, running her trembling hand

through her hair. If Mariz and Consuelo had only known how difficult it had been for her to be so hard and unyielding. What a honeymoon, she thought with a deep sigh, no husband to love me; only two women who hate me.

Lisa was out riding on one of her daily excursions when she saw a rider approach. Thinking that it might be Eric, she took off in the direction of the rider. She wasn't far away from him when she heard him call her name and she recognized the sound of his voice. It was Josh. Josh— she'd completely forgotten about him in the last months. How would she ever be able to explain to him that she'd married Eric? She hadn't written him about the marriage because she'd been too caught up in her own life to think about him. She'd been selfish and had neglected his feelings. And now he was here, probably expecting her to say she'd marry him. How would he ever forgive what she'd done to him?

Josh reined in abruptly, jumping from his horse. He ran to Lisa and pulled her from Vida's back. He swung her around in the air a few times before setting her back down on the ground.

"God, but you're a sight for sore eyes, girl. I thought I'd just dreamed you up." He put his arms around her and pulled her close. "I've waited a long time for this." He placed his mouth over hers and kissed her deeply. She tried to pull away, to tell him about her marriage, but he wouldn't listen. Finally, she put her arms between them and pushed Josh away.

"I have something to tell you, Josh. Please, wait a minute."

"It can wait," he replied hoarsely, pulling her close again.

"Josh, please. It can't wait. I'm married."

She felt the strong arms go tense around her and then drop limply to his sides.

"What'd you say?"

"I said I'm married. Come over here and sit down. It's a long story." She led him to a nearby oak tree and they sat down next to its large trunk. Throughout her entire story, Josh's face remained impassive and Lisa couldn't tell how he was reacting. When she finished, he remained silent, unmoving.

"Well, at least it's to the man you've always loved. I woulda been madder than hell if you'd gone and married someone else."

"You're not angry?"

"I didn't say that. 'Course I'm angry and my pride has been kicked all to hell. But after lookin' at your face, I can't be too mad at you. You look happier than I've ever seen you look. I just wish I coulda been the one to bring that look to your face." He reached over and brushed her cheek with his hand and then stood up. "So, when do I get to see the lucky bridegroom? Damned luckiest man I ever knew."

"He should be back soon. He's running some beef up to some of the mining camps. You won't recognize him; he looks different now. The life of an hacendado agrees with him."

"And bein' married to you doesn't hurt," Josh said dryly.

Lisa stood up and dusted off her pants, ignoring Josh's comment.

"I never meant to hurt you, Josh, I hope you believe that. You're the last person in the world I'd ever want to hurt. It's just that . . . well, when I found out he was alive and that he still loved me, I knew he was the only man for me. I feel so cruel. I don't blame you if you never forgive me."

"Don't blame yourself, darlin'."

"Who else should I blame? If I hadn't been so concerned with my happiness . . ."

"That's enough. Don't apologize for bein' happy, darlin'. I woulda done that same thing in your place."

"I'm so sorry, please believe that," Lisa said pleadingly, holding on to Josh's arm.

"I know you are. I guess it was just my bad luck to fall in love with a woman who was always in love with someone else."

Lisa walked back to the tree and sat down, leaving Josh alone with his thoughts. She didn't know how to undo the hurt she had done to Josh. A few minutes later Josh walked over to Lisa, extending his hand and helping her up.

"C'mon, let's get back to the rancho. I'm hungry as a bear and could do with some liquor. Do you suppose your husband would mind if I camped out here for a few days? I may as well stay awhile as long as I'm here."

"That would be wonderful. I know Eric will want you to stay as long as you want to."

They rode back to the rancho, their conversation much more friendly now that the bad news was out of the way. Josh didn't seem to be angry with Lisa and again she marveled at what a good and loyal friend he was. As soon as they got back to the rancho and went into the hacienda, they ran into Mariz, much to Lisa's dismay.

"You have a guest, I see," Mariz said coldly, eyeing Josh up and down. "How nice for you."

"You remember Josh Wade, Mariz? He was the one

who brought me out of the Comanche camp."

"Oh, yes," Mariz answered as if completely bored.

They exchanged a few more words and then Lisa led Josh upstairs to his room. She went back downstairs to get him some lunch and again ran into Mariz.

"Do you think it's wise to have another man in your husband's home when he isn't here?"

Lisa looked at her mother-in-law quizzically.

"There's nothing wrong with it. Josh is a good friend and I see no reason why he shouldn't stay here. Besides, you and Consuelo will be here to chaperone me," she said sarcastically.

"You are a grown woman, of course, and there is no reason for me to question your loyalty to your husband. I just thought Sandro might not like the idea."

"I'll take that up with him when he gets back. If you'll excuse me now, I'm going to see that some lunch is prepared for Josh."

Mariz smiled as she watched Lisa leave the room, a smile which contained only malice. Perhaps this man, Wade, would be the excuse she needed. Somehow she would make sure that this woman didn't remain married to her son for long. No matter what she had to do, she'd break it up. She'd make sure that Sandro saw that he'd made a mistake in marrying the little slut. And this man Wade could be the way to show him.

CHAPTER XXIV

Lisa spent all of her time with Josh, and Mariz and Consuelo always seemed to be watching them. Lisa knew that the two of them were hoping they'd find her in a compromising situation with Josh so they could tell Eric, but she didn't care. Josh was her friend and until Eric came home, he was the only reason she was able to tolerate the atmosphere at the rancho. After her initial meeting with Josh, the strain left their relationship. She talked openly to Josh about her marriage and the plans that she and Eric had made for the future. If Josh harbored any hostility toward her. Lisa didn't notice it. She and Josh enjoyed each other's company, and they were as close and open with each other as good friends should be.

They spent very little time in the hacienda. They were always out riding, or walking, or swimming. One day they rode into Monterey to watch the ships unload some of their cargoes, and were forced to spend the night there because they had stayed so late. As Hector had told Lisa many times, it was unsafe to ride alone or at night.

They dined with Mariz and Consuelo, and it was a constant battle of words, with Josh and Lisa matching wits with the other two women. After dinner, Josh and Lisa usually took a walk around the courtyard and then went to Eric's study for a game of chess, which Lisa was teaching Josh, or poker, which Josh was teaching Lisa. Sounds of their laughter could be heard in Mariz's sitting room, and she and Consuelo convinced themselves that there was something more than friendship between the two.

"Do you know, Mariz, I couldn't sleep last night, so I got up to get a book from the library? When I walked past Lisa's room I heard voices, hers and Señor Wade's."

"You're sure? But this is just what we need to tell Sandro. When he hears of this, he'll make her leave at once. Then he'll see the kind of woman he really married."

"Yes." Consuelo nodded in agreement, smiling to herself at the deft little lie she had told Mariz. She hadn't really heard Josh in Lisa's room, but what did it matter? As long as Mariz believed that she and Wade were lovers, that was all that mattered. She would plant the seed of doubt in Sandro's mind and then he would force his faithless wife to leave. And if that didn't work, she had another plan, one that wouldn't fail, one that would eliminate the girl forever.

Josh had been at the del Sol for about two weeks when he decided to ride up to San Francisco. Lisa asked him not to go, but he argued vehemently.

"A fella like me's got needs, girl," he said, smiling devilishly, "if you know what I mean."

"I know. You don't have to explain it to me."

"Good. I'd like to do some gamblin' while I'm there; maybe make me a fortune off of some of them starry-eyed miners who're ready to lose all the money they worked so hard to get."

"Will you take me to the del Mar on your way? I

don't think I can stay here alone while you're gone."

"Sure. But what's the del Mar?"

"It's Eric's grandfather's rancho. I'm very close to him, and my sister from the Comanche camp, Raytahnee, is there. I have to get out of here for a while."

"Sure. When do you want to leave?"

"Now," Lisa said emphatically. She was packed within the hour and she and Josh rode off. She couldn't find Mariz to tell her where they were going, so she told Marta, hoping that the message would get to Mariz so her imagination wouldn't wander.

Don Alfredo was surprised but happy to see Lisa. He didn't know that Eric was north and was obviously displeased at the fact that his grandson would leave his new bride so soon. He was very gracious to Josh, and when Lisa went outside to find Raytahnee, Josh and Don Alfredo were already embroiled in an argument about the waves of immigrants to the west coast.

Lisa found Raytahnee at the corral, just having come back from a ride with Miguel.

"How is it you are allowed to ride with Miguel alone when every other young maiden in California has to have a duenna with her?"

"Miguel almost always has one of his vaqueros with us; he feels that is chaperone enough. He doesn't believe in duennas. He feels they are old-fashioned."

"That's rather a modern view from a young man who belongs to such a traditional family."

"Miguel is different. He wants to make changes on his rancho, in raising cattle and in agriculture. He reads everything he can get his hands on from the East and Midwest. He feels the future of California lies in agriculture because we are too far west to drive our cattle east to the big cities."

"Your Miguel is a smart man. I think you chose well."

"Thank you. You've never before told me what you thought of him. I'm glad you approve."

"It's not for me to approve or disapprove. But if you want to know the truth, I think he's not only handsome and smart, but very astute in his judgment of women."

"What is this word, 'astute'?"

"It means shrewd."

"Yes, I think I agree with that," Raytahnee replied laughingly.

"There is one thing I don't like about him, though," Lisa said seriously. She noticed the frown which suddenly appeared on Raytahnee's face. "It's his cousin; he doesn't have good taste in cousins."

Raytahnee laughed, slapping Lisa around the shoulders.

"You haven't told me what you are doing here."

Lisa explained that Eric was away and Josh had come for a visit and they decided to come here for a while, since Josh was on his way to San Francisco.

"Mariz and Consuelo hate me so much and I'm so tired of fighting with them. And with Eric gone I'm so lonely. It's terrible living in a place where you're so hated."

"Don't let them push you out. What is Consuelo doing there anyway? It's not her home. She's a she-devil, that one. Why don't you tell Sandro what they've been up to?"

"I can't do that. I'm the one who talked him into making up with his mother. They get along so well now; I can't break up that relationship."

"Always worried about others, aren't you? When are you going to start looking out for yourself?"

364

"I do. I don't let either of them walk over me. I'm just tired of the constant fighting."

"Why don't I go back with you? I'd be glad to give you support," she said with a sly glint in her eye.

"I bet you would. You'd probably think up some Comanche torture to put them through."

"And it would probably be no more than the two of them deserve." She raised her hand up to push her hair out of her face.

"What's that on your finger? Oh, Raytahnee, that's the biggest diamond I've ever seen in my life. You didn't go and get yourself married behind my back, did you?"

"No, it's just an engagement ring. It's a family heirloom. Miguel wants to marry me in the spring when he turns twenty-one and becomes the legal heir to the rancho. I told him I don't care about the land or the money, that I want to marry him now, but he insists we wait. It will be a big wedding. I told you, he has relatives in Santa Barbara, Los Angeles, and even all the way down in San Diego. Can you imagine me in such a wedding?"

"It's what you deserve. You must know how happy I am for you. You've come a long way from that little girl in the Comanche camp."

"I feel so lucky. I feel as if it's all a dream and that I will wake up and it will all be over."

Lisa took Raytahnee's hand in hers.

"Don't say such a thing, don't even think it. You've had so much sorrow in your young life. Just enjoy all the happiness that's finally come your way."

"I will. Now, let's get in to your friend and Don Alfredo, and we'll have an enjoyable evening together."

Josh and Lisa spent three days at the Rancho del Mar and then returned to the del Sol. Josh decided to go back

365

to the rancho with Lisa because he didn't want her to ride alone, and then he would leave the next day for San Francisco. They arrived in time for dinner and after that solemn occasion, they went into Eric's study for some poker.

It was later that evening, while Josh and Lisa were still playing poker, and Mariz and Consuelo were in the sitting room, that Eric came home. At first he thought everyone was asleep, but when he heard the laughter coming from his study, he assumed his mother and Lisa were in there. He walked in and saw Lisa and Josh together on the couch laughing, his arm around her. When they heard the door open they both looked up. Lisa jumped up and ran to Eric.

"You're home," she said excitedly, throwing her arms around his neck. She kissed him, but Eric remained cool, staring at Josh.

"Eric, you remember Josh Wade? He took me . . ."

"I remember him," he cut her off abruptly.

"I told him everything."

The two men stared at each other in cold silence and then Josh got up off the couch and extended his hand to Eric.

"Congratulations, Anderson, you're a lucky man."

Reluctantly, Eric took Josh's hand and shook it.

"Thanks. What brings you to these parts, Wade?"

Josh looked briefly at Lisa before answering.

"Just some unfinished business I had to clear up."

"Be staying long?"

"Not much longer. Hope I'm not intruding."

"No, stay as long as you like." Eric walked to the door and turned to Lisa. "I had a long ride and I'm tired as hell." He looked at Lisa. "You coming?"

"Yes, of course. Good night, Josh. I'll see you in the morning."

"Yeah," Josh said pensively, watching them as they walked out. There was something wrong there, he thought. Something real wrong.

"What the hell's he doing here?" Eric asked angrily when they got to their room.

"He told you why he was here. He had some business and he stopped by to see how I was doing. That's all."

"That's all? You sure as hell didn't seem to miss me very much, did you? You certainly seem to know how to occupy your time while I'm gone."

"What's the matter with you? Josh is a good friend, nothing more. You more than anyone should realize why I value his friendship so much. And as for occupying my time, just what am I supposed to do, pine away the entire time?"

Eric's manner changed abruptly and he took Lisa in his arms.

"God, I'm sorry, Lisa. I'm just so damned tired and I rode all day so I could get here tonight. The rest of my men are still on the trail. I missed you so much I couldn't stand it. When I walked in and saw Wade's arm around you and you both having so much fun, I just got a little hot under the collar."

Lisa reached up and put her arms around his neck, pulling him close to her.

"Don't you know by now that there could never be anyone else in the world for me but you?" She kissed him deeply, running her hands over his chest. It wasn't long before Eric responded by carrying her to the bed, where his need for her became quite evident. Afterward, they lay quietly beside each other.

"The next time I go on a trip, no matter how short it is, you're coming with me. It was hell without you."

"It was for me too. I missed you so much," she said softly, swinging her long leg over his. "I had trouble getting to sleep at night. I kept dreaming you would walk in and take me in your arms and make love to me."

Eric pulled her on top of him, running his hands down the length of her body.

"Well, I'm back now and you don't have to dream anymore." Lisa sighed contentedly as his lips covered hers. It was always the same with them, as if they could never get enough of each other. That night they made up for the many long and lonely nights they had spent without each other.

Lisa was still sleeping when Eric got up to go down to breakfast the next morning. He kissed her softly and went down to the dining room, famished after his long trip and the activity of the night before. He was in a good mood when he entered the dining room, and even Consuelo's unwanted presence couldn't dull his mood. He was amazed at how the younger woman copied his mother in dress and disposition—it was obvious that she idolized Mariz. He was even more amazed to find them both up at that early-morning hour. He had never known his mother to be an early riser.

"Good morning, ladies," he said while leaning over and kissing his mother on the cheek.

"I am so glad you're back, Alejandro," Mariz said sweetly. "Was it a profitable trip?"

"Very. I got a good price for the beef. Those miners will pay any price for fresh beef. How are you, Consuelo?" he said with an abrupt change in the conversation.

"Very well, thank you. Your mother invited me for a little visit. I've had a lovely time getting to know your charming wife."

"Have you?" Eric said, surprise evident in his voice.

"Did you see Lisa last night, dear?" Mariz asked coyly.

"Yes, I saw her. We sleep in the same room, remember?"

"Oh, I thought maybe she was out with that Señor Wade again."

"Out? Why would she be out with him?"

"Well, they've been spending so much time together lately that I thought perhaps they were out when you arrived home."

"How long has he been here?"

"He arrived right after you left for your trip," Mariz lied.

"We've hardly even seen Lisa since that man has been here. They're always off somewhere together. The only time we get to see her is at dinner," Consuelo interjected. "And they don't even eat with us all the time. Sometimes they eat alone in her room."

Mariz watched as the muscle twitched in her son's jaw, a sure sign he was getting agitated.

"They even disappeared for a few days," Mariz pressed further. "They said they were going to visit your grandfather but quién sabe?"

Eric stood up and walked to the windows. He stood silently for a moment, letting himself absorb all that he'd just heard. He turned back to the table.

"You're sure they went away together? Could you be mistaken, mother?"

"Oh, no. They were gone for over three days. The only way I even knew where they went was through Marta.

369

Lisa told her, but didn't bother to tell me. Possibly she was embarrassed to tell me she was going away with that man."

Eric excused himself suddenly and strode out of the room, taking the stairs two at a time. Lisa was dressing when he walked into their room, and she turned and smiled at him when he entered. He walked over and took her by the shoulders.

"Did you spend the night with Wade while I was gone?"

"What are you talking about?"

"I asked you if you slept with Wade while I was gone. It's a simple enough question."

"How many times do I have to tell you that Josh and I are just friends. Why can't you believe that?"

"Because it seems that someone knows otherwise."

"Someone?"

"Yes, she told me you went off and spent a few days with Wade."

"That someone wouldn't happen to be your mother, would it? Oh Eric, don't you see? She's trying to break us apart and instill doubts in your mind. She doesn't approve of our marriage and she'll never accept it."

"That's crazy. She likes you and thanks you for bringing her and me together again."

"She's telling a vicious lie about me."

"Why would she have reason to lie? She knows it was you who made it possible for us to get along again. She knows I wouldn't tolerate it if she mistreated you."

"I told you, she doesn't approve of our marriage or me. She wants you to divorce me and marry Consuelo, someone who is worthy of your noble Spanish blood," she said dryly.

"Don't be bitchy, Lisa, it doesn't become you."

"And it's not like you to be so damned jealous for no reason at all. First you come in here and accuse me of sleeping with another man, and then you accuse me of being bitchy. Is there anything else you'd like to accuse me of before you leave?"

"Don't get upset, I only want to know the truth."

"I told you the truth, damn it! If you choose to believe your mother rather than your wife, then that's your mistake."

Eric went to her, taking her in his arms.

"I don't want to doubt you; it's just that I know you felt close to Wade at one time, and very grateful. And with me gone, you probably felt lonely . . . ."

"Stop it! I don't want to hear any more. If you don't believe me then I want you to get out of here right now." She quickly finished dressing while Eric watched in stunned silence and then she walked to the mirror to brush her hair.

"All right, I won't question you any more about it. Do you want to take a ride?"

"No. I'm going to stay around here for a while. Maybe I'll go for a walk later on. I just want to be alone for a while."

Eric nodded and bent down to kiss her but she turned her face away. He shrugged his shoulders and walked out.

Eric thought about what Lisa had said to him as he walked out of the hacienda. Was it possible that Mariz really didn't approve of the marriage and she was trying to instill doubts in his mind so that he would break it off with Lisa? If that were true, then she had made him so jealous that he had doubted his own wife. And why all of a sudden, was he so jealous of Lisa? It had never bothered him before that she had been raped by the other braves; it hadn't even mattered to him then. Why now, should he begin to feel this way?

Josh was sitting in the courtyard soaking up some of the sun when Eric came out. He had decided to stay for another day before taking off for San Francisco. His shirt was unbuttoned to the waist and he was lying back against the bench.

"Good morning," Eric said pleasantly as he walked up to Josh.

"Howdy," Josh replied lazily, squinting up at him. "We don't get sun like this back in Missouri. I really enjoy this."

Eric smiled and started to speak, but stopped when he saw something shiny around Josh's neck. He stepped closer to look and saw that it was the Comanche necklace he had given Lisa. He went into a sudden rage and pulled Josh up by the shirt.

"You bastard," he snarled and then smashed his curled-up fist into Josh's unprotected face. Before Josh could react, Eric had him on the ground and he was pummeling away at the blond-haired man's face. Eric was so furious, he didn't hear Lisa run up behind him and scream for him to stop.

"Eric, don't, you'll kill him. Stop it, stop it!"

Eric was suddenly aware of Lisa pulling at his shirt and arm and he stood up, looking at the bloodied face of the man on the ground. Lisa bent down next to Josh, wiping his face with a piece of her skirt. When she turned to question Eric, she saw him walking out of the courtyard.

"Where are you going?" she demanded angrily.

"Leaving you alone with your lover."

Lisa had no idea what had happened. She helped Josh

372

off the ground and onto the bench. She ripped off a piece of her petticoat and dipped it into the water of the fountain. She walked back to Josh and began to clean the cuts on his face.

"What happened, Josh?"

"I don't know. I was just sitting there mindin' my own business when that husband of yours comes up and begins beating the bloody hell outta me. He didn't even give me a chance to ask him what it was all about."

"You mean he didn't tell you?"

"No, we were talking real friendly like when all of sudden he lit into me like a bull who saw red. I don't know what in hell got into him."

"He's been acting strange ever since he got back," Lisa said absentmindedly. "He thinks you and I are lovers. Mariz and Consuelo have convinced him that we've been sleeping together while he was gone. I'm sure they had a lot of juicy lies to tell him."

"The man's a fool if be believes them. Want me to set him straight? I'd be glad to," Josh said, rubbing his sore jaw.

"No, thanks. That would only make things worse."

"He has to know the truth, and I think I oughta be the one to tell him. He's got no right thinkin' what he's thinkin'."

"No, it won't matter. I've told him the truth already but he won't believe me. He'd think you were lying to protect me."

"Well, if you're sure you don't need my help, I think I better be gettin' on my way to Frisco. I don't seem to be real welcome around here anymore."

"Are you sure you're all right?"

"Sure. I been in worse fights than this before. Gotta

say tho', I ain't never been caught so unawares before."

"Are you sure you have to go, Josh?"

"You said it yourself, darlin', I'll only make things worse by hangin' around here. He's your husband after all and you two gotta work things out for yourselves. Don't worry, I ain't leavin' California yet. I'll be back to say good-bye to you."

Lisa didn't try to dissuade Josh from leaving and he was gone within the hour. She suddenly felt closed in, lost, and completely alone. She went and got Vida and went for a ride. She didn't care what Eric said about her riding alone. She only knew she had to ride and get out in the open countryside.

She rode for hours over the land, finding new trails she'd never seen before, watching frightened deer dash out of her way as she rode by. The fresh air felt good against her skin and she enjoyed the freedom which riding provided. She stopped by the lake that she and Josh had found on one of their rides. She walked to the lakeside and stared at the clear water, stooping down to scoop some up in her hand for a drink. She let Vida graze idly on the abundance of grass and wild mustard while she walked around and looked at the flowers, just enjoying the fresh air and sunshine, and the immense beauty of the land around her. She decided to go for a swim, and looking to see if anyone was around, she took off all her clothes and walked into the cool water of the lake. She swam and tried to forget that anything was wrong between her and Eric. She still couldn't figure out what had caused his sudden change of mood. He had never been jealous before. She turned suddenly when she heard the whinny of a horse. She looked up and saw a rider on a nearby knoll looking at her. She squinted her eyes against the sunlight, but she couldn't see through the glare. She started for the bank and her clothes, but the rider moved forward, blocking her exit from the water. She backed up and sat down in the water, trying to cover herself as well as she could. The rider came even closer and finally Lisa saw who it was—Chuka.

He sat on his horse, silently staring at her, making no move to get down from his horse. Lisa backed up deeper into the water so that all that was showing were her face and neck. Chuka dismounted and walked to the edge of the water, his eyes still on her. As she looked at him, Lisa realized that he was young, Eric's age, and without the cruel look he had had on his face when he talked with Eric, he was almost handsome. There was an animal beauty about the man, a sense of power.

"You are his woman?" he asked suddenly.

"Please, could you leave so I can get my clothes?"

"Answer my question."

"I'm his wife, but I'm not his woman," Lisa said honestly. She really wasn't sure how Eric felt about her now.

Chuka smiled and Lisa was amazed at the change in his face. He looked softer somehow, more vulnerable. The sun glinted off his hair and she watched the dark eyes watch her.

"Come out of the water now, I won't hurt you. I just want to watch."

"I can't. Please go."

"No, señora, I will not go. You'd better come out of the water soon. The wind will be up from the ocean and the water will be very cold. I told you I wouldn't hurt you." He walked back up the bank and sat down by a tree, stretching his legs out in front of him and placing his

375

hands behind his head.

Lisa watched him and she knew he would stay there until she came out; he was much more determined than she. The water was already getting colder and she wasn't about to stay in it and freeze.

With as much pride as she could muster, she rose out of the water, her head held high, her eyes fixed straight ahead of her. She didn't cover herself with her arms—she refused to act like an embarrassed child in front of the man.

She went to her clothes and dressed as quickly as she could. At least Chuka was honest, he didn't harm her or even move from his spot by the tree. He sat in the same position as before, his eyes glued to Lisa's every movement. When she reached up to undo her hair, her hands trembled slightly—the man made her extremely nervous. She shook out her wet, tangled hair, running her fingers through it.

"You should have done that when you were naked—it would have been beautiful."

Lisa stood up and looked at him defiantly.

"How dare you talk to me like that!"

Chuka laughed loudly, revealing the creases on either side of his mouth. There was a time when he must have laughed a lot, Lisa thought. He stood up. He was tall and lean. Lisa thought he looked much different from the man she had seen on the beach.

"You remind me of a wild horse—spirited, long legs, firm flanks. I bet you're just as hard to ride, too."

Lisa uttered a loud, gasping sound and turned to walk toward Vida. Before she got to her horse, however, Chuka grabbed her from behind and turned her toward him.

"Let me go," Lisa yelled angrily.

Chuka held her tightly against him, feeling her firm breasts press against his chest as they heaved in anger. Lisa stared up at him as if hypnotized, her pulse quickening in spite of herself.

"What's wrong, green eyes, does it surprise you that I can make you feel as de Vargas does?"

"Don't call me that, don't ever call me that," Lisa screamed. "I don't feel anything for you."

"Tell yourself what you wish, green eyes, but you desire me. I saw it in your eyes that day on the beach."

Lisa struggled furiously, suddenly very much afraid.

"You're out of your mind, let me go. Please, I just want to go."

Chuka relaxed his hold on her slightly.

"All right, I'll let you go, but we'll meet again, of that you can be sure. I have plans for us. When my business with de Vargas is finished I will come for you. I will make you forget that de Vargas ever existed."

Lisa felt a shiver run down her spine at the decisiveness of his tone. He frightened her and she was anxious to get away from him. She pulled away, stumbling backward, but he made no motion to stop her. She quickly mounted Vida and rode off in the direction of the rancho. She thought of Chuka and how he had affected her. She had responded to him, if only for a short moment, and that bothered her. Why had he called her green eyes as Eric had done? She also thought of what he had said about his plans for Eric and for the first time, she was frightened for him. Chuka meant what he said and it was inevitable that they would meet. Equally as frightening was the thought that Chuka would take her if he killed Eric. He was both sensual and violent, Lisa thought, an extremely volatile and dangerous combination.

The next few weeks were lonely ones for Lisa. Eric refused to speak to her and he had even moved his things out of their room so that she was sleeping alone. Consuelo continued to stay, and she and Mariz were relentless in their attitude toward her, especially since they knew that Eric had moved out of their room. She was constantly near tears and she needed someone to talk to, to be with, someone who would be her friend. She thought of going to Raytahnee, but she didn't want to mar her friend's happiness with her own problems. She confronted Eric one night in his study, tired of being treated like a stranger by him.

"Why did you marry me?" she demanded to know.

He was drinking brandy, as was his custom of late, and he ignored her for a long time before he answered, his voice cold and devoid of any emotion, "I don't know why the hell I married you, but I wish now I never had."

Lisa stared at him, the shock of his words dulling her senses. She walked from the room as if in a daze. She didn't know what she was going to do now that he had finally admitted to her that he didn't love her. It wasn't long after her conversation with Eric in his study, that Lisa learned she was pregnant. She was afraid to tell Eric, afraid he wouldn't believe the child was his. He hadn't spoken a civil word to her since the day he'd beaten up Josh and she didn't know how to approach him.

The days dragged for her. The more she thought about it, the more she knew she couldn't live this way much longer. She knew she had to tell Eric about the baby. She thought it might help to bring them together again since they had talked about having a baby. She had to convince him the child was his.

The night Lisa decided to tell Eric about the baby, she didn't go down to dinner. She didn't have much of an appetite since she'd been pregnant, so she passed up dinner and opted for a bath instead. She was lazily dreaming in the tub when she heard the door open and saw Eric walk in. He closed and bolted the door and took a long drink out of the brandy bottle he was holding. Lisa could tell by the glazed look in his eyes that he was drunk and she knew this wouldn't be the night she would tell him about the baby. He walked over to the bed and sat down, an inane grin on his face.

"Too bad your lover isn't here to see you; he really is missing something. Water seems to compliment you."

"Get out. I'm not even going to waste my time trying to talk to you when you're in that condition."

"What condition? Oh, you mean the brandy bottle. Well, if it hadn't been for my faithless wife, maybe I wouldn't have to resort to this every night."

"Please, get out."

"Get out of my own room? Tired of me already, querida?"

Lisa didn't reply. She stared down at the water in the tub. She would never be able to tell him about the baby, she realized.

"I've decided it's my turn. I have a great desire for my wife tonight. So come over here, wife, and please me like you do your lover."

"You're disgusting. Why don't you just get out and leave me alone? I'm sure Consuelo would be happy to welcome you to her bed."

"She always does, but I'm in the mood for a change

tonight. Now, are you going to come over here or do I have to drag you out of that damned tub?''

Lisa looked at him and she knew that his threat wasn't idle, but she refused to be intimidated by him. She didn't move from the small tub. Eric got up from the bed and walked over to her, staring down at her for a few seconds, before quickly scooping her out of the tub, spilling most of the water on the floor. She fought him, but he half carried, half dragged her over to the bed, throwing her down on it. She stared up at him familiar with the look on his face, knowing what would happen next. She lay still, unmoving, unfeeling, as he lowered his body over hers. There was no gentleness in the act, no love, and Lisa was glad when his assault on her unyielding body was over. She didn't cry this time; she felt nothing but intense anger and hatred for what he had done, after he had promised her he would never force her again. Hatred was something she didn't think she could ever feel toward this man who had meant so much to her, but she realized for the first time, how narrow the line was between love and hatred. She didn't look at him but remained motionless until she heard his heavy, even breathing. Her decision had been made for her.

She got up from the bed as slowly and quietly as she could and dressed in her buckskins. She packed a few more things in a bag, picked up her moccasins, and started for the door. She stopped when she remembered something and she walked back to the bed. She set her things on the floor and unclasped the chain from around her neck. She looked once again at the beautiful green stones and then put them on the night table. She thought about taking off her wedding ring, but realized she would need it to prove that she was a widow. But she knew in actuality that it was only that she didn't want to give up the last little part she had of Eric, so she slipped the ring off her finger and placed it next to the necklace. She could buy a ring anywhere to prove she had been married.

She looked at her husband once more, a tight feeling in her stomach. She bent over and kissed him on the mouth. She could never hate him, she realized. He had loved her as no man would ever love her and for that, she would always love him.

"Good-bye my love," she whispered tearfully, "vaya con Dios." She touched his mouth softly and then turned and left the room.

CHAPTER XXV

Lisa had been riding for about three hours when she stopped to water her horse and rest. She was tired and needed to stretch her legs. She was sure Eric wouldn't have noticed her absence yet and even if he did, he probably wouldn't come looking for her. She didn't know what she was going to do. She knew she had to get to Tom in San Francisco and after that she would make her plans.

After a short rest during which she had eaten a tortilla taken from Marta's kitchen, Lisa mounted Vida and headed north toward San Francisco. She wasn't even sure how to get to San Francisco, but she figured if she kept north along the coast, she'd run into it. She was so deep in thought she didn't see the riders approaching from the east. When she did see them she instinctively knew that they were trouble. She kept riding northward, hoping she would avoid them, but they cut her off from the east. When she turned to go back, she found she was surrounded on all sides, unable to move anywhere. Then she saw Chuka and she never felt such raw terror in her life. The man instilled incredible fear in her.

They formed a tight circle around her and Vida became skittish, not used to the closed-in feeling. Lisa was unable to hold him when he reared suddenly, and Chuka caught her to him as she started to fall to the ground. He held her in front of him, his hands directly below her breasts.

"It seems we have met even sooner than I expected, eh green eyes? What are you doing way out here by yourself? Why isn't the patrón here to protect you?"

"Please let me go, Chuka," Lisa said excitedly, trying to struggle free of Chuka's rough hands.

"Ah, the pretty señora says please, eh compadres? I would be most happy to oblige you in that way, bonita."

Lisa watched blindly as Chuka and his men laughed at his crude joke and she knew the nightmare was just beginning. It was going to happen again—the men, the brutal assault, the pain and humiliation. She shut her eyes and tried to stop the tears. Chuka turned her face toward him.

"Don't worry, bonita, I'll take good care of you. Ándale!" He screamed to his men and they rode off in a cloud of dust. They rode eastward into the foothills until they came to a small encampment hidden back among some rocks and trees. Chuka dismounted and pulled Lisa along after him. He dragged her to a corner of the camp and tied her arms and legs and set her against a large boulder; and then walked off back across the camp. Lisa tried to maneuver into a more comfortable position, but it was impossible since her hands and feet were bound so tightly. She leaned her head back against the boulder and tried to fight the wave of nausea which overcame her. She didn't know if it was from the baby or from her fear of what Chuka would undoubtedly do to her. She thought of her unborn child and she knew that she would do anything to keep it alive. She had already lost one child and she was determined to keep this one alive. She needed this child—at least through it she could remember what it had once been like between her and Eric.

383

Eric—she thought of their last night together and again the nausea swept over her. Why had he treated her as he did, she wondered. How could he have believed the lies his mother had told him about her? Maybe he didn't want to know the truth. Perhaps what he had said about marrying her was true, that it had been a mistake. She thought back to the last few weeks at the rancho and she cringed inside. Eric had always been with Consuelo. He walked with her, rode with her, and, he had admitted, made love to her. She was angry suddenly, angry that Eric could be so hypocritical. He accused her of having an affair with another man, but he thought nothing of having another woman as a lover. It made no sense.

"You shiver, bonita. Are you cold?" Lisa shook her head. "Here, I have some food for you. It's all you'll get until tonight." He knelt down and untied her hands. "Don't try to run away, my guards are everywhere."

She rubbed her numb wrists and looked up at Chuka.

"What are you going to do with me? I have to know. At least let me know what I can expect." Her voice trembled slightly.

"I find I don't like what is planned for you, bonita."

"I don't understand," Lisa said with a puzzled expression on her face.

"You are to be killed, bonita, but only after my men have had their way with you? Entiendes?"

"But why?"

"For money; I do anything for money."

"Was this your idea or Mariz's?"

"Neither. It was Consuelo's, but I readily agreed. It seemed a good way to get back at de Vargas."

"Oh, God," Lisa moaned. "I should have known she'd never let him go."

"Why does she hate you so?"

"She hates me because Eric married me and not her. She wants him; she always has. How much is she paying you, Chuka? I'd guess not half as much as she's going to get out of it."

"She says with you out of the way de Vargas will marry her. Then we can arrange for a little accident, a fatal one. Then we will get married and we'll control almost all the land around here. The land is mine anyway, it was stolen from me."

Lisa began to laugh, sounding almost hysterical. Chuka took her by the shoulders and shook her.

"Why are you laughing? No one laughs at Chuka. No one."

"You're stupid," Lisa yelled at his shocked face. But she continued; she knew she had nothing to lose. "Do you actually believe Consuelo will marry you? Why should she? She's just using you. She's in love with Eric and she'll do anything to get him. Do you think she needs the de Vargas land or money? She's a wealthy woman. She doesn't want you, Chuka, she wants my husband. And once she gets him, she'll never let him go. Never!" Lisa watched Chuka's expression change from one of disbelief to one of anger. Lisa decided to press her advantage still farther. "Once you've killed me Consuelo will marry Eric and then she'll probably have you arrested for murder. She's the only one who knows your plan and you're the one who's taken all the risks. It's your word against hers and who will believe the word of a notorious bandit against that of a respected landowner. She told me once she would never let me have Eric and now I believe her. It's him she wants, not you. Think back to when you were children, who was it she cared for then?"

"Bastante!" Chuka yelled as he stood up. For a second Lisa was sure he was going to strike her, but he stood still, looking down at her.

"You've said far too much. I've killed men for saying less to me. I'm not so stupid as you seem to think. I trust no one, especially a woman. I have my own plans for you and de Vargas. And as for that puta," he spat on the ground, "I have a special surprise for her."

Lisa watched him walk away, breathing a sigh of relief. She was afraid she had pushed him too far, but it was too late to take it back now. She wondered what he had meant when he said he had a special surprise for Consuelo.

She leaned back against the rock and rubbed her hands together, trying to keep warm. Her feet were still tied together and she knew she didn't have a chance of escaping. She shut her eyes and tried to rest. Awhile later Chuka returned and retied her hands, after taking her to the stream to see to her needs.

The day passed uneventfully and Lisa tried to keep her mind occupied with various things. Chuka came once again in the evening to bring her another plate of food, and when she was finished, he led her back to the stream. Her hands were retied and he covered her with a blanket.

"Sleep well, bonita, tomorrow should be an exciting day." Lisa had no idea what he was talking about and she didn't try to figure it out. She was tired and her body ached all over from the hard ground. She lay down on her side and closed her eyes, pulling the blanket around her as tightly as she could. At least she was safe for the night—Chuka didn't seem to have anything in mind for her yet. She felt a slight movement in her abdomen and a smile touched her lips. She longed to reach down and feel her stomach, feel the movement of the child, but at least she knew it was alive and strong. That in itself was enough to make her strong, to keep her going. Even if she had to submit to Chuka, she thought sadly, she would do it. She would do anything to keep her baby alive.

She wondered what Chuka would do if he found out she was carrying Eric's child. Would he do something to harm the child or her? Or would he wait until the child was born and give it away. The thought made her shiver and she was determined to keep the knowledge from him as long as she could.

Lisa was untied and taken to the stream early the next morning, and she was even allowed to go for a little walk under guard. When she got back to camp she ate cold beans and coffee for breakfast. The beans and coffee were horrible, but she ate with relish, happy to have something in her stomach. She watched as some of Chuka's men rode out of camp. Before they left, Chuka walked over to her. He took a long knife out of his leg strap and reached down to her. She shook slightly but she didn't show any sign of fear. Chuka reached for a length of her hair, and after fondling it for a moment, swiftly cut if off.

"For luck, bonita," he said and walked toward his men and his waiting horse.

The day passed slowly for Lisa, much like the day before. She tried to pass the time thinking of names for her baby. She could imagine what it would look like—thick black curls, dark skin, and clear blue eyes. She smiled happily and then closed her eyes and slept for a while.

She sat up abruptly. Some of Chuka's men rode in at a furious pace, sending dust to every part of the camp. Lisa looked up and saw that Chuka wasn't among them. They were all talking excitedly about something, but she wasn't able to hear anything they said.

It was almost dark and Chuka still hadn't returned. One of his men brought her dinner and then retied her hands when she was through. She tried not to think of Chuka, but it was impossible. He desired her, that much was obvious, but whether he cared enough for her to spare her life or that of her child, she didn't know. It was late in the evening when Chuka and the rest of his men returned with Consuelo on the back of one of the horses, her hands and legs bound. She was pulled from the horse and dragged to the opposite side of the camp from Lisa. She seemed dazed and Lisa was sure Consuelo hadn't seen her. She was gagged as well as tied, and Lisa could see blood and bruises on her face.

Chuka walked to Lisa and sat down next to her, untying her hands as he did so. Lisa studied him in silence. He was a brutal, cruel man, yet he hadn't really harmed her and in fact, had treated her almost kindly. He'd been considerate of her needs and made sure that she was able to clean up, eat, and sleep with a fair amount of comfort. She wondered if he were kinder than he really showed.

"Why do you stare at me, bonita?"

For a brief moment, Lisa was taken back to that time in Nakon's tipi when he had first caught her staring at him and had smiled at her.

"I'm sorry, I was only wondering why you've treated me so kindly."

"I always treat my property with great care, and make no mistake about it, you are my property, bonita." He caressed her shoulder shoulder lightly, but she shrugged his hand off.

"It will do no good to fight me. When the time is right, I will make you mine. But I will be patient. I will wait until your husband comes for you and then I'll take you in front of him. I will get great pleasure in watching his agony as I take you. And then I will kill him. I will kill him in front of you so that you can see he no longer exists for you. You will forget that he ever existed. I will be the only man for you then."

"No! He won't come after me, he doesn't love me anymore. You're wasting your time. He doesn't even know where I am."

"But he will. Right now, one of my men is leading him here. When I cut off a piece of your hair, I gave it to Paco to give to de Vargas with the instructions that if he ever wanted to see you alive again, he should follow Paco. He should be here at any time now." He stood up, a slight smile on his face, and then he walked off in Consuelo's direction.

Lisa shut her eyes and prayed that Eric wouldn't come, that he didn't love her anymore. Nothing would save him if he came into Chuka's camp, nothing.

Eric opened his eyes to a fist crashing down into his face. He was violently pulled from his bed and thrown onto the floor, and before he could react, he felt the blows again while he was pinned to the floor. When the brutal assault finally stopped, he saw Josh Wade. Josh got up and pulled Eric up after him.

"I owed you that," Josh said angrily. "Now, while I'm here I'm gonna tell you a few things and you're gonna listen to me, even if I have to beat them into you. I ain't never been Lisa's lover. Not that I didn't try, mind you,

I'm no fool. But she never had any interest in me other than as a friend. It was always you she loved, tho' hell if I know why. When we heard you'd been killed I thought for sure she'd forget you and turn to me, but she didn't. You were still too much a part of her, even dead. She couldn't turn to another man."

"What about the necklace?"

"This? She gave it to me after I brought her here. Said it was the only thing she had to give me. It was her way of sayin' thanks."

"What about the time you spent with her here when I was gone? Did anything happen?"

"Christ, you're a bull-headed bastard. I just finished telln' you there ain't never been anything between us. When I came back here I was hopin' Lisa would marry me. I wanted to take her back to Missouri with me. But she told me about you and your marriage. At first I was angry, but I guess I knew all along she could never love me. Anyway, I stayed because she was lonely and missed you. Your mother and that bitch, Consuelo, were treatin' her like dirt. We spent as little time here as we could. Lisa was tired of all their bull."

Eric walked over to the bed and sat down next to Josh. He bent forward, running his hands through his hair.

"Jesus," he said tiredly. "I acted like a damned fool. I was so goddamned jealous I didn't even stop to listen to her. Like an idiot, I believed what my mother said—something I should have known better than to do."

"Well, you're right, you are a damned fool, but that's not gonna help things now. You gotta patch things up with Lisa. Where is she anyhow? Marta told me she was gone."

"I don't know, at my grandfather's, I guess."

"You don't know! Don't you give a damn?"

"Of course I give a damn. I just figured she needed some time to cool off."

"When was the last time you saw her?"

"Night before last. When I got up yesterday morning she was gone. I just assumed she went to my grandfather's. There isn't any other place she could go."

"And you didn't even check to make sure. Christ, you're an idiot, Anderson. The countryside is full of bandits and squatters and you let your wife ride out alone. Never seen such a crazy person in my life."

"That's enough. So I made a mistake, but talking about it isn't going to help."

"Well I'd feel a helluva sight better knowin' Lisa's all right before I go back to Missouri."

Eric nodded and got up from the bed and dressed. As he sat down on the bed again to pull on his moccasins, he looked over at the nightstand and saw Lisa's necklace and ring. He picked them up and he had a strange feeling that something was wrong. He hurriedly finished dressing and he and Josh went downstairs. They were walking through the courtyard to the stables when they saw Paco. He looked vaguely familiar to Eric.

"Don Alejandro?"

"Yes. What do you want?"

"I am to give you this," Paco said, handing Eric a note. When Eric unfolded it a piece of Lisa's hair fell on the ground. He glanced at it briefly and read the note. When he finished reading it, he bent down and picked up the piece of hair, rubbing it between his fingers. Then he walked over to Paco and took him by the shoulders.

"Where is she?"

"I am to take you to her alone, Don Alejandro."

"What does it say?" Josh asked, walking up behind Eric. Eric handed him the note. It read:

> If you want to see your woman alive again, come with Paco—alone.
>
> Chuka

"Oh, Christ, I knew it, I knew something had gone wrong. I felt it in my bones." Josh walked back and forth a few times and then came back to stand in front of Eric. "Well what do we do?"

"There's nothing we can do. I have to do what the note says or he'll kill her. I know Chuka and he'll do it."

"Who the hell is Chuka and what does he want with Lisa?"

"He's using Lisa to get back at me for something I did to him when we were kids. He means what he says, Josh, he'll kill her if I don't come alone."

"I'm going with you."

"You can't, you read the note. I have to go alone. It's the only chance Lisa has." He started to follow Paco out of the courtyard but stopped and turned back to Josh. "Do me a favor and keep an eye on my mother; I wouldn't be surprised if she had a hand in this. Wait here until you hear from me. I may need your help later."

Josh nodded and watched as the two men walked out. He felt curiously helpless. Lisa was in danger, and this time there was nothing he could do to help her.

Eric and Paco had ridden for about an hour when Eric stopped and dismounted. Paco looked at him, his hand resting on the gun in his holster.

"My horse, I think he's got something in his shoe."

Eric bent down and picked up the horse's leg, as if looking for a small stone. Growing impatient, Paco dismounted and stretched. It was what Eric had hoped he would do. He jumped Paco and knocked him unconscious. When Paco woke up later he was staked naked on the ground, the heat of the midday sun already making him sweat. Eric sat in the shade of a nearby tree, his hands crossed in front of his chest.

"You're very careless, Paco. You should've known my horse is an Indian pony and doesn't wear shoes. I lived with the Comanche a long time, Paco, and they taught me a lot about torture. There are many ways to make a man talk. Before long those leather thongs should begin to dry out and they'll be getting tighter and tighter. Your tongue will begin to swell as the thong around your neck starts to choke you. I've seen a man last three days like that."

"What do you want, señor?" he asked fearfully.

"I think you know, Paco. Tell me where Chuka's camp is and then I'll let you go. I don't have any quarrel with you."

"But I can't do that, señor, Chuka will kill me."

"You'll die anyway if you don't tell me. It's your choice. You can be in Mexico before Chuka even knows you're gone."

"I can't, señor."

Eric got up and poured some more water over the leather thongs. Paco squirmed, trying to loosen his bonds, but he only caused them to tighten painfully.

"I wouldn't take too long to decide if I were you, Paco. When the leather dries again, you may not be able to talk." Eric walked back to the tree and sat down. "I'm going to take a little rest now. I hope you come to your

393

senses soon. It may be too late by the time I wake up."

It was only minutes later when Paco screamed for Eric to untie him. He told Eric where Chuka's camp was located and Eric untied him and took him bound and gagged back to the rancho. He took him into the tack room and told Hector to guard him. He wanted to make sure he was still around in case he had lied about the location of Chuka's camp.

He went into the hacienda to get some food and bandages, and he ran into Josh. Josh insisted that he go with him, but Eric refused. He still believed the only chance Lisa had was with him. As he started out of the hacienda, he saw Mariz sitting by the fountain reading a book. He walked up to her, grabbing the book from her hand and tossing it into the fountain.

"Sandro, what are you doing?"

"You'll pay for what you've done to Lisa, Mariz, you'll pay dearly. I'll take care of you myself when I get back. I should've known better than to trust you."

"But I don't understand . . ."

"You're an expert at lying, aren't you? Like a fool I believed what you told me about Lisa, but I know the truth now. If anything happens to her, I swear I'll choke the life out of you."

Mariz stared at the furious expression on her son's face, not understanding what he was talking about.

"Sandro, please, tell me what you're talking about."

"I'll talk to you when I get back. In the meantime, Josh Wade will be here to keep an eye on you. Don't try to leave, Mariz. I told Josh to keep you locked up if he had to until I come back. You better pray that Lisa's all right."

"Sandro, come back, I don't understand. Where are you going?" Mariz's words fell on deaf ears as Eric walked out of the courtyard, mounted his horse, and rode off. Mariz didn't know what he was talking about, but for the first time she was afraid of him. Something had happened and evidently he thought she was responsible. I should never have crossed him, she thought, and now I will pay dearly for trying to destroy his marriage. God help me, she thought.

CHAPTER XXVI

Lisa was abruptly awakened by the loud, raucous laughter of Chuka's men. They had been drinking and she knew that something horrible was about to happen. She looked up in time to see Consuelo dragged from her spot in the camp, to the group of Chuka's men. Chuka said something to them in Spanish which Lisa couldn't hear, but she quickly figured out what it was.

The men slowly circled around Consuelo, and one of the men cut her ties. She tried to get up and run, but she ran right into the chest of a grossly fat man. She pulled her gag off and began to scream for Chuka to help her, but the fat man slapped her face until she stopped. Now, each man moved forward and took a turn at pulling off Consuelo's clothes. She was pushed from man to man until she was completely naked. The the fat man took her by the shoulders and forced her down to her knees, and he began to unbuckle his pants. He pulled his swollen member from his pants and shoved it toward Consuelo's face, but she turned her head, screaming. Her arms were quickly pinned behind her and her head pulled back until she was forced to submit to the outrage. Lisa turned her head at the disgusting sight and tried to blot out the sounds coming from the circle of men, and the woman they were abusing. She heard Consuelo's shrill screams and looked back to see the naked girl forced on her hands and knees, and she was entered from behind by one of the men. The raucous laughter continued unchecked.

"It's not a pretty sight, eh?" Lisa hadn't heard Chuka walk up silently next to her. He sat down. "You see, she's not such a grand lady now, is she?" He saw the worried expression on Lisa's face. "Don't feel sorry for her. Remember, that is what she had in mind for you, only after you were violated, you were to be murdered. Can you feel sorry for a woman who would condemn another woman to such a fate?"

Lisa looked at Chuka and then back at Consuelo. Her anguished cries still filled the air. Lisa knew what Consuelo was going through and in spite of what Consuelo had planned for her, she felt sorry for her. Admittedly, the Comanche had not abused her in such ways, but nevertheless, she had been abused. It didn't surprise her that these men were doing worse things to Consuelo, however. The red man was always being accused of such atrocities, but the white man and brown man was just as capable of committing such acts. She looked at Chuka, unable to restrain her anger.

"Is this what you have in mind for me? If it is, then I beg you to kill me now. I would rather die than go through that again." She turned away from him, not wanting to show him how vulnerable she really was.

"Again? When did such a thing happen to you, bonita?" He lifted her chin up. "Tell me."

"I was captive of the Comanche for many months. I don't think I have to tell you any more." She looked away, her voice sounding cold and distant. "I don't think I could go through that again; I would rather die."

Chuka pulled her into his arms and held her. She

didn't resist him. This was a woman worth having, he thought, a woman who is strong yet beautiful. She will turn to me when de Vargas is dead. She is the kind of woman who needs a man. Even now she is softening toward me, he thought with a smile.

"Don't worry, bonita, my men know that you are mine. They wouldn't dare harm you. And as for me, I don't treat my women like that. I am a man and I can make a woman respond to me without forcing her to do so." He lifted her face and kissed her lightly on the mouth. Lisa felt a slight ache in her stomach and she kissed him back.

"Soon, bonita, soon," Chuka said softly. "I don't think I will have to force you." He loosened her ties and got up, covering her with the blanket. He walked over to his men and yelled at them to stop. Unwillingly, the men listened to their leader and backed away from the battered Consuelo. Lisa saw that Consuelo was lying naked on the ground—dirty, bruised and bloody. She watched as Chuka walked over to her and covered her with a blanket.

Lisa curled up on the hard ground, thinking of the kiss Chuka had given her and the way she had responded to him. It was the second time she had responded to him, but was it really to him she was responding? Or was it the memory of Eric? She shut her eyes and for one small moment, dreamed that it had been Eric who had held her so tenderly and kissed her so softly. She drifted off into a fitful sleep and she didn't awaken when Chuka walked over to look down at her.

Chuka stood staring down at her. She looked beautiful and young, almost like a child. He was no different from any other man who had always wanted a woman to love him and give him children. He was tired of all the whores he had had and he wanted a real woman. He was sure he had found her in Lisa. He decided he would take her to Mexico with him when he was done with his business here. When he was through with Consuelo, she would give him everything she owned and he could go to Mexico a very wealthy man. He could make a good life for Lisa.

He was suddenly startled by the howl of a lone coyote. It was an eerie sound, one which he would never get used to. He looked around the camp to see if all was in order and then he went over to his pack. He thought about Eric. He thought back to the time when they were boys and Alejandro was the only friend he had had. He had forced his family and friends to accept Chuka and he had made his mother find work for Chuka on their rancho. He had even talked his father into letting him take lessons with him from the padre and the English tutor. Those had been good days. They were young and innocent and free. They roamed around the land like young explorers, and they dreamed of the day when they would both sail off to the Orient with Alejandro's father. Chuka loved Sandro as a brother and he would have gladly died for him. He had treasured the knife Alejandro had given him on his eleventh birthday. It was the same knife he had almost killed Alejandro with when he discovered him with his mother. He still carried the knife with him.

The coyote howled again and the hair on Chuka's neck bristled at the sound. He pulled his blanket around him and laid his head back against his saddle. Paco and de Vargas should have been here by now, he thought. Something's gone wrong. But what could go wrong?

Lisa too, heard the coyote and she sat up. It was odd that there was only one. They almost always traveled in packs. It reminded her of the time with the Comanche when Nakon told her that when they went on raids they communicated by way of a coyote howl. It was meant to signify that they were near. . . .

Again the howl and she knew. It was Eric telling her that he was near. She should have known he would never be caught in Chuka's trap. He had been a Comanche for too long, was too wary of traps to be caught in one. She felt safe now, as if he were within reach. She didn't know how he was going to fight over a dozen men, but she knew he had a plan. Surprise was on his side.

The howling stopped and Chuka finally relaxed. He knew he would be able to sleep now and he stretched out on the hard ground, more reassured by the quiet sounds of the night.

The three guards, one each on the two rocks above the entrance and one of the rocks above the back of the camp, relaxed their vigil after their leader had returned that night. They had been drinking some tequila and watching the other men as they had raped Consuelo, angry that they had to stay on guard. When the excitement was over and they saw Chuka go to sleep, they all decided they too would get some sleep. Surely no one would sneak into camp without them hearing. Thinking that was their fatal mistake.

Eric killed the guard on the rocks at the front of the camp first. His moccasins allowed him to move swiftly and silently. He moved to the other guard who was situated a little farther back from the entrance. He covered his mouth from behind and stuck his knife between his ribs and into his heart. The man fell limply to the ground, out of the light of the campfire. Eric then crept around the outside of the camp and back into the trees by the stream. This was the path which Lisa had taken to the stream. He walked slowly, avoiding twigs and branches. The third guard posed somewhat of a problem because he was off the path poised on a rock above the bushes. It would be impossible for him to go through the bushes without making a lot of noise, so he crept on all fours to the opening of the path. The guard was dozing fitfully, his head bobbing on his chest, his mouth open. Eric stood up suddenly and with a deft movement threw his knife at the man's chest. The guard never woke up. Eric picked up his rifle as he had the others', and then he crawled over to where Lisa was sleeping. He put his hand over her mouth and shook her awake.

"Lisa, wake up," he whispered softly.

Lisa lifted her head, startled, but she didn't utter a sound. She sat up and Eric took his hand from her mouth.

"When I cut you loose, run to the stream and wait for me there." He cut her ties and she stood up.

"Eric . . ."

"We'll have plenty of time for talk later. Now do as I say; get to the stream."

Lisa made her way quickly down the path to the stream and waited in the shelter of some trees. Eric made his way across the camp to Consuelo and picked her up, carrying her to the stream where Lisa was waiting for them.

"Let's get going."

"What about Chuka?"

"I'll take care of Chuka later. Follow me." They walked downstream to a large group of rocks. They climbed down the rocks and mounted the two horses which were waiting for them. Eric carried Consuelo in front of him.

Lisa couldn't contain the jealousy and hatred that welled up inside her when she looked at Consuelo in Eric's arms, even though she knew Consuelo was badly hurt. When they were a few miles out of camp, Lisa spoke to Eric, angry in spite of herself.

"Why did you come for me? Why didn't you just let me go?"

"I'm sorry for what I did to you that night, and there are still some unanswered questions between us. But if Chuka is more to your liking, I'd be glad to take you back up to him."

"You bastard!" she said viciously. "I wish you had left me there."

"Look," Eric said, his voice hard, "I expect a little gratitude for what I did for you. I risked my neck to get you out of there."

"And Consuelo."

He grabbed her wrist and practically pulled her from her horse.

"Stop it, you're hurting me."

"God, you're an ungrateful bitch." He pulled up and dismounted, laying Consuelo on the ground and pulling Lisa from her horse. He grabbed both her wrists and yanked her toward him.

"I don't think you really wanted me to leave you there, did you? I know you, Lisa, and I know how I make you feel, how your body opens up to mine. . . ."

"Stop it, you make it sound so dirty." She tried to pull away but Eric held on to her wrists.

"It's the truth and you can't go on denying what you feel inside. I don't care how many men you've had, I love you and I want you." He covered her mouth with his and his fingers fumbled at the buttons on her blouse.

"No!" Lisa cried and pulled away from him. "Don't you understand, there haven't been any other men but you. Why won't you believe that?" She ran off into the darkness, ignoring Eric's pleas for her to come back.

"Christ," he muttered. "Lisa, will you come back here. We've got to get out of here before Chuka discovers you're gone. We can talk later."

When Lisa didn't answer he walked around in the darkness after her and finally walked back to his horse to get his rifle. "Lisa," he yelled once more, but when she didn't answer him he began to get worried. He was just about to set off after her when he heard her scream. He rushed toward her in the darkness. Damn, he thought, we should've never stopped here. Damn!

"I suggest you stop, de Vargas, before I slit her pretty throat," Chuka said fiercely out of the darkness. Eric stopped in his tracks. "Too bad, you almost got away, but you had to have her, didn't you? You're more of a fool than I thought." Chuka motioned to his men and they lashed Eric to a tree, while some others built a fire.

"I was going to take you back to my camp but this is good enough for what I'm going to do; no one will be this far out this late at night. No one will hear your screams for mercy." Chuka walked up to Eric and hit him across the face, opening the cuts that Josh had inflicted on him that morning. Chuka hit him again and again, until Eric's face was bruised and bloodied. Eric remained impassive throughout the onslaught. Chuka took out his knife again.

"Remember this knife? You gave this to me on my eleventh birthday, remember?" He started to lift the knife toward Eric's face when Lisa broke free of the man who was holding her and grabbed Chuka's arm.

403

"Please don't, Chuka, please. I'll do anything you ask."

"Stay out of it, Lisa," Eric yelled angrily.

Chuka looked from Lisa to Eric and he realized that she did love Eric. She would do anything for him.

"All right, bonita, I'll stop for now. I've waited for this for a long time," he said, grabbing her by the shoulders and turning her to face Eric. "I will take great pleasure in watching you suffer before you die, bastardo. I will torture you in the best way I know how."

Eric stared at Chuka, a smile on his face. He wasn't afraid of any torture which Chuka could inflict on him. He knew he could outlast anything Chuka had in mind for him.

"Don't be so quick to smile, patrón, you don't know the torture I have in mind for you." He pushed Lisa forward a bit, until she was almost face to face with Eric. "Look good, because it's the last time you'll see this face." He pulled Lisa back and kissed her, ripping the clothes from her body as he did so.

"Look, patrón, is this not perfection? Have you ever seen a more beautiful body?" He ran his rough hands over Lisa's bare breasts and stomach, and down to her thighs. In spite of what she had said to Chuka, she fought him. She knew she couldn't bear to have him touch her and she fought him, but the more she fought him, the more he inflicted on her. She looked up at Eric once and the look on his face reflected what he felt. He loved her and there was nothing he could do to help her. Why did I have to fight with him, she thought. We could've been far away from here by now. The tears rolled down her face; she knew that Chuka would rape her and then make her watch as he killed Eric. Chuka saw the look that passed between the two and he hauled Lisa to the ground.

"Chuka, don't, your fight's with me, not her. Do anything you want with me. Chuka!" Eric screamed furiously, but Chuka only laughed as he straddled Lisa's body. His hands traveled everywhere and he marveled at the beauty of her body. He spread her thighs apart, ready to mount her, but she screamed and hit him across the face. He hit her back, but Lisa was able to push him to the side a little and she brought her knee up with all the force she could muster and struck him in the groin. He yelled and rolled away and she crawled away from him and got to her feet, but Chuka grabbed her ankles and pulled her back down on the ground. She tried to hit him again, but he pinned her to the ground with his hands and knees, and he hit her across the face until she quieted down.

Eric struggled against his ties, his pleas to Chuka completely ignored. He shut his eyes to the sight before him, but he couldn't shut his ears to Lisa's cries of anguish. He was afraid Chuka would kill her if she didn't quit fighting him. He opened his eyes again and saw Lisa bite Chuka's lip, in spite of the fact that he was still beating her everywhere else.

"You bitch," he screamed. "I'll show you what I do to such women."

All Lisa was aware of was the blinding, searing pain as Chuka beat on her with his fists. She tried to protect her belly, but she wasn't able to do anything against his vicious onslaught. Then she heard the shot; it sounded far off, and blessedly the pain stopped. Her last conscious thought was that her baby was dead.

The sound of the shot surprised Eric as much as it did everyone else. He looked behind him and saw Consuelo, naked and covered only by the blanket, her long hair in

405

wild disarray, his rifle in her hands.

He'd been watching the spectacle before him and dying little by little. Chuka had been right—it had been the worst kind of torture. He felt no fear of physical torture, but he couldn't cope with seeing another person whom he loved so dearly being harmed in such a violent and humiliating way. When he heard the shot, he had no idea where it had come from. He was shocked to see Chuka slumped over Lisa, a bullet hole in his back.

"The next one of you bastardos who moves will get a bullet in his gut," Consuelo screamed at the men. "All of you drop your guns and knives, and you, gordo, I want you to cut the patrón loose." The men did as they were told and Eric quickly gathered all of the guns and knives.

"Now, gordo," Consuelo said coldly to the fat man who had first abused her, "kneel down here, right in front of me." The man hesitated until Consuelo shoved the barrel of the rifle into his stomach, then he quickly complied.

"Now, open your mouth." The man looked up at Consuelo and did as he was told. Consuelo laughed and then put the tip of the barrel into the man's mouth. "How does it feel, gordo? Do you feel like such a man now?"

Eric was pushing the men against the trees and going through the saddle gear, when he turned to see Consuelo, the rifle poised in her hand, the barrel in the man's mouth.

"Consuelo, don't," he yelled.

"Good-bye, gordo," Consuelo said coolly and then pulled the trigger. She began to laugh hysterically at the bloodied stump which only seconds before had been the man's head. Eric walked over to her and took the rifle out of her hands.

"You men ride out of here as fast as you can and get as far away as possible. If I ever see any of you around here again, I'll take great pleasure in slitting your throats. Entienden?" The men ran to their horses and rode out, the sound of their horses' hoofs echoing in the still night.

Eric walked over and pulled Chuka's limp body from Lisa's and he picked her up in his arms. He covered her with a blanket and walked to the fire. She was badly bruised and there was blood running down her leg.

"She was carrying your child you know?" Consuelo said as she walked up behind him. "If it had been me I would have told you; I would have done anything to keep you."

"What did you say?"

"She was carrying your child. Rosa, her maid told me. She saw her coming out of the tub. She said there was no mistaking the fullness in her breasts and belly."

"Why didn't she tell me?" he said more to himself than to Consuelo. Then he realized how little attention he had paid to her in the last weeks.

"It seems she's a proud woman, but it doesn't matter now anyway. It looks as though she's lost the child." Consuelo knelt next to Eric. "Leave her; we can be together now. No one will stand in our way."

Eric stood up, his face contorted with rage.

"What the hell is wrong with you? Can't you understand this woman is everything in the world to me? If she dies a part of me dies, too. I was crazy to have anything to do with you or Mariz."

Consuelo stared at him in disbelief.

"But I had it all planned; we can be together now. I have gone to so much trouble for us to be together, querido."

Eric looked at her, comprehension slowly dawning on him. He walked to her and grabbed her roughly by the shoulders.

"It was you who planned for Lisa to be kidnapped by Chuka. And I thought it was Mariz. I didn't think you were capable of such treachery. It seems I underestimated you, Consuelo."

"But I did it for us so that we could be together. You came to Chuka's camp to rescue me, you must care."

"I didn't come for you, I came for Lisa. You were an afterthought," he said coldly.

She reached out to slap him, but he caught her wrist tightly.

"What was your plan, Consuelo? Was Chuka supposed to kidnap Lisa and take her to Mexico so that I'd never see her again?"

An evil smile spread across Consuelo's face, distorting her otherwise delicate features.

"It was a better plan than that. I paid Chuka to kidnap her and told him he and his men could do anything they wanted with her, as long as they killed her afterward. I told Chuka that you would marry me when she was out of the way and then he and I would arrange to have you killed, too, so I would own everything and share it with him. He liked the prospect of being a rich man. What he didn't know was how much I love you; I could never harm you. I was going to blame Chuka for your wife's murder. It was a perfect plan. It can still work, querido."

Eric looked at her, conscious of the crazed look in her eyes.

"Consuelo . . ."

"We can leave her now, Sandro, and no one will know what happened. They will think Chuka killed her."

"I love her, Consuelo, can you understand that? I love Lisa and I'm not going to leave her here to die. She's my wife and she's the only wife I'll ever want." He walked away from her, bending over to wrap Lisa in the blanket and pick her up. "I don't want to see you around the del Sol anymore, Consuelo. And if you ever go near or try to harm Lisa, I'll see to it that you never harm anyone again." His voice carried such a deadly threat that in her near-hysterical state, Consuelo knew Eric meant what he said.

He mounted his horse, holding Lisa in front of him, and taking Vida's reins. As he turned to go, he heard Consuelo screaming at him.

"You can't leave me here, I'll die. You can't leave me here you bastard! Come back here. I'll kill you someday, I swear I'll kill you for this."

Eric rode away, oblivious of everything but the woman in his arms. He held her closely as he rode the distance to the cave. It was the place where he had gone as a small boy to watch his father's ship on the horizon. He knew many of the Comanche herbal medicines and he would try to heal her. He would care for her until she was well again, and there, he would make her love him again. He would try to make up for all the wrong he had done her.

The sound of pounding surf reached his ears. He was close now. It was completely up to him to make her well again, physically as well as emotionally. He had to make her see that he loved her more than anything or anyone else in the world. He had to.

Consuelo stood watching as Eric rode off with Lisa in his arms. She ran after him, but she knew it was no use; he wouldn't come back for her. She couldn't believe what he'd told her; she couldn't believe he really did love his wife. She walked back to the camp, intending to keep the fire going to deter bears or wolves from wandering into camp. She looked around for the rifle, but she couldn't find it; she was sure she had left it by the dead man's body. Then she remembered that Eric had taken it out of her hands. Where had he put it? She walked over and stared down at the dead man's body, laughing as she thought of the look on his fat face when she fired the rifle. She looked up; something was different, something was wrong. She walked around and then realized what was bothering her—Chuka's body was gone. She was sure she had killed him. Where had the body gone? She heard a sound among the trees and stared toward them. She walked closer.

"Is someone there?" she asked tentatively.

The blast from the rifle was the only answer she would ever receive.

Josh found Chuka's camp without any trouble, but when he rode in he found it completely empty, only a few scattered campfires to suggest that anyone had been there. It was easy enough to follow their tracks out—they hadn't even attempted to cover them.

He smiled when he remembered how easily he had gotten Paco to tell him the whereabouts of Chuka's camp—Eric had probably scared hell out of him with some of his Comanche tricks, he thought amusedly. When he left the del Sol to search for Lisa and Eric, he had made sure that Paco was securely tied up in the tack room, with Hector and Vicente as his guards.

Josh saw a faint glow in the distance and dismounted, quietly approaching the dying campfire. His rifle was ready. He crept along slowly in the darkness, but when he came to the camp, he saw it was deserted except for three dead bodies. He recognized Consuelo, but he didn't know the fat man or the younger man. He examined the bodies. Consuelo had been shot twice, once in the chest, once in the stomach; the fat man's head was blown nearly clean off; the younger man had a bullet hole in his back, but was lying on his back instead of his stomach. It was all very strange. He wondered what these men had to do with Consuelo and if they all had anything to do with Lisa and Eric.

He started digging a shallow grave for them, working as quickly as he could with his hunting knife. There was still no sign of either Lisa or Eric and he was growing impatient and worried. Where had they gone? When he was finished burying the bodies, he rode back to the del Sol, hoping that Eric and Lisa had gone back there.

On his ride back to the rancho Josh was seized with a sudden panic. What if Chuka had gotten away and taken Lisa with him? Maybe Eric had followed them. He had no idea where to search for any of them, or even where to start. He had faced just such a challenge when he had searched for Lisa among the various Comanche camps and he had finally found her. Well, damn it, he thought, if I did it once, I can do it again. I'll find 'em both if I have to search from here to Mexico. I'll find 'em.

Lisa opened her eyes and looked around. It was dark except for a small fire burning close to her. She looked to her left and saw Eric sitting across from her on the other side of the fire. She tried to sit up but she groaned. She was stiff and sore. Eric heard her movement and walked over to her.

"How do you feel?"

"Sore." She looked at the fire, avoiding his eyes. "I've

lost this child, haven't I?"

"I don't think so. You lost a little blood but not much. But you'll have to feel for any movement. That will tell us for sure."

"Us?"

"It's my child, too. Why didn't you tell me, Lisa?"

"It wouldn't have mattered if I had told you; you would never have believed it was yours. It could be anybody's child for all you know."

"It's mine."

"It doesn't matter anyway. As soon as I'm well enough to travel, I'm leaving here for good. You won't have to worry about me or the baby."

"And just how do you plan to support yourself and the child?"

"It's none of your business how I support myself. I'll get along. I'll find a way if I have to become a maid to a wealthy woman."

"You, a maid? That is funny!"

"Why? I've certainly done worse things in my life."

"And do you think any woman in her right mind would hire you as a maid in her house? No chance, my sweet."

"Why not?"

"A young woman on her own, beautiful and un-attached, she'd be crazy to hire you. Once her husband got a good look at you he'd consider you his property just because you worked for him. Is that what you want for your child?"

She looked at him a moment then dropped her eyes. She knew he was right, but what could she do? She had no skills and no money to rely on. How could she support herself?

"Of course, there is one other alternative," Eric said slyly.

"What alternative?"

"Marriage," he said simply. "Marriage to me. We're still legally married, you know."

"The marriage was a farce. We both know that."

"I didn't think so and I was the one who won the bet. I didn't have to marry you. I married you because I wanted to—for no other reason."

"Then why did you marry a woman whom you couldn't trust? Did you do it just to torment me?"

"I never meant to torment or hurt you. I just found out that I am insanely jealous when it comes to you—I couldn't think straight."

"That's obvious," she said dryly.

"I was wrong and I admit it. I'm sorry. Why can't we start over from here?"

"Because there's too much that's passed between us. Do you expect me to simply forget the way you treated me the past few weeks? You accused me of sleeping with another man and you yourself treated me like a whore. And all the while you were wasting no time in crawling back into Consuelo's bed. How much do you think I can take? It would always be like that. Every time I talked to a man you'd be wondering if he was my lover. I won't live like that. Nobody dictates to me whom I can and cannot be friends with and how I should choose to conduct myself."

"Maybe you should get some more sleep, you're beginning to babble. I'm going to get us something for dinner."

"Don't you walk out on me, Eric Anderson," she yelled, forgetting about her injuries as she sat up. She screamed involuntarily from the pain.

"Are you all right?" Eric asked as he ran over to her.

413

"I'm fine, I just don't want you running out on our fight."

He smiled, his teeth contrasting with his dark skin.

"I'm glad to see your injuries haven't affected your spirit any. Seems they've just affected your mind."

"You bastard!" she screamed, reaching for something to throw, but he was already out the mouth of the cave. She lay back down on the soft bed Eric had made for her and snuggled beneath the blanket. She watched the leaping flames of the fire and she was overcome by utter exhaustion.

The smell of fresh fish roasting on the fire roused Lisa from her sleep. She sat up and leaned against the wall, watching as Eric cooked the fish. She could see the supple muscles of his back, even through his shirt, and she thought of all the times she had run her hands over them. There was no doubt in her mind that she still loved him, but she was afraid to continue on with the marriage, afraid that he would always be suspicious of her. She knew she couldn't live the way she had the last few months. She needed to be loved and wanted. As if sensing her eyes on him, Eric turned, a smile on his face.

"Hungry?"

She nodded and he brought her some fish and some fresh water. They ate in silence. When she finished, she stretched out her arms and legs and smiled contentedly.

"You're a good cook." She watched for his reaction, but there was none. He disposed of the bones outside the cave and then stretched out by the fire, propping his head on his hand.

"Why are we here?" she asked suddenly.

"It was a place I used to come to when I was a kid. I figured it was as good a place as any to bring you."

"Your face looks terrible. Chuka didn't do all that to you."

"No, your friend paid me back. I figure we're even now."

"What about Consuelo? Is she all right?"

"I don't know; I left her there. I was more concerned with you at the time."

"God, she must've hated me. She wanted to make sure she had you all to herself."

"Yeah," Eric said harshly. "What a goddamned fool I was to ever get involved with her. You almost got killed because of it."

"Well, it's over now. I'll be leaving soon and . . ."

"Do you plan to see Raytahnee and my grandfather before you go?"

"I don't know."

"They'd both be hurt if you left without saying good-bye. And what about Tom? And Josh? Are you going to leave without saying good-bye to any of them?"

How could she leave all of these people who meant so much to her without even saying good-bye, she wondered. How could she leave the people who had become her family?

"Well?" he prompted.

"I don't know. I haven't really thought that far ahead."

"Then I think you should allow yourself a little time. You can stay with me at the del Sol until you decide what you want to do. I won't make any demands on you and my mother won't be around to bother you again. The del Sol is as much yours as it is mine."

Lisa looked at him in silence. She didn't know what to do. She was afraid that if she went back to the del Sol she would never want to leave again. But it would give her time to ponder the future and make plans. She could get in touch with Tom and make arrangements possibly to live with him.

"I'll think about it."

"That's good enough." He got up and put some more wood on the fire. "It's time you got some sleep." He walked over and covered her with another blanket, making sure she was warm and comfortable. He hesitated for a moment, as if he were going to touch her, but he got up and went back to his spot.

It was a few hours after they went to sleep that Eric heard Lisa scream his name. He got up and ran to her.

"He's alive," she said simply.

"What?" Eric asked, puzzled by her statement.

"The baby, he's alive. I felt him move, or kick, I should say. He's strong like his father."

Eric took her in his arms, secure in the knowledge that their child was alive and growing. He had an incredible urge to kiss her, but he drew back instead. He didn't want to push her. He got up and went back to his blanket.

Lisa's eyes followed him back to the spot where he slept. She had thought for a moment that he was going to kiss her, and when he didn't, she had been disappointed. She had told him that there could never be anything between them again so what did she expect from him? It seemed as though she were always contradicting herself when it came to Eric. She knew that what she really wanted was for him to take her in his arms and comfort and love her, but why couldn't she tell him that?

She lay back down and watched him as he slept—the tousled black hair, the dark lashes against his face, his long legs stretched out in front of him—there was

416

nothing about him which she didn't love. The truth came to her as she stared at him, her feelings bared but not visible to him. The truth was that there could never be any man that she could love as she loved, and would always love, him. And for that reason she knew she had to leave.

Eric carried fresh game when he came back to the cave the next morning. He was tired of fish and clams. He had even found some fresh berries growing in the woods. He had decided to take Lisa out that day so that she could have some fresh air. She was healing well and it wouldn't be long before she was well enough to leave. He was hoping he could keep her here long enough to change her mind. No matter what she decided, he wouldn't let her leave.

He walked into the entrance of the cave and knew instantly that she was gone. He looked around and saw that she had taken the blanket and a few other things. He ran outside, thinking that she might have just gone for a walk, but Vida was gone and so was she. He quickly gathered his things and tied them onto his horse. She can't be far, he thought. She isn't well enough to ride far.

He rode in the direction of the del Mar, positive that she had gone there to say good-bye to Raytahnee and Don Alfredo. He knew a shortcut that could get him there hours before she arrived. He'd be waiting when she got there, and this time he wouldn't let her out of his sight. He'd never let her go again.

CHAPTER XXVII

He leaned against the veranda railing which was partially hidden by the dangling wisteria blossoms. Lisa was on her hands and knees trimming the rose bushes and pulling the weeds around the small garden. Four months it had taken him to find her. He had looked everywhere and asked thousands of questions in two languages. Finally, he found Tom in San Francisco, but Tom told him he hadn't heard from Lisa. Eric had written to Lisa's mother in Boston, but she, too, replied negatively. For a long while he believed that something had happened to her, but he knew what a gift for survival she had; he refused to believe that anything had happened. He stayed around San Francisco, hoping he would hear something about her or find her working somewhere, anywhere. He and Tom met periodically for dinner, but he always found Tom to be subtly evasive about his sister. Eric became suspicious. He knew how much Tom cared for Lisa, and Eric knew he wouldn't be so nonchalant if he thought anything was wrong.

Eric began to follow Tom everywhere; then he noticed that Tom occasionally disappeared from town for a few days. He discovered that Tom owned a small rancho outside San Francisco and he followed him there hoping that Lisa would be at the ranch. He waited until Tom left and then rode in. He walked through the small courtyard and up onto the veranda. Then he saw the movement in the garden and Lisa. He stopped by the veranda railing, watching her as she worked in the garden.

She was dressed in a pale-blue dress which was covered by a long apron. Her hair was pulled back on her neck in a chignon, but stray wisps of hair fell down around her face and neck. She sat back on her haunches, wiping her hand across her brow, and finally leaned against the garden wall. She laid her head back against the adobe with a deep sigh and pressed her hands to her large abdomen. For the first time he saw how really large she was and he felt his stomach churn. She was his wife and she was carrying his child. How could he have ever doubted her and forced her away from him the way he had? Even if she had had other lovers, why should it have mattered? She wouldn't have loved him any less as a result. She had loved him even though she knew about Consuelo. He had been so wrong, so damned wrong. He started to move forward, but stopped when he heard her voice.

"My baby," she crooned softly, moving her hands across her belly. "I yearn to see you, to touch you, to love you." Her voice trembled. "Will you look like your father and have dark hair and eyes the color of the sky? Oh, Eric," she moaned suddenly and began to cry, her shoulders shaking with her sobs. He started to go to her, but he knew she'd resent his invading such a private moment. She was quiet now and her eyes were still shut. He decided to go inside when he heard her moan and slump forward, her arms clasping her belly. He made quick and silent passage across the tile floor and knelt beside her, his hand lightly touching her shoulder.

"Are you all right?"

Her eyes opened. "Eric . . ."

"Let me help you to the bench." He helped her up and walked with her to the wooden bench. He grabbed the clay pitcher standing nearby and made her drink from it, then he took off his bandana, dipped it into the water, and gently patted her face.

"You shouldn't be out here in this sun without something on your head."

"What are you doing here? What do you want?"

"You."

She looked at him, flustered by his direct answer; she stood up.

"How did you find me?"

"Tom."

"But he promised not to tell you. I made him promise."

"He didn't tell me. I just hung around him long enough to find out that he occasionally rode out of town. I figured he either had a lady tucked away somewhere or it was you."

"I want you to go. I don't want you here."

"I'm not going anywhere unless you come with me."

"No, I want you to leave me alone. I'm happy now, I'm content."

"I don't believe that." He walked closer to her and lightly touched her cheek with his hand. "I just don't believe it."

Lisa swayed on her feet, much too aware of his presence.

"I want to go inside. It's too hot out here." Eric nodded and took her arm, refusing to let her walk by herself. They went into a small, airy room, followed by an Indian woman.

"Señora, are you all right? I tell you again and again not to go outside in the hot sun."

Lisa waved her away, resting her head against the back of the chair which Eric had helped her into.

"I'm fine, Carmen, just a little tired. Would you bring Señor Anderson and me something cool to drink, please?"

Carmen stared at Eric, a quizzical expression on her brown face.

"You are related to the señora's husband?"

"I am the señora's husband."

"But I don't understand, the señora she say . . ."

"Never mind, Carmen," Lisa said impatiently. "Just bring us our drinks. I'll explain to you later."

Carmen nodded and hurried out, looking over her shoulder at Eric as she did so.

"Why did you tell her you're my husband?" Lisa glared angrily at Eric.

"Because I am. Why did she act so surprised? What'd you tell her?"

"That you were dead."

"No wonder she looked so damned scared," he said with a laugh. He walked over and sat down in a chair across from Lisa. He saw that her face was still flushed and her breathing was heavy. She was wriggling around in the chair and she looked extremely uncomfortable. He reached over and took her hand; it felt cold.

"Are you sure you're all right? Maybe I should carry you to your room so you can lie down."

"I told you before I'm all right! You probably couldn't lift me anyway."

"Don't bet on it."

"I don't make bets anymore," she said bitterly. "Now

421

please tell me why you're really here."

"I want to be with you when our child is born and afterward, too. I always want to be with you. I've missed you, Lisa. When I came back to the cave that morning and found you gone, I went crazy. I didn't know what'd happened to you. I knew I had to get you back."

"Why?" she asked with deliberate hardness.

"Because I love you and I need you."

"You rode all this way to tell me that, knowing I would look like this?" she asked incredulously. "You must be disappointed. I know I look . . ."

"More beautiful than I've ever seen you look."

"Next you'll be telling me what a beautiful body I have," she said dryly.

"You were always a little too skinny. I like you better with a little meat on your bones."

"You're the most exasperating man," she shouted, clearly unnerved by his obvious attempts to woo her. "Where is Carmen anyway?" She looked around her as if she were very interested in Carmen's presence. Carmen walked in, carrying a tray filled with drinks and fresh fruit.

"You try to eat something, señora. I worry about you." She turned to Eric. "She doesn't eat enough, señor. You will try to make her eat, eh?"

"Don't worry, Carmen, I'll take care of her now."

"Bueno," Carmen said smugly and walked out.

"I think I should take you to San Francisco. There are a couple of doctors there who could look after you."

"I don't need a doctor. Carmen has delivered lots of babies. I'm too far along anyway; I could never make the trip."

"Then I'll bring one here."

422

"No, don't. Carmen knows as much as any doctor."

"Maybe, but I'll feel a lot better knowing a doctor is around in case something goes wrong. I'll take a ride in tomorrow."

"No," Lisa screamed loudly. "Why are you doing this? Everything was fine until you came here." Her voice was trembling and she began to cry. She covered her face with her hands. "Why did you have to come," she sobbed.

Eric got up and knelt down next to her. Pulling her into his arms he stood up.

"You're tired," he said gently, "I'll take you to your room so you can rest."

Lisa laid her head against his shoulder, too tired to argue. He took her to her room and placed her on the bed. He put a cool cloth on her forehead and sat down next to her, taking her hand in his. She fell asleep almost immediately, and soon her breathing became even. He brought her hand up to his lips and kissed it, unwilling to relinquish his hold on her. He looked down at her large belly and he had a sudden urge to touch it. He ran his hand around the large mound and stopped when he felt the sharp movement from within.

"My God," he muttered softly. He had no idea until now what it was like to feel life in another's body. He lowered his face and kissed her stomach, embracing it with both arms. "Please, God, let her and the child be all right," he murmured softly to the God he said he didn't believe in. Fear welled up inside of him as he remembered hearing the Comanche women's screams during childbirth and seeing their limp bodies carried away later for burial. He sat up again, moving the cloth over her face and neck. She would be all right, because without her, there was nothing.

* * *

It was late afternoon and Lisa started to get out of bed when she felt the gush of water down her leg. It felt warm and she knew it was time. She walked to the door and yelled for Carmen, who came within seconds.

"It's time; I'm all wet." Carmen helped Lisa change into a fresh nightgown while she issued orders to another girl, who quickly changed the linen on the bed and brought in a stack of clean towels.

"Is Señor Anderson still here?" Lisa asked tentatively, afraid Eric had ridden back to San Francisco.

"Sí, señora, he is resting. He told me he thought the child would come tonight and he wanted to be rested when the time comes."

"How could he know?"

"He said he felt the child as you slept and he knew it would be this night."

Lisa softened perceptibly, grateful that he wasn't gone and wondering about his gentle gesture. She slipped into her robe and walked around the room, refusing to get into bed despite Carmen's protests to the contrary. She went to the window and looked out; then she left the room and went into the garden. The sun was about to set and it cast an orange glow over the little garden. She bent down and picked one of the red roses. She lifted it to her nose and inhaled deeply. She was aware of the growing intensity of the pains and she grasped her stomach. She knew she would have to go back into her room soon, but she was afraid. Up until this point she really hadn't thought about the actual birth, but now that it was finally here, she was frightened of the unknown. She looked up at the rapidly darkening sky and said a silent prayer for her unborn child. She pulled her robe tightly around her and gasped at the intensity of the next sharp pain. She felt a hand on her shoulder.

"Are you frightened?" She knew it was Eric before he spoke; his touch was like no other. She nodded slightly and he turned her around to face him. "I'll be with you; I'll do anything I can to help you. I just wish I could make it easier for you." She looked at him and she felt the familiar beating of her heart. She reached up and touched his face lightly, fleetingly, and then she rested her head on his chest.

"I think I'd better go in now. The pains are closer together." He nodded and bent to pick her up, but she shook her head. "I can still walk; I'm not an invalid."

"I know. I just want to help."

"You can help me later. Just stay with me."

"I told you before, I'll never leave you again." She nodded slightly and they walked in. She went into her bedroom amid frantic cries from Carmen. She looked at the bed before getting into it. For some reason, it frightened her. She knew it was the place she would have to give birth to her child or die in the process. She shivered slightly and felt Eric's arms go around her. She wanted to be strong, to prove to him that she could bear a healthy child, but she didn't know whether she was equal to the task. She walked to the bed and sat down, swinging her legs up. She looked up at Eric and saw him standing there, so strong and healthy and alive, and suddenly she didn't want him with her. She didn't want him to be ashamed of her if she failed him again.

"Will you leave me alone for a while?" She looked up at him imploringly. He sat down next to her.

"I won't leave you."

"Please. I don't want you here. Please go." She turned

her head away from his as another contraction came and went. He turned her face toward his.

"I'm not going to leave, Lisa. I'd be a real fool if I didn't learn from my past mistakes. You are all I want, you and the child." She looked up at him and grasped his hand and held it during the next contraction. He wiped her face with a wet cloth.

"You're doing fine."

"No, I'm not. I'm afraid; I'm so afraid." She bit her lower lip with the next contraction, determined not to scream. She wanted to be strong and silent; she wanted him to be proud of her.

The evening progressed into night, and night into early morning, but still the baby showed no signs of entry into the world. Lisa's contractions were hard and close together, and she had been pushing for over an hour by the time dawn came. Carmen felt her abdomen for any sign that the child had moved, but it still felt as though it were in the same position. She motioned to Eric to follow her outside the room and sent one of the other girls to stay with Lisa.

"What's the matter? Something's wrong."

"The baby is not moving, señor. The señora has been pushing for much too long and still the baby isn't in the canal. I don't know for sure but I think the baby is in the wrong position."

"What can you do to help? You have to do something."

"Señor, the child has to be turned if it is in the wrong position. I myself have never had to do this, but I watched a midwife do it once."

"Then you must do it now."

"Señor, I must tell you that there is danger to the child

426

and the señora if I do this. I am frightened that I will injure the señora."

"The señora will be injured if you don't help her, Carmen. Please, just do what you can. Is there anything I can do?"

"Sí, if I am unable to turn the child, then you must. Your arms are longer and you might be able to do it if I cannot."

"Me? I can't. My hands are too big—I'd kill her."

"Like you said, señor, if we don't try, well . . ."

Carmen's unspoken words hammered at Eric's brain. If they didn't help Lisa then what? He knew the answer. If the child wasn't expelled or taken from her womb, she would die. She would *die*. The word was so ominous, so definite. He turned to Carmen.

"Very well, Carmen. I'll do whatever has to be done."

They went back into the room and Eric walked to Lisa. Her eyes were closed and she was panting, her face and hair drenched in sweat.

"Lisa . . ." She opened her eyes. He thought they looked enormous in her pale and drawn face. She looked so tired. "Lisa, the baby isn't moving into the birth canal. Carmen is going to try to move it. Do you understand?"

She stared at him, her eyes large and frightened.

"I knew it, I knew something would go wrong. . . ." She stopped as the urge to push overcame her. "I was so afraid I'd fail you again. . . . That's why I didn't want you here. The baby . . ." She held on to his arm as she pushed again and when the urge passed, she panted and closed her eyes. He nodded to Carmen who poured oil over her hands to facilitate her entry into Lisa's body. She waited for the next contraction to pass and was about to enter when Lisa began to moan. Carmen looked at Eric.

"Señor, I cannot do it. If something should happen, it would be on my conscience forever."

Eric walked over and grabbed her by the shoulders, shaking her violently.

"It will be on your conscience if you don't do something, damnit!"

"Please, señor."

"Oh, hell," Eric muttered angrily and turned back to Lisa. Up until now she had been silent, keeping her pain to herself. But now she was moaning loudly, and he knew something had to be done. He rolled up his sleeves and washed his hands and arms in the basin, then covered his hand with the oil which Carmen had used. He sat down on the chair at the end of the bed, watching for the end of Lisa's contraction. When it subsided he took a deep breath and put his hand into her, not knowing what he was feeling for, knowing only that he had to help her. She gasped as his hand entered her and for a second he almost withdrew it, but he knew he had to try. He probed deeper into the canal stopping when he felt the walls contract around his hand. Lisa was crying now and he knew the pain must be unbearable for her. Why couldn't he feel the child? She pushed again and this time Carmen pushed from the top, hoping that she could be of some help. Lisa groaned and he pushed farther in until he finally reached the womb. His hand touched flesh and he knew he had reached the baby, but what to do now? He waited for another contraction to pass and reached still farther until he felt his fingers on something, some part of the child's body.

"All right, Lisa, I want you to push as hard as you can. Do you understand?" He tried to talk as calmly as possible. He heard Carmen urge Lisa to push harder with the next contraction and he grabbed the child's body and began to pull. It felt like a tiny shoulder but he could not be sure. He knew only that it had moved—it was coming into the canal. The contraction subsided and he held on to the tiny bit of flesh, afraid that it would slip back if he didn't. Lisa pushed again, and this time the baby moved down of its own accord. Eric quickly withdrew his hand and watched as the crown of the baby's head appeared. He waited until Lisa pushed again, and then helped the baby out, slowly, with each successive contraction, until the entire body was out. The child was born. He held the wet, bloodied infant in his arms and instinctively stuck his fingers in its mouth to take out the mucus. He wiped its face and heard it scream when he held it up. It was a girl. A girl with red, mottled skin, and thick, black hair. He held her up to Lisa.

"Your daughter."

"Oh, God," she muttered softly, taking the tiny infant from him. "You did it; you saved her and me." Tears rolled down her cheeks. Now that the worst was over, Carmen had again assumed the role of doting house-keeper. She took the baby and cleaned her up and then came back to deliver the afterbirth, which she promptly bundled away. The baby nursed while Carmen cleaned Lisa and changed the bed. Then the three of them were left alone—mother, father, and daughter.

Eric took off his shirt and washed up at the washbasin as Lisa watched. She saw the taut muscles of his arms and back as he bent over the basin and she couldn't believe that he had just delivered their child. He had been so gentle, so caring, and he had saved her life again. If he hadn't come, she and the baby would have died. She looked down at the tiny little girl in her arms and she began to cry again. A new life. A new life created by her and Eric. And she had been created out of love.

"Crying again?"

She looked up and saw him staring down at her.

"I was just thinking what would've happened if you hadn't come. You were wonderful."

"I was scared as hell," he said honestly, sitting next to her. "I don't think I've ever been so scared in my life. The next time, you're going to have a doctor around."

"The next time?"

"If you're able, if you want to, I mean."

"Oh, I'll be able. This one just needed a little help in getting out, that's all." She reached up and touched his face. "Thank you."

He took her hand and kissed the palm.

"I told you before, there is nothing for me without you and her. I did what had to be done." He reached over and touched the baby's arm, rubbing his finger along the smooth skin. "God, she's so perfect. So tiny, yet so perfect. What shall we name her?"

"I don't know; I haven't really thought about girls' names. I was so sure it was going to be a boy. Are you disappointed?"

"Why should I be? Girls can be taught to do anything boys can be taught. I'll enjoy spoiling her, and can't you see Don Alfredo?"

"I don't doubt that you'll both spoil this poor helpless child." Lisa stopped, her tone suddenly serious. "Eric, what happens now? What about the future?"

"What about it?"

"Please, don't play games with me. I want to know."

"What do you want to know? That I love you and need you and that we'll always be together? There aren't any guarantees in life, Lisa. All I know for sure is that you are all I'll ever want or need. You and the baby. What happens after that is up to us both."

Lisa put the sleeping baby into the cradle next to the bed, and she pulled Eric toward her, moving her lips firmly against his.

"I know we'll always be together; it was meant to be. Just as it was meant for you to come here and save my life and the baby's. We can't fight fate, can we? But we can help it along a little."

"I like the way you think, green eyes," he said, nuzzling her neck with his lips. "How would you feel about living at the Rancho del Mar? Of course, it's not as grand as the del Sol but . . ."

"The Rancho del Mar," Lisa repeated softly, interrupting Eric. "Yes, that's how it should be. The del Sol is really Mariz's anyway; I never felt at home there. But the del Mar is different. It's warm and comfortable; it's home to me. I think it's a wonderful idea."

"I thought you'd feel that way. I thought a lot about it while I was searching for you, and then I realized that I didn't want the del Sol as much as I wanted to hurt my mother. Now it doesn't matter—she can have it all. I can't believe my own mother . . ."

"She didn't try to have me killed. That was all Consuelo's doing. You can't blame your mother for that."

"I know she didn't do that, but I also know that she'll never change. I can never trust her. She'll die a very rich, very lonely old lady. But I'm tired of being so full of anger and hatred. There is more to life than that. I learned that from you."

"Don Alfredo will be so happy; he loves you so much."

431

"I missed out on too many good years with him when I was gone. I want to make up to him for all the hurt he's had because of me and my mother."

"I think you already have." She laid her head on his chest and clasped his hand in hers. "It will be a new beginning for us. We will have all our children there. It will be a happy place, full of love and understanding. Our children will never feel the lack of love that we felt as children. The Rancho del Mar will live long after Don Alfredo and we are gone."

Eric ran his fingers through Lisa's hair, absent-mindedly staring out the window. He watched as the sun shone in through the panes, lighting up the entire room. He sat up abruptly, pulling his hand from Lisa's.

"What's the matter?"

"I know what we'll call her," he said with excitement. "Raya, we'll call her Raya. It's a new day, the sun is bright, and she is strong and healthy. Raya, that's it!"

"Raya," Lisa repeated. "Yes, it's beautiful." She touched his face. "I love you, Eric."

He looked at her, surprised by her frank admission of love. He pulled her to him, loving her more than he ever had before. They lay down and he held her close. The Rancho del Mar could wait for the time being; everything could wait. Now was their time, a time to mend old hurts, and a time to look forward to the future and the spirit of love forever.